Copyright © 2025 S. D. Gredell
All rights reserved.
Ebook: 979-8-9924370-2-7
Paperback: 979-8-9924370-3-4
Hardback: 979-8-9924370-4-1

WHISPERED SECRETS

PLAGUE AND MAGIC
BOOK 2

S.D. GREDELL

To my husband and the readers so far.
Thank you.

CHAPTER 1

The desperate sound of screams echoed off the crystalline walls as I was dragged from my cell despite protests. We passed through halls filled with angry, desperate or frightened Fae within them, cowering in the corners of their cages.

My bare feet scraped against the frigid polished stone, chains rattling with each stumbling step as my toes went numb. The Fae guards escorting me moved with inhuman grace. Their grip on my arms was as strong as steel, despite my struggles. Behind me, I heard the heavier clank of silver—Aldric's restraints, different from mine—crueler, as I knew it burned against his pale skin.

"Where are you taking us?" I demanded, though my voice cracked from thirst. How long had we been imprisoned in this place? Weeks? Months? Time moved strangely in the Starfall Veil, the days seeming to never end. The lack of windows in the prison did not help that feeling at all, my skin having grown even more pale—almost translucent—in the ambient light of the castle.

The guard to my left—a tall, stony-faced man, with hair like spun moonlight, so similar to my own—didn't bother to answer. None of them ever did, regardless of how hard I tried to speak to them. I don't know why I still bothered. They acted as though they couldn't even hear me.

The corridor opened into a vast amphitheater I'd never seen before. Crystalline seats rose in circles around a central dais, filled with hundreds of Fae nobles in their best finery, hints of gold and silver glimmering like stars as my eyes flit from face to face. For many Fae, looking at them was terrible to behold—their faces too perfect, too sharp, like looking at broken glass arranged in pleasing patterns. Some just looked human, others looked like monstrous creatures of times past.

Much of the creature lore in Aethralis was based on seeing glimpses of Fae, I realized absently.

How often did they venture into our realm unseen? What untold horrors had they wrought to become the villains we warn children about at night?

With a clearing of a throat, my gaze snapped to the raised dais. At the center of it all stood the King and Queen, their crowns catching the ethereal light that seemed to emanate from the very walls. Between them knelt a figure in chains—another Fae. But this one's perfection was marred by a face twisted by terror.

"Behold," the King's voice rang out, magically amplified to reach every corner of the amphitheater, "the fate of those who betray the crown."

They forced Aldric and I into seats in the front row as though we were honored guests. Aldric's shoulder pressed against mine for just a moment, and despite the silver that weakened him, I felt the tremor of protective rage that ran through his body. Through the silk-thin thread of our bond, his fury burned like starlight. As though punishing us further, Aldric's seat was jerked away from me, and Seren stood between us, her face unreadable.

The ache that bloomed as Aldric and I were separated took my breath away. It had been so long since I had been so close to him, I'd forgotten what it felt like. But before I could think too much about it, there was a stifled sob from the stage and my gaze reluctantly returned to the trio there.

The condemned Fae was someone I didn't remember seeing before—a young-looking woman, even by their standards, with golden hair and sea-green eyes. There was something familiar about her, but I couldn't quite put my finger on it. But it was the terror in those eyes that made my stomach clench. This wasn't justice. This was theater—a performance to frighten their enemies. *Or maybe something to liven up their miserable existences*, I thought bitterly.

"The crime," the Queen announced, her voice tinkling like silver bells, "is the bearing of a half-blood child. Contaminating the Fae bloodline and a complete betrayal of our sacred heritage." Her voice was frosty with condemnation.

No one else seemed to bat an eye, but I leaned forward despite myself. A half-blood child? Were they all so proud that having a child with someone other than the Fae was worthy of punishment? How did she end up with someone who was an Other? But the questions died on my lips as the King raised his hands, magic gathering between his palms like darkness itself, absorbing all light around it.

"The punishment," he continued, "is full essence extraction."

The words meant nothing to me, but the collective intake of breath from the assembled Fae spoke volumes. Whatever this was, it was horrible, even by their standards.

The mana that erupted from the King's hands wasn't the clean, sharp power I'd felt in my cell. This was something ancient and hungry, coiling around the condemned Fae like serpents made of night itself. The victim's scream split the air—a sound of such pure agony that I flinched backward into Seren's side. She was stiff, unmoving. I glanced at Seren's face to see a single tear rolling down her cheek despite her stoic expression. The pain in her eyes resonated with something deep within me. Swallowing hard, I reluctantly turned back toward the stage.

And then I watched something I would never forget.

The woman's immortal beauty began to drain away. Her golden hair dulled to brittle straw, her perfect skin grew lined and spotted. The Fae's sea-green eyes clouded further with each heartbeat until I was sure they had to be blind. But this wasn't just aging. The very essence of what made them Fae was being torn away, leaving behind something small and delicate and utterly mortal.

"No," I whispered, my hands twisting behind my back, causing the chain to strain against the delicate flesh at my wrists. I barely noticed the pain. "No, no, no—"

That…*poison* was ripping away everything that made the condemned who and what she was. Her power became less than nothing.

And still she screamed until her voice was raw and broken. Despite the prisoner's unseeing eyes, they seemed to look in my direction.

Why?

Then I realized it wasn't me, but someone else nearby.

Seren's breathing hitched, and my gaze darted back to her face, where her eyes were full of agony, her lips drawn and her skin pale. But she still held onto her pride, keeping her head held high. This person meant something to her.

The pain emanating from Seren was a reflection of my own, the helpless agony of watching someone you care about being murdered while you're powerless to help. A flash of golden eyes and blood-soaked dirt flitted across my mind, and I swallowed hard, my eyes pricking with unshed tears.

As I slowly turned back towards the King and Queen, I saw why Seren was trying so hard to look unaffected. The King's cold, calculated gaze was trained on Seren, as though waiting for something.

The process seemed to take forever and no time at all. When it ended, what remained didn't even look like the same creature. It was aged and broken, a being who crumpled forward and simply… stopped. No dramatic death. No last words. Just the absence of everything they had been as their body crumpled to ash, leaving only tattered clothes behind.

The King lowered his hands, with a few sparks raining from

his fingers to fizzle against the floor. "Let this be a lesson to all, especially those who would betray the crown."

Silence filled the amphitheater. Even the nobles seemed shaken by what they'd witnessed.

My whole body was shaking with adrenaline. The magic I'd been suppressing since my capture suddenly surged within me, responding to my horror and rage. The chains around my wrists grew hot, and I fought to tamp the power down before it made me a target. Slowly, painfully, I was able to lock it away deep inside.

This could be me, I realized with sudden clarity. This could be Aldric—or my parents. *Had something like this already happened to them?* I thought, panic seizing me tighter than any restraint they could put on me.

But then I realized, no. If it were going to be them, they would be in this 'show', not killed where I couldn't see. *All the better to break me,* I thought bitterly as my chest slowly relaxed.

The King's gaze found mine across the room, his smile sharp as winter's chill. "Take them back to their cells," he commanded. "I trust our guests found the demonstration... educational."

As the guards hauled me to my feet, Seren stepped aside. Her gaze remained trained on the remains of the now-deceased Fae, her expression unreadable. As one of the officers touched my chains, they hissed out an expletive, and Seren's eyes caught mine.

She was staring at me with an expression I couldn't quite read. Horror, yes. But something else. Something I couldn't place. Guilt? Shame?

I didn't have time to think about what that look meant right now. The guard who cursed grabbed me by the upper arm, his grip bruising my pale flesh.

Our escorts dragged us back through the crystalline corridors, but I barely noticed the path back to the dungeon. My mind was still in that place, still watching magic tear away everything that made a person who they were.

This is what they'll do to us, I thought as the sentinel threw me back into my cell. I landed sprawled across the floor, but the pain didn't even register. My mind was racing, and my breathing was fast. This is what awaits anyone who defies them.

Even as the thought formed, my magic pushed against the Fae bonds with renewed strength. It felt strange. Like my power was…hungry. A warden hauled me into a seated position and pressed a dagger against my throat. I felt a warm trickle as the blade pierced my skin. They were trying to get Aldric back into his cell, I realized dimly.

"Move and she dies," the officer snarled at Aldric.

Aldric's silver eyes blazed with inhuman fury, but he allowed the guards to unlock his cell and drag him inside. As soon as they reached for the wall shackles, however, he struck. Moving with deadly grace, he slammed the closest Fae into the bars hard enough to crack them. Another officer was his next victim, their arm snapping as easily as a stick with a wet *crack* as Aldric lashed out with his bound hands. There were shouts echoing in the dungeon, and soon the hall was filled with bodies.

It took five guards to stop him, even with the silver weakening his body. His fangs were bared, and deadly promises spilled from his lips in an ancient language I didn't recognize, but that sent chills up my spine. I cried out as the blade drove deeper into my flesh, the trickle of blood becoming a stream. Aldric immediately stilled, though I could feel the fury radiating off of him in waves.

"The King and Queen will not punish me for killing her," the officer shouted over the clamouring voices. "Do not test me, you demonic parasite!"

Aldric's eyes were filled with deadly intent, despite his compliance. When they finally clicked the wall shackles into place, they positioned him as high as they could, so his feet could barely brush the ground. Forcing him to bear his weight on the silver that bound his wrists lest his airway be cut off by the collar.

He endured it all in deadly silence, his gaze never leaving mine. The mercury within swirled with a promise of retribution for every drop of blood, every ounce of pain they caused us.

Later, after getting my neck bandaged, I stared at the floor, my mind reeling with all the revelations from today. Did we have any hope at all of escape? Were we doomed to a horrific death, too? Could I watch Aldric go through it? My chest seized at the thought. I couldn't. I couldn't do it.

"Lyra," he called softly, and even weakened as he was, his voice carried across the space between us like a caress, soothing my jumbled nerves and cutting through my thoughts. "Are you hurt?"

Hurt? *Hurt?* I wanted to laugh, but it would have come out broken. "I'm fine," I lied, testing the chains around my wrists. They felt warm now, responding to something in my magic that hadn't been there before. It felt as though my magic was trying to draw something in. But what? "Are you?"

"I've been better," he admitted, but there was something in his tone—a dark promise that made me shiver. "But seeing what they're capable of... it's put some things into place."

It did. Whatever was happening between us—whatever this tether was—I still didn't fully understand, but I couldn't let them destroy it.

I couldn't let them destroy *him.*

Mana deep within me pulsed again in response to my thoughts, and this time, a hairline fracture spread through the metal, the white runes flaring.

Hope, dangerous and fierce, bloomed in my chest.

Maybe we weren't as helpless as they thought.

CHAPTER 2

Hours after the execution, I was pulled from my cell yet again by two wardens. My legs were still shaking—the image of that Fae crumbling to nothing burned into my mind. Her screams continued to ring in my ears as if they were still happening, even now.

The guards said nothing, just wordlessly dragged me along with them. The slap of my bare feet and the smart click of their heels against the stone were the only sounds reverberating through the empty halls.

This time, they brought me to a smaller chamber—much more intimate, with sparkling walls that seemed to pulse from within with their own light. It felt much too warm compared to the chill I felt deep within. The king and queen waited, no longer in their ceremonial robes but somehow more terrifying in their casual attire.

"Sit," the queen commanded, gesturing to a chair across from the royal pair.

Stubbornly, I remained standing, my chains clinking softly as I came to a stop. "Why didn't you bring Aldric?"

"The vampire is not your concern right now," the king said, his voice as sharp as a blade and just as cold.

They began circling me like wolves, hammering me with the same questions I'd heard before.

About the plague.

My magic.

How it all began.

But their tone was different now—more pointed, more knowing.

Eventually, despite the pit in my stomach, I grew exasperated. "You've asked me all of this before. Why are you asking again? Nothing has changed," I snapped, refusing to bow under the weight of their immortal gazes.

"We've been reading some interesting journals," the queen said flippantly, producing a familiar leather-bound book. My chest clenched painfully.

Thorne's research.

"You were the first," she continued, gauging my reaction. "Patient zero. The one who started it all."

The words hit me like a physical blow. Reading the words of a madman on a crumpled, stained page was one thing. Hearing it spoken aloud...that made it more real. Griffin died for what? To save the person who killed thousands just by existing? Who the people were so afraid of that they tried to smother her gift—her very being?

My throat tightened as a wave of grief struck me, and my

mana responded to the emotional surge. The chains around my wrists grew warm, pulsing along with my heartbeat. I fought my power down and kept it contained. Pressing the manacles closer to my back, I fisted my hands, my nails digging into my palms. The pain helped me think more clearly.

"I thought so," I whispered, the words tasting bitter on my tongue. The truth slipped out.

"But I hoped it couldn't be."

"Is it so strange?" The king sat in a plush chair as he spoke, steepling his fingers and leaning forward. There was an unsettling gleam in his eyes.

"A desperate healer tries to suppress a child's dangerous magic. Instead of containing it, he accidentally taints it with his own power. The resulting corruption spreads like wildfire." He waved his hand in the air, as though the idea should be entirely obvious.

Keep it together, I told myself as my power pushed against my control. Don't let them see the cracks.

They'll kill you. Then they'll kill Aldric, a voice whispered through my mind.

It hurt, but I was determined to restrain myself. I gritted my teeth.

"What do you want from me?"

"Cooperation," the queen said simply, taking a seat next to the king. "Help us understand what you are, and *perhaps* we can find a solution that doesn't end with your essence being extracted."

The reminder of that horrible process brought my parents again to mind. Are they being experimented on? Dissected? A rush of bile threatened to come up, but I swallowed it down with difficulty.

"How can I trust that you're not harming my family? I know you have them." I sounded braver than I felt, my throat still burning with acid.

"If we were going to hurt them, they would have been dead by now," the king said flatly, his face emotionless. "But we could always make arrangements if you prefer another show?"

The threat was obvious, and the thought alone was enough to get me to comply. As they continued rattling off questions at me, my gaze drifted around the room.

Aside from the usual gaudy statuettes that the wealthy enjoyed, there was another door behind the king and queen. Two guards were stationed at either side. And one of them was Seren.

She stood at attention in a fitted metallic garb with a short sword attached at the hip. Her moss-green eyes kept flicking to me, though her expression was kept carefully blank.

The interrogation continued for what felt like hours. Eventually, it got to where I was just repeating the same answers over and over, growing more monotone each time.

I gave them nothing useful, but with each question, each veiled threat, my gift strained harder against the Fae bindings until it felt as though the metal would scorch my skin.

As my exhaustion began to show, the royals finally deigned to dismiss me. When the guards moved to escort me back, I caught Seren's eye. For just a moment, she let her professional mask slip. What I saw there wasn't the loyalty of a royal guard.

It was grief. Raw, unbridled, so intense that it took my breath away.

But why?

Back in my cell, I tested the chains around my wrists. My very essence seemed to reach for whatever was contained within the cold iron, wrapping it in my magic like a blanket.

What could this mean?

"How did it go?" Aldric called softly from across the corridor as I continued to fiddle with my bindings. The metal began to feel more brittle in my hands, like it was being rusted through.

"They know," I said simply. "About the plague and Thorne. About me being the first."

There was a long pause, tension heavy in the air between us. "And?"

"And they're deciding whether I'm more useful alive or dead. Whether my answers were enough."

Another pause, longer this time. Then his voice floated over to me, sliding down my spine like a lover's caress. "Lyra, look at me."

I turned toward his cell, and even in the dim light, his silver eyes seemed to glow with an otherworldly intensity.

"Whatever happens," he said, his voice carrying a weight that made my chest tighten, "you are not alone in this. I'm here."

The faint bond between us pulsed, warm and reassuring, though guilt washed over me. I couldn't forget Griffin, and I couldn't move on while he rotted away in that gods-damned basement. But I could do something about it, I thought, my power flaring brightly. Shadows stretched like fingers across the walls as the light faded.

And for the first time since the execution, as the chains

binding me crumbled away beneath the force of my magic, I felt something other than fear.

Determination.

The sound of footsteps in the corridor had me quickly tucking my arms behind my back as though my bindings still held me. Every muscle in my body coiled in preparation to strike. But it wasn't guards coming for another interrogation.

It was Seren. Slowly, the tension eased, leaving behind a strange sense of relief.

She approached my cell with her usual stride, but something was different. Her back was too straight, her movements too controlled—like a puppet just going through the motions.

"You need to eat," she said, sliding a tray through the slot at the bottom of my cell door. I barely spared a glance at the abysmal food I knew was waiting for me, despite the growling in my stomach.

I stared at her. In all the time we'd been imprisoned here, no one had brought me food directly. It came through magical means—bowls of slop that simply appeared and disappeared.

"Why?"

A single word with a lot of meaning behind it.

"Orders, of course."

But her expression said something else entirely—the depth of her pain making itself known for just a moment.

She passed by Aldric's cell. He'd been silent since our conversation, but I could feel his wariness through our bond. Something strange was happening, and I caught his eye, reflective in the limited light like a cat's. His gaze flicked to her, and I knew what I needed to ask.

"Seren," I called softly as she prepared to leave.

She paused, her back to me.

"At the execution today." I swallowed hard, barely able to form the words through the dryness of my throat. "Who was she?"

Seren's shoulders tensed, and she stood as still as a statue. I wasn't even sure she was breathing. For a long moment, she didn't respond.

"A traitor to the crown," she said without turning around, her voice flat, emotionless.

"That's not what I meant, and you know it."

This time, Seren turned to look at me directly. And in that moment, I saw the answer I'd been dreading. The grief I'd witnessed earlier suddenly made terrible sense. Someone she knew.

Someone used against her?

Nausea washed over me, and I swallowed hard.

"Eat," she said again, but her voice cracked slightly on the word. She cleared her throat and tried again. "You'll need your strength."

"For what?" Aldric asked from his cell, his voice deadly calm.

Seren glanced around, ensuring we were alone in this section of the prison. Then she stepped closer to my cell, her voice dropping to barely above a whisper.

"The king and queen are discussing your fate tomorrow morning. I don't know what they're planning."

My heart hammered against my ribs. "And?"

"And I've been ordered to prepare for either outcome, whether they decide to let you live." Her eyes flicked meaningfully around the inside of my cell. "Or whether they don't. The question is: what would you want to do about it?"

The weight of her words settled over me. This wasn't just information—it was an offer. An ally.

"Why?" I asked. "Why would you help us?"

Seren's jaw visibly tightened, and I could hear her teeth grinding. "Because I've seen enough innocent blood spilled for one day."

She turned to go, but paused at Aldric's cell. "You," she said to him, "I've heard the two of you talk before. Do you really believe the caste system in Vespara should be dismantled? That's been around since the inception of your kind."

Aldric shifted, and I heard the clink of his silver restraints as he hissed out, "Every breathing moment of my existence."

"Even if it meant war?"

"Especially then."

Seren nodded slowly, as if something had been confirmed.

"Eat," she said again, nodding in my direction. "And be ready."

After she left, silence stretched between our cells.

"She's going to help us," I said finally.

"Yes," Aldric agreed. "The question is why now? What changed?"

I thought about the execution, about the emotion in Seren's eyes, about the calculated cruelty of forcing her to watch.

"They broke something in her today," I murmured, my gaze tracing the pattern of the stone beneath my feet. "Something that can't be fixed."

I allowed my arms to fall to my sides, though even that slight movement felt like shards of glass in my joints and muscles. Pins and needles burst in my fingertips as blood rushed back. Slowly, carefully, I brought my hands in front of me, rubbing my wrists to assuage the feeling. There were dark, angry bruises I hadn't realized were there.

I'd lost weight, grown weak since I'd been here. Despite her restrictions, it looked like Seren had tried to get me something a little better than usual. It was a sandwich. It wouldn't have been easy to eat if my hands were still bound.

Was she being…considerate? How did she know?

I filed that thought away for later and ate with relish. Anything would taste better than the usual slop they gave me. No idea what was between the bread, but it didn't matter. It tasted glorious.

Like survival.

"How long do you think we have?" Aldric asked.

"Not long." I could feel it in my bones—tomorrow would bring either freedom or death. There would be no middle ground. Not for us.

As if summoned by my thoughts, that whisper came again: Be ready to choose. Your power or your principles. You cannot have both.

I shivered, unsure where the thought had come from. But as I looked down at the crumbled remnants of the surrounding chains, I wondered if the choice had already been made for me. With my free hand, I grasped the collar around my neck and pulled. There was a *crack* as the metal snapped as easily as dried twigs. The power contained within it rushed inside my body to collide with my own. The internal reservoir within me was overfilled in less than a second.

Agony lanced through me, stealing my breath. The food dropped to the ground, forgotten, as I gasped out. I dimly heard Aldric's voice call out to me. The wave of pain slowly receded, and I could finally breathe, leaving only an odd, languid feeling in my stomach. A trickle ran from my nose and landed on my lower lip. It tasted like copper. Warm and metallic.

Blood?

CHAPTER 3

"Lyra!"

Aldric's voice cut through the haze of tingles filling my body as the magic settled within. It felt like an old friend coming home. Like it was *mine*. "Lyra, answer me!"

I wiped the blood from my nose with the back of my hand, my vision still swimming. What was that? Did this magic... belong to me?

"I-I'm okay," I managed, my throat dry.

"You're bleeding. I can smell it." His voice was strained with worry, and something else—hunger, dark and desperate. "What did you do?"

I looked down at the remnants of the collar, now nothing more than twisted metal and fading runes. "I broke it. But the magic inside..." I pressed a hand to my chest, where it felt like my heart was trying to beat its way out of my ribs. "It's in me."

Through our bond, I felt Aldric's concern spike. But

underneath it was something else—a pull, unlike the normal urge to be near him. The excess magic inside me seemed to respond to him, reaching toward the silver chains that bound him.

"I can feel it," he murmured, his voice awed. "Your magic. I've never experienced something like this."

Before I could respond, the sound of marching feet echoed through the corridors. Not the usual two guards, but dozens of them, their synchronized steps like thunder against the crystalline walls.

"They're coming," I whispered, panic rising in my throat.

"Not yet," Aldric said, listening intently with his head cocked to the side. "They're passing by. But dawn can't be far off." I spent the next few hours pacing my small cell as much as the space allowed. Every time I stopped moving, Aldric would call my name softly, checking to make sure I was still conscious, still breathing. The bond between us pulsed with his worry, and underneath it, that strange pull—as if the magic wanted to flow from me to him.

Let it, came a whisper in my mind, layered and strange, like many voices speaking over one another. I blinked hard, and the voice became my own. *My magic belongs with him. I should stop fighting it. After everything we've been through, don't I deserve some happiness? Doesn't he?*

I froze, a chill crawling up my spine. "Did you say something?"

"No," Aldric replied, though his voice sounded far away. "But you just went still. What's wrong?"

The thoughts kept coming, unbidden. *Aldric should help me*

carry the weight of this burden. Let the power flow where it belongs. It felt like they were my own thoughts, but… wrong somehow.

"I don't know what's happening," I whispered, my heart racing. "There are all these thoughts in my head, telling me things. I don't know what to do."

Aldric's silver eyes seemed to glow through the strands of inky black hair hanging over his face. "What are they saying?"

Before I could answer, deliberate footsteps approached our section—not the heavy boots of guards, but the whisper of soft leather on stone. Seren appeared, but she wasn't alone. Behind her walked a Fae noble from the amphitheater, his expression cold as winter frost and his skin just as pale. His eyes were completely black and alien, almost reptilian in appearance. A wave of unease rushed over me.

"The King and Queen have reached their decision," he announced as breezily as if he were telling me the weather. Luckily for me, the dim lighting in this place worked to my advantage—he couldn't see the bits of mangled metal at my feet. "You will be brought before them within the hour."

"Both of us?" I asked, though I already knew the answer.

"Both. Together." His smile was like that of a shark—all sharp teeth.

After they left, Seren lingered for just a moment. She caught my eye and made a subtle gesture toward the corridor opposite the way we were usually taken. Then, she was gone.

"She's telling us which way to run," I mumbled.

"When?" Aldric asked.

The magic inside me pulsed beneath my skin, responding to his voice—desperate for me to reach him. I understood now what the voice had meant. This energy that had flowed into me—he could help carry it, if I wanted him to. But first, we needed to be free.

I looked at the remnants of restraints on the cold stone at my feet. They could no longer hold me. Not while I held this power.

"Now," I said, and let the magic I'd been holding back for so long burst forth.

The explosion of mana that erupted from me was unlike anything I'd ever experienced. This was not my transformation magic. This was different—something ancient, wild, desperate to be freed. The remaining fragments of my restraints didn't just break—they turned to glittering ash, dancing in the air around me as I rushed towards the bars of my cell.

The power reached out hungrily, tendrils coming from my body shimmering like golden thread, seeking more of its own kind. Once my hands actually touched the bars, euphoria flooded through me like the headiest wine. The bars dissolved as easily as sugar in water, their ancient magic flowing back into me in a rush that made my knees buckle.

Yes, I thought distantly, this is how magic was meant to feel.

"Lyra!" Aldric's voice was sharp with alarm, but it sounded far away, muffled by the intoxicating sensation of power flooding my veins. "You need to hurry!"

But I was already moving, stumbling on unsteady legs toward his cell. The magic thrummed beneath my skin, begging to be used again. Aldric's cell bars glowed with the same golden hue that radiated out from my body, the Fae mana imbued within trying to come home.

"Stand back," I whispered, reaching out with trembling hands.

The moment I touched his bars, the world exploded into sensation. Magic poured into me like a river breaking through a dam, and I gasped, my back arching as pleasure and pain coursed through every nerve. The bars crumbled away, their power adding to the intoxicating storm inside me.

Aldric remained chained to the wall, silver restraints biting deep into his wrists and throat. The closer I got, the worse he looked. His cheeks were sunken—there were dark circles below his moonlight eyes, and angry red welts on his wrists and neck where the restraints dug into his flesh.

"The chains," he said urgently, straining against them. "Lyra, you have to—"

I reached for the silver with confidence, adrenaline burning through my veins, but the moment my fingers brushed the metal, it was like needles jammed into my flesh. I jerked back as though I had been burned.

Not just physically, but magically—the enchantments imbued within to control Aldric were repelling the Fae magic I'd absorbed. My power skittered away from the silver like oil from water.

"I can't," I gasped, panic cutting through the euphoria. "It won't work on silver."

Aldric's face went pale, but his voice remained steady. "Then you need to go. Now, before—"

"No." The word came out fierce, desperate. I could hear footsteps in the distance now, getting closer. "You need blood. You need strength."

I dragged the unused cot in his cell with more brawn than I expected over to where he hung against the wall and bared my neck. He couldn't easily move, so I dragged a fingernail I didn't remember sharpening across the tender flesh. Blood welled immediately, and I watched as his nostrils flared, his pupils dilating.

The effect was instantaneous. His silver eyes blazed as he drank, and through our bond, I could feel just how much he needed this. But more than that, I felt the feeding itself—the intimate connection, the way my life force flowed into him. Combined with the Fae magic still singing in my veins and how desperately he needed this blood, it should have been painful, draining.

Instead, it was pure bliss.

A moan escaped my lips as Aldric's fangs pierced deeper, and I lost myself in the sensation. This was what I'd been missing, what I'd been denying myself. The magic, the connection, the feeling of being truly alive...

"Lyra." Aldric's voice was stronger now, but urgent. He'd pulled away from my throat, though his eyes smouldered with barely contained hunger. "Go. They're almost here."

I blinked, trying to focus through the haze of pleasure. The footsteps were louder now, accompanied by shouts. They'd discovered my escape.

"I'm not leaving you," I said, though my words slurred slightly. Everything felt soft around the edges, dreamlike.

"You have to." Aldric strained against his chains, tearing the skin at his wrists anew. Bright red blood ran in rivulets down his arms, dampening the haze I found myself in. "Find another way.

I'll survive this. I'll come back to you."

"Promise me," I whispered, swaying on my feet. The magic was making it hard to think clearly, everything bathed in warmth that made our desperate situation feel distant and unreal even while I was filled with a gnawing sense of loss at the thought of leaving Aldric behind.

"I promise," he roared. "Now go!"

The dominating command in his voice finally snapped me out of the euphoric state I'd been in. Before I could even think about it, I pressed a quick, desperate kiss to his lips, tasting copper and starlight, then forced myself to turn away.

"I'll come back for you," I said, and meant it with every fiber of my being.

Then I ran, following the direction Seren had shown me, my body still humming with stolen magic and the lingering tingles from the feeding. Behind me, I heard Aldric's voice, strong and defiant as the guards found him.

"She's already gone, you fools!" he hissed. "And when she comes back, you'll wish you'd never been born."

I ran faster as I heard a bellow of pain that sounded too much like Aldric, my bare feet slapping the floor painfully and my weakened muscles straining with the effort.

The corridors blurred past me, the stolen magic making every step feel weightless despite how heavy my heart was. The euphoria from absorbing so much power mixed with the lingering pleasure from Aldric's feeding, creating a dangerous cocktail that made everything feel sharp and electric.

I found Seren waiting at an intersection of hallways, her face pale with shock as she took in my appearance—blood still trickling from my throat, golden light flickering beneath my skin.

"You actually did it," she whispered, staring at me as though I were a new creature she'd discovered.

Before I could respond, the sound of running feet and shouts echoed from multiple directions.

"This way," Seren hissed, grabbing my wrist.

We moved carefully through the shining halls, ducking into alcoves when patrols passed. The magic inside me thrummed with each heartbeat, buzzing beneath my skin.

What was happening with my mana? How could I absorb theirs?

As we neared what Seren had promised was the final stretch before freedom, our luck ran out.

"Seren! You traitorous wench!"

A tall, lanky Fae with translucent skin burst around the corner, his internal organs bouncing with each step as he raced towards us. The sight was nauseating. I barely had time to notice as he was swinging a massive, heavy sword towards us.

Seren moved to intercept him, but she wasn't fast enough. Before I could even think, something primal took over me and my form changed without conscious thought.

I became something with massive fangs and eyes that saw in impossible colors. The world shifted into ultraviolet spectrums that made the Fae's magic visible like glowing veins beneath his skin. I didn't give myself time to be disoriented by the change and just… reacted.

My paw—easily as large as the Fae's torso—struck him with inhuman force. My claws sliced through his flesh like it was warm butter, and his scream was high-pitched and awful. Too loud. They would hear.

Out of desperation, thinking only to stop the noise, I clamped my enormous jaws around his torso and shook him like a rag doll until he came apart in pieces. Bone and sinew separated with wet tearing sounds, painting the walls with a nightmarish display as his cries died out.

When I dropped the mangled remains and shifted back to human form, I was covered in gore, dark blood and viscera dripping from my mouth. I spat the remnants onto the stone, wiping my face with the back of my hand.

Seren stared at me in absolute horror, her face white as snow.

The reality of what I'd just done crashed down on me, sudden and suffocating, but I couldn't process it. Not now. I grabbed Seren's wrist, dragging her away from the nightmarish scene. We slipped in the spreading pool of dark liquid that had been sprayed onto the stone and Seren began to cry.

"I'm sorry," I whispered as quiet sobs escaped her. She covered her mouth with her hand, her fingers trembling. "I'm so sorry, but we have to go."

There was a faint hum in the air as she took us to the middle of a hallway. My hand was drawn to the wall, where the vibration reverberated up my arm and I could feel the touch of magic like a caress. My breath shuddered out of me and there was a nearly inaudible click as the wall slid away, pulling some of the wild magic within me along with it.

Behind us, bellows of alarm erupted as they discovered the carnage we'd left behind.

Panic seized me and I tightened my grip on Seren's wrist, pulling her into the entrance that had opened before us. The wall slid shut behind us, trapping us in absolute darkness.

But even in this brief respite from our pursuers, I couldn't escape what I'd become. The taste of blood lingered in my mouth and for the first time in a long while, I truly felt like the monster people thought me to be.

CHAPTER 4

The darkness was oppressive. It was so heavy and all-encompassing that it felt alive. My eyes widened instinctually to try to pull in any modicum of light, but there was nothing. Seren was still quiet to the right of me, and I dropped her wrist, which had been limp in my hand.

"We need some kind of light," I murmured. Despite the softness of my voice, it echoed strangely in this place, making each word feel wrong, forbidden somehow. But as I said it, I felt the tiniest tug of magical power, similar to what I felt in the dungeons. In the darkness, straining my eyes, I could just barely see something lingering in the air. A thin, golden thread glowing with the barest hint of light. Seren didn't seem to see it, or she was still in shock. I couldn't tell which.

"Follow me," I whispered. I felt Seren grab hold of the back of my dirty, tattered shirt, still not speaking. What could she be thinking right now? My tongue felt thick in my mouth, the taste of the Fae's lifeblood lingering. It tasted like dirt, freshly torn from the earth.

I'd killed someone. They almost certainly had a family, someone who would miss them. A pit opened up in my stomach and I shoved the feeling down. I'd have to deal with the guilt later.

I had to escape—to survive. If not, as morbid as it sounded, they would have died for nothing. I just had to plan how to get Aldric out of here. Once we found our way out, I'd have to ask Seren what the best way would be.

It just felt wrong somehow to speak here, in this place. Like the walls themselves were listening, desperate to learn any secrets. The disgust that weighed me down didn't help, either. It was hard to ignore the way my shirt had dried to my skin from the viscera of the Fae I'd slaughtered.

We shuffled along in the darkness, the thread of magic guiding me down twists and turns in the passage. Whenever I'd veered the wrong way, it felt like the strand of magic would tug against my own. It was borderline painful, but there was no other option but to follow.

The purity of the Fae mana felt like getting a drink of fresh water after dying of thirst, like it was cleansing, cooling my body. Is this what it felt like for everyone?

I thought back to the prisoner on the dais crumbling into nothingness and my imagination went wild, putting Aldric in her place. Nausea roiled in my stomach, and I stumbled on a loose rock in the darkness, falling hard on my knee.

A jagged piece of stone scraped through the thin material of my pants, puncturing flesh. Warmth spread from the wound and I bit my lip to muffle a cry. Seren dropped down next to me and placed her hand between my shoulder blades. I felt her question without her even needing to ask.

You okay?

I turned and touched her arm to reassure her and stood, the thread of mana growing stronger the further along we went.

Aldric, I hope you're alright.

It was only luck that led me to being able to escape, myself. Luck, and the sacrifice of others.

I pulled on our bond as strongly as I could, and I barely felt a whisper in response. Distance, or something worse?

Had they already started removing his immortality?

My chest seized painfully, but I maintained my hold on the tether between us and thought with all my mental strength: I'll be back for you. You won't be alone. Wait for me.

Stay alive.

But I received nothing in response.

Soon, we had made it to a portion of the tunnels that looked to be headed towards an exit. The roughness of the walls had smoothed, and the ground beneath our feet was more level. There was a sliver of light at the end of this stretch, and I had to squint against it after so long in pitch-black. The hint of power in the air dissipated into nothingness. I glanced around, but there was no evidence it had ever existed.

Seren had continued to hold on to my shirt, but dropped the ruined fabric once we had a little light to see by. She probably hated or feared me after what she saw. Not that I would blame her. I'd become a literal monster. I'd killed someone in front of her. And not just killed, but maimed them. What was I thinking?

That's the problem. I wasn't. I just acted.

Just as bad as Thorne, I thought bitterly. How could I have done that? Why was that my first instinct? Was there no other option?

We should have just run. Or at least *tried* to.

Seren grasped my shoulder, and I came up short of smacking into a wall. We were at a door of some type. It was heavy, old wood, with a thick round door ring instead of a doorknob. There was no window or opening, but it was barricaded from our side with a thick wooden plank fit into an iron cradle across the door. I tried to lift the support and found it to be much heavier than it looked. I gestured to Seren and together, we strained to lift the wood out of the cradle. After some intense effort, we could slowly wiggle it until it slid out onto the floor with a deafening clatter against the stone.

I covered my ears against the sound, my heart beating wildly against my ribs. If anyone was in these tunnels, they had to have heard it. I grabbed the door ring and pulled with all of my strength. It definitely had not been opened for a long time, judging by the screech of the rusty hinges. Seren strode past me through the doorway, and I followed. This wasn't what I expected. The exit had led us to a field of lilies, both red and white. I stopped in my tracks.

There was something about this scenery that felt wrong somehow, but I couldn't put my finger on it.

"What is this place?"

Seren finally glanced back at me, her eyes haunted. She looked haggard, and I couldn't blame her in the least. Because of me, she had to betray her people, to bear witness to the atrocity I committed.

"Why do you ask?"

"It just feels...strange," I said finally, looking around. There was an energy here, but it felt different from what I'd experienced so far in the dungeon. Something even more ancient and foreboding. I felt both repulsed and intrigued by it, despite the anxiety worming around in my gut. Why would the tunnels have led here of all places?

"Strange how?" she asked carefully.

"It's like there's some kind of odd magic—I don't know, I can't explain it," I said. Seren looked at me with naked curiosity on her face.

"I'm surprised that you can tell. This is a holy place to the Fae. It's where we were first given magic," she explained, turning in a slow circle as though taking it all in herself. "Humans and Otherkind usually can't tell the difference, whether they have magic or not."

I nodded, my gaze roving over the rows and rows of flowers. I could see why they would treat this as a holy place. There was a certain mysticism to it—it felt significant. And yet, it felt wrong for me to be here. Sacrilegious, given that I was covered in gore and viscera. I felt like I was going to be sick. Seren slowly backed up, looking me up and down as though she just had the same thought that I did.

"Is there any place around here where I could, you know…" I started. I didn't want to say it.

"Later. First, we need to leave an offering for the Sovereign of Night. The deity who bestowed magic to our people," she explained quickly, striding off into the distance. I jogged to catch up with her, surprised by how quickly she moved.

"What kind of offering do you make to a deity like that?"

Seren seemed to consider my words as though weighing how much to say, her arms crossed. Her body language was closed off, untrusting. This was the first time she'd ever looked at me this way, and it left a sour taste in my mouth. I needed her to trust me. Just like the feeling that I had with Aldric, I knew in my gut that I needed her. And—and more than that, I had to admit…

I wanted her not to hate me. She would be well within her rights to, but I wanted to prove that I wasn't a bad person. No matter what people assumed about me.

"It's an offering of magic," Seren said carefully. "But I don't think you can be involved. What you became—what you did… I've never seen anything like that before."

"I understand," I said, although it pained me. "It was instinct. We had to get out of there. It felt like I didn't have a choice. I've never had to do anything like that before."

She looked away, her gaze falling to the sky off in the distance. The sun was setting, painting the sky in wine and purple hues. Stars winked into existence, becoming brighter as the sky darkened.

A small structure came into view as we crossed a hill. Once we got closer, I realized what it was.

An altar.

It stood nestled within a ring of black-barked trees, their twisted limbs arching and weaving together into a living cathedral. At its center rose a pedestal that seemed woven of night itself—it shimmered like glass, and yet it had no solid form. An endless pool of inky blackness that seemed to shift and fold in and out of itself. Flickers of starlight and nebulae winked in and out of view, like glimpsing the cosmos itself.

Small black motes floated around the altar like they were following its gravitational pull, and they seemed to shift in tune with my heartbeat. My eyes grew round and I hesitantly reached a hand towards the mantle.

Seren grabbed my wrist and forcefully pulled me back, her face dark with disapproval. She then grimaced and wiped her hand on her pants. "This is her sacred space. I don't want you to sully it," she said, her tone biting.

Without another word, she strode up to the altar, her head ducked in reverence. She held her hand out over the pedestal and, like water from a cup, vibrant green mana flowed from her fingers to gather in a bowl of night that hadn't been there before.

Shifting my weight from foot to foot, I waited, just watching. But nothing happened. Seren backed up next to me, a wrinkle forming between her brows.

The silence stretched between us, broken only by the faint rustling of leaves in the distance as a gust of wind blew. Seren's offering sat in the bowl, untouched and glowing softly. All I could think about was how much time we were wasting. While we waited here, the entire royal force could be on its way to this very place.

Then, the structure began to hum.

It was a sound I felt more than I heard, resonating in my bones. I clenched my jaw, the motes floating around the pedestal moving faster, twisting and writhing in the air. The starlight within the altar's surface pulsed, growing brighter with every beat of my racing heart.

"Lyra," Seren whispered, her voice tight with warning. "Step back. Get away from here!"

She tried to pull me away, but my body stood frozen, as though I was rooted in the ground. The sound grew louder, and I felt something calling to me from within the void. The Fae magic within me responded eagerly, reaching toward the altar like iron towards a magnet. Golden threads of power began to flow from my skin and swirl within the essence of night, an unreal sight to behold.

"Lyra!" Seren shouted, but it sounded far away.

The pedestal erupted in light—something ancient and overwhelming. Suffocating power shot out like inky tentacles, wrapping me with its sticky flesh. I felt them pierce through me, into the very core of my being.

The world went white, then black, with Seren's shouts nothing more than distant echoes as my consciousness faded.
I awoke standing in a void that stretched endlessly in all directions.

Stars whirled overhead in impossible patterns that made my head throb and beneath my feet, the ground seemed to be made of obsidian glass. The air hummed with an ancient presence so strong that my very bones ached with the pressure.

"Lyra."

The voice that called to me was haunting. It was multi-layered, like many voices talking over one another. Horror skittered up my spine, but I steeled myself against it as a figure materialized in front of me. She was slim, her skin ghostly pale, but her eyes were deep, black pits that held the depth of eternity within them. I bit my lip against the urge to flee until I tasted copper.

It stung. Wasn't this just a dream?

She wore a long-flowing robe that shifted and changed like the sky itself, and a heavy pendant shaped like a distorted moon sat between her small breasts. Pain immediately splintered behind my eyes and I found myself unable to look away, despite the agony.

The woman circled me with a predatory grace and as she did so, I saw trails of multi-hued threads falling from her fingers and lingering in the air. Something about the way they looked felt familiar to me.

"You are difficult to reach, young one," she said, the barest whisper of her robes against the glass echoing in the void. "And your magic resists mine. How curious."

I tried to speak, but no sound escaped. My throat felt like it was seizing, and panic settled within me, my heart racing. The deity smiled, her face both beautiful and terrible as she stopped in front of me. She was very tall, towering over me easily. I craned my neck back and her smile became fierce, more of a baring of teeth.

"The healer's meddling must have changed you more than I thought. No matter. You will follow regardless." She waved her hand and a series of terrible images flashed through my mind, one after the other. Aldric, mortally wounded, my parents in a crystalline room surrounded by Fae, piles of the dead, both human and Otherkind.

"Rescue the immortal prince and return to Aethralis. Claim your place," she commanded, her voice hard.

I couldn't respond, unable to even pull air into my lungs being this close to this…creature.

A cruel expression spread over her face. "Refuse and everyone will die. And it will be your fault, just like it was with the *beast* you were infatuated with."

Griffin's face flashed in my mind's eye and guilt speared through me. With those last biting words, she made a motion as though to wave me away, and my vision swam before me before leaving me again in the dark.

I woke gasping, my body thrashing against cold stone and dirt. My vision swam as I fought to focus, the taste of copper thick in my mouth.

"Lyra!" Seren said, her face coming into view. She struggled to help me sit up, my body shaking like a newborn deer. "You've been unconscious for hours." Her voice was tight with worry. "I tried to get you onto a cot, but you were fighting so hard, I thought it was best to leave you on the floor where you couldn't hurt yourself."

The world tilted dangerously, and I had to close my eyes as

a wave of nausea overtook me. When I opened them again, I was surprised to find I was some place new.

Seren noticed my questioning gaze. "We're in a bunker. It technically belongs to the royal guard, but it hasn't been used in decades," she assured me.

The walls were packed dirt, with shelves full of various foods, from breads and dried fruits and meats to flasks of water that were incredibly clear and seemed to be permanently frosty cold, judging by the condensation on the containers. I raised my brows, turning to find some rudimentary furniture, a couple of cots, some hand-carved chairs, and a table. A small bookshelf with books of various genres sat tucked in a corner, the spines showing the books were well-used.

My gaze roved over our surroundings from my vantage point of the floor, and I came up short when I saw some torches, unlit but twirling aimlessly through the air as though on invisible strings.

"Where are we? What's going on with these? How are they doing that?" I asked.

"If you mean the torches, they're enchanted. No actual flame, so it's safe, even underground. Easy to grab and go if needed," Seren said. Her voice moved away, and I heard a scrape of wood. Squinting, I opened one eye to see a couple of chairs across the room with a small, rounded table between them.

One was just plain wood, the other had a thin pad for the seat. She left the padded one for me, I noticed. I struggled to my feet and shakily made my way to the chair. It was just as uncomfortable as it looked, but I didn't complain.

Seren muttered an incantation, and the torches flared to life with an ethereal periwinkle flame, small sparks flaring up around them to fizzle out moments later. It was beautiful, I had to admit, even with the throbbing in my head.

"Is that your magic?" I asked. "It's really pretty." The blue-violet color lent a dreamlike quality to the room, making it feel like we'd taken a step out of reality. It was disorienting in a way, comforting in another. Made it easier to distance myself from everything that had happened.

Seren shook her head, her eyes reflecting the flames as she watched them flicker. "No, this was here when I first found this place. Took a while to find the words to make them work, but as you can see, I managed." Her voice had a hint of pride, and it made me wonder how long she'd had to try.

I looked harder at the torches and if I really strained my eyes and squinted, I could almost see the small threads of power that wound together to make the flames. Would I be able to see the way the world of magic flowed together if I tried hard enough, long enough? Would it feel the same way if I absorbed it into my body? Then I had a thought.

"Can you see those threads?" I asked.

"What threads?" Seren asked carefully.

"The threads on the torches. It's like they weave together to make the fire."

Seren was silent for a beat. Then she frowned. "There's nothing there. You must have hit your head when you fell."

A blush crept up my cheeks and my throat tightened with

humiliation. Could she be right?

"I need to go back for Aldric," I said after a few minutes of silence. I folded my arms across the table and propped my head up on my hand, trying to dull the ache between my eyes.

"What do you mean? We've just barely gotten out of there," Seren said, throwing her hands up in exasperation. "It's like you're trying to die!"

"They wouldn't expect us to escape just to go right back in. Besides, I don't want them to hurt Aldric. And I can't really feel him from this far away," I said with a frown. "I'm worried about him."

Seren put her forehead down on the table, her arms hanging limply by her side. "This is ridiculous. Why am I here?" she muttered, seemingly to herself. Then she lifted her head, a red spot appearing where her forehead had been on the table. "That would be suicide. Just walking into the hands of death itself."

"I had a dream while I was unconscious," I said, undeterred. "There was some figure there. It's hard to explain, but they said we needed to rescue Aldric as soon as we could."

Seren looked exhausted suddenly, a frown pulling at her lips. "I don't want to talk about some dream. This is ridiculous. You know that, right?" she asked. Then she sighed.

"We need to rest first. We can take a quick nap, then you can head out to the entrance of the tunnels and we can make our way back in, given that they haven't re-blocked the entrance."

With that, Seren stood with yet another bone-tired exhale, looking more defeated than I'd ever seen her. She slowly shuffled over to the cot nearest to her. I felt awful that I was the cause of this. I was always at the center of every problem, it seemed like.

My heart constricted, but I made my way over to another cot and settled slowly. The cot was lumpy, uncomfortable, painfully pressing into my spine. These were somehow even worse than the ones in the dungeon. But we'd make do somehow. It looked like this was built for a small squad of royal guards, as there were another two cots free. I absently wondered how many bunkers like this existed in Starfall Veil. Not that it mattered.

I lay there, turning every scenario over in my mind, anxiety causing my foot to shake. Taking deep breaths, I fought to settle down enough for a nap. We would need the rest, and I knew that. My body had been through so much in the last few days, and I'd barely made it through alive.

Slowly, my body relaxed and my thoughts fell quiet. Just before I drifted off to sleep, Griffin's mangled body flashed in my mind, turning my stomach into knots. His glazed, unseeing eyes seemed to look right in my soul, and to my horror, with the sound of cracking bones and dark fluid gushing from his mouth, he whispered.

"You'll lose him too."

CHAPTER 5

The vision was still fresh in my mind as I shot up straight on the cot, a scream escaping me. Panic erupted in my chest, and I doubled over, my arms wrapping around my waist as I struggled to breathe. I couldn't catch my breath. It was only becoming harder and harder to pull air into my lungs, to keep myself together. My heart was pounding painfully against my ribs, and I rocked back and forth, a cold sweat breaking out over my skin. My vision blurred, and my limbs were shaking.

Seren was suddenly pulling me into her arms, saying something that I couldn't hear over the buzzing in my ears. I continued to rock, trying to center myself, but it felt like I was floating above my body, my mind racing at a million miles a second. Griffin's dead, glazed eyes were still burned into my soul, and I shuddered, my heart feeling as though it were about to burst. Seren stroked my hair and tucked my head under her chin.

I don't know how long we sat like that before the panic

subsided, leaving me completely exhausted. We sat in silence, the only sound my harsh breath grating through my lungs. Seren kept stroking my back, helping me to feel centered in my body again. I glanced around, taking in the different items in the room. The books on the shelf, Seren's cot with a threadbare blanket that's mussed from her sleep, the two chairs and table, the ladder, the torches floating around. The more items I silently counted, the more my mind went quiet.

I felt like I couldn't talk yet. Vulnerability and anxiety weighed me down, making my body feel hundreds of pounds heavier than it was. Seren's hands slid slowly to my shoulders, and I felt a warmth spreading through me.

"You've been through a lot, huh?" Seren asked, her tone gentle as though I were a horse she was afraid of spooking away.

My throat tight, I nodded, but I couldn't bring myself to look at her. A shudder wracked my body, and I swallowed hard.

"You don't have to explain. We've all got some skeletons in our closets, after all," she murmured. "But it explains why you went berserk in there. Your fight or flight is ridiculous compared to most people. You didn't even hesitate to kill that Fae."

Shame colored my cheeks, and I turned in Seren's arms. I would need to explain at some point.

"You became something I don't think you would have seen in Aethralis. Do you know what you transformed into?" Seren asked, curiosity coloring her voice.

I shook my head, drawing my knees up to my chest and resting my head on them and wrapping my arms tightly around my legs.

"It's something called a Pokarnya," she said. "It's a long-fanged, long-clawed beast you may see in the wilds of the Starfall Veil, but only in the parts with the least amount of people. Have you seen one before?"

I shook my head again. It was hard to even listen to Seren talk. It was like my brain was full of fuzz, and I struggled to focus, but I tried. She was just trying to help distract me, I knew. This was important, though. How would I have become something I'd never seen before? This happened one other time, with…

You'll lose him, too.

I vehemently shook my head, trying to clear the sound of his voice from my mind. The last time it happened, I was with Griffin. Thinking about those times felt like living another life. Before long though, the image of his half-Shifted body looms like a gargantuan monster in my mind, dwarfing those happier memories.

"Has something like this happened before?" Seren asked carefully. "If it's too much for you right now, we can talk about it later, once, you know… you've had some time."

I nodded, struggling to articulate any words. It was like they just got stuck in my throat and choked me.

"Do you think you can fall back asleep? I know you must be exhausted," she said gently, slowly moving herself away. Panic threatened to seize me again, but I focused on deep breathing, biting my lip and using that pain to center myself. I had to learn to deal with this on my own. I couldn't have people coming to rescue me all the time. Sometimes, I had to be able to rescue myself.

I nodded again, turning away to face the wall and settling back down. Pulling on the bond, I tried in vain to feel anything coming from Aldric, but there was nothing. Not even a whisper.

I'll be coming for you soon. I swear it.

These words played on repeat in my mind as I finally drifted off, my mind and body giving out entirely until there was nothing left but sleep.

A too-large crescent moon hung overhead, lighting the world around me so brightly I could see as easily as if it were the sun instead. I stood on the edge of a cliff, overlooking a vast ocean. The scent of saltwater stung my nose and wind whipped against my skin as I teetered on the edge.

"You must hurry or it will be too late," came a murmur of many voices. "He cannot be allowed to die or you will not complete the task you were destined for."

I turned to look back at the speaker, but before I could catch more than a glimpse, a hard push threw me over the edge to the jagged rocks below.

My eyes shot open, but I just took a breath. What the hell was with these dreams? Why couldn't I just sleep? I scrubbed a hand over my face with a groan and sat up. Glancing over at the other cot, Seren was twisted in the blankets with an arm thrown over her head, her hair a halo of blue-black around her. She looked much more free in her sleep. I almost felt bad to wake her. But I knew there was no time to waste. I fixed my hair into a braid to keep it out of my face, and straightened my clothes, preparing myself for what may come.

Striding over to the shelves, I grabbed some type of jerky and dried fruits and shoved it into a nearby leather pack. I couldn't remember the last time I ate anything. They hadn't exactly treated it like a five-star hotel in those dungeons. Steeling myself, I made my way over to Seren's cot and put my hand on her shoulder, gently shaking her. She didn't budge at all, quietly snoring.

I shook her again, harder this time. "Seren, wake up. We need to go," I said.

She rolled over, mumbling, and I was running out of time to fight her. I pulled out a piece of jerky and chewed, mulling over my choices. The jerky was edible, not awful. I wondered absently how long it had been here and how often Seren refreshed the foods here.

As I swallowed, I had a dark realization. If I couldn't get Seren to wake, I'd have to go myself. Could I remember the way there? Could I make it back through the tunnels alone? I closed my eyes and mentally mapped the path we took here. I felt a tug deep in my gut and my eyes shot open in surprise. There was a magic deep within me that was not my own, and it reacted to the pressure I was feeling.

Was this from that… deity from the vision? Their power

seemed to fuel the ancient magic below the Fae castle. Were they helping me? My eyes fell on a wisp of a thread, pulling from the flame of the torches floating around. I dropped the rest of my jerky on the table and cautiously approached the nearest torch. As I got closer, the thread grew thicker, brighter. It seemed to be pulling towards the south. To the castle?

There's no way this wasn't divine intervention. It left a bitter taste in my mouth, but I didn't have a choice. I'd have to follow where the threads led and hope for the best. I shouldered the pack and picked up a torch, climbing the ladder. With one last look towards Seren's sleeping form, I left the bunker and set out on my own.

CHAPTER 6

The periwinkle flame continued to go out, thread by thread, leading me away from the bunker and back to the castle we had just fled. I reached into the pack and pulled out a piece of what looked like a dried fruit. If it was in the bunker, it wouldn't kill me. Hopefully. It woke me up at least, I supposed.

The sun sank below the horizon. As darkness fell, I realized the stars were brighter than I'd ever seen in Aethralis. Almost like spotlights shining down on me, but the surrounding sky was deep like an ocean, nebulas and galaxies clear to see. It was unlike anything I'd ever seen. I could look at this forever and keep finding new things to see.

I couldn't wait to show this to Aldric, I realized. I pulled on the bond between us, but there wasn't even a flutter. With a sigh, I scrubbed a hand over my face. He was alive. He had to be. Why else would the Sovereign be leading me to him?

My eyes still up on the sky, I finished chewing the fruit and immediately tripped over an exposed root and fell face-first into the hard-packed dirt. Shock had me lying there for a moment, the wind knocked out of me.

The torch fell with me and sputtered as it hit the ground, causing panic to fill my body. I scrambled back to my feet and gently blew on the flame, trying to will it back to life before it went out and left me stranded. As my breath touched the base of the fire, it crackled with power and flared a deep blue and emerald green before settling back into a periwinkle hue. That was strange. Why did everything around here have to be so odd? It had to be me, right?

With a sigh, I shook my head, resolutely keeping my eyes on the ground to avoid any other mishaps that could leave me lost. The threads floated through the air again. I followed their path exactly, my gut instinct leading me. And soon, I saw why when I was led around a clearing in the forest that would be a straight shot to the tunnels and instead saw the bright, cheery faces of the enemy Fae, spreading out in a searching pattern. More than likely looking for Seren and me. I sent a quiet prayer to whomever may be listening that Seren be kept safe, and silently crept my way around, keeping myself as small as possible.

Luckily, the light of this torch did not travel far, so I wasn't immediately noticeable. I moved as swiftly as possible and somehow managed to dodge anyone who may be looking for me.

Before I knew it, I was standing back in front of that heavy door leading back into the dungeon of the castle. I swallowed thickly, my hand tightening on the torch until wood splinters stabbed my fingers, drawing pricks of blood. After a moment of thought, I wondered something and decided to chance it. The torches floated in the bunker. Would one float here too? I cautiously peeled my fingers from the wood handle, leaving spots of red behind where the wood had dug in. It didn't drop, instead ominously floating before the door, the light flickering off of the metal accents.

Okay, that was one problem solved, I thought. I grasped the handle and pulled hard on the door. It didn't budge. Well, that wasn't going to work. I peered all around the edges of the door, looking to see if there were any gaps I could sneak through, but there was nothing even an ant could squeeze through. What could I do? I pressed a hand to my forehead, thinking hard. Could I use any of my magic somehow?

I turned and sat on the ground, leaning against the door. The torch descended to float next to me, which was creepy as hell. The spectral color of the flames made it feel haunted somehow. Maybe it was. Seren did say that she wasn't sure where that magic had come from that powered them, after all. Maybe it was a ghost or poltergeist, I thought, dread curling in my belly. Weirder things had happened around here.

A headache bloomed behind my eyes as I thought long and hard about how I was going to get through this gods-damned door.

Myrana, I don't know if you can hear me. I don't know if you're one of those deities that listens to prayers, but if you could help me out here, that would be great. I thought, sulking.

For a few minutes, I sat and planned what my next steps

would be if I wasn't able to get through this door. I knew nothing about this castle, or where else I may get inside. A breeze blew past me that carried a hint of laughter, multi-layered across many voices, which chilled me to the bone.

I straightened and quickly got to my feet, looking around. The torch continued to follow before a loud bang sounded from behind the door. Even through the heavy wood, it was deafening. If that was their way of helping, I didn't think I'd make it. The Sovereign had basically announced my arrival.

My stomach sank all the way to my feet and I fell backwards as the door opened soundlessly. Of course, this part is soundless, I thought, my mood entirely soured. There were splinters of wood littering the floor where the barricade had been blown away. Adrenaline coursed hard and fast through my veins and I shook with the force of it. This was it. Now or never. I had to get in and get out as quickly as possible with Aldric, who may be hurt, or…

I refused to consider the possibility that they took his life. There was no way. I took a deep breath and rushed inside, the torch staying just ahead of me to illuminate my way.

Following the threads coming off of the flames became easier and easier in the dark. They seemed to travel along an invisible breeze, their slight glow like a beacon in the void. It brought me through the twists and turns, avoiding any dead ends, ensuring that I stayed true to the course. I was beyond grateful, as I had a sinking feeling that time was of the essence.

I walked faster and faster until I was running full tilt, my breath sawing in and out of my lungs. I *needed* to get to Aldric. To see him. There was still no response when pulling on our bond. Something was wrong. I just knew it.

Finally, I saw the edge of a light. The exit of the tunnels. Surely they had someone guarding it? I mentally prepared myself to fight, my power surging inside of me until I felt like a balloon about to burst. I slowed my pace, trying to catch my breath. Couldn't exactly sneak up on anyone if they heard my labored breathing. Once I had myself under control, I crept towards the exit, putting my ear up to the stone and concentrating. The torch clattered against the stone, almost like it was urging me to continue, but I had to be sure. I didn't want to take any more lives if I could avoid it. Every time it was like my soul died a little.

Eventually, I would lose myself entirely. This isn't who I was meant to be, and I knew it in my bones. There had to be another way. With a slight flash of light, I became as small as possible in an attempt to sneak by unnoticed. The form I ended up taking was a ladybug. That way I could fly as needed. The torch continued to gently bounce off of the stone, but I slipped through a crevice, leaving it behind. I had to remember the way.

As soon as I made my way out, I knew that was the right choice. There were several guards standing by, chairs set up and all. One was leaning against the wall, snoring away, while several others stood at attention, some on their feet, some sat down, but all keeping a wary eye out. Regret coiled in me like a poison as I spotted the dark stain left behind by the Fae that I had killed. It looked like they had attempted to clean it up, but their life had stained the stone.

It stained my soul as well, I thought bitterly. But it was horrible that I even felt that way, given that it was my fault that they died to begin with. I shoved these thoughts down and focused. It was strange having human thoughts in the body of an insect, but I paused, hiding in the shadows on the floor as I tried again to pull on the bond. The faintest tingle whispered to me and I followed where it led, slowly making my way through the dungeon back to the cell where I had spent what felt like an eternity.

When I finally arrived some time later, I was surprised to find no guards nearby. They had tapered off the closer that I got to the hallway where Aldric would reside. I quickly turned back into myself as I approached his cell.

"Aldric?" I whispered as the inside of his cell came into view. "Are you—,"

The words crumbled in my throat as he came into view. "Wh-wh-what have they done to you?" I cried before I could stop myself.

I ran to the bars and grabbed his door. The lock shattered into nothingness as soon as my hand touched it and I flung open the door, rushing to Aldric's side, coming up short with arm outstretched towards him.

Aldric was bound in chains yet again, but this time, with enormous silver spikes going through each limb, burning away at the surrounding flesh. He looked like a bound voodoo doll someone had pushed pins into with wanton abandon. He was unconscious, blood dribbling from the corner of his mouth to pool on the floor. His breathing was ragged, and he looked as though he'd been beaten, his body marked with bruises. As I looked him over, I saw what looked like strips of flesh peeled away on his back.

What the hell had they done to him? My power bloomed painfully inside of me, almost audibly screeching to get out, to attack, to maim, to protect him. I stood there dumbly, my entire body shaking with a rage like I'd never felt before. A sliver of his mercury-colored eyes were visible, and I crouched next to him, brushing a trembling hand over his clammy forehead, pushing his ebony waves off of his face.

Whatever I felt about this bond, this…this couldn't stand. I tenderly cupped his cheek in my palm and pressed a kiss to his lips, which were dry and cracking. I channeled all of my anger into my mana, pooling it inside me until it felt like a vast cavern of magic, where it began to greedily pull the threads of power remaining in this dungeon until my skin grew almost luminescent from the force of it. This was something I'd never felt before. I felt almost like an avenging demon, ready to destroy all those who opposed me. I turned my hand this way and that, and there was a barely visible trail of light following behind, the same color as the ancient magic here.

Taking a deep breath, I used this power to become a Pokarnya yet again, my body shifting into a monstrous beast, huge and hulking. The world became a kaleidoscope of colors and my hearing went to superhuman levels, where I could hear a guard clearing his throat half-a-mile back. My ears were huge and tufted, rotating on a swivel. Gently, I picked Aldric up in my gargantuan maw, careful not to jostle him too much. I couldn't remove these spikes on my own without risking him bleeding out. Seren. She would have to help me, to make sure he survived.

My elongated fangs kept Aldric cradled into my mouth, keeping him as secure as possible while I prowled the halls, making my way back to the only exit I knew of. There were so many more colors than I'd given myself a chance to see before, which was disorienting as I was navigating my way along. It was like the world was turned up to neon and I'd only ever seen colors in pastels before. Jarring. I trot along silently on padded paws, my tail swishing behind me. Aldric didn't make even a single groan as I carried him, which urged me to move faster.

There was no time to waste. Not if I wanted him to live. My pace picked up until I was racing through the halls. I could feel his breathing become fainter, and the scent of his burning flesh was nauseating, especially with my heightened sense of smell. I could scent the Fae up ahead, but I didn't have a choice. Rounding the corner, their screams echoed off of the stone, reverberating in the small hallway. I filled the hall from wall to wall, so there was no place to run except further into the dungeon. Most didn't hesitate and tucked their tails and ran, but the few that remained were bowled over by me as I barreled through the entrance to the tunnels, careful to turn my head so that my shoulder took the brunt of the impact.

I barely felt my skin slicing open from the jagged rock, adrenaline coursing powerfully through me. Refusing to slow even a second, I completely ignored the shouts of alarm from behind me, pushing myself to run harder, faster, to make my way through these tunnels as quickly as possible. And with how agile this form was, it didn't take long at all before I was back at the door, which was still open. How no one had come to the exit baffled me, but I wasn't going to look a gift horse in the mouth.

As I bounded out, doing my best to keep Aldric stable, I came up short. Could I remember the way back? The torch had lost its flame and lay lifeless inside of the tunnel way back at the very entrance, so that wasn't an option. I took a deep breath through my nose, a myriad of smells accosting me all at once. Maybe I could figure out the way back to the bunker by the scent?

I knew I came from the South, so I turned in that direction and started off, moving swiftly and silently through the woods. The thought that as this creature, I could move so quietly, it gave me chills. If a Pokarnya were to follow me, would I notice? The taste of copper drifted across my tongue and my stomach sank, pulling me from my thoughts. Aldric. He had to hold on until I got back to Seren.

She could help me. She had to.

CHAPTER 7

Through dumb luck or divine intervention, I avoided any Fae in the forest as I quickly made my way back to where I thought the bunker was. And eventually, I caught the scent of springtime, of fur and big cats.

Seren.

Desperately, I pawed around on the ground, looking for the trapdoor. Who had covered it? Unless Seren had woken. I inhaled deeply, drawing as much information from her scent as I could.

She wasn't as close as I thought.

I made my way further south until I saw some disturbance in the leaves. There! Panic filled me. What was I going to do with Aldric? How would I get him safely into the bunker? I couldn't open the door as a Pokarnya, and I wasn't strong enough to carry him down, especially injured as he was.

With the utmost care, I gently laid him in the softest grass I could find, transforming back to my original body. I yanked the trapdoor open and jumped in. Seren was still laying where I had left her, still and quiet. Storming over to her, I wasted no time in waking her.

"Seren!" I shouted, jostling her.

It took a moment, but Seren awoke abruptly, her entire body shaking with adrenaline.

"W-what happened? The Sovereign, they—" Seren babbled, then took a moment, staring up at me with eyes as wide as saucers, her pupils huge.

"I got Aldric. I need your help. Hurry!" Without waiting for a response, I headed back up the ladder and went to sit next to Aldric, who hadn't moved at all since I sat him down, blood trickling from his mouth to stain the emerald-hued grass.

The sounds of shuffling could be heard from where I worried over Aldric, and before long, Seren's head appeared as she climbed up, dark circles under her eyes. She had a bundle over her shoulder, and her expression was kept carefully blank as she saw the state that Aldric was in.

Wasting no time, she whipped open the bundle to reveal a number of bottles, pastes, and other tinctures. Not only that, there were bandages, needles, and various other implements as well.

How she managed to fit all of that in one pack was beyond me, but she was nothing if not prepared, I supposed. That made a good leader, after all.

"Lyra, you're bleeding," she murmured, her brow furrowed in concern as she came closer, putting a hand on my shoulder. Looking down in surprise, I saw blood trailing down my shirt from where the delicate skin above my collarbone had been torn open. It must have been when I shouldered through the tunnel, I realized. The jagged rock shredded my flesh, but I couldn't feel a thing.

"I'm fine. It doesn't hurt. Please. Please just help Aldric," I begged.

My gaze fell back on the vampire, silently bleeding into the grass. He was barely breathing, and the odor of rotting flesh filled the air. I didn't know the healing capabilities of vampires, but surely they could only make it through so much until their bodies could no longer keep up.

My heart twisted in my chest as Seren moved to Aldric, her hands exceedingly gentle as she poked and prodded to see the extent of his injuries. The faintest groan fell from his lips from her ministrations, his face screwed up in pain.

"Let me know what I need to do. We need to help him, no matter the cost."

My body was practically vibrating with adrenaline—the only thoughts I had were to save Aldric.

"I—I don't know how much we *can* do," Seren said carefully, her face betraying no emotion.

Before I knew it, I was gripping her shoulders, turning her towards me. I loomed over Seren, blood racing in my veins and causing it to seep ever faster through my clothes.

"We do whatever it takes. He needs to live," I ground out from between clenched teeth. "It was *your* people who did this to him."

Seren flinched beneath my fingers, and I realized I was holding her much harder than I thought.

"I'm sorry," I said, releasing her and backing away with my hands up. "I'm sorry."

Seren straightened and brushed her hands down her shirt as though clearing unseen dust. "I understand. But remember, it was *them*. Don't take out your anger on me," she said with a sniff. "I'll do what I can, but no promises. He'll definitely need blood. And a lot of it."

Wrapping my arms around my middle, I nodded. "Whatever it takes."

Seren got to work quickly, unraveling the chains that were bound around Aldric's body. He barely moved during this process, and I knew he was close to death. Probably closer than he'd ever been. However, as soon as she touched one of the spikes, Aldric suddenly arched his spine up off of the ground, screaming.

"Get over here and hold him down before he damages himself more!" Seren shouted, trying in vain to keep him from bucking against her touch.

I swallowed thickly around the lump in my throat, tears pricking at my eyes. But I didn't hesitate, straddling Aldric's waist and putting my hands on the free spaces in his flesh that were unmarked. There weren't many, I realized, my heart shattering. Why would they do this to him?

"Lyra, help me," Aldric ground out, his voice thin and reedy. His eyes slid open, and I could tell he wasn't really aware of what was going on. They were cloudy with pain, rolling around in their sockets. "Help me."

I struggled to speak, tears choking me. "I am," I whispered, my voice cracking. "Please stop moving before you hurt yourself more."

As if I hadn't spoken at all, Aldric continued to fight as hard as he could against Seren's ministrations. I held him down with as much force as I could muster without further injuring him. Before long, the first spike came out, and with it came the horrible stench of infection.

"Please," Aldric said, and I was horrified to see tears of blood leaking from the corners of his eyes. "Please help me."

"What do you need?" I asked through hiccuping sobs. My heart was being torn to shreds, and I felt so helpless. "Tell me what you need and I'll get it for you."

As though just realizing I was there, Aldric's eyes found mine, the silver murky through his anguish. "Love, you came back," he said, with a touch of awe in his voice. "You shouldn't be here. They'll catch you."

I just couldn't stop crying. Aldric stilled, watching me, and I wiped my eyes. I hated this. I hated that he had been put through this, that this just *kept happening* to people I cared about.

Looking to the sky, I fought the urge to scream out to the Sovereign. I knew she was listening.

Silently, Seren continued to pull the spikes slowly from Aldric's limbs, leaving weeping wounds behind. What demonic entity thought of this?

Then it occurred to me. This is how I could help. Seren had finished with his arms, and he lay completely limp and placid beneath me.

"Are you almost done?" I asked, my voice soft, broken.

"Almost. As long as he doesn't fight me, I should be done in the next few minutes. Then it'll just be about finding what mixture to use for these wounds," she muttered, then began mumbling to herself, talking about different ingredients she could mix and what effects they would have.

I stopped listening, instead waiting until she was finally moving to his lower legs. Shifting myself back onto Aldric's upper thighs carefully, I reached and burrowed my hands under Aldric's arms, cradling his shoulders and pulling him off of the ground and towards me.

He looked so exhausted, with dark circles under his eyes. His skin was pale and sweat-slicked, having lost its sun-kissed glow. The more silver left his body, the more lucid he became. A wave of relief crashed over me, though I knew he was far from out of the woods yet.

"You've never looked more like a vampire than now," I murmured softly, taking one hand and brushing his hair back off of his forehead.

Aldric laughed weakly. His voice was hoarse when he asked, "Am I still the most attractive vampire you've ever seen?"

"Now, I don't recall ever saying that you were the *most* attractive," I said with a wry twist to my lips. The smile slowly faded, and I cradled his head to my chest. "You need to have some blood."

"You're already hurt, love," Aldric murmured against my skin. His lips were dry and cracked, scraping against my tender flesh.

"You're more hurt than me. Drink. Please," I pleaded, holding him tighter.

At my words, I felt a soft, hesitant touch—his arms encircling me. I heard the last *clink* of metal being dropped into the pile behind us, and I heaved a sigh of relief. Aldric was tense, his grip growing tighter against me.

Then, I felt it.

The rough touch of his tongue, lapping up the free-flowing blood from my collarbone. A ragged moan escaped him, and I matched it with one of my own, my fingers moving to tangle themselves in his dark hair. Faintly, I heard the trapdoor closing, but I couldn't focus on that now.

I knew this was exactly what Aldric needed. A memory flashed unbidden across my mind—Aldric tearing into me as he was half-dead. But it faded away, evaporating into smoke.

This couldn't be more different, the tender way he held me, the emotion pouring off of him. Tears flowed from my eyes anew, but for a completely different reason. Why had I tried to push him so far away?

I could have lost Aldric entirely. He didn't choose this bond any more than I did. But he never turned away from me. Instead, he took me, as broken as I am, and tried to make me whole, to keep me together, to pick up the shattered pieces of my being.

His tongue worked harder, and I shuddered in response. His long fingers traced up and down my spine, leaving tingles in their wake. Aldric's hands were shaking, and I could only imagine the pain he was in. Was he shielding me from it? I thought absently.

Before long, the blood coagulated there, and Aldric pulled back, his eyes already a little brighter. I shifted to straddle him more comfortably, and was pleased to see some of the smaller wounds had begun to heal already, although the holes left by the silver spikes had yet to change.

Wordlessly, I urged Aldric to my neck, tilting my head to the side to allow him better access. Aldric's hand slid up to cup the back of my head, gripping my hair and pulling hard, causing a delicious pain as my back arched from the tension. His other hand gripped my lower back, pulling me ever closer.

Soon, I felt the touch of his lips on the column of my neck, leaving soft butterfly kisses as he moved to where he needed to be. Then, a pinch as his fangs slid into my neck. A deep groan escaped him, rumbling against my delicate flesh. A wave of pleasure shot straight to my core, and I fought not to grind against him.

Much as I wanted to, now was not the time. And much as he wanted to, I thought with surprise as I felt movement beneath me.

"Aldric," I said, but it came out as a breathy moan, heat spreading from the bite to fill my entire body.

I felt Aldric's lips twitch up in a smile. "Say my name like that again, and I may take you right here."

His words caused a pulse of arousal to spear through me and I bit my lip. "Aldric, no," I panted despite myself. "You're barely making it alive. This is to help you, remember?"

Aldric growled against me, shifting to press against the apex of my thighs. "Don't say that. My life would be complete if I had you," he said, before working his lips against my throat again. The more he drank, the hotter I burned until I felt like I would combust.

"You make it out alive, and you just may," I said, writhing against him. "But not now."

Slowly, Aldric pulled away from me, licking a bead of ruby red blood from his lips. The view, even with his injuries, was incredibly erotic, and I was desperate, slick with desire. Every beat of my heart just pushed the feeling even harder until I was aching—nevertheless, I refused.

We only felt this way right now because of the feed.

The worst of the silver wounds still stubbornly refused to close, weeping and raw, like his body couldn't decide whether to heal or die. I knew once the high wore off, he would be in incredible pain, and I refused to subject him to that. But maybe, maybe when he had healed…

I shook my head and looked down at Aldric. His eyes were heavy-lidded with desire, the dark circles all but gone. His skin practically glowed from within. "Do you mean that, love? If I make it through this, I mean. No promises," he said with a wink.

"Even on your deathbed you're still a ham," I said, rolling my eyes. "But maybe."

"Maybe is enough for me," he murmured, lovingly stroking a hand down my cheek. My heart swelled in my chest.

I had almost lost him. But I wouldn't lose him again, I promised, my head falling back as I stared up at the sky. I would not lose him.

"Yeah," I murmured. I pulled Aldric close to me, and we just sat there, holding each other for a while.

"Are you two quite done?" Seren called from the entrance of the bunker. A flush crept up my cheeks, but I didn't move. My head was cradled on Aldric's shoulder, my hand tracing the planes of muscle on his chest.

I was pleased to discover that most of the skin had stitched itself back together, not even a blemish remaining. However, the same could not be said for his other injuries. Whatever they had imbued that silver with had slowed his healing to a snail's pace.

"Not quite, but please, join us," Aldric called back, a teasing note to his voice. I jumped up, thumping his chest.

"Aldric," I cried, my cheeks burning. "Yes, we're done."

He nuzzled close to my ear and murmured, "I'm not." His breath caressed me as erotically as his tongue would, and I suppressed a shudder, a spike of heat spearing me.

"You're definitely done," I whispered back.

A dark laugh escaped him, and I smiled in response. I had missed this. Aldric had been so down for so long, I realized. Because of me. Guilt crashed over me like a wave of cold water, immediately souring my mood.

After Griffin's death, I had shut down. Shut Aldric out. Because it felt wrong. To want to be around him. To enjoy talking with him. But I realized I didn't have to forget Griffin, or to pretend that didn't happen. I was with him, and I cared about him.

And it wasn't the same.

Regardless of any bond, I cared about Aldric. I wanted him safe. To be happy. And right now, with things as they were, that couldn't happen. I needed to fix it. This whole thing—the plague, Griffin's death, Aldric's imprisonment—it all began with me. And it would end with me, too.

I would make sure of it.

CHAPTER 8

Seren's soft footsteps sounded behind me, and I quickly disentangled myself from Aldric, much to his disappointment. He huffed a bit, but I saw the smile he tried to hide. It made my heart flutter and my cheeks warmed, but these feelings were still too new. Instead of ruminating on it, I turned to Seren.

"Well, if you *are* quite done, we need to take care of those silver wounds before they fester even more. Wouldn't do you any good to keep laying on the ground," she said pointedly, gesturing with the poultice she carried. "Luckily, I had a pestle and mortar stored away, so I could grind some ingredients into a paste that may just help. No guarantees, though."

Seren strode over with all the confidence of a trained professional, hauling Aldric up to his feet before he could complain and dragging him by his arm to the trapdoor. Aldric looked pleadingly at me over his shoulder, but I just shrugged. I didn't want to get in Seren's way, so I just followed silently behind, just in case.

Seren quickly descended the ladder, Aldric following more sluggishly as he carefully made his way down the rungs to avoid further injuring himself. Closing the trapdoor behind me, I slid down the ladder, wanting to get into the bunker as quickly as possible.

Seren had already led Aldric to my cot, I noticed with a tingle in my belly. But I quashed that feeling down, because now was not the time. I strode over to Aldric's side, and the pain was clear now that the high of feeding had gone. The moonlight in his eyes drew me in until I felt like I couldn't escape. He seemed just as enraptured staring into mine, and I noticed flecks of amethyst in his gaze as the color of my eyes was reflected at me.

Seren cleared her throat, and I blinked, the moment fading. She handed me the poultice, and I held it carefully, not quite sure what to do.

At my quizzical look, Seren said, "Just hold that for me. I'll need both hands to do this, and there's not enough room for me to put it anywhere that's within easy reach."

Made sense. Should have thought of that. "No problem. Just let me know if you need anything else," I said, diligently holding the poultice close to her. She used a spatula-like object to scoop some of the paste and slathered it onto one of the holes left from the spikes, then wrapped it in linen. She moved methodically, and each time, there was barely even a flinch from Aldric.

"Does it hurt?" I found myself asking, trying to keep my voice carefully neutral.

Aldric smiled, though it was a little shaky. "It's not as awful as getting stabbed through more times than I can count," he said with a dark chuckle, wincing as Seren continued working. "Once it's had time to settle in, it's kind of soothing, actually. There's a cooling effect from something in there."

"Ah, yeah, that'll be the skullcap and honeysuckle," Seren said, scraping into the jar again. The scent was surprisingly pleasant and floral. "They both help with inflammation and infection. I'm hoping that'll be enough to allow you to heal yourself."

"Why are you helping me? Aren't I the enemy? The rest of your race seems to think so," Aldric said, with a note of bitterness creeping into his voice.

Seren didn't respond, but tightened the next bandage a little more aggressively than she needed to, causing Aldric to hiss out a breath.

"Don't assume we Fae all think the same. Sometimes we do things just because we have to, and not because it's what we think is right," she snapped with a huff.

I thought back to the meal Seren brought me, even though she could have been punished. She had helped me then. After Aldric's bite, she'd helped me then, too.

"Give her some credit, Aldric. She's here, isn't she?" I said, chastising him as I watched her continue her ministrations.

"Yes, yes, you're right. My sincere apologies," Aldric said, though I couldn't tell if he meant it. Come to think of it, our bond hadn't felt quite right since I was forced to leave him behind.

I tried to pull on the line between us, however, I was shocked to find that I couldn't feel anything from him. There was so much adrenaline before that I hadn't tried, but now that we're here, right next to each other, I should be able to feel him just as easily as I could before, right?

How could I fix it? I was surprised to find how much I had grown used to feeling his presence. It had made me feel… less alone. No matter what else had been going on, I could draw on him for strength. And now, it was like my soul was bereft of a key part of myself. I searched his moonlight eyes, looking for any trace of concern, of whether he could feel my inner turmoil, how lost I felt. But there was no sign of anything but the sheen of pain as Seren finished up, leaving the jar empty of its contents.

Was this Myrana's doing? Why would she do that if she wanted Aldric and me to be together? None of this made sense. I shook my head, trying to clear my thoughts. I had to be missing something. Mentally pulling harder on that tether, I was shaken to my core to find it completely empty.

Seren seemed to sense something was wrong, and she came to gently remove the jar from my hands, which I was surprised to find were trembling. Aldric had a quizzical look on his face, his head cocked to the side as he studied me.

I didn't trust myself to speak right now. Instead, I pivoted on my heel and moved to leave. I had to get out of here. Vaguely, I heard Aldric's voice calling out for me, but I didn't stop, just hurried out and shut the trapdoor behind me.

Wrapping my arms around my middle, I took a shaky breath and strode off into the forest, determined to put some distance between myself and the bunker. I needed time to think, and I couldn't do that if I were looking at Aldric the whole time. My gaze rose to the sky, which looked like a blanket of velvet and diamonds, the stars glittering almost ominously the further I made it away from Aldric.

"I don't know if you can hear me, but if you can, what is this?" I asked no one. There was no answer, not that I expected one. Suddenly, I was filled with rage and frustration, and I punched a tree. The bark immediately flayed my knuckles open. As my blood trickled down my fingers, I struck it again and again, until my hands were wrecked, the pale trunk stained with the evidence of my anger.

Slowly, I sank to my knees, the burn of tears stinging my eyes. My lower lip trembled, and I bit down hard to still it. "Can you just tell me what you want? I don't understand. Why? You gave me this bond I didn't want, and now that I've come to accept it, you've taken it away again. What sense does that make?" I raged, slamming my fists into my thighs.

There wasn't even a single breath of wind to answer me, and I broke, a sob wracking my body as I screamed my resentment into the air. "Myrana, I know you can hear me!" I roared, my voice raw and pained. "Don't ignore me!"

Curling over on myself, I sucked in a ragged breath, my hands gripping my hair tightly. Nothing was under my control. I was just a puppet being used by everyone, with no will of my own. My eyes slipped closed, and I leaned forward until I lay prone on the ground, my body going limp in the cool grass. And I simply existed for that moment, feeling completely defeated.

Broken.

After gods know how long, I picked myself up slowly, sitting back on my heels. Everything felt like too much right now, with all the pressure weighing on me. Sucking in a deep breath, I shakily let it back out, curling my hands and setting them on my thighs. I ground my teeth against the burn of the torn skin stretching, bleeding starting anew.

My eyes were closed, listening to the world surrounding me. A faint whisper of wind through the tree branches. A faraway cry of some unknown animal, the trills of birds. The scent of the grass I'd crushed as I laid on it, the smell of earth, of moss and damp.

It reminded me of Sylvan Reach, where I'd grown up. There was an underlying current of power here that Sylvan Reach lacked, however. Almost like the ground beneath was charged with electricity and just looking for a conduit to release it.

Reaching down, I ran my fingers through the grass. It was cool and slightly damp with dew tickling my fingertips. My head tilted back to the sky, and I took deep breaths, just feeling the mana of this place. It was like an ancient being just staring down at me, cradling me gently in the palm of its hand, as though to protect me from all the harshness of reality. The energy was both intense and gentle—powerful, yet forgiving.

Eventually, the thunderous tune of my heartbeat slowed to a more steady rhythm, my breathing slowing. But as I stood to leave, there was a noise I recognized. My head tilted, listening. Rushing water. How had I not noticed that before?

Padding through the grass, it felt as though each blade was reaching for me, trying to grasp onto me. Whether to hold me back or to keep me there, I didn't know, but either way, it was eerie.

The closer I got, the louder the sound became until it was almost deafening. Soon, a river came into view.

It was beautiful. Glowing from within with a gentle light, the water was the purest blue. And it was massive, stretching miles between its banks. I couldn't tell where it started or ended, my gaze traveling from one side to the other.

The water was rushing impossibly fast. If I were to fall in, there was no way I could ever get myself free. I peered into the water and froze with shock. Despite how fast the water was moving when viewed from afar, the surface seemed to be flat and smooth, reflective like a mirror.

That wasn't right.

My breath hitched as my face came into view. There were streaks of dried, flaky blood in the mass of white hair on my head. It was a tangled mess. I had smudges of purple under my eyes, and the violet within them was dull and dark, almost black. Honestly, I looked like someone who'd given up. It was hard to tell myself that wasn't true.

I reached for the water, wanting to at least wash my hair and face. But just before my fingertips broke the surface, I looked deeper, past my reflection, and saw something else. Bracing myself on the riverbank, I leaned in a little closer, my nose almost brushing the surface.

As the object came into view, I screamed, scrambling back away from the water, my heart pounding against my chest so hard I thought it might explode.

It was a face.

As I turned to flee, my body stopped responding. It was like my flesh had turned to stone. Panic arced through me like a lightning strike, and I glanced around, terrified.

What was happening?

I heard a splash behind me, and my lungs seized, leaving me short of breath. It felt like I was going to have a heart attack. What was with this place?! I thought, my anxiety rising.

My blood was rushing in my ears, and I strained to hear anything. There was the sound of wet footsteps approaching me, slapping against the grass. My eyes darted around wildly, desperate to see what was surely about to kill me.

"Hey, sorry. This isn't the most ideal way to meet, I know," came from behind me. My mouth opened in a scream, but nothing came out.

"There's no need to be afraid. I mean, I could have thought about that before I left you stuck, I guess," the voice said, sounding sullen. It was a man's voice, soothing and soft, like the burbling of a creek. As it washed over me, my pulse immediately slowed, and I felt my muscles relaxing against my better judgement.

Suddenly, I could move again. Immediately, my body tried to go limp, but a pair of powerful hands caught me, hauling me back to my feet. He turned me so that I was facing him as easily as if he were turning a page. This guy was *strong*, I realized. Just who was he?

"Yeah, I know, I know. Really scary, huh?" he asked sarcastically. I was taken aback. He had long black hair that looked as though it was made of silk. It went straight to his shoulders. He didn't have a shirt on, I realized.

My gaze went lower, and I realized he was wearing a pair of loose, flowing pants that tapered at the ankle. They were fitted at the waist, and seemed to allow for a lot of freedom of movement. The pants themselves were dark blue.

His feet were bare—his toes were surprisingly well manicured. Slowly, my gaze went back up, where I noticed he was muscular despite being lean. Finally, I reached his face. He had dark circles under his eyes, which were a deep shade of pink. His skin was dusky gray, his ears pointed like the Fae.

He had thin lips that were a shade of mauve. His eyes glowed from within, leaving a gentle hue of pink on his face. This was both the strangest and most interesting man I'd ever met. Who was he?

"Are you done ogling me yet?" he asked wryly, his lips twisting up in a facsimile of a smile.

I startled, not realizing just how long I'd been staring. "I'm sorry," I muttered, looking down. "Didn't mean to stare."

"It's quite all right. Mortals don't often see people who look like me, after all," he said. "Which is good for you."

"Mortals?" I asked, my gaze snapping back up to his. I didn't realize how tall he was — at least a couple of feet taller than me. It was hard not to feel dwarfed by his presence, though he had a kind energy to him.

"You bet. I'm what you might call a god," he said, raising his arms and wiggling his fingers at me. "You scared yet?"

"W-wh—," I sputtered, then took a breath and tried again. "What in the world? What do you mean you're a god?"

"Surely I'm not the first one you've met. I mean, I know

Myrana's energy when I feel it," the man said, crossing his arms and widening his stance. "She's such a sourpuss."

"Why do you talk like that?" I blurted. "You just…don't seem like a god."

"Not everyone takes things so seriously, you know," the man said. "Some of us aren't in the wheelhouse of trying to terrify mortals into obeying us. Some of us just exist and are content that way."

"So… why are you here? And where is this anyway?" I asked, gesturing to the river.

"Ah, this is like a mini-realm, if you'd prefer to call it that. You're in my domain. I rule over the rivers in the Starfall Veil, among other bodies of water. There wasn't one nearby, so I brought you to one so I could pop in and see how you were doing."

"How I'm doing?" I asked, incredulous. "What do you mean? How would you expect me to be doing? Do you even know what's been going on?"

The man moved to sit, and I fully expected him to fall, but to my surprise a wave flowed up from the river, seeming to take solid form beneath him, though it still rippled and flowed. My mouth gaped open. Okay, he was definitely a deity of some type. He steepled his fingers under his chin, resting his elbows on the arms of his seat.

"Oh, I'm well aware. We all are. All of the others have turned away, content to let things continue as they may. But I heard you. When you cried out, your voice was so full of pain. And I realized I didn't want to just sit idly by and let Myrana just continue to play with innocent lives."

"Just who are you?" I asked cautiously. "Why help me?"

"My name is Ler. And I'm not just helping you. The path that Myrana is trying to set you on is one that would hold much more bloodshed than I think you're ready for."

"I'm not ready for *any* bloodshed. I don't want anyone else to die," I said, my voice surprisingly steady despite how shaky I felt inside.

"That's what I thought. And that's why I'm here. It's not typical for gods, deities, whatever you choose to call us, to meddle in each other's affairs. I didn't want to shrug this off like the others."

"Is this…dangerous for you?" I asked. "The Sovereign seems pretty strong."

"She has a heftier domain than I do, that's true. But that's why I'm being a little sneaky bringing you here," he said with a wink. He was much more playful than I expected from a god. He brushed his hair back away from his face, and it fell through his fingers like liquid silk.

"What do you mean?"

"Each deity's domain is cut off from the rest, except in very rare circumstances. She can't overhear us in this place, unlike if I tried to meet you where you were," Ler explained.

I tapped my finger to my chin, then winced as I felt the torn skin pulling on my knuckles.

"You looked like you were really going through it down there," Ler said gently. "Are you alright?"

"It's—it's hard to explain," I said, hesitant to share my feelings. Would he use this against me? How can I trust him—

deity or no? Every legend about gods and goddesses says that they're cunning, conniving, bored with eternity and wanting to use lesser beings as forms of entertainment. Was Ler like them?

"It's the bond, isn't it?" Ler asked, curiosity plain on his face. "What happened?"

"How do you know about that?" I snapped, frustrated. "Why is everyone so involved in every aspect of my life and my being?"

Ler raised his hands in an attempt at placating me, though it did nothing to dim the fire roaring inside of me. "It's a topic among the gods. Do I agree? No, but it's like Myrana is trying to replicate the same events that almost tore Aethralis asunder thousands of years ago."

"Nothing in my life has felt like mine. My powers, this plague, this *bond*, and then as soon as I decide to give Aldric a chance, the bond is gone!" I yelled.

"Gone? It's still there," he said, his dark brows raised.

"I can't feel anything. I try to pull on the tether, and it's like there's nothing there."

Ler cocked his head to the side, considering. He sat back. "Have you thought about cementing the bond between you?"

I crossed my arms, mirroring his expression back at him. "What do you mean by cementing the bond?"

"Well, how long has it been since you had his blood?" Ler lowered his arms, tucking his hands into his pockets.

"I—I don't know how long it's been. A while. He just had some of mine, though," I said, thinking back. Not since that incident with Thorne. Just how long had it been? Time felt like it was going by so quickly, but also slogging along like it was dragging through tar. I furrowed my brow as I tried to count back the days, but it was impossible. Back in the dungeon, I didn't know when the time would change from day to night.

"Maybe that's your problem. See if he wants to do a formal blood exchange. If he does, taking and giving your blood at the same time should solidify the bond between you two, making it more permanent," Ler said, gesturing vaguely with his hand.

Despite his odd appearance, he felt like a very warm person. I couldn't help but think he was being genuine in his wanting to help. Why else would he be telling me this?

"What would that mean for us? For my power?" I asked. "I know I'd been told before that a bond between vampires increases the powers higher than they would be as individuals. Would that be the same for me and Aldric?"

Ler glanced back towards the river before tilting his head back with a sigh. "Honestly, I don't know. When this happened before, the bond was incomplete. They never actually hit the point of a full blood exchange. Which was a good thing, honestly, given how everything went." He shook his head as though brushing away that memory.

"I just don't understand, though. Why a mage and a vampire? Did Myrana set up this bond between us?"

"Yes and no. But you don't need to worry about that now. You should get back to your people before they freak out about your being gone. You've been here longer than you think," Ler said, turning to look at the horizon. The sun had begun to rise, leaving the sky awash in rosy pink and lilac hues. Had I really been here all night?

"How do I get back?" I asked. "I hadn't exactly planned to come here to begin with."

"Just turn around and walk away. You'll end up back where you started," he said, giving me a gentle wave and a surprisingly genuine smile. "We'll talk again sometime. Hopefully before you have an entire mental breakdown again, but we'll see." Ler chuckled, and I scowled back at him.

"That's not funny in the least," I said, heat rising to my cheeks in embarrassment.

"Oh, before you go, head over to the river and dip your hands in."

"What—why?" I frowned, taking half a step back. I don't know why, but the thought of putting my hands in that water gave me chills.

"Just do it." Ler circled me and gave me a gentle push towards the river. I stumbled forward a couple of steps, and then cautiously made my way towards the water. The sound of the river rushing by became deafeningly loud.

Once I got close enough, I leaned over, glancing into the pristine surface yet again. I still looked like a mess, my hair tangled almost beyond repair, dried brown patches from my bloody hands. But I wouldn't be defeated so easily.

I took a deep breath and shoved my hands below the surface.

CHAPTER 9

The water was bitingly cold, numbing my fingers almost immediately. A gasp escaped me and I lurched backwards, falling back onto the muddy bank. Just great. Exactly what I needed, to be covered in muck and who knows what else.

I spit the hair out of my mouth, dragging it out of my face. Bracing myself for the pain of my split knuckles, shock filled me when it didn't come. I brought my hands up to my face, turning them this way and that. All the wounds had mended, leaving not even a single mark behind. Like it hadn't happened at all. I was flabbergasted. There wasn't even any blood left.

I scrambled to my feet, struggling in the slick mud. Turning back, I found Ler watching me with an amused expression.

"You're welcome," he said with a barely concealed laugh. "Now go. Before they send out a search party for you."

I snorted. "A search party of who? We're on the run."

"You'd be surprised with what that Fae woman can come

up with," Ler said cryptically, shooing me out. "Get out of here."

I swatted at his hands before making my way opposite of the river.

"I'm sorry we couldn't have met under better circumstances. But remember, this doesn't have to be your life. You can do things your own way. Don't forget that," Ler called.

I glanced over my shoulder and he sent me off with a wave. I held my arm up in a return wave before turning away completely, heading back in the direction I'd come from, ready to get back to Aldric.

The sound of rushing water faded quickly, and before long, it was just the sounds of the forest surrounding me. I breathed a sigh of relief. This was much nicer.

"Where have you been?" a voice said from behind me, beyond irritated.

I spun on my heel to find Aldric behind me, leaning far too casually against a tree for the tone of his voice. His arms were crossed, and his legs were also crossed at the ankles. He was wearing a loose long-sleeved tunic over a pair of too-small brown pants that rode up on him. He also had the thick, black waves of his hair pulled back to the nape of his neck. Seren must have had spare clothes in the bunker tucked away somewhere.

"You know how it is. I just got randomly dragged to a whole other realm against my will." I crossed my arms, mirroring his pose against another tree.

"You know, I don't know if you're being serious or not, or if you just don't want to tell me what's going on."

"Serious as the grave."

"Are you going to explain why I could scent your blood on this tree?" Aldric asked with a frown. "And in your hair? I don't see any injuries on you."

"It's that whole dragged-to-another-realm thing I mentioned earlier. That, and I may have been taking out my frustration on that tree," I said, dragging my hand across the back of my neck.

Taking a deep breath, I decided to ask the one question that had been plaguing me since I rescued him.

"Why haven't you mentioned anything about our bond?"

Aldric's dark brows rose, the silver in his eyes catching the sunlight and glowing from within. "What do you mean?"

My eyes pricked with unshed tears and I furiously blinked them away, surprised by the sudden emotion. "I haven't been able to feel anything from you. It's like our bond isn't there anymore."

Aldric pushed off of the tree and stopped directly in front of me. His fingers flexed as though he wanted to reach out, but restrained himself. "You can't feel me? That's strange."

"I do think there's something going on. I know it's still there, but it's just like a void coming from you," I wrapped my arms around my middle, turning away from him.

Aldric hummed, and I felt his arms slide around my waist, his large hands cupping my forearms and seeping warmth into me. "Why are you turning away, love? I'm still here. I've been here the whole time, just waiting for you."

He nuzzled into my hair with a sigh. "I'd noticed that I felt less, but I thought you were just closing yourself off from me again. Did you think I'd shut you out?"

Wordlessly, I nodded, leaning into his touch just a little. The weight of his arms around me was grounding, helping to pull me out of this dark pit I'd fallen into.

Before I could react, Aldric spun me around to face him and put his hands on my shoulders. He leaned in close and I craned my neck to look up at him. His expression was fierce, his eyes shining with unsaid emotion. "Love, I would never turn away from you. I would never abandon you, nor would I shut you out."

He paused, then his voice rumbled across my skin.

"You have *no idea* how long I've waited for you."

Aldric walked me backwards until my back hit the rough bark of the tree, caging me in with his powerful body. My heart fluttered in my chest and a small gasp escaped past my lips as the scent of storms and wilderness enveloped me. He leaned closer until we were just a breath apart.

"Thousands of years of night, and you crashed into my life like a falling star, shining so very bright it hurts to look at you. But I'd rather burn than live another day in darkness without you." His voice deepened, growing husky and gliding over me like silk. "Your presence is like a drug, and I am absolutely an addict."

His words circled in my mind, driving out all other rational thought.

"I-I want to complete our bond," I blurted, my cheeks ablaze. It felt like I couldn't catch my breath. Being so close to Aldric, it was as though my body was on fire, every nerve ending singing with an awareness of our proximity. Aldric's eyes darkened to the color of storm clouds, and a small shudder ran through his muscular frame.

"Lyra," he groaned, my name like a prayer on his lips. His hand came up to cup my jaw, the calluses rough on my skin. He traced my bottom lip with his thumb, the sensation leaving tingles in its wake. "Do you understand what you're asking? What that would mean?"

I swallowed hard, my mouth dry. It was impossible to think straight with him so close to me. But, I knew I wanted this. "I do. Aldric, I almost lost you. And I never want that to happen again. I want to experience everything with you, and become yours. Completely."

A growl rumbled deep in his chest, the sound sending goosebumps across my flesh. My tongue darted out to lick my lips, and his gaze dropped, watching the movement. "Once I claim you, there's no going back. You know this, right? You would be mine forever. No matter how far apart we may get from each other, no matter how much time passes."

His other hand slid down to grip my hip, kneading. He pulled me closer until I was flush against him, the hard planes of his body contrasting with my soft curves. He dropped close enough that I could feel the whisper of his lips against mine. "Tell me again. Tell me you want this."

Breathlessly, I nodded. My heart was pounding against my ribs. This was going to happen.

Aldric's hand slid down to my neck, and he smiled against my lips. "Tell me."

"Yes. I want this, Aldric. I will be yours, and you will be mine," I rasped, my pulse beating wildly against the pressure of his palm. Before I could find a reason to talk myself out of it, I pressed my lips to his. A deep groan escaped him, and he slanted his mouth across mine.

He tasted of starlight, of strawberries and wine. It was intoxicating. I moaned, my hands finding their way into his hair as he cupped the back of my head, deepening the kiss. His tongue traced my lower lip, requesting access. I opened to him with a soft moan, arching against him. His hand left my hip to pull me closer, crushing my breasts to his chest.

Our tongues met in a sensual dance and the world fell away, leaving just the taste of him, the way our bodies fit together, as though made for one another. Each stroke of his tongue sent sparks of pleasure through my body, lighting me up from within until I felt like I could burn to ash. He kissed me like a man starved, like he wanted to devour every whimper and moan that escaped me.

I gripped his hair tightly, and he smiled against my lips before pulling back, much to my chagrin.

"Not here. Not yet," he said, just as breathless as I was. His eyes were glowing like the purest moonlight.

I whimpered in frustration, aching in a way I'd never felt before. I pressed my thighs together to assuage the feeling, but it didn't help in the least. Reaching up on my tiptoes, I pressed another kiss to his lips before sinking my teeth into his lower lip, hard enough to cause pain.

Aldric pulled my hands from his hair and pinned both of my wrists above my head against the roughness of the tree bark, the discomfort doing nothing but heightening the pressure building in my body.

His voice was low, dangerously erotic as he said, "Now, why did you have to go and do that, love?" His tongue traced his lower lip, and my eye was drawn to the movement. "You're unfortunately still going to wait, no matter how utterly tempting you may be. It may leave you vulnerable, and I can't risk anyone coming upon us."

I leveled a scowl at him, rotating my hands around in a non-verbal request to release me.

"What, you think *I* want to wait?" Aldric asked with a quiet laugh. "If any more of the blood in my body migrated south, I very well may go unconscious."

Heat rushed to my cheeks at his words, but I couldn't help the laugh that escaped me. The sound seemed to please him—his grip on my wrists loosened slightly as a now-familiar roguish smile spread across his face.

"That would be a real shame, huh?" I teased, trying to get my mind off of how he made me feel. "Can't have you going weak in the knees on me."

"Love, you make me weak everywhere," he murmured, but released my wrists to take a step back and put some distance between us. My body immediately felt a chill once I was away from the heat his proximity offered. His eyes still were storm-cloud dark, and I swallowed hard at the emotion contained within. "As much as I would *love* to show you just how weak you make me, we should probably head back before Seren comes looking for us."

Before I could stop myself, I strode forward and tucked

a loose strand of black waves back behind his ear, my touch lingering there. "You're probably right. And it is important to stay safe. I just…this is important, too. I wanted you to know."

With that, I turned and strode back towards our little hideout, and away from the heaviness that weighed inside of my heart, the spark of guilt that lingered there. Golden eyes flashed in my mind, souring my stomach.

Seren was sitting cross-legged on a tree stump near the edge of the forest, waiting for us. She wore an intense scowl.

"Just what were you two thinking?" She gestured angrily at Aldric. "You've just barely healed enough to safely walk around and you decide to traipse after Lyra like nothing even happened."

She jabbed a finger at me, her eyes flashing with irritation. "And *you*! Where do you get off just wandering off in a magical forest with no one to guide you? Did you even know where you were going? The risk you put us under if you didn't come back?"

I hung my head in shame, my hair falling like a curtain over my shoulders. Feeling like my mother was berating me, I apologized. "I know, I'm sorry. There's no good explanation. I just had to get away from here for a bit." At her look, I held my hands up. "It's private. And hard to explain."

Aldric shoved his hands in his pockets, completely unapologetic. He wore a smirk, as though finding her ire amusing.

"I had to find her. There is no way I was just going to leave her alone in this place."

"Whatever. I won't chase after you two fools. If you want to risk getting caught and killed, that's on you," Seren said with a huff, turning up her nose at us.

I thought about telling Seren about Ler, but something told me to keep it quiet for now. Instead, I asked, "Is your beast able to make it to Aethralis?"

Seren narrowed her eyes in suspicion. "I don't even know if I have access to her right now. And for the second time, she's *not* a beast. She's a Feralumin. Why?" She crossed her arms over her ample chest, looking less than cooperative.

"I've been wondering, why haven't you tried calling your—Feralumin," I said, catching myself before I called her a beast again.

Sadness crossed her face, and I almost felt bad for asking. "Koto and I—we've been together for a long time. They can live for hundreds of years, and we've been together for most of her life so far. I'm worried if I try to call her to me and she's caught, they may kill her. I'm considered a traitor, after all. At least if she stays in the kennels, they may try to bond her to someone else."

"Can you just use your power to shift her to us?" I asked, pushing my hair back out of my face. Ugh, it felt like cotton. It was going to take forever to detangle my hair.

"No, she's in the royal city. Remember? We talked about this before," she said, exasperated.

I thought back to when I was first being brought to the royal city, Everall. I asked why we had to walk, and she said the city is warded against stuff like that. With a sigh, I nodded. "You're right, I forgot. I was just thinking we could use Koto's ability."

"For what?" Seren uncrossed her arms, leaning back on the stump.

"To track down the person who started all of this. Thorne," I said, feeling a rush of determination. "We need to go back to Aethralis and take care of him once and for all before he makes things even worse than they already were. He's stolen some of my power, or at least tried to, and I don't know how long that will last."

Seren tapped a finger against her chin, thinking.

"I see. So you would want to use Koto's ability for tracking magical signatures to locate him. It could work if we had access to Koto. But there's no way to get to her." Seren looked down at her feet, a furrow between her brows as her raven-colored hair fell across her face like a curtain. "I refuse to put her at risk of death for this. I'm sorry."

I nodded and sighed. I couldn't ask Seren to put her closest friend at risk just for me. I'd have to find another way. Aldric stepped close and put his hand on the small of my back, his touch burning like a brand through my thin shirt, but I was grateful for it.

"I understand. We'll figure something else out."

Seren glanced up at me, her moss-green eyes bright with unshed tears. It was one of the few times I'd seen genuine emotion from her—real vulnerability. It was like a punch to the gut. "Thank you," she whispered. "I can't lose Koto, too. Even if she'll no longer belong to me, at least she'll be safe."

"Let's settle in to rest," I said, turning my gaze up to the visible patches of sky between the trees. "It's been a long night. I'm sure we can all agree."

With murmurs of assent, we all climbed into the bunker below. Aldric eased the trapdoor closed, leaving us in darkness. Soon, we slept.

CHAPTER 10

I was in Aldric's arms, held tight to his chest. His heartbeat was sure and strong against my ear, and I felt safe. I opened my eyes and looked up to see him staring down at me, his eyes bright with affection. A smile curved my lips in response, and I nuzzled against him, my arms wrapped around his waist.

"I never want to let you go," Aldric murmured, his voice rumbling through me.

"Don't. I want to stay here forever," I whispered, a warmth suffusing my chest.

"Be mine, Lyra. Bond with me," he whispered back, shifting until our faces drew closer and closer. I wet my lips in anticipation, my eyes sliding closed.

The kiss was tender, sweet, his mouth moving gently and lovingly against mine. But there was something off—a different scent than the storminess I was used to. My eyes popped open, only to see a golden gaze staring down at me.

Griffin's voice was broken as he rasped, "Was I so easily forgotten?"

I sat up straight on the cot, panting. The ghost of leather and citrus lingered in my nose, making my stomach churn. In the ethereal light cast off by the torches, I saw a flash of Aldric's silver eyes, the sight of them sending a pang of guilt stabbing through me.

"Another nightmare?" he murmured, his voice carrying to me despite Seren's gentle snores in the background. Through the tenuous thread between us, I knew he could tell it was more than just that. A whisper of concern traced against me like a spectral finger. I drew my knees up to my chest and turned away. I didn't want to look at him right now. Didn't want to admit how I really felt in this moment.

My throat closed up around the words—that I was dreaming of kissing another man, the one who died because of me. That while I wanted our bond so badly, I couldn't stop being torn apart by guilt. Tears pricked my eyes, leaving hot tracks down my cheeks as they spilled. My body shook with silent sobs, and within moments, the scent of storms and wilderness surrounded me as Aldric's arms encircled me, pulling me onto his lap and tucking me under his chin.

"I never got to bury him," I whispered, my voice cracking. "I just… left him there. In that basement, where he died. Alone."

"Oh, darling," Aldric's voice fell over me like a weighted blanket, offering me more comfort than I deserved. "It wasn't your choice. There was no opportunity for you to lay him to rest. If he truly loved you, he would understand. I know it."

I shook my head, the vision of his body haunting me. "He died because of me, Aldric. He died for me, and all he got was to rot away in some dingy basement because of *my power*. I should have died instead," I sobbed, curling in on myself. "Then he could have lived, and you never would have gotten hurt."

Aldric turned me in his arms, the faint glow in his eyes highlighting his features. The seriousness of his gaze caught me off guard. "Darling, listen to me." His voice was firm, but gentle.

His calloused fingers caught my chin, turning my face up to him. I tried to look away, unwilling to see the emotion clearly on display, but his grip held firm. "Every one of us makes our own choices. Griffin protected you because he saw what I see—someone who is worth protecting, someone worth dying for. And I would have made the same choice a thousand times over."

A fresh wave of tears spilled over and my voice trembled as I choked out, "That's exactly what I'm afraid of. I can't…I can't watch someone else die for me. Not again. Never again."

"You're not responsible for other's choices, love," he said, his thumb brushing away the wetness on my cheeks. "And you don't get to decide if you're worth dying for. That's not your choice to make."

I jerked my chin out of his hand, anger burning through my grief. "Then whose choice is it? The gods? Fate? I'm so tired of everyone else deciding everything for me!" The words ripped from my throat in a scream, my voice raw, ragged.

"No," Aldric said quietly, his voice impossibly loud in the silence that followed my outburst. "It's my choice. Just like it was Griffin's choice. And neither of us made that choice lightly, I promise you."

The words hit me like a smack to the face. Aldric wordlessly held his arms open to me and I collapsed into them. His heartbeat was a steady pattern against my ear, reminding me that right now, he was alive, and this is what he wanted. And what I wanted, I admitted to myself finally.

"I'm sorry," I murmured. "For all of this. For all the baggage that comes with me." Wiping my eyes, I sniffled.

Aldric nuzzled into my hair, his arms wrapping around my waist like an anchor, keeping me steady. "You are worth all of this and more. And I will never turn away from you."

"I need to go back," I whispered. "To Sylvan Reach. I need to give him the peace he deserves. To lay him to rest."

Aldric's arms tightened around me. "Then that's what we'll do. We'll go back. Together."

I pulled back to gaze into his eyes, his expression earnest and open. "Are you sure? We need to worry about Thorne right now—,"

"That may be, but charging in while your head is swimming like this won't save anyone," Aldric interrupted, hushing me. His raven-black hair tickled my cheek as he pulled me back to his chest. "Some debts need to be repaid first."

For a long moment, we sat in silence, the dancing light of the torches sending shadows skittering across the walls. I shifted in Aldric's arms, but he held tight.

"When should we set out?" he asked, his thumb rubbing soothing circles against my forearm.

"As soon as we can," I said, my voice wavering. "I know we shouldn't waste the time, but…,"

Aldric's hands were strong and warm as they gripped my chilled fingers. "We'll need Koto to track him anyway," he said softly, his voice reassuring. "And frankly, love, I still need to heal from these injuries. It may not look it, but on the inside, I'm still weak from the silver. A few days to take care of this, to lay your friend to rest, won't set us back too much, if at all."

"He's right, you know," Seren said from behind us. I jumped, startled. I hadn't realized she'd woken up, though I should have figured from my earlier outburst.

"Seren!" I exclaimed, my hand jumping up to my throat. "I'm sorry if I woke you."

"It's okay, truly. I understand how you feel, and how hard it is to feel so out of control," Seren said, her gaze distant. After a moment, her eyes refocused on my face.

"If the King and Queen had actually treated you as a person, instead of as a villain, this whole situation could have been avoided. But they kept you locked up. To torture you."

She jabbed a finger at Aldric. "None of that was right, none of it was okay. And even though I didn't agree, I couldn't disobey without being seen as a traitor."

Silence lapsed, heavy with unsaid words.

"I'm sorry," I whispered.

"Don't misunderstand me," Seren said with a heavy sigh. "I chose to do this. It wasn't because of you. Your situation was just the tipping point on an already full plate. It would have happened at some point or another." She tucked an inky strand of hair behind her ear and leaned back on the bed.

Aldric lay back on my cot, bringing me with him and tucking me against his body. We fit together perfectly, as though made for each other. The thought warmed me despite the tears still running down my cheeks. I wiped my nose unceremoniously with a discarded shirt.

"Thank you both. I don't deserve either of you," I said with a shuddering breath.

"You're right. We're way too good for you," Seren said teasingly, though her eyes were still sad.

"We need to get some rest, especially if we are aiming to head out when we wake. Do you plan to join us, Seren?" Aldric asked, his voice flowing over me like a physical touch.

Seren scoffed. "Like you could do it without me."

"We would figure it out," I insisted.

"No, I mean, you literally can't do it without me. You couldn't cross the Veil on your own," Seren said with a dry laugh, sliding back down onto her cot. "So I don't have much of a choice. Though, I will admit, it's an honorable thing that you are choosing to do, so I would have done it, anyway. Aldric is right though. Let's get some rest." She waved a hand, and the torches dimmed, the room seeming more intimate in the limited light.

Wordlessly, I snuggled back against Aldric and his arm slid around my waist, anchoring me to him. And in that moment, I'd never felt more safe, despite the dread curling around us like smoke from a dying fire.

When we awoke, I had the uncanny feeling that something was wrong. As I slowly sat up in the darkness, I realized just what it was. The torches had all gone out. I blindly reached out and found Aldric's sleeping form next to me, except he wasn't breathing. Panic rose in my throat, threatening to choke me.

Ancient magic crawled over my skin like frost, raising goosebumps all along my flesh. *Myrana?*

The absolute stillness around me felt wrong, as though the world was frozen in this moment. Aldric's body was unnaturally rigid, like a marble statue instead of a person. I put my head against his chest, listening for the steady thumping of his heart that I'd fallen asleep listening to, but there was nothing. I stood, my magic crawling beneath my skin like a living entity.

All the air felt like it was sucked out of the room and I fell to my knees, gasping for breath. There was a malevolence in this darkness, ancient and unforgiving. The magical threads in the air felt like shards of glass, slicing against my skin, rebelling against my magic.

I didn't understand—why was this happening? The magic had flowed gently around like dandelion seeds, and yet now it was like a weapon, shredding me from within.

A voice, grating like shattered glass, multi-layered and filled with maternal disappointment, filled my mind. *Why are you wasting time on a dead mutt while your true enemy grows ever stronger?*

The casual way they insulted Griffin rankled me, and my magic flared in response, burning away the hostile threads around me. But the pressure within me was so strong, my head felt full to bursting. I doubled over, hissing through my teeth.

Your power was not gifted to you so you could waste it on sentimentality, little one. There are greater purposes waiting. Your destiny calls you.

"I didn't ask for any special destiny," I ground out through clenched teeth. The pressure in my head grew stronger until a scream ripped itself from my throat. It felt like my eyes were going to fly out of my head.

No? The voices held a note of amusement. I wanted to rage against them, to yell and fight, but I could barely hold myself together. *Then perhaps I was wrong about you. Perhaps you lack the strength to lead the people to their rightful places. I thought you different than the last ant that I gifted with this power—yet here you are, choosing a beast over your own kind.*

Your power is a gift from me. And you can only wield it because it is my *will.* You'd *best remember that.*

The pressure suddenly vanished like opening a release valve on a water pipe. Air rushed back into my lungs as the torches flared to life, leaving me wheezing as I caught my breath. Sweat ran in rivulets down my spine, cooling rapidly against my skin.

Aldric quickly sat up next to me, his silver eyes wide with concern. Seren was already climbing to her feet, moss-green eyes tracking the shadows as though something were about to leap out at her—and with how things are going, who knows? The thought made me sick.

"Darling, what happened?" Aldric's voice was rough, deepened with sleep and concern. His hand reached up and brushed under my nose, coming away stained with red. "Your nose is bleeding."

I opened my mouth to tell them, but a sinking feeling in my gut told me to keep it to myself for now. Whatever the game was that the Sovereign was playing, I would not be their pawn.

"It's nothing. Just had a nightmare. The nosebleed must be from the dry air," I lied, forcing a smile. I could only hope they didn't see through me. Aldric brushed my hair back over my shoulder.

"Are you sure, love? Nothing else is going on?" his eyes searched my own, the swirling depths within almost begging me to reveal the truth, but I didn't want to put him at risk and make him a target.

I beamed at him, even as I felt warmth trickling down from my nose. "It's nothing. Let's get ready to go."

As I climbed out of the cot, I noticed that my hair was stuck to the sides of my face. While Aldric and Seren were busy packing our meager supplies, I left the bunker under the guise of a restroom break, making my way down to where I'd seen the river earlier with Ler.

Whether by coincidence or fate, the sound of rushing water greeted me right where I'd seen it before. I had little time, and I didn't want anyone to come looking for me. As I approached the surface and looked in, horror chilled me, turning my blood to ice in my veins. There were deep purple smudges beneath my eyes and dried blood flaking off of my face. Moving my hair, I had to peel it off of my face where it had stuck to my skin, revealing twin tracks of red running from my ears.

I knew, without a single doubt in my heart, that Myrana could have killed me just then, as easily as crushing a grape between her fingers. Then why let me live? Why continue this farce—unless she still thought I'd come back under her thumb?

She wanted *something* from me. Said I was betraying my people. But did what she mean?

These thoughts sent white-hot anger burning through me, chasing away the chill that had settled in my bones. I would *not* be a pawn in these games. I've had enough of everyone deciding for me what my life would be.

It was time for me to choose for myself.

CHAPTER 11

After washing away the evidence of my meeting with the Sovereign, I made my way back into the bunker. The bruising under my eyes remained, but there was nothing I could do about that right now.

Ever since meeting up with Myrana, my magic felt off somehow. Less constrained, harder to control. But no matter how much it hurt, I kept it shoved down. I would learn to control it whether Myrana wanted me to or not. It was *mine,* and I didn't care that it belonged to her first.

As I climbed down the ladder to rejoin my companions, Seren laid out travel supplies on the small table—dried food, water skins, and some type of map. Aldric was slowly putting a shirt over his head, but he was stiff, and I saw fresh blood on his bandages, so I rushed to his side, stilling his movements.

"Here, let me help. You don't have to do everything on your own, you know," I admonished. He protested, but I was already pulling the linen over his head, where it draped perfectly on his body. I cleared my throat and looked away.

"That's rich coming from you," Seren commented dryly, not looking up from the table as she made selections for her travel bag.

"What's that supposed to mean?"

"You have dried blood in your hair. I may not know exactly what happened this morning, but I know it's not as simple as you're making it out to be." She finally met my eyes, her gaze looking chipped from jade.

"I—It's nothing you need to concern yourself with, Seren. I have things under control."

The fewer questions they ask me, the better.

Aldric sighed, and I felt faint disapproval from the connection between us. "We're meant to be a team, you know. How can we work properly together if you won't trust us enough to tell us anything?"

A pang of guilt hit me, and I swallowed hard. He was right, but now wasn't the right time. "Not now. Later." At their skeptical looks, I held my hands up. "I promise. But not now. Let's just focus on getting back to Aethralis."

"Let's just focus on what we need to do right now. Getting ready to go," Aldric said, stretching. Once he lifted his arms overhead, he hissed out a breath and hunched over, pain causing his face to pale. "Not quite ready for that yet, I suppose," he bit out between clenched teeth.

"Are you okay?" I asked.

How long would these wounds take to heal?

Aldric held up a hand. "I'll be okay. Don't strain yourself too much, love." He straightened his spine, his movements rigid.

"What about you?" Seren asked, stuffing her pack with dried fruits. "You look like death warmed over. Are you good?"

I waved her off, despite the headache pounding behind my eyes. "I told you, I'm fine. What's the plan for getting back to the other side of the Veil?"

Seren rolled her eyes, and the next item went into her bag a little harder than necessary.

"There's a thin spot not too far from here. But we'll have to scout the area thoroughly. I'm sure the guard patrols have been increased since our escape."

"How far from Sylvan Reach will we be?" Aldric asked. His voice was deceptively casual, despite the way his hands shook.

"A few days, if we're lucky. Longer if we happen to run into trouble, which, knowing you two, is bound to happen," Seren said dryly. She traced a finger down the map, showing a side path I'd never taken before. "This will keep us off the main roads. We don't know what lies on the other side anymore, after all."

The thought of days of travel with Aldric in this state made my stomach clench, and I absently rubbed at my abdomen to soothe the ache. Aldric could barely walk, and my magic felt like glass under my skin, but there was no choice.

Griffin had waited long enough—it was time to put his memory to rest.

An hour later, we were ready to go. Once we cleared out the bunker, Seren carefully covered the hatch leading below.

"Just in case," she explained.

The early morning light bloomed between the branches of the nearby trees, though it paled in comparison to the stars twinkling overhead. That was about the only thing I would miss once we left. The way the sky glittered like a million diamonds, no matter the time of day.

Glancing around, the forest was eerily still and silent, as though holding its breath. I pulled the hood of my borrowed cloak high over my head, covering my mass of white hair. Seren had found some less conspicuous clothing for all of us to wear, allowing us to blend in smoothly with the foliage.

I carried mine and Aldric's packs, and Seren took point, silent as death as she traversed the forest. She effortlessly avoided every twig, every dried leaf, as though this was second nature to her.

Aldric was hiding a limp, but I could feel the haze of pain through our bond. Seren had no more medication to give him, so for the time being, he just had to suffer, which twisted my insides.

Aldric stayed despite the danger, and he's choosing to stay even now. And no matter how I felt about it, he made his choice clear. He would stick by me, regardless. Reaching out, I steadied him as he stumbled.

"I'm fine," he whispered, pushing my hand away. "I'm a big,

strong vampire prince, remember?" His voice held a shadow of its normal teasing tone, but his face was pale and drawn with pain.

"Aldric, if we're a team, let me be here for you," I murmured back, though the words tasted bitter on my tongue.

He scowled like he wanted to argue, but as he took another step, a shock of pain flared between us, and I wrapped an arm around his waist, helping to support his weight. Wordlessly, he squeezed me against him.

My eyes tracked the surrounding forest, looking for any hint of movement. We needed to be ready, no matter what came up. Swallowing hard, and with the weight of Aldric's arm around me, I knew I would do whatever I needed to in order to keep everyone safe.

Seren held her hand up, her head cocked and listening to something that I couldn't hear. Aldric and I froze, refusing to even breathe. I strained my ears, listening hard. There was a very faint crunching of leaves fading off into the distance. I released my breath silently, bracing myself for us to continue.

Seren waved us forward, and we crept along, careful to avoid attracting any unwanted attention.

We continued like this for about an hour, slowly making our way towards the thinnest part of the Veil in the area. Out of the corner of my eye, I would sometimes see a wisp of magic, floating on the breeze like a jellyfish. But whenever I would turn to look, it would be gone.

Was Myrana truly in this much control—did she truly hold this much mana to her breast?

I'd grown up thinking that magic was wild, just an untamed entity that blessed a select few, but she made it sound as though it was *her will* each time someone was gifted.

I scowled. It wasn't the time to worry about this. We were finally closing in on our destination, I realized. There was a haze, a shimmer in the air in the middle of a group of trees. It reminded me of heat rising off of sun-baked sand. We'd been insanely lucky not to run into anyone, and I would not waste this opportunity, quickly dragging Aldric along. His muscles trembled, and sweat raced down his back, but he soldiered on, doing his best to keep up.

Once we reached those trees, the air pressure changed, becoming thick like molasses. It was hard to breathe, and I took great gulping breaths with increasing difficulty.

Seren wrapped her arms around Aldric and me, and the world spun into nothingness.

CHAPTER 12

The world reformed back around us in a kaleidoscope of colors, nausea rising inside of me. I barely stayed on my feet, retching loudly. My mouth filled with saliva, and I forced the feeling down, sweat beading on my forehead. Aldric was hardly bothered, and I glared at him.

Of course, he wouldn't be.

Seren's arms fell away from Aldric and me, and she immediately put some distance between herself and us. I staggered a bit, and Aldric caught me, an amused glint shining in his eyes.

"That was… interesting, to put it lightly. It was like being unmade and reformed between one heartbeat and the next." His moonlight eyes were bright with curiosity.

My scowl only deepened. "How are you so calm about this? The first time I Shifted I threw up for ages."

"Ah yes, but you, my love, are not a vampire. I'm not as affected by these types of things, luckily for me." He wore a ghost of his usual smirk, then winced. "Although I still wouldn't recommend it with silver wounds. Makes things a little spicier than you'd expect."

Seren huffed a sigh, flipping her hair out of her face and over her shoulder. "Are you two done comparing notes? We need to get moving. The Veil isn't exactly subtle when it's crossed, and now the royal guard will know where we've gone."

She was right.

I glanced around. We'd emerged in a dense section of forest that I didn't recognize, but the magic here was more familiar. It caressed me almost lovingly, which was incredibly welcome after the harshness of the wild, untamed Fae mana towards the end of our journey.

I slowly spun in a circle. "Do either of you know where we are?"

Seren sighed again, and it rankled me for reasons I couldn't explain. "Yes, we need to go to the West in order to find that path I had mapped out."

"You don't have to be snippy about it, Seren," I said, crossing my arms.

"Well, only one of us seems to know what we're doing, isn't that right?" Seren said shortly, giving me a look.

Aldric stepped between Seren and me, holding up a hand to both of us. "This has been stressful for us all. Let's just get to Sylvan Reach. We'll figure out the rest afterwards."

I scrubbed a hand down the back of my neck. "You're right. I'm just—this isn't going to be easy for me. I'm sorry, Seren. You're right, I should be more prepared. Ever since you and I met, I've just been a pain in the ass."

Seren walked over and touched my arm, sympathy plain on her face despite her earlier frustration. "It's okay. The Fae haven't exactly been kind to you, either. And I know how you feel—I've had to lay comrades to rest countless times. It never gets any easier."

I nodded, my eyes prickling with sudden tears. But I didn't let them fall—not yet. Resolute, I turned to Seren.

"Lead the way. I'll follow you."

Seren had definitely earned her position as head of the royal guard. She tracked effortlessly and kept us both in line, aware of all threats, real or imagined. We'd been walking for hours, and despite his best efforts to conceal it from me, Aldric was quickly deteriorating. Fresh blood seeped through his shirt where it had soaked his bandages, and his breathing grew more ragged.

"We should rest," I said gently as Aldric stumbled over a loose branch.

"I can keep going," Aldric insisted, despite the pain that echoed within me.

Seren held up her hand, effectively silencing both of us. Her moss-green eyes narrowed as she studied our surroundings, then scanned Aldric up and down. "There's a shelter about a half-mile ahead. We can stop there for a bit." Her gaze stopped at the obvious red splotches on Aldric's shirt. "Those bandages need changing, anyway. We might get lucky on the way and find some herbs that I can use to help with the pain."

Even without the bond, I could feel Aldric's resistance, his pride warring with his obvious need to rest. But resignedly, he gave a tight nod. Even royals had their limits. I moved closer, careful not to touch any of his wounds, as I wrapped an arm around Aldric to support more of his weight while we continued to hobble along.

The familiar magic of Aethralis swirled around us, so different from what we'd left behind. But something felt off. Ever since that 'visit' with Myrana, my connection to magic felt raw, like rubbing sandpaper over my skin. That combined with my power feeling like broken glass inside of me, left me feeling on edge.

I took a deep, centering breath. This wouldn't last. Looking deep within, it felt as though my mana recoiled from me in a way I'd never experienced, almost like we were two opposing forces. The more I distanced myself from the Veil, hopefully this feeling would dwindle.

Aldric's hand crept up underneath my cloak, rubbing gently at my shoulder as we trudged through the forest. Seren continued scouting ahead, leaving us in relative privacy.

"Darling, are you okay? I know that we're getting close to putting…him to rest. I'm here if you need to talk," he said, his tone gentle and warming me as easily as a wool blanket, despite the guilt that I carried like a shroud.

"It's not just that, but I can't talk about it yet," I murmured, looking anywhere but him. If I meet his eyes, I don't think I'd have it in me to avoid the subject. "Soon. When we rest."

Aldric stopped on unsteady legs, pulling me to stand

in front of him. He reached a tremoring hand under my chin and tipped my head back so that we were looking eye to eye. I squirmed under the intensity of his gaze, his emotions laid bare in the swirling mercury depths.

"If it's something dangerous, please tell me, love," Aldric said, his hand sliding from my chin to cup my cheek. I leaned into the touch despite myself, holding his arm. Gently, I stroked the sensitive skin on his wrist, careful to avoid any wounds.

"It's nothing I can't handle," I said, pressing a kiss to his palm. "We need to get going before you collapse right here."

"Ah yes, what would we do if I fell right here, only to pull you atop me? How awful it would be for you," he said, his voice deepening and sliding over me like a caress.

"Aldric, you can flirt with me when you're not about to die," I said with a laugh despite the tension that lingered between us.

"I'll flirt with you until I die and even afterwards," Aldric said with a dark chuckle. "You can't escape."

Despite his words, he pulled me back under his arm, where I resumed supporting him as we caught up with Seren, who impatiently waited a couple dozen paces ahead, barely visible through the trees.

"You two are a mess," Seren said as soon as we reached her. "Every time I turn around, you're trying to pull each other's clothes off or disappearing on me."

My face warmed, and I looked away. "This wasn't that. It wouldn't be right. Not when we're going to—you know." I gestured vaguely with my free hand, trying to force the words out. "Put Griffin to rest."

It was still hard for me to talk about. Every time I did, I got flashes of his body rotting away in the basement of Thorne's house. A pit opened up in my stomach. Every moment I spent not mourning him felt wrong, disrespectful to his memory.

A chill ran up my spine, and I just felt awful holding Aldric, like I couldn't wait to move on without giving time to grieve Griffin.

"Seren," I called.

She stopped a few feet ahead of me and gave me a look over her shoulder. "What now?"

"Can you help Aldric for a bit, please?" I asked, despite how the words felt sour in my mouth. No matter what I did, I was hurting someone.

Seren raised a dark brow, but stopped, waiting for us. Aldric gave me a concerned look, but said nothing. I ignored him, and once Seren was close enough, she slid into the spot I had just vacated, although she was much shorter than me. Aldric was a lot more stiff with her, careful not to touch her anywhere he could avoid it.

Despite her stature, she was strong, hefting Aldric's weight like it was nothing. Jealousy burned within me at the sight of her holding him, even though I knew it wasn't what either of them wanted, and I strode off ahead, disgusted with myself.

I pushed ahead through the trees, guilt warring with envy and leaving me sick to my stomach. Behind me, I could hear

Aldric's labored breathing and Seren's murmurs about where to step. Every sound between them twisted the knife in deeper, because the only reason they were working together was that I couldn't handle my own emotions.

The wrongness of the magic here, along with my own, was pissing me off on top of it. I hit my palm against my forehead twice and shook my head. This funk couldn't last, or I'd be useless.

"There," Seren called softly behind me. "Beyond those trees."

I looked back and followed where she pointed, seeing what equated to little more than a small hunter's cabin, off in the distance. But it was off the beaten path, and we wouldn't be easily found there.

"I'll go scout it out," I said, rushing forward.

"Lyra—," Aldric started, but I pushed ahead and his voice faded in the background. I needed to do something, anything, to feel less useless. Slipping through the trees, I took off at a run until I made it to the cabin. They'd be at least a few minutes behind me at Aldric's pace, and I needed that quiet.

The shelter was empty, covered in what looked like years of fallen leaves. It was otherwise intact, with a surprisingly solid roof. As I cleared out space inside, moving broken furniture and old rucksacks caked with dust, I coughed, waving my hand to clear it out of my face. Pulling my shirt up over my nose, I kept working. My thoughts were just running in circles—Griffin's body waiting in that basement, Aldric's injuries, the echoes of Myrana's voice in my head. I was so lost in my spiral that I didn't hear Seren approach.

"Come with me," she breathed, making me jump.

Aldric sat hard on a nearby wooden chair, which creaked dangerously, but managed not to collapse under his weight. I looked at him concerned but couldn't bring myself to say anything. Shame bubbled inside me like acid, and I turned away. Seren grabbed my hand and pulled me outside of the shelter, a few paces away so we could have privacy.

She pulled me down to sit on the ground and sat on her knees before me, putting us at more of an even height. She grasped my face in both hands, turning me so I was forced to meet her eyes. The pressure of everything going on made my throat tighten, and I didn't know what to say.

"You know," she murmured, her surprisingly callused hands gentle on my face, "you're allowed to care for them both. It's okay."

Her words hit me like a physical blow, and suddenly, I couldn't breathe. My face flushed, and tears burned my eyes, rushing down my cheeks in twin rivulets.

"Oh, Lyra," she said, wiping my tears with her thumbs. "How long have you been holding this in?"

She pulled me towards her, resting my head on her bosom. Seren gently stroked her hand up and down my back as I clung to her, sobbing. This couldn't be what Griffin would have wanted. For me to be with Aldric.

"If he loved you, he would have," Seren whispered into my

hair, and I realized I must have spoken aloud. "It's okay to wish that you had more time together. But you can't keep living like this. Torn apart from every positive feeling you have just because he isn't here."

I only cried harder, my body shaking. "He and I barely had any time at all. He was—he was the first one to accept me. And he died for it."

"Honey, he may have been the first to show it, but he isn't the last. Look at what Aldric has done for you. What he continues to do. And me, I accept you too. It doesn't diminish your other relationships, Lyra," she gently admonished. "He'll always be special to you, and that's okay. But just don't push everyone else away because it's what you think you *should* do."

"It's just hard. I don't know what I should do or who I should trust. I thought I could trust Thorne, and he tried to kill me," I sobbed. "And he killed Griffin, too."

"Well, you trust me, right?" Seren asked, tipping my chin up to meet her gaze. It was gentle, like fresh spring grass. "And you should trust Aldric. After all, with the bond between you, you'd know if he wasn't being true to you. Have you ever felt that he wasn't honest with you?"

I shook my head.

"Well, there you go! You'll meet people over time—some will be awful. But others, they're gems in the rough. Like you, Lyra. I trust you, and I know Aldric does." She continued to rub soothing circles on my back, and my tears slowly subsided. I took a deep, shuddering breath.

"Thank you, Seren. It's—it's hard to talk about. As soon as

I began to discover what it meant to be with another person, to be more than *just* a transformation mage, that opportunity was ripped away in a horrible tragedy."

I looked away, the memory flashing in my mind. But Seren shook my shoulders gently, pulling me from the vision of his death.

"It'll take time, Lyra. But just remember, we're here for you. You're hurting yourself by pushing us away." With that, she nudged me backwards so she could stand, and held out a hand to help me up. "Let's go get back to bitey boy before he collapses in there."

I nodded, shaking off the last of the heaviness that had settled over me as I grabbed her hand. She pulled me to my feet with surprising strength, and I almost tipped forward before I steadied myself.

Seren chuckled, and started off towards the cabin, leaving me behind. I tipped my head back, looking up at the sky. *The sun will be setting soon*, I thought.

The stars seemed extra bright just then, and I turned away, determined to ignore it.

CHAPTER 13

Opening the door to the cabin, I found Seren attempting to help Aldric undress. I strode over quickly and stilled Seren, replacing her hands with my own.

"Let me do that," I murmured, and Aldric visibly relaxed under my touch, fanning the flames of my guilt. Within moments, I had him undressed down to his undergarments, while Seren gathered her supplies for changing his bandages.

There was a faint odor of infection in the air, and I looked up at Aldric's face, where he was intently looking at me, his gaze open and trusting.

"I'm sorry, Aldric," I said, dropping my eyes. "I shouldn't be taking out my emotions on you. All you've done is to be there for me." I cleared my throat, determined not to cry again.

Aldric reached out and held my hands in his own, his touch incredibly warm. "It's okay, love. I understand what it's like to lose someone, and grief is complex."

"You forgive me so easily," I said, swallowing hard. "Why aren't you more upset?"

"Because I understand you," Aldric said, with a tenderness in his voice. "And you've gone through a lot recently. Enough to break most people, but yet, here you are. Still with me."

He cradled the back of my head in his hand, and I met his eyes. "That's the most important thing. You've stayed, even though I know you've felt terrible about it. You could have left me behind when I was in the Veil. It would have been easier for you to do that. But you didn't."

I shook my head, my hands finding their way to his waist, his muscles jumping beneath my fingers. "You're wrong. I couldn't have. You—you mean too much to me for me to leave you behind," I said the last in a whisper, my voice cracking with emotion.

"Then it sounds like we're stuck together, doesn't it?" he said, his tone teasing.

"I guess you're right," I said with a soft laugh, the tension finally melting away just a little. And with that, my power flared like melted iron beneath my skin. Before I could even react, it spread to my fingertips, where it met with Aldric's flesh. He stiffened, then arched his back with a pained groan. Seren rushed over and jerked me away from him. I tripped over a broken piece of furniture and landed sprawled on the floor in a *poof* of dust, panting.

Just what the hell was that?

WHISPERED SECRETS

My magic writhed within me like a living thing, desperate to reach Aldric again. I found my body moving on its own before I caught myself, and panic spread like a lightning strike at the sight before me. Aldric strained in the chair, his eyes completely silver, with no hint of a pupil remaining. He convulsed, foam frothing from his mouth, tinted with pink.

Seren turned to me, her eyes wide in horror. "What—what is happening? Something is wrong!" Her hands hovered uselessly over Aldric's quaking form.

A voice like wind chimes filled the cabin, layered one over the other.

Why do you resist what must be? Let your power flow freely.

The scent of wild magic, like freshly turned earth and wildflowers, permeated the air and wrapped around us like silken chains. My magic revolted against me, like boiling magma searing its way through my flesh as it tried to escape my control, desperate to force me back towards Aldric. The bond? This wasn't right—this isn't how this was supposed to happen!

Through the tenuous thread between us, I felt Myrana's influence trying to twist what Aldric and I had into something darker—more monstrous.

The pain radiating from him tore a scream from my throat, and my legs gave out. I curled over in the fetal position on the floor, rocking back and forth as I tried to control this invasion of my mana.

You hesitate too much. Why are you so weak? Myrana's voice crooned, sweet like syrup coating poisonous apples. *I gave you this gift, and you squander it.*

Let me show you how to use it the way it was intended.

My magic felt like molten glass in my veins, but I refused to let go—to let Myrana corrupt what should be our choice—one made of love, and when we were ready. The gentle facade broke as my resistance continued.

You dare to defy me? The voice asked, sharp as a blade. *I MADE YOU WHAT YOU ARE! YOU WOULD BE NOTHING IF NOT FOR ME!*

The energy in the air turned violent, whipping around us as furniture shattered against the walls. Seren screamed, covering her ears. With effort, I glanced up at Aldric to see his mouth open in a silent scream, light pouring from within. *This will kill him if I don't do something,* I thought desperately. *But what can I do?*

I closed my eyes and dropped my head to the floor, drawing deep to visualize the cavern inside of me where my power dwells. There was darkness, shadowed tendrils spreading outward and flowing into me. I took all the willpower I could muster and envisioned walls pressing in, smothering the darkness.

You can't hold out on me for long, little one, the voice crooned. *Your life is mine to control, and you* will *do as I wish.*

As the pressure within me loosened, I scrambled over to Aldric, who was still seizing, and dragged him down to the floor next to me so he was out of danger from the flying bits of wood and debris that whipped around us. I carefully cradled his head in my lap.

"Get out of him," I snarled, my hands cradling either side of Aldric's face. His skin burned like fire beneath my touch, and a spike of fear shot through me. "He's not yours to control!"

Such defiance from someone so insignificant, Myrana drawled, her voice holding a note of amusement. *But your power answers to me.*

The darkness within me surged, and I screamed as my muscles stretched like they were being ripped apart, my bones creaking under the pressure. Warmth ran down my face, and each heartbeat sent a fresh wave of agony tearing through my body as I tried to contain the writhing mass of power inside of me.

My vision blurred until I could no longer see, the world growing dark. I could hear Seren yelling, but it sounded like she was speaking underwater, the words warbling and unclear. I struggled to stay upright amid the maelstrom around us, curling over Aldric's body protectively. There was a crack—whether it came from above us or within me, I couldn't tell.

My entire being was pain.

I dove deeper within myself, to where my power dwelled. That darkness had spread like a cancer, pushing through every crack in my makeshift walls until they crumbled. I tried in vain to strengthen those barriers, to separate Myrana's power from my own. There was so much pressure, it felt like my skull was being split in two, and an inhuman noise tore from my throat.

I pried my eyes open, the agony so intense it felt as though I would shatter like glass.

Foolish little one. Let me show you the price of your defiance, Myrana crooned, her voice like velvet over steel.

My back arched, my eyes burning as though they were on fire. What little remained of my vision turned red. But through it all, I held Aldric, whose convulsions were growing more frantic, and as I looked down at him, the silver light pouring from him was growing murky, tainted with strains of black, dark as night itself.

"No," I ground out, my voice raw and bloody. "This is mine. My power. *My choice.*"

I held Aldric tightly to my chest. "It was gifted to me, and you can't take it back," I roared, my vocal cords shredded.

The magical pressure increased until I felt my ribs creaking, and the sound of a *snap*. I tasted copper and swallowed hard.

Would Aldric die here?

The thought ignited something within me, and even though my body was being torn apart, my power responded to my desperation. Not to Myrana's command, but to *me*. Not to obey her, but to protect what was *mine*.

The magic surged within me, and I welcomed the hurt, used it to fuel my rage. It like liquid nitrogen within me, freezing everything it touched and cooling the fire that had been consuming me from the inside.

You cannot resist me for long, Myrana said, her voice sounding less certain now. *Your body will give out.*

She were right—I could feel my body failing. My muscles were growing weak, and I had to fight to stay conscious. But I wasn't done, not yet.

Not even close.

I pressed my forehead to Aldric's, feeling the corrupted magic trying to rend his body from within.

"You want to see what I can do with your *gods damned gift?*" I snarled. "Just watch."

I plunged deep into that well of power inside of me, past the anguish, past the darkness, trying to consume everything like a black hole. In the deepest trenches, at my very core, there was something else—something that belonged *only* to me. It was clear and bright, and burning cold. I wrapped myself around it, letting it fill me entirely.

The pressure in my skull built until I thought my head would explode. Something wet dripped from my eyes, whether blood or tears, I couldn't tell. But I could feel it working, the purest part of my power forcing the darkness from my body like sludge, the chill seeping through it like the first winter frost.

What are you doing? Myrana demanded, with the first note of fear tinging her voice. *Stop this! You cannot!*

I ignored her, focusing everything I had on the tenuous bond between Aldric and I, forcing my power along that thread until it reached him, surging into his body like a dam had broken. His back arched impossibly high, the silver light flowing from his eyes and mouth almost blinding.

But I held strong, closing my eyes and continuing the assault on the void that threatened to consume him. My body grew weaker still, trembling like a newborn fawn. Despite it all, I maintained the connection between us, and slowly the shroud over us drained away, and Myrana's screech of rage echoed in the tiny cabin.

All the debris flying around the room suddenly stopped, and everything was silent. Aldric was completely limp against me, and I struggled to open my eyes to make sure he was okay.

I fell onto Aldric's chest, and tears of relief escaped me when I heard his heart beating and felt his steady breathing. But the hush was too oppressive, too thick. A whisper reached my ears.

You think you've won, don't you, child? A dark chuckle layered with thousands of voices rattled in my skull like shards of glass.

You've not shown me anything new, little bird. I can reach you anywhere, and you will soon know the price of your defiance.

Blood dripped from my lips as I rasped, "I'm not afraid of you. I won't be your pawn."

The pressure suddenly vanished, leaving me gasping. Echoes of pain traveled up and down my body, and Seren was suddenly by my side, her hands unsteady as she hesitantly touched me.

"Lyra! Oh gods, you're both bleeding everywhere." Her voice sounded so far away, and I struggled to open my mouth, to say anything, to assure her I was okay. I tried to push myself up, but my arms gave out.

The world tilted sideways as darkness crept in from the edges of my vision. The last thing I felt was Aldric's hand finding mine and weakly grasping my fingers before my consciousness slipped away entirely.

CHAPTER 14

Consciousness returned in fragments.

Seren's voice floated to me, urgent and worried. There was a bitter taste of liquid being forced between my lips, making me cough and gag.

There was the feeling of being moved, my body screaming in protest. Everything hurt. My bones, my muscles, my very *essence* writhed in agony.

"...have to get the fever down..." Seren's words faded in and out, muffled, like I was hearing her talking from far away. "...infection spreading too fast..."

I tried to reach for Aldric through the bond, but just that minor effort sent waves of anguish coursing through me. There was no response from him, though I heard a faint sound from somewhere nearby. So he was alive, at least. Finally, some part of me that had been wound into a spring could relax. The sound of tearing fabric reached me, along with Seren's muttering.

"...need blood soon, or he won't..." Her voice gained sudden clarity. "Lyra, can you hear me? I need you to wake up."

I somehow pried my eyes open despite the impossible weight of my eyelids. Seren's face slowly swam into view, lines of tension around her emerald eyes. She had stripped down to an undershirt, which was stained with blood. Mine or Aldric's, I didn't know. The cabin slowly spun behind her, and I blinked hard, trying to orient myself.

"There you are. Finally," she said, relief clear in her voice. "Stay with me this time."

She gently patted my cheek, and I pushed her hand away with monumental effort. "How..." I swallowed hard. My voice was barely a whisper. Speaking felt like I'd swallowed glass. "How long?"

Luckily, Seren knew just what I was asking, and she gave me a sympathetic look. "A few hours. I—I don't know what happened, or what you did, but I've seen nothing like that before, not once in all of my years of existence."

She dabbed a cool cloth across my forehead, and it provided immense relief to my burning skin. "Myrana, she..." I began, but Seren shushed me.

"Don't worry about that now. For the time being, we've been left alone. Let's not jinx it by calling her name," she said, shaking her head.

A low groan from beside me drew my attention. Turning my head, a wave of nausea slammed through me. I swallowed the rush of moisture filling my mouth and saw Aldric lying on the ground near me. His skin had taken on an ashen hue, and fresh blood seeped through his bandages. I reached out a hand, straining to reach him.

He looked awful, a sheen of sweat causing waves of his raven-black hair to stick to his forehead.

"He needs blood," I croaked, pushing up on my elbows, a stabbing pain in my ribs causing me to gasp. Was it broken?

"You're in no condition--," Seren started, but I cut her off with a wave of my hand.

"He'll die without it." I could feel how weak he was. I could *see* it, even without the battered tether between us. "Help me sit up."

Begrudgingly, and with concern etched into her features, Seren gently placed a hand at the small of my back and slowly moved me into a sitting position, careful not to jostle me too much.

"Lyra, I really don't think this is a good idea—," she tried again, but my sharp look cut her off.

"Are *you* going to give him blood?" I rasped out angrily.

Seren's look of disgust told me enough, and she went silent.

"Do we have a bowl or cup? I don't think I can feed him any other way."

I slowly swayed and fought to stay sitting despite the agony flowing through my body in waves. Black spots danced in front of my vision, and I tried to blink them away. Seren stepped away, holding her hands up as though ready to catch me at any moment. I shot her a grateful smile, though it wobbled.

She started throwing around the bits of shattered and broken furniture while on the hunt for our packs. After a few minutes of listening to Aldric's labored breathing and carefully scooting towards him on the floor, I could finally grasp one of his clammy hands. His skin was blazing hot, and the closer I got, the more the stench of infection reached me.

He was barely holding onto life right now, and I knew it. I swallowed hard past the lump in my throat. Listening to Seren's creative string of curses in the background as she rifled through the debris, I slowly stroked my thumb over Aldric's hand. His fingers curled against mine, and his eyes rolled in his head as though he were dreaming.

"Aldric, I'm here," I whispered, despite the discomfort. "Can you hear me?"

There was no response other than his ragged breathing, and my heart sank. I didn't know how much of my life's essence I could feasibly give him, but I was determined to do everything I could. My free arm was banded around my waist trying to help the ache there. As I shifted, I felt something grinding beneath my skin, and I knew things were worse than I thought. I took careful, shallow breaths and leaned to my left to take some of the pressure off of my ribs.

Finally, Seren reappeared at our side, carrying a couple of our backpacks, covered in splinters and dust. She dropped them unceremoniously a little ways away from me and immediately began searching through them, coming up with a wooden cup a few moments later.

"I knew there was one of these in there," she said triumphantly, brushing off any dirt before presenting it to me.

Every breath felt like blades were being driven into my lungs, and a bead of sweat ran down my spine, my hands shaking as I took the cup. Seren's jade eyes were intense, worry radiating from her.

"Do you have a knife?" I panted, my vision swimming. It felt like I couldn't get enough air, but trying to breathe any deeper was tortuous.

"Lyra..." Seren murmured, kneeling on the ground beside me. "You're both close to death. I know you want to save him, but..."

A surge of protectiveness flared within me, and I slammed my free hand on the floor. "I *will* die," I gasped, my vision swimming as my muscles spasmed on my right side, "before I let him succumb."

My body was trembling from the adrenaline, and I struggled to stay conscious, my vision narrowing to Aldric's form. When Seren didn't make a move, my power crooned to me, urging me to use it. Hesitantly, I let a trickle of it flow forth, and my teeth elongated into fangs, stabbing into my lower lip. I ran my tongue over the sharpened points and knew what I needed to do. I brought my wrist to my mouth and tore into the tender flesh.

There was a sharp, burning sensation as my fangs pierced deep into the tissue. An awful tugging sensation came with every movement of my jaw, the skin stretching and snapping. A horrified gasp came from next to me, and Seren immediately tried pulling my wrist away. A rumbling growl echoed in my chest, and she held her hands up, a trace of fear in her eyes.

Warmth dripped down my chin, and a metallic taste bloomed in my mouth, but it was the look on her face that pulled me from the darkness. I dropped my wrist, which fell limply to my side. My fingers twitched uncontrollably on my right hand, the nerves screaming in protest of my actions.

"Seren, help me," I said desperately, my vision blurring. There was a clatter as the cup fell from my numb fingers. I felt her carefully pick up my injured arm before the world fell out from beneath me, my body refusing to listen to my commands.

A groan escaped my lips as I tried to understand what I was seeing. I was just sitting, and now I was looking up at the ceiling.

Seren's voice floated in the fog, but I couldn't make out the words.

My head throbbed violently as I fought to stay conscious. My wrist burned like a brand, the muscles and tendons ripped all to hell. I'd be lucky if I didn't permanently damage myself, I realized with a start. The world was dark, but Seren's hand was holding mine so delicately, almost as though she was afraid she would break me.

My entire body trembled like a leaf in the wind, and I realized I could easily die. My body has gone through so much trauma so quickly. It was a wonder I was even still alive.

Seren carefully tapped my cheek, and my eyes opened. I didn't realize they had closed. Her face was blurry, and I tried hard to focus on her features.

"I've got enough. I'm going to bandage your wrist, and then I'll give him everything I could get out of you," she said from very far away. Furrowing my brow, I tried to make sense of her words. My world was a mass of pain and confusion, spots intruding on the periphery of my vision.

She took off her undershirt, leaving her only in her undergarments and ripped the bottom of the fabric with her teeth. Once she was satisfied that she had enough, she laid my wrist across her lap, taking exceeding care to bandage my mangled flesh as well as she could. Once she was satisfied, she put the remains of her undershirt back on and picked up the cup.

I could only hope she had enough. She *needed* to have enough.

Seren moved out of my view, but I heard her lilting voice as she encouraged Aldric to open his mouth.

Distress colored the sound as she continued trying to coax him, and my hand fumbled across the floor as I reached for Aldric. It felt as though I was hovering above my body, watching as my form desperately tried to reach Aldric, to become one with him, to offer comfort in the only way I could despite how broken I was.

It made me feel incredibly sad for the person I saw down there. So alone, so hopeless on her journey of belonging. Every person she grew close to suffered for her presence. Such a bleak existence. Slowly, I looked down at myself, hovering there. Just a being of light, made of tiny threads of gray woven together.

Strange. Was a soul made of mana?

Tapping my finger on my chin, I could feel the sensation, which was odd. Glancing around, the people surrounding my body also had light within them. Seren had a kaleidoscope of colors within her—red, yellow, green, blue, indigo, and violet. She was truly a beautiful person, inside and out.

Aldric's had offshoots of black, and it reminded me of a galaxy, sparkling with turquoise and blue and bits of red. But his light wasn't as bright as Seren's. It was fading. Moving closer to him, I saw Seren fighting to get him to open his mouth and take the blood ready to be given to him, but he was struggling. He seemed to be trapped in a nightmare, his body jumping and tense, his eyes darting around beneath his lids.

Slowly, I drifted back down to my physical body, bracing myself for the pain that I knew awaited me. I had to get to Aldric before his light faded completely.

Each movement was hell on earth.

Laying on my back, I slowly pushed myself towards Aldric with my legs. Every single shift, every twitch, and I felt my shards of my rib jabbing against my insides. The pain stole my breath away, leaving me gasping. Seren glanced towards me. But she was fighting her own battle and trying not to spill any of the precious liquid she held.

My arms and legs trembled uncontrollably and finally, I bumped into something hard and too warm.

"Aldric," I breathed. "Open your mouth." With my uninjured hand, I blindly reached up to him, despairing at the struggle we're having to get him to cooperate.

A gentle chill flowed from that cavern deep within me, my magic creeping along my skin where we touched, so different from the darkness that assailed us earlier. It seeped into him, and his movements slowly dissipated until he lay still.

"Aldric," I repeated, my voice cracking as I struggled to raise my voice above a whisper. "Open your mouth."

Time was of the essence, and if he didn't hurry, he'd never survive. Tears flowed freely down my cheeks, and I found his arm, tugging it closer to me with all of my remaining strength.

"I'm here," I breathed.

Slowly, Aldric's arm lifted and fell over my chest, the weight heavy and comforting.

"He's awake," Seren cried, her voice cutting through the tension.

Relief immediately coursed through me, and my body went weak. The part of me so determined to stay conscious for Aldric faded like smoke in the wind.

The world crumbled, and the maw of darkness enveloped me.

CHAPTER 15

The bitter taste of herbs burned my tongue as Seren forced more liquid into my mouth. Every breath felt like daggers being driven into my lungs, and I could barely manage tiny, gasping breaths. Lightheaded, I struggled to turn away from the hand cupping my cheek.

"Please," Seren's voice cracked, pleading. "Please, just drink a little more. I don't know what else I can do."

I tried to obey, despite the sharp pain every time I tried to swallow, like razor blades down my throat. There was a rasping cough and the rattle of breath coming from nearby. My gaze slowly found its way to Seren's eyes, and they were so beautiful, shiny with tears.

"Aldric isn't getting better," she whispered, remorse filling the air between us. "He drank the blood, but his infection... I've tried everything. And you're not much better."

She put a fist to her forehead, closing her eyes.

"Gods, what am I supposed to do?"

Twin streams flowed down her cheeks, which shone like jewels even in the minimal light of the destroyed cabin. I wanted to comfort her, but I could barely keep myself awake. My fingers twitched, but I couldn't lift my hand. The room was too quiet and cold, shivers wracking my body. The only sound was Aldric's labored breathing.

Seren abruptly straightened her spine, wiping her cheeks with the back of a hand. She slowly rose to her feet, silent as a cat as she slunk towards the battered door, peeking through a crack in the wood.

"Stay quiet," she murmured, so quietly I could barely hear her. Not that it mattered. I could barely speak anyway. "If it's the royal guard—if they somehow found us here—we're dead."

There were faint sounds of trees creaking and branches snapping while the ground trembled lightly beneath us. Whatever approached was huge. Adrenaline coursed through me, my heart racing as I lay still on the ground. Blood was rushing impossibly loud through my ears, but I still heard a whisper of leather as Seren drew a dagger from a sheath at her hip.

There was a hint of luminescence that made its way into the room, and I held my breath. What had they sent after us?

"It can't be," Seren whispered, her voice thick with restrained emotion.

"What?" I rasped almost silently, my throat raw and sore.

A low rumble floated through the air, causing goosebumps to appear on my arms.

Seren stood, yanking open the door with enough force that

it slammed into the wall on the other side. She was silhouetted against the scarlet and tangerine of the sky, but even with the shadows I could see her body trembling.

"Koto?" Seren asked, her voice breaking.

There was a grumble in response, and Seren rushed forward into a moving mass of shadows, a sob escaping her. Slowly, Koto's enormous form came into view, the luminescence of her eyes flashing in the darkness as the gloom melted away from her fur. A massive pair of antlers shone in the little sunlight that was left, and Seren had buried her face into Koto's neck. I struggled to lift myself, but my body was too weak.

There was a deep, low purr emanating from Koto's chest, and I couldn't help but smile despite the pain.

"H-how did you manage to get here?" Seren asked, her voice muffled by Koto's fur.

There was a series of chirps in response, and Seren nodded as though Koto was speaking perfect English. Slowly, the Feralumin nudged Seren aside, and she forced her way through the narrow door, cracking the frame as easily as breaking a twig. At this rate, I didn't know how much more this cabin could take.

Koto stood over Aldric's body, her breath ruffling through his matted hair as she inhaled his scent. She grunted, then stepped carefully over him and reached me. Up close, Koto was terrifying. She had huge, intelligent eyes the same shade as Seren's, a beautiful green that made you think of the first shoots of grass breaking through a snowfall.

Her pupils narrowed to slits as she lowered her face near

mine, her giant fangs peeking through the edge of her lip. I swallowed hard, tension radiating from my body. She seemed to look me over, then huffed out a breath as though disapproving. Koto nudged my uninjured hand, and I hesitantly lifted my arm. She rumbled with approval and bumped my palm with her massive head, nuzzling against it.

I'd never really thought about what she actually felt like before, but her fur was surprisingly soft, the slight iridescence making her fur look almost like an oil slick in the sunshine, all colors at once in very muted tones. It must be what allowed her camouflage to work as well as it did.

Her black nose was cold and wet, and it surprised a laugh out of me when I felt the rough texture of her tongue on my fingers. I immediately regretted it when my lung felt like a dagger had been driven into it, taking my breath away. I coughed and tried hard to brace against the pain.

Seren approached silently behind Koto, and the Feralumin made a strange yip sound at her. She started rifling through her fur at the thickest part of her neck, seemingly looking for something. Koto continued to mew and squawk as she did, almost like she was lecturing Seren.

"I get it, okay? It's kind of hard to find what you're talking about in here," Seren snipped back.

After a few more seconds, Seren gasped, pulling a leather pouch on a cord from Koto's neck with some maneuvering.

"Is this it?" she asked, holding out the small bag to Koto. She made a hum of approval, and Seren walked over to Aldric.

He didn't respond to her presence, quiet aside from the rattle of his chest as he struggled to breathe.

Watching carefully, I held my breath as she pulled the pouch strings, opening it to reveal a small vial with a shimmering silver liquid.

"Just what is this, Koto?" Seren asked, turning the small tube in her hands. "Is this safe to give him?"

Koto rumbled in response, silently padding over as though to supervise Seren's actions.

"If you insist," she said with a sigh.

Seren carefully uncorked the vial, and the scent of rain and the ocean filled the room. She kneeled beside Aldric, her hands trembling as she lifted his head gently. Koto chirped, and Seren's face tightened with concern. I desperately wished that I could understand Koto the way Seren did.

The moment the liquid touched Aldric's lips, his body convulsed violently. His eyes shot open, completely black. Before any of us could react, he jerked away from Seren's grasp and rolled to his side, heaving forcefully. Black sludge poured from his mouth, spitting and hissing as it touched the planks of the floor.

The fierce retching sounds coming from Aldric scared me, and I fought to pick myself up despite the searing pain. Koto was suddenly there, her massive head tipping towards me, where I carefully grasped an antler and used it to help me sit up. Her eyes were wise and pitying in a way I'd never expected from an animal.

"Just what—," I started, wheezing, "—what is happening?"

"It must be purging something from his body," Seren said,

her brows furrowed as she slowly backed away from the pooling tar. The stench of decay filled the air as more and more of the foul substance poured from between Aldric's lips.

As I looked on in horror, I just knew—he'd lost all the blood I'd managed to give him. There was no way he could be so forcefully sick and keep it down. A pit opened up in my stomach. What were we going to do?

Letting go of Koto's antler, I gently stroked her head. "Can you please get me over to him?" I asked, my voice soft.

Koto grumbled in response, offering me her neck. I carefully gripped her fur with my uninjured arm, staggering to my feet. I stumbled forward a few steps, but Koto was like an immovable object, incredibly steady and seeming to know exactly how I needed her to move to keep me upright. Bracing my ribs as well as I could with my injured arm, I sat down hard next to Aldric, jarring my injuries and making me lose my breath.

It felt like a hot iron was being stabbed into my lungs, but I couldn't worry about myself right now. I reached over Aldric's shoulder and pulled his hair away from his face, and stroked his back as he continued to retch.

Aldric's body stiffened again, and his fingers left deep gouges on the wooden floor. His wounds leaked the same tar, and dread filled me.

Koto made a series of hums and chirps as Seren turned towards the door.

Panic seized me in its icy fingers as I watched, slack-jawed, as she started to open the door, Koto heading out, leaving Aldric and me alone. "W-what are you doing?" I gasped out.

"Lyra…" Seren began gently. "He won't live without blood."

"What are you going to do?" I managed to rasp.

"Whatever we have to," she said grimly, meeting my eyes. There was steel in her gaze. "Unless you somehow have more to give?"

At my blank stare, she silently turned, and the door slammed shut behind her.

My entire body felt like a bruise, and I carefully lifted my shirt to see a bloom of mottled blue-black on my right side across my ribs. Aldric's entire body shook like a leaf, and I continued gently stroking his back. Could I allow them to bring a person here—to sacrifice someone so that Aldric could feed?

I knew the answer. I didn't want Aldric to die, no matter what that meant. As it was, the bond between us was tenuous at best. As soon as he got sick, it felt as though it was muffled under hundreds of pounds of snow, barely there at all. But I had to have some kind of faith that this was temporary.

Using my uninjured hand, I slowly unwound his dirtied bandages. It couldn't be good to leave that sludge trapped there. Aldric inhaled sharply as his wounds hit open air, and I cringed, but continued my efforts. We'd have to clean these out if he had any hope of getting better.

My muscles were becoming so tense from the effort of sitting, and I leaned to my left in order to take some pressure off, though it didn't help much. Breathing shallowly, I tried to figure out the best way to get to my feet. There had to be water somewhere that I could use to clean Aldric's wounds.

With monumental effort, I managed to shift to my knees, holding my breath against the pain. Black spots started swimming in my vision, and I tried to breathe through it, but I could barely expand my lungs. There was a grinding in my ribs and sparks of flame shooting through my chest as I braced my uninjured hand against the floor.

Agonizingly slowly, I got my feet beneath me and tried to stand, despite the shaking in my legs. My abdominal muscles were starting to cramp from the strain, and I struggled to stay upright, or as close to it as I could manage.

Staggering over to our bags, I went to my knees and rifled through them, ignoring the shock with every movement. Finally, I found a waterskin and struggled to crawl back over to Aldric, who was vomiting anew, though it was much less than before.

His skin had taken on a grayish hue, and his wounds were festering. I pulled the cork from the waterskin with my teeth and poured it as deliberately as I could over each of his wounds until the water ran out. It took away the worst of the gunk from his injuries, but he definitely needed more help than I could give. He moaned as his retching finally slowed, his face a mask of distress.

"I'm sorry, Aldric," I murmured, stroking his sweat-slicked cheek. "Just hold on a little longer. It'll be okay. I'll make sure of it."

I didn't know if he could hear me, but his expression relaxed slightly and the knot inside me loosened just a little. Just what had they given Aldric? What was it meant to do? The thread between us felt one step away from being ripped away entirely. What would happen if we lost it? Could we still complete the bond?

A sound from outside made me freeze. Footsteps. My heart thundered against my battered ribs as a voice drifted through the damaged door. It was Seren. Her familiar tone immediately provided me with some relief. Had they brought someone? I swallowed hard as the door opened.

The sun was quickly lowering, leaving us mostly in darkness. The slight glow of Koto's eyes was stark against the shadows, highlighting the outline of a body in her jaws.

"What—who is that?" I asked, stumbling over my words.

"It doesn't matter. They were unconscious when I found them. There were a lot of dead bodies in the village. I'm surprised they were still alive, to be honest," Seren said darkly, waving Koto inside.

She held up an unlit torch, which sparked to life in her hands, the color of the flame a sickly green. She placed it in a sconce near the door, which wasn't too badly damaged by Myrana's earlier tirade.

"I managed to get this from the village too, but it was dry, so I had to light it myself," she explained at my confused look.

I fought to take a breath, ready to ask about what they were going to do with the person they brought in, when Koto gently laid them on the floor. Leaning as much as I could, I saw it was a young man, his body completely slack and his eyes closed. He looked so young, probably late teens or early twenties, with straight dark hair bound into a bun on top of his head and threadbare brown pants, along with a worn linen shirt that looked like it used to be white a long time ago.

"What are you going to do?" I rasped, each word sending a stab of pain through my ribs.

"What we have to do. Unless you'd rather just let Aldric die?" Seren asked, her gaze intense on my face.

Shame colored my cheeks, and I looked away. I couldn't say the words, but she knew what my answer would be.

"Do you need Koto to take you outside while I do this?" Seren asked, her voice deadly quiet.

I swallowed hard, my stomach churning. It felt wrong to have Seren take care of Aldric like this, but this felt like more than I could handle.

"No," I said finally. "I'll stay."

The words tasted like ash in my mouth, but I just couldn't leave them to do this alone. It wasn't fair to Seren.

Seren nodded, her expression grim as she moved to kneel beside the boy. "I just need to make sure he's alive. I don't know if it's true, but I've heard if vampires drink dead blood, it's worse for them. Not like we can ask Aldric right now," she said the last on a murmur, pressing her ear to the boy's chest.

After a moment, she moved to his face and lifted an eyelid. Satisfied, she let go of the lid, and as it closed, I *swore* that the boy's dark eye rolled to fix directly on me. There was urgency—horror—in that gaze. But when his body didn't move despite Seren's manipulations, I reasoned I must be imagining things from the stress.

"He's alive, but just barely. His pulse is weak and thready. Perfect for what we need. He shouldn't suffer," she said, reaching for the knife at her hip. With a whisper of leather, she nodded to Koto, who brought over a satchel. It wasn't one of ours. She must have gotten it from the same village.

The green glow flickering through the cabin made me think of a poison, slowly reaching its sticky fingers into us. A chill raced down my spine, and I shuddered before gasping at the shock of pain.

Seren rifled through the satchel and pulled out an aluminum cup. After no more than a moment's hesitation, she propped the boy's body up on her lap and sliced his wrist, holding the limp weight over the cup, where the blood appeared black in the light. I turned away. I couldn't watch this happen, but I could still hear *drip* falling into the receptacle.

There was another retch from Aldric, and I was reminded of the situation we were in. There was no choice here. Not if I wanted Aldric to live.

I realized with a start that I would sacrifice others if it meant he would survive. Feeling like a monster, I gently stroked Aldric's back. Luckily, despite the retching, nothing was coming up. So, it sounds like whatever blood he gets, he should be able to keep down.

He took a shuddering breath, and his gagging slowly subsided. It felt both too long and too short of a time before Seren was suddenly in front of Aldric.

"Help me with him so we can get him drinking this down," she said, gesturing with the cup. She was holding the boy's arm up in the air with her other hand, trying to prevent any extra blood loss.

I tried to shift Aldric, but the searing agony of my ribs stopped me short. Looking helplessly around, Koto carefully trod over, surprisingly light on her feet even with such a small space to work in. She carefully hooked the shoulder of Aldric's shirt with a tooth and dragged him into my lap.

There was a small bloom of blood where her tooth must have nicked him, but he didn't react, completely slack where he lay against me. I carefully tipped his head back, his mouth open. Seren handed me the dark liquid, using both hands to staunch the flow of blood coming from between her fingers on the young man's arm.

Gripping Aldric's jaw with one hand, I tipped the cup until a light trickle of liquid went down his throat. To my immense relief, he quickly swallowed, though his eyes didn't open. I poured faster until he was readily guzzling the contents. As soon as there was nothing left, Aldric's eyes finally opened, and the look in them was terrifying, animalistic.

A growl like nothing I had ever heard came from his lips, and he reached for me before Seren screamed at him.

"Over here!" she yelled, practically dangling the boy in front of him like a piece of meat. He leaped off of me with preternatural speed, causing me to fall backwards. All of my air whooshed out of my lungs as I felt a sharp, stabbing pain, which worsened with each breath.

"Seren," I rasped, almost soundless. It felt like I was suffocating. There was a sound of wet, tearing flesh coming from somewhere in the cabin. Koto appeared in my vision, wavering as though I was viewing her from underwater.

A heaviness spread in my chest on my right side, and I coughed. *That was a mistake*, I thought dimly, as stars burst behind my eyes. Koto hummed, and something else came into view. Seren?

I couldn't think straight, gasping for each breath. Was I going to die after all?

Seren was saying something, but it was hard to make it out. "I can't breathe," I said, or tried to say. There wasn't enough air in my lungs to push the words out.

Seren put her ear to my chest, then bolted upright. "One of her lungs is punctured," she said urgently to Koto. The words were strangely muffled, and I couldn't slow my breathing. It felt like I couldn't get enough air, and I was panicking.

There were awful lip smacking sounds in the room as Seren struggled to pick me up without jostling my injuries any worse, and she carefully laid me on Koto's back, climbing up behind me.

"Do you know any healers around here?" Seren asked, her face close to mine. I blinked blearily, trying to see more clearly.

"Louise," I mouthed. "Haleshade."

Koto rumbled beneath me, the vibrations sinking into my back. "We don't know where that is, Lyra," Seren said, her tone taking on a hint of desperation. "Is there anyone we may have met from there?"

"Griffin," I gasped out, my heart racing as I struggled to form words. "Werefolk. Wolf. In Sylvan Reach."

The world was going black as I fought to get enough air to stay conscious. Nausea roiled within me, and I started to choke.

"Shit," Seren bit out before turning me so I could vomit on the floor. The agony of the movement felt like a lightning strike burning through me. My vision went white.

Then, there was nothing at all.

CHAPTER 16

Consciousness came in flashes. The wind whipped past. Seren's arms braced my ribs against the rhythmic movement of Koto's powerful stride beneath us. Each breath was agony, and every time I was jostled, the world would go black again.

I couldn't get enough oxygen. I would die soon if nothing was done.

Darkness took me.

When awareness returned, the scent of death was heavy in the air, so thick you could taste it. Through blurred vision, I saw dirty streets, doors left open on broken hinges. But the streets weren't empty. There were bodies left everywhere—some partially covered, others left to the elements. This couldn't be Haleshade. This place was a tomb.

"Where…" Seren's voice cracked, and she cleared her throat before trying again. "Where is everyone?"

I wanted to point her to Louise's house, but I couldn't lift my arm. Luckily, Koto seemed to have picked up the scent of someone living. She slowly and carefully weaved through the bodies. I made a point not to look too closely, too afraid of seeing a familiar face mottled by death.

My breath was coming too close, too fast. Chilled, my body trembled uncontrollably. Seren ran a hand comfortingly over my arm, but even that movement was too much for me, and I fell into unconsciousness yet again.

When I came to, it felt like I was coming up from underwater.

I could hear frantic voices, along with someone who sounded so resigned, so exhausted. I was lying on a hard cot or table, something uncomfortable on my back. But there was no way Koto would fit in here. Relief that I'd be unconscious for the transfer flowed through me, despite the pounding in my head.

"She's going to die, please," Seren insisted.

"There's not much I can do for her without going through more effort than I'm comfortable with," Louise said with a sigh.

"I've dealt with enough death. Take her somewhere else to die."

"You can't be serious. She asked for you specifically," Seren exclaimed, frustration coloring her words.

I fought to pry my eyes open—a monumental effort in itself. When a sliver of the world came into view, I saw unfamiliar walls, the scent of old blood and infection lingering in the air. This must be Louise's house. I'd never been inside because, luckily for me, I'd never had to.

"Louise," I rasped.

At the sound of my voice, I heard a scrape of wood against the floor as Louise stood, coming to the edge of my vision.

"Lyra?" she asked. "Why do you look like this? What happened to you?"

That's right. She'd only ever seen me disguised by my magic, I thought airily.

"She's always looked like this," Seren said impatiently. "And soon she'll look like a corpse if we don't get a move on. You see how only one side of her chest is expanding? She's got a punctured lung. You need to help her, or she won't make it through the night."

"Where's Griffin?" Louise asked. "Don't tell me he…" She didn't finish the sentence, but the words lingered in the air. I turned away from her, and I heard a sharp inhale.

"Oh gods, oh no… Not him too," she breathed, the words tinged with bone-deep sadness. "There's been so much loss lately. But at least I can help you. And then maybe I can get an explanation."

Her hair was twisted into a knot on top of her head, and though her moss-green eyes were tired, there was a hint of familiar determination in their depths. She came back into view wearing a white apron with some dark stains I didn't want to contemplate too much.

"You're going to want to drink this," Louise said, holding up a potion bottle with a viscous, muddy-looking liquid inside. Seren came up behind me and carefully lifted me as much as she could to make it easier for me to swallow.

As the fluid slipped down my throat, the world dimmed. I heard voices from far away.

"You're going to have to help me with this…"

Then nothing more.

Consciousness returned slowly.

The first thing I noticed was that it felt like I could breathe again. The second was pain—but this pain was different from before, less severe, more localized, rather than the suffocating agony I'd experienced earlier. There was also something tightly wrapped around my chest, restricting my movement.

I slowly opened my eyes, relieved that the world came into clarity somewhat quickly. The scent of various herbs and the metallic scent of old blood lingered in the air. I was lying on a cot in a clinical-looking room. Pale morning light filtered through grimy windows, illuminating dust motes as they bounced through the air. How long had I been out?

"Welcome back," Louise said from somewhere to my left. Her hair had mostly escaped from its neat bun, highlighting new gray streaks that hadn't been there the last time I saw her, shining through her honey-blonde tresses. She looked even more exhausted than before, dark circles marring the pale skin around her eyes.

Her movements were stiff as she approached me, telling me her usual aches and pains must have been exacerbated by whatever was done to me. "Try not to move too much. I had to piece you back together like a patchwork quilt. Surgery has never been my strong suit, but I didn't have a choice."

"Thank you, Louise," I said softly. Looking down, I saw I wasn't wearing a shirt. Rather, a threadbare blanket was thrown over me.

"I had to cut your shirt off. And since I have to keep an eye on your wound, I didn't bother with anything else," she said at my quizzical look.

"Where's Seren?" I asked, savoring every breath I could take. There was still a lot of tenderness, but it was leagues better than I'd been dealing with before.

"The Fae?" Louise asked dismissively. "She went to collect some other member of your travel party, I suppose. Or that's what she said at least. She's been gone for a while though."

I nodded. We must have had to leave Aldric behind. I only remember tiny bits and pieces of the journey, so I'm not sure how far away we are from that cabin. But I trusted Koto to keep Seren safe.

"When Seren gets back, there's a man—a vampire—he's going to need help," I said cautiously, not sure how she would take that information.

Louise scrubbed a hand over her face. "It's been a mess around here, and you're just bringing me more trouble," she said, exasperated.

"What happened since we left?" I asked, the question burning inside of me.

"What didn't?"

She gestured angrily around. "Nearly everyone's dead, and the ones that didn't die left. I couldn't handle everything on my own, but I stayed because I thought—I thought you and Griffin would…" Her eyes grew bright with unshed tears, which she scrubbed away viciously.

"I know," I whispered. "But things didn't turn out the way I wanted."

"Who even *are* you, Lyra? Why do you look so different?"

This was the question I'd been dreading, but I knew I couldn't hide myself any longer. What was the point?

"Lyra Graves. My parents are part of the Order of Mages, but I ended up with a power I shouldn't have had." I looked away, shame burning through me. "True transformation."

"You think that matters around here? You didn't have to lie. That's probably why people had trouble getting close to you. They felt you were hiding something," Louise asked, each word like a dagger in my back.

"What did you expect?" I snapped, fury coursing through me and giving me the energy to sit up despite the throbbing ache inside me. "Ever since I got cursed with this gods damned power, everyone either tried to kill me or avoided me like a leper. I just wanted to belong!"

"Well, you can't belong if you're not being yourself," Louise said, crossing her arms over her narrow chest.

"What does it matter now?" I bit out. "Everything that could go wrong has. And now we're here."

"You're right about that," she murmured, leaning her hip against the cot. She'd removed the stained apron, I realized. Now she just wore black pants that had turned gray with age and a tank top the same shade of green as her eyes. "What happened? After you left, I mean."

Rubbing a hand against the back of my neck, I rolled my head, trying to loosen some of the tension.

"It was Thorne. He said you knew him," I started.

"Thorne?" Louise said, tapping a finger against her chin. "He was the head healer in the Order for a while. We worked together while I was getting established and learning my power. But we didn't talk much after that."

"He said he knew you very well," I murmured. Then it struck me. "Why aren't you more upset about my ability? Most mages would have already tried to kill me by now."

"Who gives a shit?" Louise said bluntly, the crassness of her words almost humorous coming from such a delicate-looking woman. "The world's gone to hell in a handbasket right now. Besides, didn't you ever wonder why there would be another mage who made a point to stay out of Sylvan Reach?"

"I know you went back to visit on occasion, so I never really thought about it," I said.

"I went as much as I had to, no more. Not every mage agrees with what the Order does," she said, waving a hand before re-crossing her arms. "So what they're afraid of—who they choose to ostracize—doesn't really matter to me. I don't consider myself part of that organization. They don't scare me."

Had I thought wrong all these years, hiding myself, so afraid of being found out? I shook my head, putting my hands in my lap.

The past was in the past.

"Thorne is the one who killed Griffin," I said, the words bitter in my mouth. "I was going to head back and bury him, but there's some primordial god or something like that who's trying to force me onto some path I don't want to follow, and it's what led me to end up here."

"That's some crazy shit," Louise said, her eyes widening. "You should be patched up enough to go wherever you're going though, if you're careful."

"His body is in Sylvan Reach."

"Good luck, that's all I'm going to say," she said, pushing off of the cot with her hip and pacing. "There's been so, so much death, and the people who are left are scared. Violent. They won't accept people coming around, so you'll have to stick it out in the forest and hope no one's returned to the village."

"Are you the only one left here?" I asked cautiously. "Outside… It was horrible."

"Yeah. Imagine living in it," she said viciously. "This whole thing has been completely fucking awful, and I've been stuck dealing with it all alone. Everyone else either fell to the plague or left. And the only people who are here are victims, whom I'd been struggling to keep alive. They were the last ones who have gotten sick, and it's because they stayed to help me."

Her eyes were haunted, shadows swirling in their depths, and I could only imagine the horrors she'd endured, failing over and over to save these people who she knew so well.

"I'm sorry, Louise," I murmured, tucking my hair behind my ear. "I should have been here."

"It is what it is. I just hope we can figure out how to help the people who are left," she said sadly, looking as though she'd aged ten years just in the time we've been talking.

"We'll do what we can."

CHAPTER 17

The sound of Koto's heavy footfalls resounded in the small room as she approached outside. Louise tensed, her hand automatically going to a small dagger at her hip. I looked up at her face, surprised to find an intensity in her gaze that I hadn't seen before.

"It's just Seren," I said, holding my hands up. The pull of the stitches on my abdomen made me wince, but slowly I brought myself to my feet, shuffling to the window and looking outside to see Seren walking behind Koto's hulking form. Aldric lay limply on his stomach across the Feralumin's back.

"Can't be too careful these days," Louise said grimly. "We've had raiders coming through, looking to pick over anything that's left. That's why there are so many broken doors and windows around here—people searching for medicine, food, anything they can steal from the dead and sell."

Frowning, I gazed out at the village to see evidence of her words. There were doors hanging off of hinges, splintered wood on the ground and glass scattered about. Things had gotten much, much worse than I thought in the time we'd been gone, a sinking feeling in my gut.

Deliberately skating my eyes over the many still forms lying in the streets, I turned as the door creaked open, Seren entering the room, looking more exhausted than I'd ever seen her. Her inky hair was windblown, and she was moving slower than usual.

Koto struggled to maneuver herself through the entrance, but she was just too large. She huffed and lay next to the door. My heart raced as I held my wound, slowly making my way over to Aldric.

His skin was pale, ashen, and though his silver wounds were no longer leaking that tar-like substance, they looked angry, inflamed, and the smell of infection was strong enough to wrinkle my nose. Louise trailed behind me, with a wary expression on her face.

"Is this the vampire you mentioned?" she asked, crossing her arms. She hesitantly peered over my shoulder, as though afraid he would leap up and attack her.

As I got a closer look, I understood why she would react that way. He had dried blood on his face and hands, I noticed, though I forced myself not to think about why.

"Yes, it is," I murmured, tracing the line of his jaw. "Please. He needs help. I don't know what to do." My throat tightened, cutting off my words. "He was impaled with silver and isn't healing—,"

Louise waved me off and cautiously approached. "You there, Fae. Help me get him in here."

Seren slowly shook her head, as though trying to clear her thoughts. "No problem," she murmured, tucking her shoulder under Aldric's arm and dragging him off of Koto, who sighed as though she was being incredibly inconvenienced. I moved to help, but Louise looked at me incredulously.

"Girl, you are barely being held together right now. Go sit your ass down before I make you," she lectured, cursing under her breath as she took Aldric's other arm and heaved him over to the nearest cot. He must have been heavy, because his feet were dragging behind them.

With an *oof*, Louise dropped him heavily onto the thin mattress, and Seren went to flop in a nearby chair with a sigh. Louise straightened her spine and rubbed her right fist into her lower back. I remembered how much my body ached when I wore her form.

"Are you doing okay?" I asked, guilt seeping through the words.

"It's nothing I'm not unused to," she said, groaning. "But I'm not the patient right now. Let's see what we can do for this bloodsucker of yours."

A blush crept up my cheeks at her words, but I carefully rolled a stool over to where Aldric lay, moving his hair out of his face. He was clammy and completely unconscious. Ignoring the burning feeling as the stitches pulled, I leaned over carefully and pressed a light kiss to his cheek in an area not marked with blood. He didn't stir, and anxiety sparked within me.

"What do you need me to do?" I asked, my legs bouncing with nervous energy.

"Just keep yourself calm. Only one of us is a healer, remember?" Louise said, spinning on her heel and strutting out of the room, her movements stiff. I heard glass clinking together and the sounds of cabinet doors opening and closing as she rifled through what I assume was her potions closet.

After what was probably a few minutes but what felt like hours, she returned, a bundle of herbs in her hand and a couple of bottles perched precariously in her arms. I hopped up to help her, despite the severe look she gave me. Despite my achiness, I felt immensely better than I had when I arrived, and I was desperate to be of some assistance.

Taking a fat, round bottle from her curiously, I swirled the contents. It looked like little more than milky-white water.

"Don't go shaking that too much," Louise said, warning ringing clear in her voice while she set her other supplies on a small table nearby. I lowered the bottle and looked at her face, her jade eyes growing bright with unshed tears. She cleared her throat and looked away. "I made that for Griffin, actually. In case—you know…Werefolk and silver don't tend to mix."

The bottle felt like lead in my hands, and my throat grew tight. Griffin had told Louise more about himself than he'd ever told me, I realized. He had trusted her enough to divulge his secret willingly, to help prepare for worst-case scenarios. Did I mean as much to him as he had meant to me?

Shaking my head, I pushed those thoughts away. Now wasn't the time to dwell on something like that.

"I never got the chance to give it to him," Louise whispered, her voice cracking on the words. She wiped her hands aggressively on her pants and cleared her throat again. "But I guess it can help someone else now."

I swallowed hard.

"He would have wanted that."

Louise nodded sharply, rolling her shoulders as though her whole body had grown tense. "Right. Well, those wounds aren't just infected. There's silver still in his system. Normally, vampire healing would push it out, but there must be something hindering his healing capabilities. We need to clean these properly first, then see if we can draw out whatever is left in his blood."

From her chair, Seren made a soft sound, her eyes heavy-lidded. Koto grumbled from the doorway, turning to peer inside with a huge, emerald-hued eye. There was a hint of concern there, but I had other things to worry about right now. Besides, Seren had been running herself ragged, taking care of Aldric and me. She deserved a break.

"First time I've had to use this," Louise muttered, pulling glass-like iridescent leaves from a branch. She walked back into her ingredients closet and returned with a mortar and pestle. It was speckled dark gray and white, and seemed incredibly heavy by the *thud* it made as she placed it on the small round table with her ingredients.

"Griffin used to come by and help test this recipe, though. It took months to really perfect it, and even then, I don't know if it's really up to snuff. We never got there in the end," she said, dropping the leaves into the mortar. With practiced skill, she quickly worked them into a paste.

"Go get me some moon-flora oil from the ingredients closet. It'll be in a blue glass bottle near the back. Should help with drawing the metal out," she said, waving me off.

I wasted no time and immediately took off towards the closet, a hand pressed against my stitches to help with the pain of walking.

As I crossed the threshold, the scent of liquorice and mint assaulted my nose, along with something vinegar-y. Liquid filled my mouth as nausea roiled in my stomach, but this was no time to run away.

Moving quickly with my free hand covering my nose, I strode directly to the back of the closet, eyes roving over the shelves as I searched for a hint of blue.

There were dozens of different bottles, herbs hanging from the ceiling, medical implements, not to mention medical journals. This closet was packed tight with everything a healer could need. How long did it take her to accumulate this much stuff?

"No, no…Not this," I muttered to myself, picking up a teal-colored bottle that was marked as containing comfrey root.

Carefully setting it aside, I got onto my tip-toes to see further in.

There, at the very back, sat a deep cerulean-colored orb with a cork in it. Stretching my arm, the sound of glass tinkled together as my hand bumped the bottles. I finally closed my fingers around my target and pulled it from the confines of the shelf.

My wound burned like a lick of flame as I drew my arm carefully back out, careful not to knock anything off. Sweat broke out on my skin, and my body trembled from the pain, but this was for Aldric. For him, I would suffer endlessly if I had to.

As long as he could live.

Tears pricked my eyes at the thought, but I refused to let them fall. Slowly making my way back to Louise, I closed the closet door behind me, effectively confining the intense smell from within.

I held up the bottle of moon-flora oil. It shone with a light from within, almost like I carried a star in my palm. Passing the orb to Louise, she deftly opened the cork with her teeth, spitting it on the ground nearby, then poured the entire contents into the mortar. There was a spark and a small *poof* of smoke. The paste mixed with the oil seamlessly to create a galaxy-like liquid. It was strange watching it being made.

The ingredients alone didn't look like they would make something like this. A thick black paste, glimmering with white light that burst from within. I'd never seen anything like it.

"Okay, now the fun part," she said with a sigh, brushing her wheat-colored hair from her forehead and tucking it back behind her ears. Slowly getting to her feet, she stretched, and then carried the mortar over to Aldric's bedside. She opened a drawer in the bedside table, where there was something that looked like a… paintbrush?

"I don't know how he'll respond to this."

I glanced over at Seren, but she was asleep, her head tucked into her crossed arms. Looks like it was just up to me to help.

"Just in case, let me get you something to help with the pain. I may need you to help hold him down, and I don't want you to let up because you're sore," she said, bustling off again and returning with a vial of what looked like plain water. "Drink up. The whole thing."

Hesitantly, I popped the cap off and sniffed the contents. It smelled of fruit, sugary sweet. I tipped the glass against my lips, and the taste of wine and chocolate burst forth. Easily downing the liquid, a strange feeling filled my body, starting from my stomach and working its way through all of my limbs. My head grew fuzzy, but it felt more like I was becoming wine-drunk than anything.

"It's a fast-acting pain reliever. You might feel a little high or drunk, but you'll stay conscious," she said, eyeing me up and down as though to monitor my reaction.

The ache in my side melted away, and I straightened my spine for the first time since I woke up.

"Just because it doesn't hurt doesn't mean that you *aren't* hurt though—bear that in mind," Louise lectured with a sniff. "Now get over here and help me."

Wasting no time, I strode over to Aldric's side, putting my hands on his arm with the utmost gentleness that I could muster. He's been through a lot since he ended up with me, I thought sadly. But if anyone could help him, it would be Louise.

"He ah…" she coughed. "He needs to be undressed for this. Not completely, but down to his undergarments at least."

Shocked, my gaze flew to hers, but there was only a cool professionalism in her eyes.

"If that's what we have to do," I said, though a blush crept up my cheeks.

Louise and I carefully disrobed Aldric, who remained out cold. Unease crept through me the longer he remained unmoving, but that's why we were here. I had faith in Louise's ability. Once we had him down to his undergarments—a pair of tight black boxers—the reality of his injuries came to light.

There were obsidian-like tendrils across his skin, creeping through his veins, and there was mottled blue-black bruising all over his body. How much was he suffering? Was he in pain even now, unconscious as he was? Anguish blossomed in my heart at the thought, and I stroked his face, sending him as many good feelings as I could as Louise started to work.

Dipping the tip of the paintbrush into the mixture, she slowly painted it along his skin, where it settled like ink into his flesh. There was no response from Aldric. He lay completely still, almost unnaturally so, his breathing so slow and minute that I had to put my hand on his chest just to feel it rise.

I traced my fingers along his arm, trying to comfort him as best as I could. There was no hint of the bond between us, and it unsettled me in a way I couldn't explain.

I'd grown so used to his feelings, his *essence* within me, that being without left me feeling more alone than ever. Slowly, methodically,

Louise covered more and more of his body in the dark substance. His skin was beginning to look like the night sky. It was beautiful, the way it glimmered in the limited light of the room.

She traced the brush along his neck, his abdomen, down his legs, and eventually she got to his face.

"Do you want to do this part?" she asked, her voice soft. "It always feels strangely intimate, so I thought…"

"Yes," I said, cutting her off. "I'm sorry. I mean, if it's no trouble."

Embarrassment warmed my cheeks, but I took the mortar as she held it out to me. Sitting the heavy stone bowl next to me on the other bedside table, I carefully saturated the brush and stroked the bristles down his cheeks, across his aristocratic nose, his full lips. He looked so otherworldly, so ethereal, like a being made of night. Suitable for a vampire, I supposed, I thought, a hint of a smile cracking my lips.

I…I just hoped he would wake.

He had to.

CHAPTER 18

As the last dregs of the mixture were saturating Aldric's skin, I looked up at Louise.

"So now what?" I asked. "He's not waking up. Should he be waking up by now?"

My body practically vibrated with nervous energy, and as I dropped the paintbrush back into the stone bowl, my hand crept up to my hair and began nervously twisting the strands between them.

"Now, it's a waiting game. It'll will take time to work, to draw the silver out of his body," Louise said, stretching her arms overhead. There was the sound of bones cracking with the movement, showing just how tense she'd been.

"Now would be a good time to get some rest."

The warm, fuzzy feeling in my body slowly leeched away, leaving uncertainty in its wake. "Are you sure it will work? Is there anything else we can do?"

"There's nothing else. Judging by the blood on him that's *not* his, he's fed recently. Or just tore someone apart, I suppose…" she murmured the last, a hint of disgust on her face before the mask of professionalism slipped back into place.

"Your friend—is she usually this tired?" Louise asked, approaching Seren, who lay curled silently in the chair.

"No, not usually. But we had a long journey. We got attacked by…well, you wouldn't believe me anyway," I said, a bone-aching weariness settling into my body.

"By what?" she asked, curiosity shining in her eyes.

"By, well…a god," I mumbled, feeling like any normal person would think I was crazy.

"A god? How'd you manage that? They don't exist here," she said easily, waving a hand as though dismissing the idea entirely.

"Wait, so you know they exist?" I asked, incredulous.

"Well, of course. Where do you think magic comes from? But they don't exist *here*," she said, pointing to the ground for emphasis. Her tone was like she were lecturing a small child, and it rankled me.

"I'd never heard of them being real before I ended up in Starfall Veil…" I murmured.

"You crossed the Veil?" Louise asked, disbelieving. "We need to have a chat."

Grasping my wrist, she pulled me into a side room.

WHISPERED SECRETS

There were a couple of plush chairs and a single couch, along with a coffee table and bookcases packed to the brim with novels of all kinds. This must be her study, I realized.

Louise gestured to one chair and sat in the other. I carefully lowered myself onto the cushion, which I sank into easily. This was one of the most comfortable chairs I'd ever sat in. It reminded me of the one that Griffin had made for me. The thought caused a pang of sadness to spear through me, but Louise wasn't going to give me time to think too much about it.

"Tell me about crossing the Veil," she said, crossing her arms over her narrow chest.

"After what happened to Griffin," I started, my voice cracking. I cleared my throat and tried again. "After what happened, Aldric and I were gathering information from Thorne's house. Thorne had gotten injured and had fled, and Sylvan Reach, well… Everyone had left, so it was just us."

"They left?" Louise seemed to consider something, but waved a hand for me to continue. "Go on."

"Seren showed up and captured the two of us. Aldric first, then me. Next thing I knew, I was in the Veil," I said, shrugging. "We got thrown in jail for who knows how long, and I… escaped."

"How did you manage that?" she asked, her pale brows rising. "The ancient magic there couldn't have been easy to bypass."

"That's where it gets strange…" I told her everything that

happened, from the Fae magic being unable to contain me, to the monstrous form I had taken, to the Fae I had killed. By the end, Louise had a guarded expression on her face, her hands in her lap.

"So this god, she told you to come back and to bring those two?" she said cautiously.

I nodded, my skin crawling as I thought about our last encounter with Myrana.

"The Order may have been onto something," she mumbled, looking at the stacks of books, her gaze unfocused.

"What was that?" I asked, leaning forward despite the pull on my stitches.

"Don't concern yourself yet. I don't know for sure, but I'll find out what's going on," she said cryptically. "In the meantime, please. Rest. I can give you something to help you sleep." With those words, she stood, and I followed her back out into the medical room.

Louise's bare feet made barely any sound as she padded back over to the closet and came back out moments later with a small flask. She led me to the only other cot in the room, across from Aldric. The small amount of space between us felt like miles, and I found I missed having him nearby.

Seeing the look on my face, Louise sighed and flipped a lever on the other cot, allowing it to roll to the other side of the room. I hadn't noticed before that there were wheels, but she easily brought it over to Aldric's side, pushing the bedside table out of the way so that both cots could be pushed together to make one larger bed.

"I can tell that he means a lot to you," Louise said, clasping a hand on my shoulder. Her fingers were icy against my skin, but her voice was warm. "Griffin really cared for you, you know, but this… this is something else. If I didn't know any better, I'd say you two were made for each other, the way your eyes soften every time you look at him."

As she spoke, a flutter began in my stomach, and my throat grew tight. My vision blurred with unshed tears. "He—I really care for him a lot. I just need him to be okay."

"We'll do our best, don't you worry. Take this and go get some rest," she said, handing me the tincture before flipping the same lever to lock the wheels. She dropped her hand and strode back into her study.

Taking the potion, which tasted much worse than the last one, I put the empty flask on the bedside table. Crawling into the cot beside Aldric, I scoot myself over to him, carefully picking up his arm and draping it around my waist as I snuggled against his chest.

As I drifted off, I thought I felt the smallest twitch of his fingers against my skin.

It could have been hours or days later when I finally awoke. There was a puddle of drool on Aldric's bare chest, I realized as I lifted my head, mortified. There was still the same inky blackness that was there when I fell asleep, only now there was a shimmer of silver in spots along Aldric's body.

As I carefully tried to extricate myself, I hissed out a breath where my wound had grown stiff, tugging and pulling against the stitches, but before I could actually maneuver into a sitting position, Aldric's fingers tightened against my shoulder.

"Leaving so quickly, are you?" a voice rumbled against me, hoarse, but achingly familiar.

"Aldric?" My eyes widened into saucers, tears immediately warming my eyes and spilling down my cheeks. I threw myself back onto his chest, wrapping my arms around him tightly despite the throbbing and stinging in my side.

"Careful, darling. I'm awake, but still sore," he murmured, though his arms settled over my body like a comforting blanket.

Burying my face against the hard planes of his chest, I couldn't help the sob that escaped me. "I thought you were going to die," I said through tears. "I thought I'd lost you."

"You can't get rid of me so easily, no matter how much you may want to," he said, his hand stroking along my spine.

"I never want you to go," I whispered against his skin. "Not ever."

"Then you'll have me," he said easily, his hand climbing from my back to my hair, delving his fingers through the messy white waves.

Aldric and I stayed that way for a while, the thrum of his heart beating in his chest relaxing the last of the tension out of my body.

He was alive. Louise had done it.

After the initial shock wore off, I slowly raised my head and glanced around the room before my gaze fell on Aldric's face. His silver eyes were stark against the inky blackness of the mixture on his skin. He looked like a god himself, crafted from the very fabric of night.

"How long have you been awake?" I asked.

"Long enough," Aldric said, his voice low and melodic. "You were snoring."

"Y-you're lying! Why would you tell me that?" I asked and sat up, mortified. His hand dropped with the movement, but his lips quirked up.

"Why not? It's true," he said, his normal teasing tone back in his voice.

"You're awful," I said, turning away as I climbed off of him to sit on the other cot. "Where's Louise?"

"Is that the other mage?" he asked, slowly maneuvering into a seated position. I could tell by the way he moved he was still very sore, though his wounds seemed much better than they were, no longer as red and inflamed.

When I nodded, he shook his head. "I know at one point there was another mage here, but she was already gone when we awoke."

I rubbed my chin in thought. Where had she gone? She said she was going to figure something out, but what?

Glancing around, I saw Seren was still asleep in the chair.

How long had we been out?

"Do you know how long we were asleep for?" I asked, concern growing within me.

"No. I wasn't conscious for at least part of it, so my sense of time is skewed," Aldric admitted sheepishly. "Do you happen to know if there's a bathroom of some type here though? I want to wash this…" he gestured to himself, "…off of my body."

Humming, I carefully stood, my hand immediately going to put pressure on my wound. The skin felt tight and uncomfortable under the bandages. My eyes drifted around the room. There were four doors in here. One led outside, the other was Louise's supply closet, then there was her study… So the bathroom must be that room on the left.

"I think it's over here," I said, shuffling my way over to the heavy oak door. Once I got it open, there was a pristine white bathroom with a shower, a toilet, a mirror, and a sink. The room felt very sterile and had a scent of cleaner that was so strong it stung my nose. How had she managed to get a shower in here?

All the other villagers had bathtubs, from my knowledge. But then again, maybe someone owed Louise a favor and set her up with this shower to help her clean up after any healing sessions. Regardless, I could not be more glad about it. There was also a boar bristle brush sitting on the edge of the sink, the only non-white thing in the room. It was ruby red with cream-colored bristles.

Finally, maybe I could work the mats out of my hair. And Aldric's, if he wanted me to. For some reason, the thought of taking care of him like that made a blush creep up my neck, but

I shoved those thoughts away.

"Yeah, it's here," I said over my shoulder, reluctantly turning away from the bathroom.

Turning on my heel when Aldric didn't come over, I saw him sitting on the edge of the cot, looking…embarrassed?

"I may need your assistance," he murmured, looking anywhere else but me.

"My help with what?" I asked, oblivious.

"With bathing. I'm still incredibly sore, and I don't know if I would be very steady on my feet," he admitted sheepishly, his fingers gripping the sheet tightly as though it was hard for him to show weakness like this.

My mouth immediately went dry, and I swallowed thickly, the image of him naked dancing through my head. Dismissing the thought, I was immediately frustrated with myself. How could I think of him like that when he was in such a vulnerable position?

"I-if that's what you need, I will do my best. But you should know, Louise had to perform surgery on me, so I can't do as much as I would like," I said, gesturing to my bandaged chest. "She said I punctured a lung."

Horror crossed Aldric's face, and he crossed over to me on unsteady legs, crushing me against his body in a desperate embrace. A sharp sting erupted on my side and I grunted. He immediately released me, gripping my shoulders as he looked sternly into my eyes.

"You could have died!" he said, aghast. "You should have told me so earlier."

"I didn't have much of a chance to, you know," I said, though guilt still crept through the words. "Besides, *you* could have died, and that was more of a pressing issue for me."

His mercury gaze flared brighter, surrounded by that inky black substance painted on his skin. "Nothing is more important than you, my love," he murmured, eyes roving over my body as though checking for every scrape and bruise.

"Not true, and never say that. You're important," I said, scowling. Aldric started to turn me this way and that, trying to eye every inch of my body, but I planted my feet, reaching up and tipping his chin so that he would look at my eyes instead. "I'm okay. I'll heal. Let's take care of you right now."

After a bit of a staring contest, Aldric looked away, and I carefully put his arm over my shoulder, helping him stay steady as we shuffled towards the bathroom. His skin felt too hot against my own, and up close, I could see small beads of metallic-looking sweat. The mixture must be working to draw out the silver, I realized.

"I'm going to help you first, then I'll worry about myself," I said, eyeing the shower uncertainly. "Are you going to be able to stand on your own if I help you get in?"

Aldric's lips quirked up with barely contained laughter. "I'm sure I can handle that much at least, darling." Despite his words, his hand gripped my shoulder tightly as he climbed into the tub, turning towards the showerhead mounted on the wall.

"Are you—can you undress yourself?" I asked, my cheeks warming. "I should have thought about that before helping you in."

"It's okay, Lyra. You know, I don't know if I can," Aldric murmured, his body trembling slightly.

Clearing my throat, I tried to put on the cool professionalism that Louise held, and carefully removed Aldric's undergarments, throwing them into a nearby clothes basket. Careful not to let my eyes drift, I turned the water on. Within seconds, steam rose, and I adjusted the temperature until I was satisfied Aldric would be comfortable.

I offered my arm, and Aldric cautiously shuffled forward until he was under the stream of water. Almost immediately, the water at his feet turned an inky black, much deeper of a color than one would expect for how thin the layer was on his skin, but it didn't seem to want to wash off.

There was a set of folded body towels on a nearby shelf, which I took advantage of. Taking a small rag, I scrubbed it against a bar of soap until it was sudsy, then slowly and gently began clearing all the grime from Aldric's skin. Each pass of the cloth brought out the paleness of his skin that I'd grown to appreciate. The water at the tub's bottom sparkled like starlight from the hints of silver throughout it.

As Aldric slowly shook from the effort of standing, he turned towards me, bracing his hands on my shoulders as I worked him over from top to bottom, making sure that there were no lingering bits of darkness on his skin. Finally, I made sure that his hair was well and truly saturated with water, the blue-black waves cascading over his shoulders.

"Sit here," I murmured, pointing to the squared edge of the tub.

Wordlessly, Aldric followed my command, settling himself onto the porcelain. I strode over and grabbed a couple of bottles, marked as shampoo and conditioner, then drove my fingers into the mass of his silken hair, gently scratching my nails against his scalp. Aldric moaned huskily, his head lolling back at my touch.

A blush crept up my cheeks, and a flutter blossomed in my stomach at the sound. It was…incredibly erotic, as though I was doing something much more sensual than helping him get clean. Squirting some shampoo into my palm, I worked until white bubbles popped up between my fingers, and Aldric arched into my touch, as though starved for it.

My fingers stilled, and Aldric groaned, "Don't stop, it feels so good."

I swallowed thickly, then resumed my ministrations, working my way through his waves. Ignoring the salacious sounds coming from him, I was determined not to respond. Not while he was ill.

Eventually, I got the worst of the filth from his silken strands, tapping him on the shoulder. "Let's get this rinsed out, then I can condition your hair," I said, tucking my arm under his armpit to help him get to his feet. He seemed to stand straighter, taller than before, almost like the work that I was doing was helping him more than it should.

He held his head under the water until it ran clear, which took longer than expected.

"I must have smelled awful," he murmured, the sound muffled by his mop of hair.

"Honestly, not really," I said with a shrug, though I realized he couldn't see it. "I've never been bothered by your scent. I like it."

He tilted his head, and I caught a glint of silver in his waves as he laid an eye on me. "Oh, you do, do you?" he asked, his voice husky. "The more we're together, touching, the more you'll smell like me. Just something to consider." His voice flowed over me like a caress, and unwittingly, my thighs clenched.

Even when he's practically on death's door, he's still so frustratingly tempting. So dangerously alluring.

He moved with a bit more grace to sit on the side of the tub once again, flipping his hair back and causing water droplets to fly all over the bathroom. A hint of a smile curled his lips at the look I gave him. He definitely seems to be feeling better, I thought, though I figured I may as well finish up.

"You need to get clean too, don't you?" he asked, his voice low and seductive.

"Why not join me?"

CHAPTER 19

Faced with the thought of being naked in front of Aldric, my stomach seized, even as a rush of warmth flooded me.

"I shouldn't," I said, a blush creeping up my cheeks. "If you need help, it's easier for me to be out here than in there with you."

"You're making excuses, love. Come, get in here with me," Aldric said, his eyes alight with desire, and something else. "Don't make me beg."

He paused. "Or do."

Stifling a laugh, I reached for the hem of my shirt. Aldric's eyes blazed against my skin as I slowly lifted the shirt, stopping just shy of my breasts. When I didn't move, his eyes jumped to mine.

"Beg," I said, my voice breathy despite the restrained laughter.

His gaze traced my body, the feeling as intense as if it were his fingers instead of his eyes. Slowly, so slowly, his heavy-lidded stare fell on my face again. "Please," he said, his voice deep and rough. Aldric's hands fisted on his pale thighs as though resisting the urge to rip me out of my clothes himself.

A deep, aching want settled within me, heat pooling deep in my core. My hands trembled slightly as I pulled the shirt over my head and let it fall to the floor in a heap. My nipples beaded from the air, and I raised an arm to cover them. A low growl came from within Aldric's chest.

"Don't hide yourself from me," he said, his gaze darkening as hunger simmered below the surface. "Now for the rest."

With only a moment's hesitation, I peeled off the pants and underwear that I'd been wearing, tossing them atop the shirt. There was a rumble of approval from Aldric.

"Give me a spin, darling. I've imagined this thousands of times, and yet nothing I could conjure could possibly compare to you," Aldric said, his lips parted slightly as though tasting the air between us. The air between us was charged, crackling with intensity.

Slowly, I spun on my heel, feeling a little silly, but I wanted to indulge him, anyway. When I faced him again, his breath was coming faster, uneven, like he could barely restrain himself. "Come," he said, holding a hand out to me. As I slipped my hand into his, I carefully stepped into the tub.

"Let me help you with your bandages before you get in the water," he said, his voice low and melodic. Every time he spoke, it was fanning the flame within me, driving my desire higher.

"You know, if you took some of my blood, it would help accelerate your healing."

"And if you took mine, it would help you," I said cautiously. We were treading a dangerous line, and we both knew it. Aldric gripped my wrist and spun me, pulling the bandages free and slowly unwinding them from around my ribs.

There was a fierce ache as the support of the bandages was wrested away from me, but I was so attuned to Aldric's fingers that it was easy to ignore.

When the angry line of my wound was brought to light, Aldric sucked in a breath. "This looks awful. You should feed from me, Lyra," he murmured, all traces of desire gone from his voice.

"But what about you?" I asked, a little disappointed despite the pain blooming across my ribs.

"We'll worry about me later. I'm already healing much better than I was," he said, gesturing to his wounds, which looked like little more than angry puckered flesh at this point. It was astonishing how quickly he'd healed once all the silver was drawn out of his body.

"Let me finish getting you clean. Then whatever it is you're proposing… we can do that afterwards," I murmured, picking up the conditioner.

Pouring the vanilla-scented mixture into my hands, I rubbed them together and slowly worked through his waves, detangling as I went. Twice, Aldric had to re-wet his hair to ensure that it was completely dripping wet. That way, his hair would be slick enough for me to work my fingers through.

He was much more steady on his feet and rinsed his own hair before turning back towards me. He sidestepped me and gently pushed me towards the steaming water.

"And now your turn," he murmured, picking up the bar of soap.

WHISPERED SECRETS

The water sluicing down my body didn't sting as much as I had expected, though I was careful to keep my injury out of the direct spray. Glancing down, it looked awful. The line of stitches was red and angry, and there was mottled black and blue bruising along my ribs.

With the utmost care, Aldric gently washed my body, the act incredibly intimate. He treated me like glass, as though I could break at any moment. All the stress and grime melted away in the suds as they flowed down my body and down the drain.

It finally felt like we could relax.

Before my eyes, Aldric's wounds were slowly stitching themselves back together, and I was astounded at the rate of his healing. His strength was returning quickly, color flushing his cheeks. There must have been a lot of silver in his system for it to have delayed his healing so severely.

Without so much as a word, Aldric lifted me up, my legs automatically wrapping themselves around his waist. Our bodies slid together as though they were made for one another, and my breath caught in my throat. His body was hard against me, muscles bunching, but he acted as though I was weightless. Before I could even respond though, he gently sat me on the side of the tub, my legs dangling out and dripping water on the floor.

"Aldric, what are you doing?" I asked a little too loudly, my cheeks burning. I gripped the side of the tub with white-knuckled intensity.

"Shhh. Don't worry, love. I just need a better angle to work on that mane of hair you have," he murmured, his voice sultry. I heard him rubbing his hands together, the shampoo making them slick as he worked his fingers into my hair. My back arched, and a groan escaped my lips as he dragged his fingernails against my scalp.

Now I see what the appeal was for him, I thought, a smile curving my lips. As he slowly detangled the worst strands of my hair, each stroke of his hands sent sparks of pleasure down my spine. I couldn't help the soft sounds I made as he continued his efforts.

"Lean back," he said, his voice husky and deep.

Wordlessly, I complied. One of Aldric's hands supported me so I didn't lean too far, and that simple act was enough to make my stomach do flips. Once Aldric was satisfied that my hair was clean and had been rinsed, he reached for the conditioner.

He meticulously worked through the last of the knots in my hair, showing utmost care while he did to ensure he didn't tug or pull too much.

"Your hair is beautiful, you know," he murmured, his voice rumbling through me. "Ever since I first saw you, I've thought that. It took a lot of restraint for me not to touch it. Do you remember when we first met?"

"Of course," I replied. "It wasn't that long ago, you know."

"Wasn't it? Feels like it just happened, but also like it could have happened centuries ago. Time is strange when you're a vampire," he said, running his fingers gently across my scalp. My back involuntarily arched from the sensation, and a deep, sensuous laugh came from behind me.

"You're easily pleased, aren't you?" Aldric said, his usual teasing tone back.

"No, not particularly. Must just be you," I said, teasing back. It felt good to just have a normal moment with him, no gods, no fights, just us.

I felt warmth at my back a moment before Aldric pressed against me. His fingers lightly played with the hair at the nape of my neck, twirling it around his fingers. I shuddered, and his other hand gently caressed my throat.

"I often think about the first time I tasted your blood," he murmured, his hand dropping from my dripping waves to slide down my shoulder. He pulled me more firmly against him, and my eyes widened as I felt the evidence of his arousal against my back.

"It was like... *ambrosia*," he said, a groan coming from his lips. A warmth spread low in my belly at his tone, and my breath hitched. "Never before and never again will I taste something quite as sweet, as decadent, as the nectar you offered me that day. You've ruined me for anyone else."

I didn't know what to say. He'd ruined me for anyone else, too.

He pulled the mass of white locks behind my back. "Let's get this rinsed out before any other devious thoughts come to mind," he said, a smile in his voice. "We need to get you all healed up before anything more... strenuous can happen."

A blush crept up my neck, and I nodded, leaning back again. Aldric's hands were exceedingly delicate as they rinsed my hair, and finally, I was completely clean. Or, well, mostly.

"Aldric, would you mind stepping out?" I asked, the words catching in my throat.

"Why ever for?" Aldric asked, crossing his powerful arms across his chest. My eyes traced the movement as I glanced at him over my shoulder. It took everything within me not to let my gaze drop lower, and lower still.

"I just want to, you know, finish cleaning up," I said, avoiding eye contact. "And I don't need your help for this part."

He chuckled, the sound distinctly masculine. He wrung out his hair, leaving gorgeous waves behind. My fingers itched with the urge to run through those blue-black tresses, but I refrained, climbing down from the side of the tub.

"As you wish, my love," he said, bowing gallantly. Or as gallantly as you can while buck-naked in someone else's bathroom.

He wandered over to the linen closet and pulled out a beige towel, slinging it low over his hips. A dusting of black hair peeked over the edge, flowing down from his navel. My mouth went dry, and I averted my gaze, quickly cleaning myself in my most intimate areas. There was more sensitivity than I expected, and my eyes found Aldric again, who had turned away from me. Tracing the muscles of his back with my gaze, I swallowed hard. What would it feel like beneath my fingers?

A throbbing ache blossomed at my core, and I bit my lip to stifle a moan. There was a sharp pain as I straightened, reminding me of why we couldn't do this. But, gods damn it, I wanted to. Supporting my ribs, I quickly rinsed the last of the soap from my body and turned the water off.

"All done?" Aldric asked, still facing the wall, though he shifted impatiently from foot to foot.

"Yes," I said, wringing my hair out. It felt blessedly clean and soft. Finally.

"Let me get you a towel, then," he said, reaching into the closet again.

As Aldric wrapped me in cotton, his fingers traced the angry line of stitches in my ribs. The discoloration looked awful in the harsh light of the bathroom. Water dripped down my back, and I shivered, though not from the cold.

"We need to heal this," he murmured, his fingertip trailing lightly along the edge of the towel. "You're in pain, and I don't want to worry about you when we travel again."

I stepped back, putting some distance between us. The air felt charged, heavy with unspoken tension. Swallowing hard, I said, "Aldric… We're in Louise's house. Not only that, but we have other things to deal with right now. I still need to make it back to Sylvan Reach."

My mind flashed to Griffin's body, trapped forever between Shifts, and my stomach roiled. Guilt twisted in my belly. "You know that."

"All the more reason to help you heal, my love. It'll make traveling there easier," Aldric said, his voice soft, tempting.

Before I could protest further, he drew a fingernail along his throat, a thin line of red welling up. The scent of storms and moonlight filled the space between us, and my mouth watered despite itself.

"We shouldn't do this," I whispered, though my body betrayed my words and took a step toward him. A drop of blood slowly traced down the column of his neck and his chest. I had to stop myself from allowing my tongue to trace the path it took. "Louise could come back any minute."

"A few drops," he murmured, reaching for me. I stepped into his embrace, unable to stop myself. "Just enough to ease your pain. Nothing more."

I hesitated, my morals warring with my desires. In the end, my desires won, and my tongue darted out, wetting my lips. My wound throbbed, almost as though encouraging me to take the healing that he offered in the form of his life's essence.

Aldric's arms cradled me, and he urged me towards his neck. I reached up on my tiptoes, pressing my lips to the small cut. The rich taste of wine and chocolate bloomed on my tongue, and I couldn't stop a moan from escaping my lips. Aldric's deep groan answered mine, and he held me tighter, his hands roaming over my back as if to pull me impossibly closer.

A tingle started from my mouth and spread throughout my body, my thighs instinctually clenching against the assault on my senses. My arms wrapped around his waist, tugging him closer. I made a tight seal against the column of his throat with my lips, drawing as much of his essence in as I could.

Aldric's shuddered breath rumbled through me, and I couldn't stop myself from biting down, my teeth sinking easily into the soft flesh. Aldric growled darkly as he hauled me up, turning to pin me against the wall. My legs wrapped easily around his waist. I felt the evidence of his arousal through the towel around his waist, and it took every ounce of my willpower not to push the cotton down, so there was no barrier between us.

My core throbbed with such intensity, I knew I must be embarrassingly slick and needy for him. I moaned against his neck, unable to get enough of his taste. Is this what bonding would be like?

"Lyra," Aldric groaned, my name like a prayer on his lips. "You need to stop, or I won't be able to control myself."

He pressed against me, and I could feel the heat of his manhood even through the fabric between us. I wantonly ground myself against him, and he shuddered, another rumbly growl escaping him.

"You love to test me, don't you? If this isn't what you want, you need to stop now," Aldric warned, pressing back against me. The fold of his towel parted, and I felt the smooth head of his arousal prodding my entrance. Almost every part of me wanted to sink onto his length, but I had to restrain myself.

With an audible pop, I released my mouth from his neck. A bruise remained, a visual reminder of how desperately I had pulled blood from his body. Aldric's eyes were dark and stormy, arousal burning in their depths. A droplet pooled at the corner of my lip, and my tongue darted out to catch it, Aldric's gaze tracing the movement. With great effort, he adjusted himself and slowly lowered me back to the floor, where I landed on shaking legs.

I was relieved, but also savagely disappointed.

This wasn't the time, I thought as I wrapped my arms around my middle. The sting of my wound had already abated, and I peeled the towel back to find the skin had sealed itself back together, the ache almost entirely gone from my ribs.

"Thank you," I whispered, unable to meet his gaze.

"Of course, darling. What kind of mate would I be to let you suffer so?" he asked, his tone deceptively casual. This was the first time he'd referred to me like that, and my body reacted, pulsing with desire. My core clenched, aching with need, but I couldn't give in. Not yet. Not here.

I had to put my past to rest before I could give myself fully to Aldric.

And he deserved nothing less.

CHAPTER 20

After dressing in a set of clean clothes Louise had lying around—I'm assuming as spares for patients since they weren't her size—I made my way out of the bathroom on slightly unsteady legs, Aldric close on my heels. The heat of his body radiated against my back, a reminder of what had almost transpired between us. My cheeks reddened at the thought, and I scowled.

Seren was exactly where we had left her, curled up in the plush armchair. Her blue-black strands of hair fell across her face, and her chest rose and fell almost unnaturally slowly. Something wasn't right. A chill raced up my spine, and I made my way over to Seren.

"She should have woken up by now," I said, carefully brushing her hair away from her face. My fingers shook, and I fisted my hands. Glancing around, I saw the luminous green glow of Koto's eyes through the window as she peered in at us, a low rumble reaching my ears. The Feralumin's tail twitched back and forth, a sign of unease I've come to recognize over our short time together.

Placing the back of my hand on Seren's forehead, her skin was cool to the touch. Too cool. There was a *clack* as Koto now had her massive face pressed against the window, her ears pinned, and her antlers jammed against the glass. Her gaze was zeroed in on the chair Seren was in, as though she could sense her despite being unable to see her.

"Aldric," I called, worry saturating my voice. "I think something's wrong."

From outside, a keening call erupted, the sound making the hair on my arms stand up. I'd never heard an animal make a sound like this before, full of emotion. It made my heart race, and I fought the urge to cover my ears against it. I turned, Aldric close at hand.

"She's awake in there," he murmured, his brow furrowed. "I can smell her fear."

He leaned down, lifting one of Seren's eyelids. Horror crawled through me as her jade eye rolled to look at him, terror in its depths.

"Seren, you're awake?" I asked incredulously, and aside from her gaze snapping to mine, her body did not react. The realization hit me like a physical blow, and I wrapped my arms around my middle, my mind racing. I'd seen this so many times before—in the villagers of Haleshade, in my own parents, in passers-by who seemed more sluggish than normal. The exhaustion setting in, and the unnatural stillness that came afterwards.

The plague had taken Seren.

WHISPERED SECRETS

Koto was trying to push her way through the door, but it just wasn't wide enough for her. The wood of the doorjamb began to splinter against the force, and her claws left gouges in the floor as she tried to force her way inside.

"Koto, stop! We'll take care of Seren. Please," I cried, dropping to my knees beside the chair Seren was slumped in. Koto paced outside, the movement punctuated with distressed growls.

"This isn't right," I whispered. "The progression is too fast. She was fine just a few hours ago!"

Aldric dropped to a crouch beside me, his silver eyes luminous in the limited light. "Could it be because she's Fae? If it affects magic, Fae are creatures of mana, after all. Maybe it affects them differently."

He wrapped an arm around my shoulders, and I realized my body was shaking with adrenaline. This couldn't be happening. Seren afflicted with the plague? How could this have happened?

"Seren, can you move?" I asked, my eyes tracing her face for any hint of movement. Nothing. My heart hammered against my ribs. I slowly reached up to her face and lifted her eyelid again, and there was panic blooming in the depths of her meadow-green eyes. "Look up if you can hear me."

Her eyes rolled upwards before refocusing on my face, and some tense part of me loosened ever-so-slightly. I squeezed her arm with my free hand. "Can you feel this? Look up for yes, down for no."

Her eyes rolled up a second time. At least she wasn't paralyzed, I thought.

"What about Louise? She's been treating this plague. She must know something about how to treat it, right?" Aldric murmured, his arm dropping to his side as I shifted closer to Seren.

"She's gone. Did she say where she was going?" I asked Seren, my throat working as she looked to her feet. "Did she say anything identifying?"

She looked up.

"Was it about the plague?" She looked up again before her gaze landed on my face with a strange intensity.

"Wait, wait—Koto!" I called. "Koto can help us figure out where Louise went." Koto's bright green eyes zeroed in on me, and my stomach tightened. "Can you lead me to Louise? Is she far?"

Koto hummed and chirped with a nod, turning away from Louise's house.

"I can't go with you, my love," Aldric said sadly, standing and leaning back on the balls of his feet. "Where ever she has gone, one of us needs to stay with Seren. I don't think it would be safe for her to be on her own."

"Could we bring her with us?" I asked, hesitant to leave them both behind. "Koto's carried all of us before."

"I know, but do you really think it would be wise to bring Seren to an unknown location, unable to fend for herself? What if we were attacked? She is entirely vulnerable."

I cursed under my breath. He was right, of course. And he

could scent her emotions, so it would be easier for him to take care of her than for me to. With a groan, I scrubbed my hand down my face. At least my rib had healed.

Padding over to the door, I pulled on my boots while Aldric followed behind.

"I will be back soon," I said, resolute. "And I'll bring Louise with me."

Aldric grabbed my wrist as I straightened and brought it to his mouth, his lips gentle as he pressed a kiss to my pulse.

"Come back to me soon, my love. I will be thinking of you." His eyes were like starlight, drawing me in with gravitational force until I pressed myself into his arms, pulling my wrist free.

I wrapped my arms tightly around his waist, my throat tight with unshed tears. Seren would be okay, I told myself. Louise will know what to do. Shoving the thoughts of all the bodies that littered the streets out of my mind, I tipped my chin up towards Aldric.

"Keep her safe," I whispered. Pushing up onto my tiptoes, I hesitantly pressed my lips lightly against Aldric's, my eyes slipping closed. A low groan escaped him, and his hands landed on my hips, pulling me closer.

He deepened the kiss, driven with an intensity that I'd never seen from him. He slid one hand up my back to cup the back of my head, his tongue swiping against my lower lip, requesting access.

Hesitantly, I opened for him, and his tongue swept inside, sensuously gliding against mine in a claiming kiss that stole my breath. His mouth crushed against mine, demanding and deep. The taste of him was dark and heady, like something forbidden, something I could drown in.

I felt a growl against my chest as it rumbled through me, and he begrudgingly parted from me, his chest heaving and his eyes dark with barely restrained passion. "Come back to me. Soon," he said, his words heavy with possessive intent.

Swallowing hard, I turned towards the door, refusing to look back lest I be tempted to stay.

CHAPTER 21

The wind whipped through my hair as Koto bounded through the forest, her massive paws barely brushing the ground. Every leap sent us sailing over fallen logs and underbrush, the Feralumin's speed unmatched by anything I'd ever experienced as her muscles bunched and moved beneath my body.

I clung desperately to the thick fur at the base of her neck, my fingers tangled in the iridescent strands. I kept my head down as the blur of colors caused nausea to roil in my stomach.

We'd been traveling for hours now without rest, following some invisible trail that only Koto could sense. She barely seemed out of breath, each exhale sending a puff of mist into the crisp morning air. Koto moved with a singular purpose—to find Louise and return her to Seren. To save her bonded master.

Her desperation matched my own determination to save her. Every minute that we spent journeying was another minute that

Seren may not have. Another minute for the plague to tighten its grip on her.

I hesitantly opened my eyes and peered up at the sky, where I saw dawn breaking, painting the sky in pastel hues of blue, pink and gold. Trying to get a gauge of our location, I glanced around, the speed of our movement making it difficult to determine exactly where we were. But I could tell from the feel of the air that we were in the forest of Sylvan Reach. Had Louise returned to the village?

Why would she do that?

Koto abruptly slid to a stop, and my entire body almost flipped off of her from the sudden change in momentum, my legs going airborne. The air *whooshed* out of me as my stomach smacked back down, and I fought to right myself on Koto's back.

I was about to complain when Koto chirruped, nodding her head towards the distance. There was a swirl of smoke rising nearby, completely out of place. We hadn't seen any evidence of another living being here. Now that we were still, I noticed that even the typical wildlife was nowhere to be found, the woods eerily quiet.

Koto's ears swiveled, her head cocked as she listened to something beyond my hearing. She lowered her body closer to the ground, silently prowling forward. I flattened my body against her, the scent of wilderness and ancient magic drifting up from Koto's fur. Within moments, we crested a small hill, and I peered over Koto's head to see who had created the fire.

My throat seized when I saw the crest of the Order glinting with firelight on a group of mages, their robes surprisingly clean and their attitudes seemingly unflustered by their situation, given how they casually spoke and laughed amongst themselves.

I scanned their faces to see if there was anyone familiar, but none of these people stuck out to me. Koto's natural camouflage was working to our advantage, given that we wouldn't be easily spotted by the group.

I strained my ears to see if I could pick up anything that they were talking about, but it was just a faint din of conversation, nothing that I could clearly make out.

But why were they *here*? It didn't make any sense. All the mages had fled Sylvan Reach when I was there last. Were they trying to return? Had Thorne reached out to them?

Koto's muscles tensed beneath me as though holding herself back, and I laid a calming hand on her shoulder. "We need to get closer," I whispered, my lips barely moving. "Can you circle around?"

The Feralumin responded by backing away quietly before padding through the underbrush. She moved like a shadow, completely silent, each step carefully placed despite her massive size. We skirted the perimeter of the clearing, approaching from downwind.

As we drew closer, snippets of conversation drifted toward us.

"...won't talk, no matter what we try. I'm trying to avoid damaging her too much," a deep voice complained, and I saw a tall male mage throw his hands up in the air.

"The Magister said to bring her back if she proves difficult," another replied, higher-pitched and reedy. Looking amongst the group, I thought this was an older mage, but I couldn't tell given that they all had their backs to me. "But I'd rather not travel with a prisoner. Too risky."

"She's just a healer—"

"A healer who was breaking into Thorne's residence," a third voice interrupted sharply, their voice authoritative and strong. They must be the leader of this troupe judging by how the others' spines straightened in response to their voice. "Nobody goes near that place without authorization. Especially not now."

My blood ran cold. They must be talking about Louise. I can't imagine who else would want to go to Thorne's house. But why? What could she have been looking for?

Koto silently inched forward, allowing me to peer through a larger gap in the foliage. Five mages circled the fire, their cerulean and silver robes marking them as members of the Order's enforcement division. I'd only seen them once before, when they took away a child whose gift was too powerful—fire magic that they couldn't control.

The child had burned down their house and was at risk of more destruction when they arrived. No one spoke of it again, though I saw their mother crying for a long time afterwards.

There.

Seated on a log with her hands bound before her, was Louise. Her gray-streaked hair had escaped its usual neat bun, falling in tangled strands around her face and matted down with dried blood on her forehead.

A bruise darkened her left cheek, and her posture was rigid with defiance. Despite her disheveled appearance, her eyes burned with contempt for those mages surrounding her.

"Why the hell isn't the Order doing more?" Louise spat, her voice carrying clear across the clearing. "People are dying. The plague is spreading faster than before. Whatever Thorne was working on, it holds the key to stopping this."

A tall woman scoffed, her face screwed up with disgust. "The plague is contained. Sylvan Reach has been evacuated."

"Contained?" Louise's laugh was bitter, dripping with acid. "Is that what they're telling you? Do you know I've seen cases that progress in hours rather than days? I bet those bastards never told you that, did they?"

This question caused a ripple of unease among her captors. They exchanged glances, their previous confidence faltering. I had to wonder how long she'd been arguing this point with them.

"She's lying, of course," the reedy-voiced person—a man insisted, though uncertainty crept into his tone. "The Magister would have informed us."

"Would he?" Louise challenged, her eyes blazing. "The same Magister who ordered all research on the plague destroyed when it spread?" At the widening of eyes around her, she laughed, the sound harsh.

"Oh, didn't expect me to know about that now that I wasn't in Sylvan Reach, did you? I've been fighting this alone for *months* and you're so ignorant you don't even know what's happening outside of your little group."

"That's enough!" The woman stepped forward, grabbing Louise's arm roughly. "You're interfering with Order business. Thorne's residence has been sealed for a reason."

"Because you're afraid of what I might find," Louise shot back, her head held high. "You've suspected from the beginning that the Order knew about this all along, haven't you?"

The tall woman raised her hand, magic sparking between her fingers and throwing a sickly yellow hue over their surroundings. "I said that's enough."

My heart hammered against my ribs. I needed to help Louise, but confronting five powerful mages directly would be suicide. I glanced at Koto, who was watching the scene with intelligent eyes, her muscles coiled and ready.

"We need a distraction," I whispered. But what? My transformation magic would immediately mark me as the very person they might be hunting.

As if in answer to my thoughts, one mage suddenly straightened, peering into the forest opposite our position. "Did you hear that?"

The others tensed, hands moving to their sides where I could now see ceremonial daggers hanging—tools for channeling magic rather than physical weapons, but dangerous nonetheless.

"Probably just an animal," the reedy-voiced man said, though he didn't sound convinced.

"There are no animals nearby," another countered. "Haven't been since we arrived. The forest has been dead silent."

The severe-faced woman gestured to two of the mages. "Check the perimeter. The rest of you, stay with the prisoner."

As two figures broke away from the group, heading away from our position, I saw our opportunity. I leaned close to Koto's ear. "Can you create a distraction on the far side of the clearing? Something to draw them away from Louise?"

Koto's eyes glinted with understanding. She lowered herself to the ground, allowing me to slip off her back. I crouched in the underbrush, watching as she silently padded away, her fur shifting colors to blend with the forest.

Minutes passed, each second stretching into eternity as I watched Louise sitting rigidly among her captors. What had she discovered in Thorne's house that was worth risking her life? Did she know how to help Seren? My fingers dug into the soft earth beneath me, anxiety churning in my stomach.

Then it happened.

A bone-chilling roar erupted from the far side of the clearing, followed by the sound of trees crashing down. The remaining mages jumped to their feet, faces pale.

"What in the name of—" The severe woman didn't finish

her sentence as another roar split the air, closer this time.

"Monster!" one of the mages who'd gone to check the perimeter came crashing back through the underbrush, his robes torn and face scratched. His eyes were wide with panic. "Some kind of beast—it's huge!"

"Secure the prisoner!" The woman barked, already gathering magic between her palms, the surrounding air distorting with power. "The rest of you, with me!"

Two mages remained with Louise while the others raced toward the commotion. Perfect. Two I might be able to handle, especially with the element of surprise. I waited until the others disappeared into the forest before carefully making my way around the clearing's edge, approaching from behind the remaining guards.

Louise's eyes suddenly went round as she caught sight of me, but she quickly masked her reaction, dropping her gaze to the ground. The guards, focused on the distant sounds of Koto's rampage, didn't notice.

I closed my eyes, focusing on a small, innocuous transformation. My teeth elongated into fangs, and my fingernails hardened into claws—changes small enough to be concealed, but giving me the weapons I needed. I couldn't risk a full transformation, not with Order mages so close.

Moving swiftly, I emerged from the underbrush behind the first guard. Before he could turn, I struck—a quick blow to the back of his head with the hardened ridge of my hand. He crumpled without a sound.

The second guard spun, his eyes widening at the sight of

me. "You—" Recognition flashed across his face, confirming my worst fears. They knew who I was.

He raised his hands, magic gathering between his fingers, but I was faster. I lunged forward, my clawed hand slashing across his chest—not deep enough to kill, but enough to disrupt his concentration. As he staggered backward, I followed with a kick to his midsection, sending him sprawling. His head cracked off of a rock and he fell silent. A pit opened up in my stomach. That could have killed him, I realized, as dark blood spread from where he lay.

"Lyra!" Louise gasped as I rushed to her side, using my claws to slice through her bindings. This wasn't the time to worry about someone else. I had more important priorities. "What are you doing here?"

"Rescuing you," I said, helping her to her feet. "We need to go. Now. Koto can't keep them distracted forever."

Louise's eyes narrowed. "Koto? Seren's Feralumin? Where is Seren?"

My throat tightened. "She's sick. The plague—it came on so fast. We need your help."

Understanding dawned in Louise's eyes, followed by grim determination. "I knew it. The acceleration pattern is consistent with what I found in Thorne's records."

"You were in his house? Why?"

"His research journals." Louise glanced toward the forest where shouts and crashes could still be heard. "They contain the original formulas he was working with—and notes about how the magic changed when it interacted with yours. I was right all along—it's not just a disease, it's—"

A blast of energy struck the ground beside us, sending dirt and debris flying. I whirled to see the severe-faced woman emerging from the trees, fury etched into her features.

"The transformation mage," she hissed, magic crackling around her like lightning. "The Magister will be pleased we found you."

Louise grabbed my arm. "Run," she urged. "His house. The basement. What I found—it's our only chance to save your friend."

Another blast scorched the earth where we'd been standing a moment before. We fled toward the trees, dodging and weaving as magic exploded around us.

"Koto!" I shouted as we ran. "To me!"

The sound of pounding paws answered my call as the massive Feralumin burst through the underbrush, her fur rippling from forest green to deep black as she raced toward us. Without breaking stride, she lowered her shoulder, allowing Louise and me to scramble onto her back.

"Hold on!" I yelled as Koto pivoted sharply, narrowly avoiding a sizzling bolt of energy.

"Stop them!" The woman's voice rang out behind us, but we were already moving, Koto's powerful legs carrying us away from the clearing.

"Thorne's house," Louise gasped, clinging to me as Koto bounded through the forest. "We need to get back there. What I found—" She broke off, ducking as a low-hanging branch whipped past us. "The journals explain everything. Why the plague happened, how it spreads, and most importantly—how it might be stopped."

My heart pounded in my ears as we raced through the forest, the shouts of the mages fading behind us. Thorne's house. Where Griffin still lay. Where everything had begun.

"What about the Order mages?" I asked over my shoulder. "They'll be waiting for us there."

"Not all of them," Louise replied grimly. "They've set a perimeter, but most are patrolling the village borders. There's a way in through the back—through the old storm cellar. That's how I got in before they caught me."

Koto slowed slightly, her head turning as if asking for direction.

"Do you remember where Thorne's house is?" I asked her.

She chirped in response, changing course with confident strides.

"What exactly did you find?" I pressed Louise as we traveled.

Louise's grip on my waist tightened. "Thorne was experimenting with blood magic," she said, her voice low. "Combining it with transformation magic. He believed he could stabilize your powers that way, when you were young."

Ice spread through my veins. "Blood magic is forbidden."

"Exactly why the Order is so desperate to keep it quiet." Louise's voice was bitter. "Thorne was one of their own, working with their blessing. Until it went wrong. But they didn't risk taking his journals, just so they could say he was working alone."

"And this helps Seren how?" I demanded.

"Because I found his notes on the core magical pattern of the plague," Louise explained. "And a formula he was developing to disrupt it—using the same principles that caused it in the first place."

"A cure?" Hope flared in my chest.

"Maybe." Louise's tone was cautious. "But we need to get to those journals. And..." She hesitated. "The formula requires the original source of the transformation magic that merged with his."

My blood. Of course, it would come down to that. Everything always did.

"Fine," I said, steeling my resolve. "Whatever it takes."

We fell silent as Koto carried us deeper into the forest, toward Thorne's house and the answers we desperately needed for Seren—for everyone affected by this plague.

And toward Griffin, waiting all this time for me to return.

The weight of it all pressed down on me as we traveled, a burden I'd carried since fleeing this place. But now I was coming back—not just to lay Griffin to rest, but to stop this plague once and for all.

No matter what it cost.

CHAPTER 22

Thorne's house loomed before us, a dark silhouette against the brightening sky. Koto slowed her pace as we approached, her muscles tense beneath me. The windows were dark, empty eyes staring back at us, but I couldn't shake the feeling that we were being watched.

"There," Louise whispered, pointing to a small depression in the ground behind the house—the storm cellar entrance, partially hidden by overgrown weeds. "That's our way in."

We dismounted, my legs unsteady after the long ride. I turned to Koto, placing a hand on her massive shoulder. "Stay close, but hidden. If Order mages return..."

A low rumble vibrated from her chest—understanding. Her fur shifted colors, blending with the surrounding foliage as she melted back into the tree line, her luminous eyes the last to disappear.

Louise moved swiftly despite her earlier captivity, pulling back the storm cellar doors with practiced ease. They opened with a groan of rusty hinges, revealing stone steps descending into darkness.

"We need to be quick," she muttered, already taking the first steps down. "I'm sure they know I'd come straight back if I could."

I followed, each step down feeling like a step closer to Griffin. My heart tightened in my chest. Was I ready to see him again? After all this time?

"The journals are in his study," Louise continued, oblivious to my inner turmoil. "Hidden behind a false panel in the bookcase. He always thought he was so clever."

At the bottom of the stairs, Louise produced a small crystal from her pocket. With a whispered word, it glowed to life, casting eerie shadows around us. We were in a narrow passageway, the walls packed earth reinforced with wooden beams.

"This way," she said, moving forward confidently. "It connects to the basement."

The basement. Where Griffin…

I pushed the thought away, focusing on the task at hand. Seren needed us. I couldn't falter now.

The passage opened into a larger space, and the familiar musty scent of Thorne's basement hit me like a physical blow. Memories flashed through my mind—fighting for my life, Griffin's transformation, his body on the floor…

"Lyra?" Louise's voice cut through my thoughts. "Are you alright?"

I realized I'd stopped moving, my body frozen at the entrance to the basement. "I'm fine," I lied, forcing myself forward. "Let's find those journals."

I kept my eyes fixed straight ahead, refusing to look at the spot where Griffin had fallen. Not yet. I couldn't face that yet.

We climbed the narrow stairs to the main floor, entering the house proper. Everything was exactly as I remembered it—books and papers scattered across every surface, half-empty potion bottles gathering dust. It was as if time had stopped here the moment we fled.

"His study is this way," Louise said, leading me down a hallway.

The study was a chaos of scrolls and tomes, shelves overflowing with arcane texts. Louise went straight to a bookcase against the far wall, her fingers tracing the spines until she found what she was looking for. With a practiced motion, she pulled one book halfway out, and a soft click echoed in the room.

"He showed me this once," she explained, sliding her hand behind the now-loosened panel. "Years ago, when we were both still working with the Order."

She withdrew a leather-bound journal, its pages yellowed with age, followed by two more. "These contain everything. His early attempts to stabilize your magic, the blood rituals he performed, and the subsequent plague development."

My stomach turned. "Blood rituals? On me?"

Louise's expression softened. "You were very young. Your parents were desperate—they knew what would happen if you were found out." She placed the journals on Thorne's desk. "He thought he could help."

"By using forbidden magic?" The anger in my voice surprised even me.

"The Order sanctions more than they admit publicly," Louise replied, her tone bitter. "Although in this case he worked alone. Despite his faults, he cared for your mother." She opened the oldest journal, flipping through pages of cramped writing and complex diagrams. "Here. This is what I was looking for."

I leaned over to see an intricate magical formula, symbols I didn't recognize flowing around a central diagram that looked vaguely like a human form.

"Thorne developed this as a theoretical cure," Louise explained, her finger tracing the pattern. "Based on reversing the original blood ritual he performed. It would use the source of the transformed magic to neutralize the plague."

"So we just need my blood?" I asked, hope rising. "That's simple enough."

Louise's expression darkened. "If only." She turned the page, revealing more complex formulas. "Your blood is just one component. According to his notes, the plague has developed a magical signature of its own—it's no longer just corrupted transformation magic. It's something new, something that resists conventional magical cures."

"Then what do we need?" I pressed, aware that each minute we delayed was another minute Seren suffered.

"That's the problem." Louise ran a hand through her tangled hair. "Thorne theorized that to create a true cure, we'd need to combine your power with something else that could purify and stabilize the magic. But he'd never figured it out despite hundreds, thousands of tests."

My mind flashed to the Starfall Veil, to the ancient magic that had seemed to call to me there. "Something like Fae magic?"

Louise's head snapped up, her eyes wide. "What do you mean?"

"I've been to the Fae realm," I said, the pieces clicking into place. "Their magic is different—older, more primal. It seemed to respond to me differently than it did to others."

Louise flipped frantically through the journal. "I think that might be just what we need! If we can somehow imbue your magic with that power…"

"I think I may be able to do that," I said, thinking of the way the ancient power was drawn to my own. "Or at least, I did it before."

Hope flickered in Louise's eyes. "Did you bring any with you? Any artifact or substance imbued with Fae magic?"

I shook my head, disappointment crashing over me. "Nothing. We barely escaped with our lives."

Louise fell silent, her fingers drumming on the desk as she thought. "Perhaps we don't need a physical sample," she drawled. "You said the Fae magic responded to you differently?"

"Yes. It was like…" I struggled to find the words. "Like it recognized me somehow. Like it wanted to join with my magic. And when it did, it was exhilarating." Just the thought made my body buzz with approval.

"Join with your magic," Louise breathed, excitement building in her voice. "Thorne writes here about the plague creating a barrier between your original magic and his own power—a defense mechanism of sorts. But if we could break through that barrier…"

"How?"

"With the right ritual, we might be able to use you as a conduit." Louise was speaking faster now, flipping between the journals. "Thorne was experimenting with blood as a magical conductor—that's what started all this. If we reversed the process, used your blood not to contain your magic but to release it in its purest form..."

"I could absorb the plague back into myself," I finished, understanding dawning. "Purify it with whatever connection I have to the Fae magic."

"Theoretically." Louise's expression grew serious. "But it would be incredibly dangerous, Lyra. If the Fae magic isn't strong enough in you, or if the connection isn't as deep as we need..."

"I could die," I said flatly.

"Or worse." Louise closed the journal with a resonating thud. "Your magic could be permanently corrupted. You could become a source of an even more powerful plague."

The weight of the choice settled on my shoulders. Risk everything—my life, my magic, potentially the lives of countless others—on the chance that this would work? That my mysterious connection to Fae magic would be enough?

But what choice did I have? Seren was running out of time. My parents were still trapped by this plague. And how many others were suffering while we debated?

"We have to try," I said, my voice steadier than I felt.

Louise nodded, her expression grim but determined. "We'll need to gather supplies for the ritual. Specific herbs to enhance blood conductivity, focusing crystals..." She turned, scanning the study. "Thorne would have kept most of what we need here."

As she began gathering ingredients from Thorne's shelves, my thoughts drifted back to the basement. To Griffin. I still needed to lay him to rest, to say goodbye properly. And perhaps... perhaps seeing him one last time would give me the strength for what was to come.

"Louise," I breathed. "There's something I need to do first."

She paused, arms full of bottles and pouches, understanding dawning in her eyes. "Of course. Take your time. I'll prepare what we need here."

With a deep breath, I turned and walked back toward the hallway, toward the basement stairs. Toward Griffin. Each step felt heavier than the last, but I forced myself forward.

I owed him this much. Before I risked everything on a desperate cure, I needed to face what I'd left behind.

CHAPTER 23

Slowly, carefully, I made my way into the basement, my mouth dry and my hands shaking. The smell wasn't as awful as I remembered, a faint scent of rot beneath the mustiness. My hand gripped the bannister with trembling fingers, my feet mechanically moving down the stairs.

As I rounded the corner, my eyes immediately fell to where Griffin's body lay.

Or where it should be.

Instead, there was a dark stain on the ground where he had been, but no sign of his body. Panic gripped me as I raced over to the dirt, my fingers raking through it as though his corpse would have buried itself. Tears burned their way down my cheeks as I tore through the earth, desperately looking for his remains. A hiccuping sob escaped me, shame ripping through my body.

Who had taken him? Why?

I curled over myself, my failures weighing on me like a smothering cloud, blotting out all light.

I don't know how long I sat there, covered in dirt and tears, before Louise silently came up behind me, placing a comforting hand on my shoulder. She got down onto the ground next to me, a maternal sigh escaping her as she gently pulled me away from the stain that represented his body—his death.

"You were looking for Griffin, weren't you?" she asked softly. "I should have told you—I buried him myself. I found his remains and buried them under the large oak tree just outside of Sylvan Reach. It felt right to put him there."

"It should have been me. I left him here," I cried, pain spearing through me. "I couldn't say goodbye. He would be ashamed of me."

Louise turned me towards her, tipping my chin until I looked her in the eyes. Her face wavered through the sheen of my tears.

"Lyra. You know he wouldn't be. He knew the risks that would come with protecting you, and he chose to do it, anyway. Thinking any less of him is disgracing his memory."

Her thumbs tenderly wiped the wetness from my cheeks. "I know it's hard. You two had barely just begun to know one another when you lost him. He'd talk about you often when he came to visit me."

"I knew him," I denied viciously, pulling my face out of her grip. "We…we were together." Color rose to my cheeks, and I looked away, unable to meet her eyes any longer.

"Oh, dear." Louise's voice was achingly gentle and without judgment. "I know you cared for each other deeply. And I know that what you shared was real and meaningful."

She settled more comfortably down on the floor, her hand compassionately patting my knee, drawing my gaze to her fingers as she spoke, "Griffin… He'd lived a very long life, you know? Much longer than what you would have thought. He'd seen things, experienced loss in ways that shaped him as a person." She paused, choosing her next words carefully. "He'd loved before. Very deeply. He had to make a hard choice about his pack, about the direction they were taking. He had to walk away from everything—his people, his home, and the woman he'd planned to spend his life with—because she couldn't leave them the way he did."

I wiped my nose with the back of my hand, my eyes still on her fingers, though not really seeing them. "What do you mean?"

She sighed, tucking her hands in her lap.

"His pack was becoming more aggressive and territorial. They wanted to push out the nearby Werefolk to expand their lands. Griffin couldn't stomach it—all the senseless violence. So he left everything behind—including her."

The words settled over me like a weight I hadn't expected. "So he settled for me?"

"No, sweetheart. Never that." Louise's voice was firm. "He genuinely cared for you. But…" She hesitated before she continued, her voice soft. "He knew what it was like to love someone completely, to find that once-in-a-lifetime type of connection. And he was honest enough to recognize that what you two shared, while real and precious, was something different."

Fresh rivulets traced their way down my cheeks. "You mean he knew I wasn't her."

"Lyra, you knew he wasn't your forever either," she said softly, tenderly. "Didn't you? Deep down?"

The truth of it hit me like a brick, because she was right. What Griffin and I shared was beautiful, but it also felt… safe. Comfortable. Not the all-consuming connection that I felt whenever I thought about…

I pushed that thought away. It didn't feel right to think about him here, in this place of grief. Louise seemed to see right through me, anyway.

"He spoke of you with such fondness," she said. I looked up to see a ghost of a smile on her lips. "But he also hoped that someday you'd find that deeper connection. The kind he had to leave behind."

Slowly, the tears stopped, and Louise opened her arms to me. I collapsed into them and she hugged me fiercely. "I know you've not had a proper mother in a long time, and we may not know each other as well as I'd like, but you're not alone in this, Lyra."

Returning her hug, I took one last, shuddering breath and pushed to my feet. Louise picked up behind me.

Despite everything, I felt lighter—ready to face what was ahead.

As Louise gathered all the supplies she'd taken from upstairs, the hair on the back of my neck prickled. I reached out to Louise silently. A sprinkling of dust came from above us, though there was no noise. The mages must have caught up with us.

Koto must have fled before they noticed her presence, I realized. Louise just nodded towards the back of the basement, and I wordlessly followed her lead. There was nothing there, just a packed dirt wall. There was a creak of floorboards from upstairs, and I swallowed hard, patting my hands along the wall. Louise was carefully packing the supplies into a satchel she'd had tucked away under her clothes, doing her best not to make any noise despite the glass bottles she'd picked up along the way.

The more I felt along the wall, the harder my heart pounded until it was buzzing in my ears. There was nothing here. No way out. We would have to go upstairs. Louise caught me by the arm and shook her head, a trace of her magic escaping from her fingers. It was unlike any magic I'd beheld so far, opalescent and unfurling in tendrils of living light. My eyes went round at the sight. It was beautiful.

There was no itch inside of me to take control of it, to absorb it into myself, like I felt with Fae power. Instead, I was so focused on what her mana looked like that I'd missed what she'd done. She nudged me with her elbow, and I shook my head, snapping out of the trance I'd been thrown into to find the wall shimmering like a pool of water.

"What is this?" I mouthed, unsure.

Louise just gave me a push towards the rippling mass of earth, and my mouth went dry as I pushed my hand through it. There was an extremely uncomfortable feeling of suction, as though the wall was trying to absorb me within it. It made my skin crawl, but just as I hesitated, there was a shout behind us.

Louise didn't give me a moment to think and shoved me through, coming flying out after me and landing in a sprawl, though she quickly got to her feet. The world went dark and twisted into a black hole that opened out in the forest of Sylvan Reach.

My heart was up in my throat as my vision righted itself. I turned to see where we'd emerged, and it was from the trunk of an enormous tree. Without pause, Louise gripped my arm with bruising strength and dragged me towards a path.

"We need to go. They won't be far behind," she said, her voice practically vibrating with adrenaline. Her hair was a wild mane, so unlike the poise and proper Louise I was used to, but her eyes blazed with determination.

"That Fae beast will know to find us, correct?"

All pretense of the touching moment we'd had in that dank basement gone, destroyed the moment that we'd been discovered.

"She can track us, yes," I stammered, practically jogging to keep up with Louise's longer stride. "And she's quick."

I felt a sudden tug in my gut, along with an impending sense of doom. The bond. Fear, anxiety and urgency crashed over me like a tsunami. Aldric.

The sensation hit me so hard I stumbled, my hand flying to

my chest as though I could physically grasp the feelings that were screaming at me. Louise caught my arm, steadying me.

"What is it?" she demanded, immediately on high alert.

"There's something wrong. With Aldric, with Seren, I don't know, but there's something wrong." The panic was so intense it was making it hard to breathe, to stay standing. "We need to get back to your house. Now."

Louise's back stiffened, and she pulled me again, not giving me a moment's respite. "All the more reason to keep moving. We're not too far from Haleshade here." Her jaw was set, with the barest sheen of sweat on her brow. The urgency burned in my chest like a hot coal. I let it sear through me as we ran.

We moved as quickly, yet as quietly as we could, aware that at any moment, there could be pursuers following us. Our surroundings became more familiar, the forest bleeding out onto the path I knew led to Haleshade. Louise was right—we weren't far.

I suppressed a scream as Koto suddenly and soundlessly appeared at my side. She chirruped, and I took the hint, grasping the ruff of her fur and climbing up. Louise followed, and I heard the clink of glass as she slid onto Koto's back behind me and wrapped her hands around my waist.

"Go! Hurry, Koto!" I whispered fervently.

She raced as hard as I'd ever seen her, her muscles bunching and flexing beneath me at a rapid-fire pace as we practically flew into Haleshade. As soon as Louise's house came into view, Koto skidded to a stop. Louise and I slid off and flung the door open. It slammed off of the opposite wall with a resounding thud, and my brain short-circuited at the sight in front of me.

Aldric was holding Seren in his lap, his wrist pressed to her lips.

CHAPTER 24

The world narrowed to a single, devastating image: Aldric's wrist pressed against Seren's lips, her unconscious form cradled in his lap like something precious.

Something that belonged to *me*.

The rational part of my mind recognized what I was seeing—Aldric saving Seren's life the only way he could. But rationality had nothing to do with the surge of possessive fury that erupted through my veins like molten fire.

His blood belonged to *me*. He was my vampire.

Mine.

"Get away from her." The words tore from my throat, raw and commanding, as I crossed the room in three swift strides.

Aldric's silver eyes snapped up to meet mine, widening in surprise. "Lyra—"

"I said, get away from her!"

Before he could respond, before I could think, I was

hauling Seren's limp form away from him, my hands gripping her shoulders with enough force to bruise. The sight of his blood on her lips, the lingering scent of starlight and wine in the air—it sent something primal and desperate clawing up from the depths of my chest.

"Lyra, what are you—" Louise's voice cut through the haze, but I barely heard her over the buzzing in my ears.

All I could focus on was the man sitting before me, looking stunned and beautiful and entirely too calm for someone who'd just been sharing the most intimate act a vampire could perform with someone who wasn't me.

"I had no choice—" Aldric began, starting to rise.

"I don't care what she needed." My voice was shaking with an intensity that should have embarrassed me. "You're mine. No one can have that part of you but me."

Warmth bloomed in Aldric's mercury eyes, but I hardly noticed as I realized I was still holding Seren in a crushing grip. I consciously eased my fingers around her, carefully lowering her to the ground. A tingling rose up my arms from where I had been touching her, something familiar—something pure.

Fae magic.

I finally looked down at her face to see her pallid skin, the sweat that had beaded up on her forehead. How much had I taken from her in that moment? Could I give it back? Her mana flowed through me like a cooling stream, swirling around the deep reservoir inside me as though begging for entrance, but I put up a wall. This needed to go back to Seren.

I took a deep, centering breath and focused on pushing it back where it came from. The magic resisted, sticky like molasses, but it begrudgingly returned. As it did, the color slowly returned to her cheeks, and her breathing eased.

My body still practically vibrated with adrenaline.

Louise dropped her satchel somewhere behind me with a clink of glass, then gently pulled me away from Seren. She gave me a pointed look, and I took the hint, stomping towards the front door.

Then I thought better of it, turned around and grabbed Aldric by his uninjured wrist and dragged him along with me as I rushed out of Louise's house.

Luckily for him, he chose not to resist.

I was a whirlwind of emotions and had to bite my tongue as I fast-walked to the only place in Haleshade that had ever felt like home to me, away from the scent of death and decay that tainted this village now.

The cabin.

It was both painful and a relief to be back in this place. I pushed the door open without hesitation and strode inside. It was dark and dusty, but it held good memories. Aldric came in behind me, his eyes flashing in the limited light like a cat's. I went to the drawer with matches in it, lighting candles until it looked less like an abandoned building and more like the home it once was.

"You gave her your blood."

The words came out like an accusation, raw and jagged. I couldn't stop pacing, my hands shaking with an energy I didn't know how to cope with.

"Lyra—,"

"No!" I whirled on him, my chest heaving with fury. "You let her drink from you. You held her to your body while she took what is mine. What *belongs to me*!"

Aldric went preternaturally still, though I could see the tension coiling in his shoulders, the way his jaw tightened.

"I don't know why I'm so angry," I continued, my voice cracking. "I know you saved her. That you had to do it. But I—you—I can't stop feeling like this. Like I want to tear something apart. Like I want to—"

I broke off, pressing my hands to my too-warm face. This rage—this all-encompassing feeling of *possession*—was unlike anything I'd ever experienced, and it almost scared me with its intensity.

"You're mine," I said, the words ripping from my throat as my hands dropped into fists at my sides. "You belong to me, and watching someone else have even a drop of your blood made me want to…"

"Want to what?" Aldric's voice was low, a promise of something dark and dangerous and oh-so-tempting.

My gaze snapped to his, tension crackling between us like an open flame, filling the room.

"I wanted to hurt her. For touching what belongs to me."

Primal heat bloomed in the stormy depths of Aldric's eyes, though there was something else there—anger.

"You're angry about something *I* had to do, but you had the gall to bring me to this place?" His voice was a growl, the sound tracing over my skin like a caress.

"You think I don't know what this place is?" he bit out, taking two long, predatory strides towards me.

I found myself pressed back against the small wooden table in the center of the room, his hands bracing on either side of me, caging me in. The table edge bit into my lower back as I leaned away from the heat radiating off of his body, but there was nowhere to go.

He loomed over me, his silver eyes blazing with something wild and possessive. "You think I can't smell him all over this place? Smell the two of you together?"

His voice was rough and deadly quiet, though the way he had me trapped between his arms made my pulse race for reasons that had nothing to do with fear. The table creaked under his grip, and I could feel the barely leashed power in his frame as he held himself just a breath away from me.

"You brought me to where you lived with *him*." His voice was made of secrets and sin, seeping into my pores, and my body reacted, tightening, aching, blossoming with heat. Aldric's nose flared, and a warmth crept up my cheeks as I became aware that he knew.

"Tell me, did he take you here?" His hand slid further on the wood, bringing his face so close that every breath almost caused our lips to touch. All I could see were the endless pools of mercury in his eyes, something ancient and unforgiving unfurling in their depths. "Did he mark you like I could?"

His words sent a quiver through my body, my core going molten with desire.

"You have no idea what it does to me—to smell *him* on you. To know that he had touched your skin, that he dared try to possess something that belongs to only me. But you weren't ready yet, and I didn't want to push you away. I had to act so damned *civilized* rather than claiming you as soon as I could." The shadows between us curled tighter, thick with want.

"You are mine, Lyra. You think it makes you angry that I had to save a life—a life *you* wanted me to protect? Imagine watching me be with her, the way I had to watch you and *him*."

I scoffed before I could think better of it. "You never had to see it. The way he touched me when we were alone, like how I had to see you holding her. I don't care if it was to save her life. You are mine."

"I want to ruin every memory of him. To fill you so completely that there is room for no one but me. The scent of your arousal… It's sweet and deliciously tempting. Addictive." Aldric's voice was dark, a whisper that dragged across my skin like claws. I swallowed thickly and said what had been building up within me.

"Then do it. Mark me, possess me. Make me yours." The words escaped me on a low moan, my body arching towards him of its own volition.

Those words were enough to crack his restraint, and his hands grasped my hips with bruising force, pulling me flush against him. "You want me to mark you? To make you mine completely?" He dropped his head to my neck, inhaling my scent and shuddering out a breath. "Be careful what you wish for, my love. Because once I start, I won't stop until you can't remember anyone else ever touching you. Until the only name on your lips is mine."

He pulled back slightly to look me in my eyes, his gaze drawing me in until he was all I could see.

"Aldric," I whispered, wrapping my arms around his neck and slamming my mouth against his.

He responded in kind, his hands sliding down to my backside and lifting me onto the table. His kiss was desperate, claiming. But there was something I needed from him first. My canines lengthened of their own volition, and I nipped his lip, the taste of his blood exploding into my mouth like the sweetest starlight.

My body shuddered, and the core of me throbbed at the flavor that was uniquely *him,* and he groaned, his hardness pressing at the apex of my thighs through the fabric between us. With feverish intensity, we pulled and tugged at each other's clothes, desperate to get skin to skin. Our mouths parted only to pull our shirts away, and then it was back to the slide of his tongue against mine, his hand splayed against my lower back and the other tangled in my hair.

Our bodies were now gloriously bare, and the heat radiating off of him felt as though it would sear my skin, but I couldn't get enough. Aldric pulled away, breathing hard.

"If you agree, I will never let you go. Do you understand me?" he asked, his voice rough with need.

"Keep me forever," I breathed, and he dragged me to the edge of the table, dropping to his knees before me. He kissed and licked his way from my knee up my thigh until his mouth reached the most sensitive part of me. My back arched up off of the table, and his name escaped my lips like a prayer.

I couldn't think. Couldn't feel anything other than his mouth pressed to my core. His tongue worked my flesh as though his entire destiny whittled down to this moment, like he was starving and I was the only sustenance he desired. His low groan reverberated through me, and before I knew it, I came undone. My cries echoed off the cabin walls, and my fingers wound their way into the inky waves of his hair, gripping tightly as my eyes slid closed.

He didn't stop. If anything, my desperation only spurred him on. His hands anchored me to the table, forbidding my escape. The bond between us flared, bright and aching. My magic swirled within me, pressing against the walls I'd placed up against it as though aching to be released.

One of his hands slid from my hips and before I could register it, I felt a finger prod my entrance. I gasped, and my hips bucked against his mouth, and I felt him smile. Slowly, teasingly, he eased his finger inside. My body welcomed the intrusion, and I came apart easily, my moans more breathless, more desperate.

"So soft," he said with a low growl that vibrated against me. "So very ready for me."

He eased a second finger in, and I gasped, my entire world zeroing into the way he curled his fingers just right, as if he knew my body already.

"That's it, love," he whispered, as his mouth found me again. He kissed me there as my thighs shook from the pleasure. He drove me towards the edge with ruthless precision, as though his entire existence was dedicated to unraveling me, thread by thread.

A primal, sinful sound escaped his lips as he made his way up my body, his fingers still working that sweet spot inside of me. My fingers slowly disentangled from Aldric's mane of black waves. I felt him looking at me, and my lashes fluttered open with some effort. His eyes were like molten silver—his gaze hot enough to burn.

"You are mine, Lyra, and mine alone," he said, a warning wrapped in desire that slid over me like the smoothest silk.

"And you are mine," I whispered, baring my throat to him. Inviting him to take me in every way.

He went still, his breath shuddering out of his body. Slowly, carefully, he removed his fingers from me and wrapped his hand across my lower back, the other cradling my neck as he brought me closer to him.

He peppered my collarbone with kisses before a languid brush of his tongue traced my pulse.

"You have no idea how long I've waited for this," Aldric murmured, rolling his hips until his hardness pressed against my folds, creating a delicious pressure. I fought the urge to sink onto his length, wanting to savor this moment we had waited so long for.

He slowly, deliberately rubbed himself against me. The movements were smooth and slick with want. My pulse fluttered against his lips, and I felt him smile. His fangs grazed my throat.

"Please, Aldric," I panted. "I need you."

"That's right, love. Only me," he said, his voice smoky and rich. He finally gave me just what I wanted as the points of his teeth sank into my flesh. His lips sealed against me and he took my essence in long, intense pulls.

The bond between us roared to life, and I was suddenly overwhelmed with sensation. My magic burst from me, flowing into him and back as though he were the moon, and I was the ocean, drawn to his gravity.

His own power, dark and seductive, trickled into me. It was unlike anything I'd ever experienced—ancient and *hungry*. It sank into my internal reservoir as though it were made for me. This was his very being, making space for itself within me. His tongue worked against my pulse, and the pleasure was almost overwhelming.

Aldric's fingers tangled in my hair, gripping tightly as he pulled back, blood glistening on his lips. His gaze was as intense as a lightning strike, glowing from within.

"You taste like the stars were made just to worship you," he rasped. "But I will worship you just as reverently."

Then he pressed into me.

He entered me in one slow, fluid thrust. He filled me completely, every inch a claiming. I clung to him, my nails digging into his shoulders as he began to move. Gradually, my body adjusted to the thickness and length of him.

As Aldric felt me relax, his last thread of restraint broke, and he gripped more of my hair, pulling my head back and baring my throat again. His fangs sank into my flesh just as he thrust in earnest, our bodies moving as one.

The combination of his lips on my pulse and the desperation in his movements was my undoing. His name left my lips in a breathless cry, Aldric groaning against my skin. I wrapped my legs around his waist, determined to be as close as possible. The raw, primal sounds of our bodies meeting filled the room, Aldric releasing me as his back bowed and he finally found his own release, throbbing and filling me with warmth.

Aldric curled over me, breathing hard. His heart thundered against my breast and I traced my fingers lightly over his back. I cringed slightly as I felt a sticky wetness against his back and realized I had broken skin. Aldric peeked up at me through the tangled mass of his hair, warmth and laughter in his gaze.

"Marks that I can wear proudly," he murmured. "I love you, Lyra."

I froze in panic. It felt too soon, too raw. My mind raced, unsure of what to say, what to do.

"It's okay, love," he said against my skin. Warmth blossomed between us, the bond tingling and fresh. Whole. Finally complete.

"As long as you stay with me, I can wait."

CHAPTER 25

I fumbled with my shirt, hyperaware of Aldric's gaze on me as he pulled on his own clothes. Through the bond, I could feel his contentment, his satisfaction, and underneath it all, a steady warmth. It was overwhelming, feeling his emotions while trying to sort through my own tangled feelings.

He hummed under his breath, seemingly without a care. Wordlessly, I took my pants and undergarments to the small bathroom so I could clean up. Once the door closed, I took a steadying breath. Just what did I do?

I didn't regret completing the bond with Aldric—not exactly. But I wish it hadn't been driven by such intense jealousy and instead from a place of caring, and not *here*.

The scent of Griffin still flowed with the dust motes here, warm leather and citrus. But I found I wasn't as sad as I would have been before talking with Louise. She was right. What I felt for Griffin wasn't love, though it wasn't any less meaningful.

I knew that as soon as Aldric and I met.

The realization hit me like a physical blow, and I braced myself against the small sink. When I was still raw from Griffin's death, some part of me knew, even if I refused to admit it to myself. The way my magic reached for him—the way he could break down every barrier I had in place like they didn't exist.

A flutter of curiosity brushed against my mind, and panic speared me. Trying to project calm, I splashed a bit of cold water on my face. Could he feel all of this turmoil inside of me? What was he thinking?

Was I just experiencing the bond, or were these true feelings?

Love seemed too big of a word. I wasn't sure yet what that felt like. Was it the urge to be near him? The urge to possess him? That didn't sound right to me.

Frowning, I wiped the water off of my face with the hem of my shirt, centering myself with a deep breath before opening the bathroom door and striding out into the living room, where Aldric waited.

The room was filled with our scent, wine and starlight. My cheeks burned.

"You look positively… ravishing," Aldric said, his lips quirked up in a smile. "I enjoy seeing my mark on you."

My throat tingled, and I unconsciously covered the bite with my hand. My core throbbed at the memory, and my breath hitched.

Aldric's eyes grew dark and stormy again as he strode up to me, slowly pulling my hand away from my throat and threading our fingers together.

"Are you okay, love?" Aldric asked, his brows furrowed. "I know it's a lot."

His concern flowed across the bond to me like cool water, soothing my frazzled nerves.

"I'm fine," I said automatically, then winced at how unconvincing I sounded. "It's just—I have to get used to this."

His thumb stroked across my knuckles gently before bringing them to his lips. "I understand, darling. It takes time to adjust. This is all new to me, too."

"Can you feel mine too?" I blurted, then my cheeks went scarlet. "My emotions, I mean."

A gentle smile curved his lips. "Your walls are formidable, even now. But I catch glimpses. I hope to break those walls down, to have you completely." His mercury eyes searched my face. "But I won't take it from you. You need to give yourself to me freely."

Swallowing hard, I straightened my spine to show more confidence than I felt. "We should get back to Louise. Make sure that Seren is okay."

With that, I turned towards the door. Aldric followed behind after snuffing the candles' flames, leaving the cabin shrouded in darkness. When he closed the door, it sounded louder than it should have in the village's silence, as though cutting off that part of my life.

Aldric's long stride caught up to me easily, and his presence beside me was comforting and warm. The tether between us was ever-present, reminding me of our act. Each time the thought passed through my mind, my body tingled expectantly, despite the achiness from our tryst.

Aldric lifted his arm, drawing my eye, but he was just pushing back his unruly waves. His gaze caught mine, and he smiled, so blissfully happy. My stomach did flips, and I caught myself smiling back at him. I felt like a teenager again who had just admitted their feelings to their crush, only for their crush to reciprocate those feelings.

The comparison made me stumble over my feet. But before I could fall, Aldric's hand shot out, steadying me with a firm grip on my elbow. A wave of amusement flowed over to me, and I scowled at him.

"Careful," he murmured, his voice carrying a sensuous undertone that made my pulse quicken. His thumb stroked my skin before he released me. We walked in silence for a few minutes, the familiar route to Louise's house feeling different. The last time I took this path, the village was still lively, despite the illness that was already beginning to spread.

The closer we got, the more the stench of death permeated the air. It couldn't be healthy for Louise, I thought absently. We needed to find a safe place where she could stay, too. There was no saving this village. The only person left alive was Louise herself. The thought was sobering, and any remaining warmth I had inside was smothered.

As we rounded the corner, I realized what was different. All the bodies that had littered the streets—they were gone. My gaze roved over the village in shock. Aldric fidgeted next to me, something completely out of character for him.

"Did you do something, Aldric?" I asked, stopping in the middle of the path.

The question made him uncomfortable, and a hint of pink kissed the tips of his ears. "I couldn't very well leave them all here, could I?" he said, though he didn't meet my eyes. "This place means a lot to you, and it wasn't exactly hygienic having bodies all over the place."

My jaw fell open, and I snapped it shut with an audible click. "What did you do with all the bodies?" I asked, aghast. Though I hated myself for it, my first thought was the bodies lying in a pile somewhere out of view.

Aldric put a hand to his chest as though he knew exactly what was on my mind. "Lyra, give me some credit. I didn't play a game of 'stack the human body' over here. I buried them all in the forest nearby. There was a clearing that was suitable… Besides, there weren't *that* many."

Warmth flooded my eyes at his words, and Aldric finally glanced at me before sputtering, pulling me into his arms.

"Aldric, y—you didn't have to do that," I said through a hiccuping sob. "This wasn't your village to fix."

"But it was yours. And that's enough, my dear," he said, stroking my back gently. "I was just waiting for your return, and I didn't want that to be the first thing you faced when getting back. Seren was stable, and I could hear her breathing and heartbeat even from outside of the house, so I knew she would be okay while I took care of it. Besides, some of them…"

He paused, then cleared his throat.

"Some of those afflicted were younger than I would have liked. It pained me to see them, too."

I wrapped my arms around his waist, clinging to Aldric as though my life depended on it. "You are too good of a man for me," I murmured into his shirt, the words muffled.

"Ah, there we must disagree," he said, reaching down and tipping my chin up to look at his face. "You were made for me."

I swallowed hard at his words, released my grip and resumed my walk to Louise's house. He wordlessly followed, though I could feel a brush of disappointment against my mind. I just needed to know if Seren was okay. Then I could sort my feelings afterwards.

There was a cheery light coming from Louise's window, a sharp contrast to the tumultuous hurricane raging inside of me. My hands shook slightly as I reached for the doorknob, but before I could touch it, Aldric smoothly opened the door for me, ushering me inside. And I was not prepared for the sight that greeted me, not in the least.

I walked in to see Seren sitting up, drinking a cup of hot tea. She looked haggard, but she was talking with Louise.

How?

My heart clenched painfully with a combination of relief and anxiety. She was alive. Something we did worked.

"Seren?" My voice came out as a whisper, disbelief coloring every syllable.

"Lyra," she said with a weak smile. Her voice was soft, but clear.

She'd been about to die when Louise and I first arrived. Was it Aldric's blood? My stomach dropped at the thought, but I knew I'd sacrifice whatever it took to stop this sickness from spreading any further—even if it tore me apart inside.

I blinked hard, my gaze roving over Seren. Her skin was glowing, a beacon of health. But there was also something strange—an aura of power about her that wasn't there before.

"How?" was all I could manage. I didn't expect an answer, but I couldn't stop myself from asking.

Louise set down her own cup, her moss-green eyes bright with excitement. "She woke up about an hour ago. Just opened her eyes and asked for water, as though nothing had happened."

"But how? The plague doesn't just—people don't wake up from it," I said, my legs shaking.

Aldric gripped my elbow to steady me, and I jumped, having forgotten that he was there. Warmth spread from where his fingers touched me, as though my body were resonating with his presence. I swallowed hard.

Seren's jade gaze snapped to where his hand held me, then slowly trailed up to my face. "It was something you did, Lyra," she said, her voice deadly soft. "When you touched me, something changed. Like a poison was leeched from my body."

"B-but that can't be true," I whispered, my voice shaking. "I don't know how to cure anyone. The plague came *from* me."

Even as I said the words, though, I remembered dragging Seren away from Aldric and the push and pull of power between us. How did I do it? Could I do it again? Was it even safe?

"Lyra," Aldric murmured, moving closer to me until I could feel the heat radiating off of his body.

"No." I backed away from him, my breathing becoming shallow and rapid as my heart raced painfully in my chest. "If I could cure people…"

The world became spotted with black as the thoughts whirled through my head. "How many have died? How many could I have saved if I had just tried?"

I fist my hands in my hair and dropped to a squat, the room spiraling.

The weight crashed over me like a tidal wave. All the villagers. The *children*. Countless others who had succumbed while I wandered around Aethralis, stifling my power instead of learning to use it.

Aldric appeared in my vision, wavering through my tears. He dragged me into his arms, murmuring into my hair. "You couldn't have known, my love."

"But I should have!" I cried. The words ripped from my throat, raw and broken. "I should have tried! It came from me. I should have realized I could help."

Louise reached out to me, gently disentangling my fingers from the white waves of my hair. "Listen, dear, I've been dealing with this sickness since it first began, and *I* didn't know. I didn't think of it either. You're still a child compared to me."

She slowly stroked my back, maternal energy emanating from her. "If anyone should have realized, it should have been me. But now's not the time to have a breakdown over it. We need to figure out if you can do it again."

Aldric scooped me up as though I weighed nothing and sat in a nearby chair, nestling me into his lap.

"Now?" he asked, concern leeching through the bond and brushing against my consciousness, though there was a hint of something else there. Pride? Why would he be feeling pride?

My confusion must have shown on my face, because he turned his mercury gaze down at my face. "You may not know how, my love, but you did it. There is hope."

I buried my face in Aldric's neck, breathing in his familiar scent. Slowly, my heart rate slowed and my breathing returned to normal. "I don't know what I did. Or, I do, but I don't know how I did it," I said, my voice muffled against his skin.

"We'll figure it out," Louise said cheerfully behind us, a scrape of wood telling me she'd likely returned to her seat next to Seren.

"Thank you, Lyra," Seren's voice carried over to me. "You saved me."

I turned in Aldric's arms until I could see her, her mop of blue-black hair in desperate need of a brushing and a liveliness in her jade-green eyes I'd not seen in a long while.

"I wanted to save you. Sorry about how I reacted to Aldric… what Aldric was doing," I muttered, my cheeks flushed.

"If not for that, I may very well still be afflicted with the sickness, so we're just going to call it a happy accident," Seren said, a wry twist to her lips. "Besides, I know how it is with bonded mates."

Something within me loosened, allowing me to breathe

easier. Guilt had been eating away at me ever since I first put my hands on Seren. Something about her statement stuck with me, and I filed that information away for later. "Whether or not you understand it doesn't make it right. I hope you'll forgive me."

"Given everything that's happened, you don't even need to ask, Lyra. Just try not to do it again," she said with a laugh.

That expression on her face warmed me from the inside. Aldric gripped me just a little tighter, as though he could feel it, too.

I straightened on Aldric's lap, just realizing what a compromising position I was in. Grabbing his arms, I pulled them from my body, then wiped any remaining wetness from my cheeks. My face burned, and I quickly stood, a hint of displeasure reaching me through the bond.

"So, what now? How do I try again?"

"We need to find more of the sick," Louise said, poised as ever. "I don't know where we can find them, but if you have any ideas, I'm open to anything."

There was a clearing of a throat. All our eyes turned to Seren, whose spine straightened. She slowly set her teacup down on the table in front of her. "Koto can probably track them based on the magical signature the plague inflicts."

A huff came from the doorway, and I jumped. "Koto!" I admonished, whipping around to see the Feralumin's large face in the doorway. "You scared me."

But she ignored me, her enormous eyes locked on Seren's form. The Feralumin tried to push its head through the doorway, but Seren stood on shaky legs, instead making her way over to her companion.

"I'm okay, Koto," she murmured, draping her upper body over Koto's muzzle. Purring rumbled in the house, the floor vibrating under the force of it. "Were you worried about me?"

I didn't even know they could purr to begin with, I thought absently. But Seren definitely had the right idea.

"I think Koto is our best bet," I said, my eyes locked on the pair, a pang in my chest at how lovingly Koto nuzzled into Seren's abdomen. For being so massive, she really was just a cat at heart. "Those two found Aldric someone when he needed blood. Someone who was afflicted." My stomach tightened painfully as I thought back. I could have helped that person.

"She is an excellent tracker," Seren said, patting Koto's muzzle affectionately. "Give us a few hours, and I'm sure we'd have someone for you."

I startled when I registered Seren's words. "You *just* woke up, and you're already talking about going out?"

Louise clucked her tongue like a mother hen, her hands on her hips. "I agree with Lyra. I can go with Koto, as long as you tell her to listen to me. You need to get your rest. I don't care if you're Fae or not, you're still recovering."

Seren rolled her eyes and sighed. "After spending the last however-long lying around, you want me to just go straight back to it?" She turned, folding her arms across her chest, and leveled a stony stare at us.

Koto, as if in agreement with Seren, chuffed and stomped a meaty paw on the ground. Never in my life did I think I would see a giant Fae-beast throwing a tantrum, but here we are.

"What if you both went?" Aldric asked smoothly, crossing his legs elegantly as though discussing what to have for brunch. "Lyra and I can stay here and see whether we can… recreate the circumstances that led to curing Seren."

My eyes went round as I stared at him, aghast.

Seren laughed, the sound full of mirth. "Oh, I'm sure. You think I haven't seen that mark on her?"

A blush crept up my neck, burning my cheeks. The urge to cover the mark caused my fingers to twitch, but I resisted.

"Not exactly subtle, dear," Louise said, barely holding back a smile.

"I'll be right back," I blurted, desperate to get away from their teasing. It was setting me on edge, though I couldn't exactly say why. I power-walked towards the bathroom, which only reminded me of washing Aldric…

Splashing cold water on my face, I half-expected steam to rise from my cheeks from the embarrassment. I shouldn't be ashamed of what we did, but at the same time, talking about it was just too much. It was still too fresh. Too new. I was still coming to terms with the fact that I was now officially bonded to someone.

A bond was like a marriage, right? I thought. Everything felt like a whirlwind. Learning about Griffin, to coming back and seeing Aldric feeding Seren, to now becoming bonded. I felt like I could barely breathe with these changes. It was giving me emotional whiplash.

Slowly, I breathed in through my nose and out through my mouth, trying to center myself. A trickle of concern brushed against my mind, but I ignored it, focusing on my breathing. After a few minutes, there was a knock at the door.

"Lyra?" Aldric's buttery voice floated through the wood. "Are you okay?"

"I'm fine," I called, though my voice sounded hollow. Clearing my throat, I tried again. "Everything is okay."

"Seren and Louise have left," he said, and I heard a sound as though Aldric laid his forehead against the wood. "Can I come in?"

Looking in the mirror, I took in my appearance. My violet eyes were tired—I had deep bags underneath. My snow-colored hair was a tangled mess, and there was a bruise marring the pale skin at my neck. Tingles erupted in my stomach at the thought of it, and I heard an intake of breath from the other side of the door.

"Lyra?" he called.

"Yes, Aldric," I said, though I was hesitant. Could he understand how I'm feeling, or would he be hurt?

The door opened with a faint creak of the hinges, and Aldric sauntered up behind me with all the confidence an ancient vampire could muster. He slowly snaked his hands around my waist and laid his head atop my own. The contrast between us was beautiful. He was the dark to my light, his inky waves falling over my pale strands, his sun-kissed glow complementing my own pasty skin.

"You look absolutely ravishing, as always, my dear," he murmured, the words sliding over my skin like the smoothest silk.

"I look like the dead," I said with a grunt.

"What's troubling you, my love?" Aldric asked, his eyes dark and stormy with concern.

I looked away, unsure of how to form the words.

"Is it me?" he murmured, his long fingers tracing soothing circles on my abdomen.

My gaze snapped to his reflection. "It's not you, Aldric," I said instantly. "It's just… it's everything right now. I don't know how to deal with this."

"You don't have to deal with everything at once," he said quietly into my hair. "We need to take things one step at a time."

"What does that even mean, though?" I asked, frustration coloring my words. "What if Seren was just a one-off? What if it was a coincidence?"

"Then we'll find another way," he said easily. "But you cured her, Lyra. That wasn't luck or chance—that was *you*."

We lapsed into silence, Aldric swaying gently from side to side in an effort to comfort me.

"Everything is happening so fast," I whispered. "The bond, Seren, and now I have to try to heal someone else. I feel like I'm drowning in these expectations, these obligations, and what can I do? I'm just one person with a cursed power."

Aldric turned me in his arms so that I was facing him directly. "Look at me," Aldric said, his voice low and commanding. I craned my neck up to look at his face, though it was hard to meet his intense silver gaze. "I've lived for a long time. Too long. But the most important things always seem to happen quickly, and you just have to figure it out in the moment. I'm here."

His hand cupped my cheek, and he stroked his thumb across my skin. "We'll figure it out. No matter what it takes."

CHAPTER 26

Aldric led me out of the bathroom by my hand, his fingers incredibly warm around my chilled digits. My gaze was trained on the floor, overwhelmed with everything happening at once. My thoughts were racing in my head like a mouse stuck in a maze, desperate for the exit, but there wasn't one.

Aldric sat on one of the sick cots, picking me up as though I weighed nothing and placing me next to him. He urged me down, and I lay in the fetal position, curled tight around myself. Wordlessly, Aldric nestled in behind me, the scent of storms and wine filling the air. There was silence for several minutes before either of us spoke.

"Did I ever tell you about my childhood?" Aldric murmured against my skin. The touch of his lips sent a shudder through my spine.

I shook my head, my eyes sliding closed as I listened to his voice, smooth as silk.

"My family wasn't always considered royal. When I was a child, it was actually a different clan. The Ravenwoods—which is the most vampire-like name, I know," he said, and I felt his lips twist into a wry smile against the nape of my neck.

"You're not wrong about that," I murmured, a begrudging smile tugging at my mouth.

"Regardless. They were another set of living vampires. We were much more numerous back then," he explained, his hand sliding smoothly over my hip and warming my flesh through the thin fabric of my pants. "This was thousands of years ago now."

I made a noncommittal noise as I listened, curiosity burning within me. He'd never volunteered information about his past before, and I would take everything I could learn from this.

"They had a son who was around the same age as I, along with an older boy. The Crown Prince of the Ravenwoods," he continued. "The younger boy—his name was Julien. Julien was my best friend until the war."

"What happened?" I asked, unable to help myself. My eyes opened, and I turned my head to see him with a faraway look, gazing into nothing.

"The previous transformation mage happened," he said flatly, his voice tinged with sadness. "They manipulated the Crown Prince, Sebastian. Told him they could make him more powerful than ever before, if only he would submit to them and become their bonded mate."

"That doesn't sound like it would work, knowing you," I said, propping myself up on my elbow. Aldric's grip on me tightened, and he pulled me in closer, ensuring our bodies were melded together.

"Yes, well, Sebastian evidently felt the same way. He rejected her, and she just couldn't take it. Next thing you know, it's a full-on war. I know she was behind it." His eyes had gone stormy and dark. He tucked his head into my neck, inhaling my scent as though he needed it to breathe.

"Did you see them? This other transformation mage?"

"Yes, unfortunately. Her name was Virelia. She was a beauty—her skin was alabaster white, her hair like golden honey. She had the eyes of everyone in the court. I was a child, of course, but even I could admit that there was a certain magnetism about her."

The burn of jealousy settled in my stomach listening to Aldric, but I swallowed my pride so I didn't interrupt his story. As though sensing the darkness blossoming within me, Aldric nuzzled me, planting a gentle kiss on my shoulder. "She couldn't compare to you though, love. That's like comparing the moon with a mere reflection in water."

Warmth suffused me, and I felt a blush creeping up my neck. I slid my hand over his own, weaving my fingers with his.

Aldric's voice dripped with venom as he recounted the next memory. "Virelia used her powers to sabotage the Ravenwoods. She would imitate the members of the royal family at various gatherings, spreading animosity until they were reviled wherever they went. Sebastian knew what was going on, but he had hoped he could contain it by doing damage control. There was no way to tell the difference between Virelia and a member of the royal family without tasting her blood, however. And no one would dare drink from royalty without an invitation."

A low growl fell from Aldric's lips, rumbling along my skin. "No matter how hard Sebastian tried, he couldn't stop it. He was the first to fall. And once he was dead, it was a free-for-all. Death around every corner."

I turned in Aldric's arms, tucking his head against my chest and burying my fingers in the dark waves of his hair, stroking my nails against his scalp. He shuddered, a faint groan escaping him as he tucked me tight against his body. I threw a leg over his own, getting as close as possible.

"You're so warm, love," he mumbled, his words muffled against my shirt. Tingling suffused my body at his words, and I continued to stroke his hair.

"It's difficult to talk about. It was one of the darkest points in recent Vesparan history. The deaths of so many families…" He trailed off, his gaze fogged over with the weight of the memories.

My free hand trailed down his back, tenderly running over the tense muscles there. I gave him time, waiting for him to continue.

"Eventually, there were so few of us left. My family hid for much of the war. It lasted a few years, which is barely a blink of an eye for vampires. The Vesparan War was incredibly violent and bloody. Towards the end, with a full family mostly intact, the Winters could take the opening left over by all the others."

"And that's how you became royalty?" I asked, pulling his

shirt up so I could reach bare skin. His muscles jumped at the touch of my fingertips. "That sounds like an awful time."

"It was, truly. But in a way I'm glad for it. It led me to you, Lyra," he said, his voice earnest as I've ever heard it as he nuzzled into my breasts. "You've made every cruelty in my existence worth it just to be graced by your presence."

"Oh hush, Aldric. I am not worth the horrible things that have happened to you."

"You're worth all of that and more," he murmured, pressing a kiss to the swell of one breast, and then the other. "You are mine, my love."

I tugged him closer to me, my leg tighter around his hips. His manhood pressed right into the apex of my thighs through our pants, and I gasped. Aldric peered up at me with a roguish grin.

"Baring my soul just does it for you, hm?" Aldric asked, a dark chuckle escaping his lips.

"Apparently it does you as well," I said with a laugh.

"What can I say? I love a woman I can be vulnerable with," he said, pulling my shirt down and exposing the creamy skin beneath. He kissed me there, and I felt the lightest graze of his fangs.

Goosebumps spread over my body, and I moaned before I could stop it. Aldric's answering sound had an ache spreading from my core. His hands crept up underneath my shirt, caressing my back. I ground myself against the hardness nestled against the apex of my thighs, and Aldric groaned, the sound smoky and darkly erotic.

Aldric pulled himself free from my embrace and rose above me, pushing me onto my back. He settled his weight between my thighs, which fell open. My breathing quickened, and Aldric reached down, gripping both of my hands in one of his and pulling them above my head, pinning me.

My heart raced, and my lips parted of their own volition. Aldric's eyes blazed with a silver flame, and his tongue darted out to wet his full lower lip, drawing my gaze there. I struggled against his grip, but his hand was like an iron manacle around my own, though his expression twisted into one of dominance and desire as my struggling further rubbed my core against the bulge straining against his pants.

"You are such a temptress, my love," Aldric murmured, his gaze roving over my body. "I want to take you right here, regardless of who may see us."

His words caused a spear of arousal to shoot through my body. As though he could sense it, his pupils dilated, and he inhaled deeply.

"You smell as sweet as honey, as decadent as the darkest chocolate. I would ravish you, my dear," he said, leaning down until our lips almost touched.

"Then do it," I challenged, surprising myself.

A deep growl rumbled over my skin as Aldric devoured me in a kiss, our tongues fighting for dominance in our mouths as I struggled against him. I wanted to take him, to make him mine as much as he wished to do the same, and I would prove it to him.

Finally, I managed to work one hand free, and I gripped the back of his neck, pulling him closer to me. I bit his lip, drawing blood. The taste of starlight and everything that was uniquely *him* spread across my tongue, and Aldric groaned into my mouth, his pelvis driving into me through the thin fabric of our clothes as though he could not contain himself.

My hips moved of their own volition, meeting him thrust for thrust. I drew his lower lip into my mouth, pulling more of that sweet taste and suffusing my body with his essence. Then, a naughty thought occurred to me, and I dragged my tongue against the point of his left fang, drawing blood. An inhuman sound rumbled into my mouth, as though just through that small act, I'd driven him to the brink of losing control. And that made me feel *powerful*.

Here was this ancient vampire, driven to the edge just from *me*. The hold I held over him was intoxicating, and as his tongue entangled with mine, sealing his lips around it and drinking me in, release ripped through my body with such ferocity that I could do nothing but arch into him. Any sounds that escaped me were swallowed up by him, and he gripped my wrist even harder.

He finally broke our kiss, panting. The silver in his eyes had darkened to molten shadow, heavy with desire. With his free hand, he pulled my shirt up over my breasts, his breath sawing in and out of his lungs as though he were an animal starved with a meal displayed just out of reach.

His gaze was like a physical touch, roving over my body

and my nipples beaded, as though desperate for his attention. My hand slipped from his neck, falling limply at my side as I struggled to catch my breath. Aftershocks rippled through my body even now, and evidence of my arousal made the thin fabric of my pants slick with desire.

"I could just…devour you, my love. You are a forbidden fruit, and I am a starving man," Aldric said, his voice achingly soft and deep. "But, much as I would love to continue, we will have guests shortly."

It took a moment for his words to register, and once they did, all I could say was, "What?"

Before I could even react, Aldric sat up, pulling me until I was nestled against his side. He deftly wrapped the both of us in a blanket, as though we had just been cuddling and talking, waiting for Seren and Louise to return.

My mind was whirling as I struggled to lose the haze of lust that clouded my thoughts.

"I love you, Lyra," Aldric murmured, nuzzling into my tangled hair. "Every part of you, regardless of what may happen."

With those words, the door to Louise's house opened, and my heart jumped into my throat.

I was not prepared for this.

CHAPTER 27

Louise and Seren wordlessly strolled into the house, oblivious to what Aldric and I had almost done on this cot. I squirmed slightly, and Aldric slid his arm around my waist under the blanket, as though reassuring me.

Koto waited outside, a lump barely visible in her fur. Louise and Seren dumped all of their belongings on the ground, then walked back through the door carrying a person. He was a young boy, probably no older than sixteen. His skin was pallid, slick with sweat.

His hair was stringy and greasy, dark brown strands sticking to his forehead. The boy's mouth hung open and his eyes were closed. If I didn't know better, I would say he had already died. I shot up off the sick cot, the blanket falling away from me. Aldric smoothly stood behind me, guiding me away and clearing the way for Louise and Seren to lay the boy on the cot.

Any remaining fog in my brain had been cleared away the moment that I saw this poor kid.

"Where did you find him?" I asked, my gaze bouncing from each of the three people in front of me.

"He was one of the only remaining humans alive in one of the closest villages, and it looks like we may have gotten him just in time," Louise said, her voice soft and protective as she brushed away the hair from the boy's face.

Gently, she closed his mouth and bustled around the house, gathering items she needed to stabilize him.

My hands shook as the reality hit me. I needed to cure him. This child would die if I could not.

Aldric smoothly ran his hands down my arms and wove his fingers in with mine, stopping the trembling. A tingling flowed from the bond, as though Aldric was reassuring me from within. It helped to soothe my rattled nerves, and I was grateful. Aldric pressed a gentle kiss to the top of my head and slowly released me. I looked back at him, and he smiled, his expression radiant as though he had no doubts within him I could do it.

I only wished I could be as confident as Aldric. Slowly, as though approaching an injured animal, I crept towards the cot. Seren waited for me there, her emerald eyes earnest and bright with curiosity. Not that I could blame her. She didn't *see* what happened to her, only felt it.

Sinking to my knees beside the boy, I picked up his clammy hand in mine. It felt so frail, like a dying leaf, desperately clinging to its branch as it dries.

Swallowing hard, I looked back at everyone. Louise was on the other side of the bed, working diligently to set up an IV and help hydrate the weak body before us. I exhaled shakily and reached out to the boy's shoulders. He barely felt alive, his chest rising only slightly.

Reaching within my internal reservoir, I tried to coax my power out. How did I do this before?

Why couldn't I remember?

I pulled magic from Seren, I think. Sending tendrils of my essence into the boy, I fought to find any magic within him. But he appeared to be human, not a mage. What did magic in a human look like?

My mind raced, and panic was setting in. I gripped his shoulders harder, as though that would help me. Closing my eyes, my breath came faster and faster, until I was almost hyperventilating. I jumped when I felt Aldric's hand on my spine, as though reminding me of his presence.

Seren gently pried my fingers from the young man's flesh, and I was aghast to see bruises blooming from where I had touched him.

"Maybe I can help," Seren murmured. "I felt it from within, so I may have a better idea of what we need to do."

Seren replaced me at the boy's side, her hands gently cradling his own. My stomach churned at the sight, and my hands fisted, my nails digging into my palms.

Seren took a deep breath, and as she breathed out, a light bloomed between them. This didn't happen before when I had cured her—I was certain. What was she doing? The scent of wildflowers and spring bloomed, the light shifting to a mossy green.

My ears popped as there was a large shifting of power coming from Seren, her magic flowing into the boy like a river bursting through a dam. Then, just as quickly, it returned, and she was done. I grit my teeth as the boy's cheeks blossomed with pink and his breathing eased ever-so-slightly.

How?

How could she do it so easily? What was wrong with me that I couldn't? Was I just doomed to fail again and again? Is this the curse Myrana placed on me?

Aldric sensed my inner turmoil, and I felt him approaching again, but I couldn't take it right now. My magic tore through my internal reservoir as though rebelling against what was right before me. Staying here would not be safe.

Without a word, I turned on my heel, chest burning with shame, and sprinted out of the house.

My lungs felt like they would burst, but my feet kept pounding the ground as I raced away, trying to escape my failure. Darkness fell with each step, reflective of the sadness within me.

I was pathetic.

Running from my problems, never able to help clean up my own messes. What was wrong with me? The world passed me by in a blur until finally, I found myself in front of a river snaking through the forest. I didn't even know how long I had run, or in which direction. I collapsed on the riverbank, my chest constricting.

Was I worthy—was I even worthy of living? It is because of me that this sickness even exists. It is because of me that all these people have died. I get *one* chance to fix it, and I screw it all up.

Darkness threatened to swallow me whole, and I just sat there, drawing my knees up to my chest and wrapping my arms around them. Every time I turn around, I'm either hurting someone or faced with my own inadequacies.

What can I do? I screamed internally. *Why am I being put through this?*

My mind went to the previous transformation mage. Virelia. Had she felt the same way? Or was she content to just sew discord wherever she went?

Stomach dropping, I fought to bring my magic back under control. It rippled beneath my skin as though begging to be used, but for what? There was nothing I could do to help. No part of me to hold on to as something 'good'.

With some effort, I shoved my power back into my internal reservoir, leaving me feeling bereft. The sound of the rushing water soothed my nerves slightly, pulling me out of my pity party. I always felt comforted being in places like this. It made me feel so much closer to nature.

Slowly, I lowered my arms and crossed my legs, just watching the river rush by. Occasionally, a fish would appear near the surface, and it brought the barest hint of a smile to my face.

A fish wouldn't care what kind of person I am. They'd just keep mindlessly swimming, oblivious to anything outside of looking for their next meal. Creeping closer to the water's edge, my chest eased.

Serenity.

That feeling didn't last long, however, as I realized there was a face in the water staring back at me. A scream was caught in my throat, and the face rose from the water, shifting like the river itself. Soon it formed into a humanoid figure.

The features were hard to make out, changing like the tides, and they wore no clothing. Though interestingly there were fish within their body, lazily swimming about from their feet up through their torso. Never in my life had I ever seen something like this, and I had no idea how to react.

"The transformation mage," the creature said, its voice burbling like a brook.

Wordlessly, I nodded, my hand covering my mouth. Something about this was familiar. Maybe it was the energy coming from this entity, ancient and wild. Slowly, I got to my feet, careful not to show it my back.

Even if I didn't feel any malice coming from the spirit, I couldn't trust it.

It cocked its head as though curious about me. My skin crawled when one of the small fish worked its way up the neck of the elemental and peered at me from where its eyes would be.

"What do you want?" I said, finally finding my voice.

"Where the river and ocean meet, there the water is the purest," it said cryptically.

"What does that even mean?" I asked, my hand dropping to my side. I was so tired of all of this.

"A stream may drink from the rain, but only the sea remembers the sky. Where they meet, any impurities may drown," it said, frustratingly vague yet again.

Slowly, it began to sink beneath the river's current, its body becoming one with the racing waters. My heart beat painfully, my mind racing.

"What does that mean? What do the river and the ocean have to do with this?" I asked, scrambling over to the riverbank.

But it was too late. The spirit was gone, and there were no traces that it had ever been here.

The hair on the back of my neck prickled, and I knew he was there before he said a single word.

"Aldric, why are you here?" I asked, exhausted. I sank back onto my behind, sitting in the mud without a care. My skin was streaked with earth, but it didn't matter.

"I came to check on you, my love," he said easily, sitting next to me with a *squelch*. He looked completely unbothered by it. Instead, his gaze was lit up with concern as he looked me over.

"I'm fine—," I started, but Aldric didn't let me finish.

He pressed a finger to my lips before pulling me against his chest, wrapping his powerful arms around me. We sat like that for a while, my ear pressed to his chest while I sat between his legs.

The steady beating of his heart and the rhythm of his breathing brought me more peace than I'd like to admit. The warmth and scent of him surrounded me, and I found myself melting into his embrace.

"I'm sorry," I said with a sigh.

Aldric pulled my hair away from my face, carefully disentangling the waves.

"I understand, darling. It's hard to understand how the magical world works sometimes. You could heal Seren, but not this boy. Why?" he asked, pressing a kiss to the top of my head. "The important thing is, Seren could help. Unfortunately, as much as I know we both have wished it, some things you can't do on your own."

The weight of his words settled in my stomach like lead. It was a bitter truth, but he was right. I never could have made it this far without Aldric and I found my mouth forming the words as the thought passed my mind.

"You're certainly right about that one. Your life would have been *dreadfully* boring if I weren't around, my dear," Aldric said with a Cheshire smile, his fangs flashing in the limited light.

"It's not about being boring. It's about survival. I…I need you, Aldric," I said seriously, the lavender hue of my eyes reflected in the silver of his.

Aldric's hand lovingly cupped my chin, his thumb gliding down my cheek. "And I you, my love. My Onyra."

My brow scrunched as the word flowed over me. It felt binding, like an oath. "What does that mean?" I asked, a tingle blooming in my stomach.

"It's an old Vesparan term of endearment. It means '*my forever one*,'" Aldric said with a shyer expression than I'd seen from him.

Was he…*embarrassed*?

"Why now?" I wondered aloud, thinking over all the other pet names he'd given me in our time together.

"It's used for bonded mates, as a proclamation of love," he said, not meeting my eyes as a hint of a blush crept upon his cheeks. He somehow looked both roguish and adorable simultaneously. "It means there will be no other. If not you, then no one."

"So, is it just a term for women?"

Aldric scoffed. "No, it is a term that can be used for men and women. An Onyra is something that comes once in a lifetime. For some, it never comes at all. But when it does, it is such a treasure," he murmured, his voice like cool silk sheets on a hot summer night, inviting you in.

"So, you would be my Onyra," I whispered, testing the word.

Aldric took a sharp inhale of breath, his pupils expanding as we made eye contact. "Tell me again."

Before I could think too much, I reached out and held his face in my hands, streaking it with the wet earth surrounding us.

"My Onyra."

WHISPERED SECRETS

There was only a moment's pause before Aldric crushed his mouth to mine, his tongue sweeping inside, claiming me as thoroughly as if he'd branded me with his name.

I responded with the same fervor, clods of wet earth flinging away from our bodies as we faced towards one another. He was addictive, meeting me kind for kind as we devoured each other.

Pulling myself from the muddied riverbank, I straddled Aldric's lap, to which he loosed a rumbling growl of approval. My hands caressed his muscles as I reached under his shirt, the gentle dusting of hair tickling my fingertips before I tore his shirt off over his head and threw it into the shadows outside of our view.

Aldric's eyes flashed like moonlight in the dark. Ancient, primal energy radiated from him. We were both breathing hard already, the urge to absolutely ravage him tearing through me like wildfire. So this time, I didn't wait for him. I used all of my weight to push his shoulders down until he lay in the wet earth, his hair like a halo of ink around him. He was *beautiful*.

Sodden earth streaked across his chest like war paint from my touch, and I couldn't help the throb at my core at the sight of him. Dirtied by me. Marked by *me*. I felt in control, powerful. This ancient vampire was *mine*.

Aldric watched me with a look of both hunger and arousal. "Take me as you wish, Onyra. I am your instrument of pleasure," he said, his voice sinfully deep.

That's right. No more hesitation. This was about what *I* wanted. He was telling me I could take what I needed.

I planted my hands on either side of Aldric's head, careful to avoid the mass of his hair, and kissed him as though I was trying to pull his soul from his body. Nipping, biting, the energy between us was electric.

The familiar scent of wine and magic flowed between us, driving the heat even higher. Dragging my mouth from his lips, I bit and kissed my way down his neck and chest, my hands following the same path. Every groan or gasp that Aldric made stoked the fire inside of me.

I glanced up to see Aldric's gaze trained on me, his eyes blazing in the surrounding shadows. My nails dug in, leaving raised skin behind. I could feel Aldric's arousal pressed against my core, which pulsed with the need for relief that only he could provide me.

Grinding against him with wanton desire, Aldric's hands flexed at his sides as though he wanted to drive himself into me right then and there.

A feeling of pride spread through me. He wanted me as much as I wanted him. I pulled my shirt over my head, tossing it in the same vague direction that I had thrown his own. Aldric's hands came up to caress my breasts, his fingers tweaking my nipples. I moaned, rubbing myself against him like a cat in heat. The soaked earth left imprints of his touch on me, driving our need even higher.

I fumbled with his pants, and Aldric growled, "Ruin me, Onyra," as he tore at the fastenings himself and shoved his trousers down his hips. I could immediately feel the warmth emanating from his member as it throbbed against me.

Loosening my own bottoms, I ripped them off and finally, sweet relief. The slickness of my arousal was intense, allowing me to glide across his length effortlessly. Aldric purred, low and dangerous.

"My love, please," he rasped. The sound was guttural, less begging and more of a warning. His hands fell to my hips, his grip tightening.

I smiled, leaning down over him and biting down on his throat, the sweet taste that was uniquely him blossoming across my tongue as my teeth lightly pierced his skin. As the intoxicating flavor swirled in my senses, I adjusted so that he was right in my sweet spot. Before he could react, I seated him to the base, filling me completely.

My mouth left him with an audible *pop,* and we both moaned, Aldric bucking up against me instinctively. As I adjusted to his girth, his hands loosened their grip slightly, caressing the sensitive skin at my hips.

"You feel like home, Onyra," Aldric murmured, his voice like sin itself.

In response, I clenched my internal muscles, eliciting a gasp from his lips. "You are where you are meant to be, Aldric," I whispered. With that, I began to move in earnest, my hands planted on his chest.

Every stroke drove us both higher and higher, the tension coiling low in my belly until I almost couldn't take it anymore. Aldric's right hand slid down to the apex of my thighs, reaching between my folds to my most sensitive area. He applied just the right amount of pressure and motion for me to shatter completely, his name escaping my lips in a cry.

With that, Aldric's tentative hold on his control snapped, and his hand returned to my waist, driving himself into me with enough force that my legs almost left the sodden earth around us. He was absolutely feral, pumping his hips with an intensity that left me breathless. I wanted him to pull from me the same way that I did from him, that trickle of darkness at his neck a reminder of his taste.

Aldric's left hand slid up my spine, dragging me down until I lay across his chest, planting his feet for leverage so he didn't have to stop his thrusts. I tilted my head to the side, exposing my throat to him. Aldric did not hesitate, his fangs sinking painlessly into me. He snarled against my skin, pulling from me deeply as he drove into my core.

The sensation of him drinking from me and filling me completely was enough to undo me a second time, stars blooming behind my eyes from the intensity. Though it was a new word to me, my lips formed the word "Onyra," as I came, and Aldric released me with a roar, bucking his hips with animalistic fervor, his release tearing through him in a shuddering wave as he spilled into me.

I collapsed against Aldric, and we both lay there panting. For the first time in a while, my mind was empty.

All I could focus on was the sensation of Aldric's body beneath mine, his heartbeat against my chest.

CHAPTER 28

We lay there together for I don't know how long, just the sound of each other's breathing and the sound of the rushing river to keep us company. I lay with my head on Aldric's chest, the mud on my skin having dried to crackling dirt. For once, my mind was quiet, empty, and there was a sense of contentment. From Aldric or myself, I didn't know.

Then his voice, low and velvety, broke the stillness.

"So," he drawled, his hand tracing a line up and down my spine. "What exactly were you doing out here, sitting in the mud looking like a drowned kitten? I could feel the storm within you, but you're still blocking me out."

I grimaced against him. "It wasn't like that."

"Don't lie," he said lightly, though I could hear the edge underneath his words. The gentleness of his touch caused tingles to break out over my skin, coaxing me. "Your walls are high enough to keep out the most mighty of armies. And yet, you cannot hide from me, Onyra."

I sighed, turning my face towards the stars, their serene light flowing down onto us like a sprinkling of rain. It was a harsh contrast to the turmoil twisting me up inside.

"Aldric, I…" I frowned, the words escaping me. "How do I put this?"

I paused, mulling the words over in my head while Aldric continued his fingers' delicate path over my flesh. "I feel like I'm just failing, over and over." My chin quivered as silent tears welled in my eyes, but I bit my lip, willing them away.

Aldric hummed, giving me a squeeze. "How do you figure, my love?"

"I don't know how I healed Seren. I poured magic into her, and it was like something shifted inside of her, but I don't know *why*. Then, I tried the same thing with that boy, but it didn't work." The admission tasted sour in my mouth. "And yet, Seren could do it. Why? How?"

I squeezed my eyes shut, the starlight just reminding me of Aldric's silvery gaze.

"Maybe it's just not something you can do yourself," Aldric murmured. "The Fae magic is ancient, wild. Not something easily understood by the mages of today—maybe that's why there was no cure before."

"You mean like I'm filtering my magic through her?" I asked, incredulous.

As soon as the words came out of my mouth, I went silent, thinking hard back to the water spirit. "Before you came, there was a creature that appeared in the river."

Aldric cocked an eyebrow while I continued, "I can only guess it was from Ler, but it was telling me something about a river and ocean. That where they meet the water is purest."

Pushing myself up off of Aldric's chest, I sat straddling his lap, adrenaline coursing through me with enough force that my hands began to shake. "Maybe that's what it meant! I am the river and she is the ocean, and it's through combining my magic with hers that we can spread the cure."

I slapped a hand down onto Aldric's chest in excitement, bouncing in place. A playful glint sparkled in his eyes as he placed a hand on my thigh, stopping my movement.

"If you keep that up, we'll have to celebrate now and not later," he purred, and my cheeks reddened as I felt his enthusiasm grow.

I cleared my throat, looking away from his smoky gaze. "I don't think now would be the best time. Let's get cleaned up and head back—I think it would be a good idea to talk to Louise about this."

But despite my words, I couldn't help but tease him, rolling my hips against him before standing. Aldric stood naked in all his glory, his perfection only highlighted by the streaks of earth on his body. My gaze trailed down his body, getting stuck on a… particular part, before sliding back up to his eyes. He had the same teasing warmth within them I'd grown to appreciate.

After a quick cleanup in the river, we stood dripping with water but much cleaner than before. I wrung my hair out unceremoniously a little ways from the river in a patch of grass, hunting for my clothes. With a blink, my eyes changed into a cat's, allowing me to see better in the dark. I quickly located my pants and shirt, pulling them on and cringing as I felt the sodden mud that still clung to the fabric.

Aldric followed closely behind, caressing the curve of my backside through my pants, causing me to shiver. I felt his satisfaction flowing through the bond and allowed him to feel some irritation back, though it was false. He chuckled, throwing his own clothes on as we readied to head back to Louise's house.

Eventually I found my shoes, tugged them on and we circled back to where the rest of the group waited for us. Koto chuffed in disapproval when she saw us, and I fought the urge to look away from her luminous emerald eyes, giving her a pet instead. She nosed my hand, and we opened the door, heading inside to see what awaited us.

The boy was sitting up, a blanket wrapped around his thin shoulders. He had bright yellow eyes, and when he looked at you, it was unnerving. Almost like you were a mouse and he, the owl that waited to clutch you in its talons. I suppressed a shudder and turned to Louise and Seren. Aldric slid his arm around my waist, grounding me.

"Sorry," I blurted. "For running away, I mean."

Louise chuckled. "We've all had days like that, Lyra. And given everything that you've been through, I think it's understandable. You're just lucky you have such a man to bring you back instead of someone like my ex-husband." Her face twisted in disgust. "Looked like a toad—and acted like one too."

Her words caused my lips to quirk up in a hesitant smile. Seren stood, walking over to me and taking my hands in hers. Her dark hair was a halo of shadow around her face, her moss-green eyes vibrant and full of life. She truly looked like one of the Fae—mysterious, timeless, with centuries of wisdom behind her gaze.

However, as soon as her hands touched mine, my magic tried to pool between us, and I recoiled, unsure what to feel or do.

The boy silently watched the exchange, Louise as well. Aldric's body was warm at my back, and I returned my hands to Seren's, taking a deep breath.

"There was a creature in the forest," I murmured. "One I think was sent by someone I know. A river spirit. It told me I need you, Seren."

My magic stretched between us, filling every crack and crevice it could find before washing back to me like a tidal wave, almost like it was marking something within Seren.

"I had a feeling that was the case," she whispered. "It was something about your power—or no, our power together. That is what I felt when you healed me. And it left a trace behind. That trace flowed into the boy and is what allowed him to wake. Here again, as we touch, it does the same, replacing what was lost and given to him."

She gestured at the boy, slowly pulling away from my clammy grip. "He has been awake for a while, but he hasn't had much to say.

Have you?" she said, turning to look at the young man.

He shook his head wordlessly as Louise stood, bustling around the kitchen and returning with a cup of tea for him. He looked down into the amber liquid, but grimaced and set it aside. Louise just tutted and returned to her seat.

"He won't eat or drink anything either," Louise said disapprovingly. "But he is so awfully thin."

Guilt trickled through me as I saw the hint of a bruise underneath the blanket, and before I could think better of it, I sat on the cot with the boy. His eyes were lifeless. His jaw tightened as I got close, and he fisted his hands in the blanket as though ready to flee at a moment's notice.

There was something about him that resonated with me.

Something familiar in the way he glanced towards the door and back, the fear that emanated from him. Instinctively, my hand reached for his, and before he could pull away, my fingers brushed his. In that singular moment, my power touched something within him I hadn't been able to feel before, and I understood.

"I see," I murmured, my gaze tracing over his face, the bags under his eyes, the way his clothes hung off of his slight frame. "It must be hard for you."

The boy scoffed, though he said nothing.

"Darling, be careful," Aldric warned, though there was no reason. This child wouldn't hurt me. Something inside me knew it with the utmost certainty.

I waved him off, and Louise picked up the tension, shooing Aldric and Seren out of the room and leaving the young man and me by ourselves.

"So, you're some kind of mix, huh?" I asked when we were alone. The boy started as though I had shocked him, sputtering.

"How could you possibly know?" he finally said, eyeing me suspiciously. His voice was soft, melodic. It reminded me of the way Aldric spoke.

I just stared at him, not sure how much to say. But then I decided to be honest. "I have transformation magic. Part of that allows me to become other people, so I can feel their power within them too."

His face shifted between disgust and curiosity, finally settling on the latter. "Anyone?"

I nodded my head slowly. "Yeah."

His face twisted in disbelief in a way that only a teenager's could. "Prove it."

Reaching my hand out to his clammy fingers again, I transformed into the young man in front of me, and he gasped, pushing me away. That fast, I was myself again. It had been a long time since I'd used my powers that way, and I cringed, rubbing at my stomach a little while my magic settled back into its place.

"How can you even *do* that?" he asked, aghast. He lost what little color he had in his cheeks and looked almost like he would lose consciousness again.

"It's the curse I was given," I said with a shrug, shoving a strand of white hair behind my ear. "And here I am, trying to find a way to live with it."

Silence lapsed between us for what could have been minutes or just a few seconds before the boy hung his head with a sigh. "I know how that feels."

I crossed my legs at the end of the cot, facing towards him. "Do you feel comfortable telling me about it?"

He refused to meet my eyes, his gaze trained on the floor past my shoulder.

"There's not much to tell. I lived in a village not too far from here. Everyone got sick—most of them died or left. I didn't get sick. Not at first, at least," he mumbled. "But my family…"

His eyes grew bright with unshed tears, and his voice faded into nothingness.

When he didn't continue, my gut twisted painfully. "I'm sorry."

The boy clenched his fists, shaking his head slightly. "It's okay. They weren't *really* my family anyway, I guess. That's what they told me at the end."

He closed his eyes and flopped back on the thin pillow, one arm flung over his face. "I don't think they told me to be mean. I think they just wanted me to know. They loved me. Or at least I think they did."

I hesitantly placed a hand on his bony knee. "I'm sure they did. What's your name?"

He shifted his arm just enough that I could see his eye looking at me from underneath. "Casper. You?"

"Lyra."

Feeling stupid, I held my hand out for him to shake. There was a beat where he didn't move, but he slowly sat up and gripped my fingers in his, tentatively moving our hands up and down before releasing me.

The silence was intensely awkward. How do people deal with teenagers?

"So what are you going to do with me now?" Casper asked, shadows crawling within his luminous gold eyes, dulling them.

His question caught me off guard. I didn't know. There was just a part of me that felt protective of Casper, despite not knowing him. He reminded me of…myself. There was no one to protect me at his age.

"What do you want to do?" I asked in return.

Casper's eyes went round with surprise. "Why are you asking me? I'm just a kid."

"Because you should have some say. Besides, you're almost an adult," I said with a wave of my hand.

He didn't seem to know how to respond. His expression was dark, his sunken cheeks making it look more severe.

"You don't have to decide right now," I said gently, making my way off of the cot and planting my feet on the floor. "In the meantime, why don't you have some of this tea?"

Casper shook his head slowly. "It doesn't taste good."

Cocking my head to the side, I meandered over to the side

table with the tea set still sitting there, steam rising. It must be enchanted to keep the tea warm, I realized. Giving it a sniff, I slowly took a sip. The flavor of fruits and honey burst across my tongue, and my eyes slipped closed of their own accord.

"What do you mean? Have you tried it?" I asked, savoring the taste.

"Nothing tastes good since my family died," Casper said, melancholy.

He carefully disentangled himself from the blankets and tried to stand before falling back onto the bed. Before I even realized what had happened, the tea was forgotten on the side table and I was by Casper's side, easing him down.

My heart sank as his fragility really sank in. He felt too light, too easily broken.

"Was your family human?" I asked.

Casper looked exhausted just from that small movement but nodded his head weakly. "At least, I think they were. They told me I wasn't…that I am what I am."

Helping him back into the cot, I scrambled around Louise's home while hunting around for pillows to help Casper sit up. He seemed much more comfortable after that, able to see around the entire room despite his lack of energy.

Considering his words, I gave a quick incline of my head and straightened my spine.

"Okay. I think you should get some rest, Casper," I began. At the panic blossoming in his eyes, I couldn't help but soften towards him, my hand reaching out to touch his too-thin arm.

"I'll still be here. I just have to go talk to everyone else for a bit."

Casper glowered, his lips tugging downwards. He looked like he wouldn't say anything, but as I walked towards the front door, his voice floated after me.

"You're really not going to leave, right?"

I couldn't help my lips from quirking up, though I didn't show it. Still facing away from Casper, I held my hand up. "Just call for me if you need me. I'll be just outside."

When a quiet 'okay' reached my ears, I tugged open the heavy wooden door and stepped out into the remnants of Haleshade.

CHAPTER 29

A little ways from Louise's cottage, but still close enough that I'd be able to hear Casper if he called out, there was a bench. I plopped down on it, scrubbing my hands over my face.

The last time I saw this bench, there were children hanging all over it and the scent of fresh-baked bread in the air. The sound of laughter.

Now it's too quiet, and there's a faint odor of decay. I hated what Aethralis had become. Without this sickness, Casper would still have a family.

Pressing the heels of my palms into my eyes, a throbbing pain flared in my head. There were too many considerations to make. How did Casper's family know what he was? Why did they keep him if they were human? Just what was he? There were two conflicting wavelengths within him that made a discordant harmony, rather than flowing like magic typically would.

How could I help him eat? What could make food and

drink taste better? If that didn't get figured out, he'd soon die just from malnutrition or dehydration.

A faint sense of curiosity crawled up my spine. The scent of night, of wine and storms surrounded me as Aldric sat next to me, his arm immediately curling around my shoulders.

"I take it your talk went well?" Aldric purred in my ear, causing goosebumps to rise over my skin.

"As well as it could have, I suppose," I grumbled. "But I don't know what to do about it."

Aldric leaned into me, his chest brushing my cheek as he moved closer. Without thinking, I laid my head there, listening to the steady thumping of his heart through the threadbare fabric of his shirt.

"That's right, Onyra," Aldric murmured, his voice growing throatier, more smoky. "Come."

Color crept across my cheeks as his words evoked a different thought, but I cleared my throat, determined not to get distracted. "Casper's not human."

He chuckled, nuzzling into my hair. "Of course not. Casper is the boy's name, I assume?"

I dipped my chin once in response.

"Did he tell you what form of mutt he is?" Aldric asked casually. Almost too casually.

I sat up and slapped his arm away, and I knew my face was flushed with anger. "Don't call him that. He can't help being what he is."

Aldric slid a hand behind my neck and gently persuaded me back against the hardness of his body, which I begrudgingly allowed. "My apologies, Onyra. My upbringing comes out sometimes despite my best efforts," he said, his voice earnest.

"Don't say something like that around him or I won't forgive you," I threatened, my voice sharp.

"You have my word. I can't have that," Aldric said, his hand sliding down my side and settling on my hip.

"I mean it," I said firmly.

"As do I," he said, giving me a squeeze. "It would crush me to have you angry with me. At least, for more than a few seconds. I can't be perfect *all* the time, after all."

Scowling up at him, he pressed a kiss to my lips, chasing away any other complaints or threats I might have made.

I don't think I'll ever get used to the way he can make me feel with such a small gesture.

"Casper is something I've never heard of or felt before," I began.

"At least part vampire, correct?" Aldric said, though he didn't look at me. His gaze was far away as though he were lost in his thoughts.

"How can you tell?" I asked, incredulous. "I couldn't figure it out even after touching him."

"Give me a little credit, my love. Like recognizes like, after all."

Mulling his words over, I nodded. It made at least some kind of sense that Aldric could tell even if I couldn't, given that he was born and raised among vampires his entire life.

Then it occurred to me. "Aldric, Casper told me that since his family died, no food or drink tastes good to him. Do you know why that would be?"

Aldric's gaze slowly refocused on me as he rubbed my hip. "If I had to guess, his family may have known of his…affliction, and was supplementing his food and drink with blood."

Is that what we would have to do, too? Could he get used to going without?

"I think he's part living vampire. He's certainly got a heartbeat, and I don't know if he could survive being undead as a mix of two Otherkind," I murmured.

"I think you're right, Onyra. But if that's the case…I'm not sure what to do with him."

"What do you mean, 'do with him'? He can stay here, right?"

Aldric's gaze softened, and he cupped my cheek. "Being a living vampire is not a boon. Others will see him as a threat. And if I could recognize him, so will others. It wouldn't be safe for him to be here."

"So what do we do? I'm not going to just throw him out into the world when he doesn't have anyone else," I said, more harshly than I intended. Adrenaline shot through me as I remembered exactly what that felt like. Being completely alone, no one to turn to but yourself. But at least I knew what I was. Casper doesn't have the same benefit.

My voice grew quiet. "He asked me to stay nearby. I think he's afraid of being alone."

Aldric nodded. "Then I will have to help him learn to hide, to survive. I need to find out the range of his vampiric power, but I think we can give him a better chance."

Aldric disappeared into Louise's house to speak with Casper, and I set out to find Seren. It felt like there were too many unknowns—too much I needed to learn about how our power would work together. How to fix this sickness. How to spread the cure across Aethralis and the Starfall Veil.

There was a subtle pull leading me into the forest, and I followed it. After a while of wandering, I found Seren sitting on a tree stump, her legs crossed underneath her. There were animals subtly watching her from the trees, which made me smile. It was like she was the princess of the forest. I could see the appeal. She looked as if she belonged here.

Seren's head hung low, and a curtain of black hair shielded her face from view.

"Where's Koto?" The Feralumin was usually glued to Seren's side, but she was nowhere to be seen.

Her head shot up as though she had been shocked, and I realized she must have been deep in thought.

"Koto wanted to stretch her legs, so I told her to go out. She'll be back before nightfall," Seren said after a moment, her voice whisper-soft.

"Are you okay?" I asked.

"Fine. Just thinking."

Despite her words, her tone was flat. I approached slowly, sitting on a fallen tree. Maybe the same tree as the stump Seren was resting on, though it was hard to tell.

"What are you thinking about?"

"Thorne. How we're going to find him. Where he could have gone," she said with a sigh, shoving her hair back away from her face. "There isn't exactly information brimming out amongst the villages. Most of the people are d—"

She stopped herself short when she saw the look on my face. Seren cleared her throat and dropped her hands into her lap.

"The villages around here are empty. So I'm not sure where to get started," she continued after a moment. Her usually vibrant eyes were dark, shadowed with the weight of her thoughts.

"Where's Louise?" I looked around, but there was no evidence of the healer nearby.

"She went to see if she could find any word of where he might be. I thought it was a good idea. Not wasting time, you know?" The Fae planted her hands behind her and tilted her head up, looking at the clouds lazily drifting past.

My chin dipped, and I mirrored her, my gaze going to the puffy masses floating by. When it was so quiet, it was easy to forget all of your problems. There was no cursed magic, no sickness killing off the world, no responsibilities. Just this moment of calm.

We sat there for a while in companionable silence, neither of us wanting to break the hush between us. However, before long, the sound of crunching sticks and leaves reached our ears, and we sat up, turning almost in unison to the source of the noise—Louise.

She had a wide smile that almost looked out of place on her face. My brows rose in response, and I straightened my spine.

"What are you looking so cheery about?" I asked before I could stop myself.

"I may have a lead," Louise said, her eyes bright.

CHAPTER 30

I stood up so fast I got a head rush and had to steady myself. Seren did the same, and we glanced at each other before turning to Louise.

"A lead how?" I asked, my mouth going dry. I swallowed thickly. This seemed to go too fast.

Louise held her arms out to her sides, as though bestowing a gift upon the forest itself. "I ended up going with Koto. Thought it might be a good idea, given her speed and tracking ability. We ended up a ways away in a town that was touched by sickness but not obliterated by it. There was something different about it that Koto was able to identify."

I was hanging off each word, adrenaline coursing through me. "What do you mean, different?"

"There was something 'off' about it. Almost like someone was trying to re-form or alter the magic that is causing the plague. And the only person who could do that is?" she asked expectantly, her gaze searing into me.

"Thorne," I stated, my hands shaking.

Louise nodded, excitement radiating from her. "Koto is trying to follow the trail before we lose it. But even if she loses track of it, we at least know what direction to search."

It was hours before Koto returned.

In the meantime, Louise, Seren and I had been discussing next steps. The trace power that they had been tracking led to the East, which crosses into Werefolk and human territory. Humans were very particular about who they let into their kingdoms, so it seemed strange that they would allow Thorne. But then it occurred to me.

Just before Thorne had trapped me in his basement in Sylvan Reach, he had given me a special tea. He said it was a gift from the human kingdom of Cairnard in exchange for his healing a member of the royal court. Maybe he used that as leverage to travel there? They would have some amount of trust in him at that point, I would assume.

Louise and Seren easily agreed that could be the case. Otherwise, he could have ended up in one of the Werefolk villages, which would probably have been easier to hide in. The Werefolk were cautious, but not to the extent that humans were.

We would reach the shifter villages before any human towns, so it would be easy enough to follow whatever tracks are left. At least, that was the hope.

Koto was whisper-quiet when she appeared in our midst. There was just the murmur of our voices, then a giant Feralumin was at the edge of our circle, shadows stretching and forming around her. She was panting, which was a strange sight. Even when racing across Sylvan Reach, she'd never once shown any sign of exertion.

Seren's brows rose, and she reached up to bury her fingers in Koto's soft fur.

"You must have gone far," she murmured, stroking the beast's neck.

Koto chuffed in response and unceremoniously flopped down into the cool grass. She curled her paws under her body, becoming a loaf. My lips curled despite themselves. The image was enough to make me laugh, though I stifled the urge.

"Where did you end up?" Seren cocked her head as though listening, despite no words being spoken.

She crossed her arms under her breasts, stiffening. Louise and I glanced at each other before turning back to the pair in front of us.

"It sounds like we'll be crossing the river," Seren said with a sigh. She dragged her fingers through her pitch-black hair, looking suddenly exhausted.

"Let's hope not. You know the legends about the Serathine," I murmured, standing to stretch my legs. It had been a while since I had left Aldric and Casper, and I was starting to get antsy. "I would like some time to discuss this with Aldric and see how he feels about it."

"Missing him already, eh?" Louise asked with a conspiratorial laugh.

My cheeks reddened, and I bit my tongue, holding back a retort.

"You and I can continue discussing next steps, Louise," Seren said easily, drawing the attention away from me. I cast her a grateful look and started back off towards Haleshade. I trusted Aldric, but there was still this niggling feeling in the pit of my stomach that something could go wrong.

Pushing through the rough wooden door, I was greeted by the scent of something delicious. Something rich that filled my senses like a caress. My gaze was drawn to Casper sitting up in bed, heartily digging into a stew. Aldric was sitting on a nearby chair looking smug.

"Lyra!" Casper said excitedly, his mouth full of food. "It's good." His eyes were brighter and more vibrant than I'd ever seen them, and he actually had energy. It warmed my heart to see.

"Don't eat too fast or you'll make yourself sick," Aldric admonished, standing from his perch to come and envelop me in his arms. I melted instantly, the stress I hadn't realized I'd been holding onto leaving my body like smoke in the wind.

Some part of me had been afraid that Casper would say or do something that would require Aldric to retaliate in some way, even though I knew that wasn't logical. If it came down to it, I know he'd come and find me rather than hurt the boy.

The sounds of slurping and chewing filled the air, and I cringed. I was happy, yes, but also, gods, that was uncomfortable to listen to. The color had returned to Casper's cheeks, and he already looked much stronger than he did when I left.

Aldric led me to the corner of the room, where he sat on an armchair. He dragged me down onto his lap, and I snuggled in. It felt both strange and natural how easily my body fit against his. How easy it was to give in to this feeling between us. Almost too easy.

In a way, it was almost like I didn't have a choice. This is where I was meant to be, whether I wanted it or not. Aldric's arms snaked their way around me, lovingly caressing the exposed skin between my shirt and breeches.

For once though, I was just going to enjoy it.

Warmth spread everywhere our bodies met, pooling in my core. I buried my face in his neck, inhaling the scent that was uniquely *him*. The scent of wine and thunderstorms, with a hint of darkness underneath.

One powerful hand crept through my hair and tugged, pulling my head back as I gasped. Taking advantage of my surprise, Aldric crushed his lips to mine, his tongue invading my mouth.

My body was ablaze, yearning for more, but within moments there was an overly dramatic gag and I ripped myself away from our kiss, snapping back into reality. Aldric's sensuous chuckle reached my ears, and my cheeks burned.

"I'm trying to eat over here. Gross," Casper said, scowling. "Get a room."

"Technically, this *is* our room," Aldric said smoothly, mirth lighting up his eyes.

"Well, get a different one," the teenager bit back, full of vitriol.

"That sounds like a good idea," Aldric replied, his eyes sliding down my body before reaching my face, which was still hot with embarrassment. He cradled my body against his, and in a few long strides, we were outside. I heard Casper sputtering behind us, but Aldric just called out that we would be back soon and to keep eating.

"Where to, madam?" Aldric asked, laughter underlying his words.

My mind was completely blank, so I just stared at him until he loosed a dark laugh that flowed across my body like a physical touch. "Sounds like my choice then."

He craned his neck this way and that, looking for something in particular.

"This looks like the fanciest house in this village. Let's go there," he said easily, his long legs eating up the distance before I could reply. I turned to see where we were going and found that it had been the blacksmith's house.

Desperately, I hoped the blacksmith had just left Haleshade, but the more logical side of my brain didn't hesitate to paint all kinds of morbid scenarios.

Those thoughts were dashed when Aldric cracked the door open. There was a screech from the hinges, which desperately needed oiling. There was no odor of decay, no dark spots on the floor. It looked as if he had just moved away. Relief had me going limp in Aldric's arms, and his silvery gaze fell on me, his lips quirking up.

"You should really use your power more, my dear," he said smoothly. "If you did, you could have scented out this house easily."

I looked away, guilt creeping up. "I know I *could*, but just because I have the power doesn't mean I need to use it for something so small."

"And why not? What is the harm?"

"It just doesn't feel right, Aldric," I said firmly, scowling. "It's my magic to use as I wish. That's the only thing I can control out of everything else. Myself."

Aldric gave me a squeeze. "Of course, my love. I understand. But you should still think on my words. It is indeed *your* power, and you shouldn't be ashamed or afraid to use it."

With that, he loosened his grip, and I slid down his body, my feet landing flat on the ground. This *was* a very nice home. Or just a house at this point, I supposed. No one here to make it a home anymore. The furniture was covered in a fine layer of dust, undisturbed for who knows how long. Aldric lit a candle on a nearby end table. I raised my brows, and he winked.

"Pilfered these from Louise's house."

I frowned disapprovingly, and he pushed his inky hair back with his free hand. "How else would I have lit the stove to cook for the boy?" he asked haughtily.

He had me there.

Speaking of… "How did you get him to eat?" I wondered aloud.

"I cooked a delicious stew, of course."

"You know what I mean. He said *any* food tasted bad to him, regardless of how it was prepared."

Instead of answering, Aldric strode to a nearby sofa, dusting it off aggressively. I waved my hand in front of my face, coughing. He stretched out on the couch, taking up more room than one person had any business taking.

"You won't like it," he said cryptically.

A flicker of unease flared to life within me, and Aldric's silvery gaze burned into my flesh as though he could feel it himself.

"Still don't trust me?"

His voice had a soft undertone. Hurt. I carefully made my way over to Aldric, being mindful of the other furniture and fallen bits and bobs on the wooden floor. The blacksmith must have been in a rush when he left.

I perched on the opposite end of the couch, between Aldric's spread legs. "It's not that," I said softly. "I just worry about Casper."

"You must see a lot of yourself in him," Aldric murmured gently. My gaze snapped up to his.

Instead of answering, I suddenly found the dust motes floating through the air very interesting, my jaw tensing.

Silence stretched uncomfortably between us. This was one of the first times in a while I hadn't wanted to talk to him. Talking about my past was… difficult. And the last person I opened up to was no longer around. A flash of sunshine eyes going dull flitted through my mind, and I shook my head, shaking the thought loose.

I hadn't thought of *him* for a while.

Aldric sighed and sat up, pulling away from me. I refused to acknowledge the sting that caused.

"I put blood in his food," Aldric drawled. At my stunned expression, he continued. "It was the only way to keep him from starving. His human family must have been doing this for him for a long time, which is why he's been so confused about why food doesn't taste good anymore."

"Did you tell him?" Despite myself, I was getting worked up.

"Of course not. He is just coming to terms with what he is. Would you rather I tell him and he choose not to eat?" Aldric asked, his mercurial eyes growing dark.

"I feel like he should be able to choose for himself."

"Even if he dies? Is that really what you want, Lyra?" Aldric spat back. "I was doing what I had to do. When he is more healthy, I will tell him."

A pit opened up in my stomach. I knew it was the best thing for Casper, but it still felt *wrong*. And yet, seeing how happy Casper had been with the stew cooled my indignation.

I sighed, my body slowly losing its tension. We can give him the choice once he gets some strength back. Who knows if he's even well enough to make that decision now?

I put my hand on the cushion between us, and without a single hesitation, I felt Aldric's callused hand encompass mine.

"We just need to focus on getting him more stable. Then we can all talk," he said easily, as though the strain between us had never existed to begin with. "But with the flavors of Otherkind that he is composed of, don't be surprised if he bounces back fast."

"What do you mean?"

"Living vampires are quick to recover once they receive blood. I assume it would be the same for whatever else is flowing through his little body," Aldric started. "Besides, I used my own blood."

My eyes went round, and I pulled my hand away from his, ignoring the chill left behind. "Your blood? Why?"

"Would you prefer I go and pilfer some blood from an innocent person? Or are you offering yourself up?" he asked flatly, throwing his arm over the back of the couch and reclining.

Frowning, my mind raced with other options, only to find none.

"Besides, my blood is powerful. It should help bolster him more than some weak, sickly human's. No offense."

"What will it do to him? Will it make him more vampire?" I asked.

"Not unless it is given with that intent. And it wasn't. Besides, in his case, I'm not exactly sure," Aldric admitted. "It just felt like the right thing to do."

After a pause, he nudged me with his fingertips, and I leaned back into the side of his body, melting into him.

"You know, I came here with more salacious thoughts in mind rather than a talk about morality and some other man," Aldric said breezily. "A young man, but still."

I slapped his arm, a laugh bubbling out of my throat. "You can't be serious."

His arm curled around my waist and lifted me to place me on his lap, showing just how serious he was.

"Allow me to see if I can set the mood," he said before descending upon me like a man starved.

CHAPTER 31

A short while later, the sun had descended, and a chill laced the air. My clothes were carefully back in place, my hair smoothed. And, surprisingly, no love bites to show off. A smile curved my lips, and Aldric sighed pleasantly, tucking my hand into the crook of his arm as we made our way back to Louise's house.

When we crossed the threshold, my stomach dropped. Casper's bed was empty. Adrenaline blasted through my veins like lightning, and I raced over, throwing the blankets as though he could be underneath the thin fabric. Aldric put his hand on my back and jerked his head towards the bathroom, where I realized we could hear water running.

"Casper?" I called, my voice sounding higher-pitched than I would like.

"Yeah?" Casper's muffled voice floated out from underneath the door.

After a beat, I took a breath and let it out of my nose.

"Nothing, just making sure you were okay. Take your time."

My legs gave out, and I collapsed onto Casper's bed, shaking.

Aldric was in front of me in the space of a single breath, taking my face in his hand. "Are you okay?"

I nodded, suddenly exhausted. "I just don't know what to expect anymore. Someone could have taken him."

"He's almost a grown man, my love. Much as he feels like a child. And we were close enough, we would have heard if he called out."

My chin dipped again, then fell back. I felt so drained all of a sudden. I shouldn't be this up in arms about some boy I'd just met, but it felt like I needed to protect him. Like something in me recognized something in him, and he just couldn't come to harm.

"I'm sorry," I mumbled. "I shouldn't have overreacted when he was gone."

The bed dipped as Aldric sat next to me. "It's understandable, love. You've got strong maternal instincts, it seems. Suitable for a future queen," he said, mirth in his voice.

My eyes snapped open, and I picked my head up, glaring at him. "I will never just be an incubator—much less a queen. Besides, children have never been a conversation for us."

The words came out more forcefully than I intended, but at the same time, an image formed in my mind of a chubby baby with a mop of inky waves and amethyst eyes. The perfect mix of the two of us.

But who knew if things would ever be peaceful enough? I would never bring a child into a world this tumultuous.

The thought dissolved in my mind like ash, and Aldric's hand slid up my hip. "I know you, my Onyra. Someday," he said teasingly.

Ignoring the heat radiating from his touch, I let my head hit the bed and slid my eyes closed yet again. All the emotions lately are really wearing on me.

I felt a powerful pair of arms slide underneath my body and carry me over to a different cot, chilly from the emptiness, but soon warmed with Aldric's body as he cradled me against him. My mind went blank, and I knew no more.

The sound of the door closing jolted me out of sleep, and I sat up, wiping drool from my cheek with a grimace. Casper was sitting in a chair nearby, Louise and Seren looked shocked. And I could see why. He was almost a different person. Lean muscle filled out his clothes, and his cheeks were no longer sunken in, his eyes bright with energy and intelligence.

"What happened to you?" I asked, mouth agape.

"Nothing. I just started feeling way better after I finished the food that guy gave me, so I wanted to get cleaned up," Casper said, looking confused.

"You mean Aldric?" I asked absently, my mind racing.

Is this what he meant when he said living vampires recover

quickly? *This* quickly? That was unbelievable. He went from looking at death's door to looking almost completely healthy in a matter of hours. It didn't even feel possible.

"Yeah, that guy," he said, nodding to the body behind me.

I turned to see Aldric with his head propped up on his hand, smiling at me like a cat with a bowl of cream as though to say, 'I told you so'.

His hair cascaded down his shoulders like a waterfall of night, stark against the off-white of his shirt, and his eyes were luminous.

Scowling at Aldric, the expression melted from my face as I turned back towards the young man across the room. "How do you feel?"

"Normal, I guess. Why?" Casper asked, frowning.

My eyes met Seren's over his shoulder, and she wore an expression of bafflement that I'm sure mirrored my own.

"Just wanted to check."

It occurred to me that Casper must not have realized just how bad off he was when he got here. It's not like we held a mirror in front of his face showing just how skeletal he had looked.

"You look great!" Louise burst out. "I'm so happy."

Her eyes were like emeralds, bright with excitement and joy. I couldn't help but return her smile. Some part of me that had been twisted up inside loosened, and I couldn't help but chuckle with relief.

Aldric nuzzled into my shoulder, and I felt a tingle as his fingers traced a line up my spine through my top. I shuddered involuntarily and leaned back against him, grateful despite how I felt about the deceit involved in helping Casper.

The teenager looked between each of the adults with a befuddled expression before joining hesitantly in the laughter filling the room.

All the stress crushing me seemed to melt away, and I couldn't stop giggling, tears running from the corners of my eyes. Finally, something good. We did something right. My stomach ached, and I leaned over, wheezing. Casper's laugh turned genuine, and he pointed at me as though to ask, 'what's wrong with you'?

I couldn't breathe to respond, but slowly the cackling subsided, leaving me feeling light as air.

It was some time later that Koto returned.

We had shared a meal—Aldric handling Casper's bowl—and talked about our lives. Mostly Seren. We were all so curious about what it was like in Starfall Veil. She regaled us with tales of growing up as a Fae in a world saturated entirely in mana.

How she and Koto met and became friends, about her family and how unusual it was because she had more than one sibling. Most Fae chose to have smaller families, except for hers.

She had such a luminous smile on her face as she recalled life in the Veil, it made me feel a pang of guilt that she had to come here with us. Though I tried not to show it, Aldric pulled me closer as though he could sense my discomfort. Maybe he could—it was hard to tell sometimes.

Seren had turned towards the door before Koto announced her arrival with a chuff. The joy in the room seemed to be sucked out like a black hole, because we all knew what this meant. She had information for us. Seren glanced back at me with a subtle nod before unfolding her legs from beneath her and striding outside.

Casper frowned, the sudden change in tension clear.

"Are you guys okay?" he asked, glancing between Louise and me.

"Yeah, we're fine. We just have someone we're trying to find," Louise said darkly.

"I see," he said, though from the tone of his voice, he didn't understand. "Why did Seren go outside? And what made that noise?"

Of course. Casper had been mostly unaware of what was going on when he was brought on Koto's back to come here.

"Don't be afraid, but it's a Fae beast," I said hesitantly. "They're called Feralumin in Starfall Veil."

Casper's expression was blank. "What is a Fae beast?"

Aldric slid out of the cot, prim as ever, and motioned at Casper. "I'll show you."

Casper followed Aldric outside without hesitation, and I heard a noise of surprise as the door shut behind them, though it was quickly stifled. Between one breath and the next, he jerked the door open with force, slamming it into the wall, and hurried back inside.

His eyes were almost comically wide, and he was breathing hard. Aldric came strolling back inside without a care in the world.

"What the hell is that thing?" Casper gasped out. "It's huge!"

"I told you. It's a Feralumin," I said gently. "People don't normally see them. They are native to Starfall Veil and aren't usually around different Otherkind."

"I can see why!" he said, indignant. "They would try to kill them!"

I shook my head. "Her name is Koto. She's the one who brought you here."

I don't know how it was possible, but his eyes opened even wider. "I was *on* that thing?"

My chin dipped, and I waved my hand. "We've all been on Koto at some point or another. She's really not that scary once you get used to her."

Casper stiffly sat in the chair near the cot I was perched on.

"Are there more…*things* like that?" he asked quietly, his yellow eyes fever-bright with adrenaline.

"I'm sure there are. But Koto is usually pretty good about keeping us safe. Don't be scared. She wouldn't be here if she were a danger to us," I said matter-of-factly. "Besides, you heard Seren. They grew up together. She knows Koto like the back of her hand."

"The way she talked about Koto, I thought she was a *person*, not a monster!" he hissed.

I furrowed my brow, the corners of my mouth lowering in disappointment. "Don't call her that. She's our friend. And Fae creatures aren't the same as animals are here. They're incredibly intelligent, and Fae they are bonded with can communicate with them. She's not just some dumb animal."

Casper's gaze slid towards the door, distrust emanating off of him in waves.

"You'll see. She's not bad," I said firmly. "Besides, you have us to keep you safe too."

Aldric sidled up next to me, giving Casper a conspiratory wink. "She won't be hungry for a few days, anyway. So even if you were on the menu, it wouldn't be for a while yet."

Casper's mouth fell open, and I slapped at Aldric's arm, shooting him a glare. "Don't listen to him. Feralumin don't eat people."

"I'll have Seren introduce you to her properly later," I assured him. "She's really not that scary."

Casper glanced between the door and me, clearly not trusting it. "We'll see about that."

Seren came in about fifteen minutes later looking somber. Koto's silhouette was visible through the door behind her before she gently closed the door. The Feralumin's face popped up outside the window near the door, nosing at the glass. Seren slid the frame of the window open, allowing Koto to feel included.

"She told me there's a town to the east that's saturated in mana. It appears to be full of Werefolk," she started, scrubbing a hand down her face. She shoved blue-black strands of hair behind her ears, sighing.

"How far?" Louise asked, taking a sip of tea while sitting in the single armchair in the cabin.

"If we could all ride Koto, about three days' travel."

Casper made a noise beside me, but I ignored him.

"And if not?" I asked.

"It would take a few weeks. It's across the Serathine River."

CHAPTER 32

Stillness fell over the room like a living thing. My heartbeat was pounding in my ears. The Serathine. It was only spoken of vaguely in ancient stories in Sylvan Reach. All we knew was to never go there. No living mage even knew what it looked like. Or at least, none I knew.

Aldric was deathly quiet next to me. How much did Vesparans know about this place? It wouldn't be of much consequence to the vampires, given that the river veered away from their kingdom, but he'd also lived so long, he must know about it.

There was no avoiding it. Louise clapped her hands together with a sense of finality. The sudden sharp noise caused me to jump. She stood and began rifling through cabinets, throwing various things into a pack.

"What are you doing?" Seren asked, her gaze snapping from one person to the next.

"No time to waste, dear. We have somewhere to be. Right?"

Louise sounded so matter-of-fact, it was hard to disagree with her.

I slowly stood and began packing my own meager belongings.

Aldric made a noise of protest, but I ignored him. He must have felt my determination flowing through our bond because he sighed.

"Off we run to death yet again, I suppose," Aldric said with a dark chuckle.

Dawn trickled through the canopy overhead in a pastel kaleidoscope of colors. Finally. After weeks of trudging through deep thickets of woods, barren fields, and at one point, a shoe-stealing mud pit of a marsh, the trees were thinning.

Somehow, Aldric managed to…acquire a couple of horses. He had returned with a devilish grin, though I knew better than to ask how he'd gotten them.

Casper was atop a chestnut mare, and Louise rode a painted gelding. The mare was on the older side, so our pace had to go a little slower than expected, but still faster than walking. Casper absolutely refused to ride on Koto, so we had no other choice aside from leaving him behind. But every part of me screamed I couldn't, so horses it was.

An earthy, mineral scent lingered on the air, and I could hear rushing water ahead. The sight that greeted us wasn't what I had expected. The few people we had encountered on our travels pointed us in this direction, but what came into view was a cliff. Sliding off of Koto's back, I hesitantly approached the edge, careful not to get too close.

Below, I could see a river writhing like a serpent, dark currents twisting beneath the surface, slamming into one another with a violence that made my breath catch in my throat.

A boundary that whispered of deadly secrets.

This was the Serathine.

Slowly we made our way down the cliff face, thin trails scarring the rock and earth. Koto merely jumped off of the edge like it was little more than a house cat going from a coffee table to the floor, but even Seren did not trust riding Koto's back during that freefall.

The horses navigated the terrain with surprising ease, so we had the horses in front and did our best to follow the path they laid out. After some time and a few scares, we finally reached the riverside.

The water up close was different from what I'd seen from the cliff. It was like a dark void with a mirror's sheen surface. What happened to the chaos from above? The waves clashing? It was almost like we were in a completely different place. A pit opened in my stomach, every instinct urging me away from the water.

A hand landed on my shoulder, and a yelp escaped me before

I could stop it. Aldric leaned in close to the curve of my ear, his voice soothing my frazzled nerves.

"There is something wrong here, Onyra. I don't know what, but I don't like it. We should try to find a way to cross quickly."

I could see the same unease reflected in each of our faces—even the horses danced in place as if eager to depart.

"Is there a bridge or a ford or something?" I asked the group.

Koto huffed and turned north, her silent footfalls eerie next to the still water of the river.

My gaze slid towards Seren, and she shrugged, her trust in Koto absolute. Once Koto realized we were following, she waited to allow some of us to hitch a ride. Casper continued to look at us with disgust, but he still cautiously followed, back atop the mare, his golden eyes dark and wary.

Louise trailed behind Casper, the gelding dancing nervously. I glanced back to see her rubbing her hand along its broad neck gently, her lips moving as she whispered to the young horse. Whatever she had to say seemed to relax the horse, though it stayed as far from the water's surface as it could.

There was a sense that there was something *alive* about the river. Something that was watching us. Waiting. *Hungry*.

After a couple of hours, we came across the remains of a stone bridge. Parts had crumbled away with age, but what was left was beautifully reflected in the water. It created a perfect circle, almost like a portal to another realm. As we approached, the remaining stonework was worse than it looked from afar. There were sizeable gaps in the foundation, and it seemed like only one arch remained, leaving only enough space for us to travel across one at a time.

The Serathine seemed impossibly wide, and I swallowed hard at the prospect of such a small space preventing me from touching the surface of the water. Aldric, sensing my growing dread, wrapped an arm around my waist as he helped me off of Koto's back.

Seren was looking between Koto and the remnants of the bridge, a furrow forming between her brows. The tension was palpable. The bridge was too narrow, the river too wide for Koto to cross. She seemed to have the realization at the same time I did, her hackles raising and a low rumbling growl erupting from her chest.

Seren immediately tried to soothe the Feralumin, speaking to her in hushed tones.

"Koto will have to stay behind," I murmured, though the words carried over the smooth surface of the water.

Casper slid off of the mare, who whinnied as if in protest.

"Well, that's not a bad thing is it?" he asked, seeming far too chipper for what we were facing.

"Yes, yes it is. We'll have to make the rest of the journey

mostly on foot," Louise said matter-of-factly. "There aren't enough horses for everyone."

Casper scowled as if she had kicked a puppy.

"I could always...procure us more transport," Aldric interjected smoothly.

Louise also joined us on the ground, the gelding moving to stand by the mare as if seeking protection. "You can't do that if there are no people nearby. Use that ancient brain of yours before it turns to ash," she said, disapprovement dripping from her words.

Hurt flowed from Aldric, and I reached a hand out to him before I even thought about it, gripping his callused fingers in mine. He gave me a grateful squeeze.

"Well, do we know *where* the nearest village is around here?"

Louise sounded exasperated. "I swear, none of you kids know anything about geography."

She clucked her tongue and pulled a compass out of her bag, along with a curled piece of paper with some vague lines etched onto it.

"This is the best idea I've got—we on the West side of the Serathine don't make this journey much. Especially not since..." her words quieted, but her gaze slid to me with an almost guilty expression.

"But nevermind that," she said, clearing her throat. "When I realized where we would have to go, I pulled this old—and I do mean *old*—map from my stores. It may not be all that accurate anymore, but the Werefolk tend to pick a location and stick to it, so we may get lucky."

"How do you know that?" Casper asked, his dark brows raised.

Again, moss green eyes fell to me and slid away. "I knew someone once. He came from around here."

A pang of sadness prickled at me, but less than before. Slowly, I was moving on. The memories were becoming less painful, the loss less fresh.

Seren meandered over to the group hesitantly. "Koto isn't happy about this."

Louise waved her off with the grace only someone with a lot of hard years under their belt could have. "We don't have a choice. And neither does she. It will be safer for her on this side. Unless she wants to cross herself?"

At those words, a deep huff sounded from Koto's direction, and I glanced over to see her pacing back and forth, puffed up with agitation.

"I don't trust Koto getting into the water. There's something…off about it." I glanced at the water, which seemed to stare back. A shiver ran down my spine that had nothing to do with the chill in the air.

"Can you talk her into staying in the area?" Aldric asked, his dark brows drawing downward.

"I can try," Seren said, making her way back over to her furred friend.

After some time, Seren returned.

"She is going to find another way to cross that is safe. She'll be able to find us. If she cannot, she will wait here for our return," Seren said, a hint of pride in her voice. Koto was resolute, the words barely leaving Seren's mouth before she bounded off into the distance.

The sun was high overhead at this point, the sky a warm blue that seemed to chase away the coolness in the air. And yet, the water of the Serathine was pitch black, as though light could not penetrate the surface.

"Let's not waste any time then. Who's first?" Louise asked, her gaze falling on each of us expectantly.

Swallowing hard, I cleared my throat. "It would be safest for me to go first."

Aldric immediately interjected, "Absolutely not. You are not going across that pit of death before we know it's not dangerous."

"If the bridge crumbles, I can transform into something that can fly. I'm the least likely to actually fall in," I said, scowling. I was not weak. My power may be hated across Aethralis, but it did have its uses.

Louise nodded. "I agree with Lyra. She would be the best person to go first."

Aldric crossed his powerful arms across his chest, tension making his muscles strain against the fabric of his tan shirt. "And why not you, then? You're like a fine wine—well aged. Less to lose."

Louise scoffed. "If that bridge crumbles, I'll be crumbling right along with it. But I'm the only one who knows proper healing magic in this group. It wouldn't be wise to lose me now."

She was right, of course.

"The elf then." Aldric was not giving up.

"I'm not an elf. I'm Fae," Seren said, affronted. "There is something off about the river. And as powerful as I am, I cannot levitate."

Aldric clearly wanted to argue further, but thankfully he did not even try to suggest that Casper cross first. The young man was silently standing in the background, seemingly wanting to disappear, judging by his hunched posture.

"What if we sent one of the horses?" Seren suggested, her brows climbing towards her hairline. "If that bridge can support a horse, it can definitely support one of us."

Aldric's eyes lit up like the moon, bright with excitement. "That, my dear, is an excellent idea. As long as it's not my Onyra. I would go myself first."

"You would not," I admonished. "Everyone needs you."

Aldric strode towards me purposefully. "You mean *you* need me, surely?" He tipped my chin up with a finger until I was looking in his eyes. He stole my breath every time with his beauty, but now was no time to revel in the feelings he brought forth.

I jerked my head back, and Aldric chuckled. Louise was giving us a knowing look, and my cheeks flared with heat.

"Which horse?" I asked, desperate to break the tension

between Aldric and me.

"I would say the mare," Louise said, jerking her thumb at the horse for emphasis. "She's older, more careful. She would be the most likely one to cross safely. The younger one is too skittish, I think, and he'd need someone to lead him."

Aldric was nodding along with her words, emphasizing each point.

He clicked his tongue at the mare, and without hesitation, she trotted over to his side. The ease with which he could communicate with this horse brought to mind the one he had lost when we were first brought to Starfall Veil.

Nocturne. The inky black stallion. I hoped fervently that he was still alive out there somewhere, living happily with his counterpart, Lune, who was as pale as winter frost.

I would have to ask Aldric about them later. Would they know to go back to Vespara? He did say that they were incredibly intelligent animals. I shook my head, dislodging that random train of thought.

While I was lost in memories, Aldric had led the mare over to the edge of the bridge. It was a sight, for sure. That bridge, despite how derelict it had become, still created a perfect circle with its reflection. The craftsmanship was something to behold. But it was steep. Aldric urged the mare to start the journey to the other side, and she hesitantly began to walk.

The sharp click of hooves rapping against stone rang out, slowly fading as the equine got further and further along. It was a slow and meticulous trip, but eventually she had reached land on the other side. There were a few instances where dust fell to mar the surface of the river for but a moment, nothing substantial.

My gaze locked with Aldric's, and I could sense his anxiety, but with a deep breath, I started towards the stone bridge, ignoring the prickling of my skin.

CHAPTER 33

The moment my booted foot landed on the bridge, it felt as though a spear of ice shot through me. There was just something inherently *wrong* with this place.

But I didn't have a choice.

I grit my teeth and pushed on, each step slow and deliberate. There were a few gaps I had to be mindful of, but there was enough of the bridge remaining that I didn't worry about falling in.

At the apex of the bridge, I nearly lost my footing and stumbled. Aldric called my name, but I held a hand up to show I was fine. My gaze had dropped to the waters below, and what I saw there had my skin crawling. I could see myself reflected in the Serathine. But it wasn't *me*, but some distorted version of me. My skin was rotting away. My eyes had sunk into pits on my face. Bile rose in my throat, and I forced it back down.

For a split second, there was a figure next to me. I caught the impression of dusky gray skin and pointed ears.

"The twisted trees hide the disorder. Don't forget this," a smooth male voice murmured into the shell of my ear. A violent shiver wracked my body in response. My head snapped up, and I spun, trying to catch whoever had spoken to me, but there was no one.

"Are you okay, Onyra?" Aldric called.

Shaking my arms out to break away from the nervous energy, I called back that I was fine and continued the journey to where the mare waited, watching with wide eyes.

It must have only been a few minutes, but it felt like hours before I was back on solid ground and away from that hellish river. I strode several paces away before my knees gave way beneath me from the relief.

Only seconds later, Aldric appeared next to me, enfolding me in his arms. The scent that was uniquely *him* soothed me even further, and I sighed, nestling into his touch.

"Please don't do anything like that ever again," Aldric murmured into my hair. "I can't tell you how nervous that had me."

"Me too," I admitted, a shaky laugh leaving my lips.

"Go keep watch for the others," I said, shooing him away. Regret immediately filled me as the warmth of his touch left me feeling bereft.

I watched Aldric call out a few times to Casper, offering guidance on where to step and what to avoid. His hair was a mess, but he was still a sight to behold no matter what. Warmth blossomed in my chest. He really cared about Casper, too. It was nice to see.

As if sensing my growing emotion, Aldric glanced over his

shoulder at me, the silver of his gaze intense. His eyes lingered on me for a moment before he turned back, barking out orders as Casper nearly lost his footing.

Finally, almost the entire group had made it. It was just Louise and the gelding left on the other bank of the river. The horse jerked its head as she attempted to guide it across the cold stone of the bridge. Louise never faltered though, gently persuading the young gelding to move.

Casper appeared next to me, his attention rapt on Louise's careful journey over the unnatural stillness of the water below. She had been watching carefully, each step deliberate and sure.

The colt, however, was less confident. The whites of his eyes were on prominent display, his hooves clattering against the rock.

Then the trembling creature slipped—and was simply gone. Louise yelped as the lead was ripped from her fingers and leaned into the gap the young bay disappeared into.

He fell into the water with not even a splash. Not a single ripple. Even after seeing it with my own eyes, it didn't seem real. Like a void had just opened and swallowed him whole. Louise cradled her right hand to her chest and soon joined us on solid ground, looking defeated.

I stood and rushed to her side.

"Are you okay, Louise?" My voice was soft, careful.

Her eyes were dark with melancholy. The breadth of it almost took my breath away, but she simply nodded in response.

Aldric stepped up and took her injured hand, turning it over to see the damage. There was missing skin on her palm, ripped away in an angry-looking strip. She hissed as Aldric stretched her fingers to assess the wound. There were raw marks across each finger in a line.

"What do we need to do?" Aldric asked, his voice smooth and low, almost as if he was afraid she would break.

"I have a salve in my bag that will help with the pain and speed up the healing some. It's dark green."

As she spoke, Seren rifled through the contents of Louise's pack. The Fae was at our side in seconds, a small jar in her hands.

Deftly, Seren applied the ointment and wrapped Louise's hand with clean, dry bandages.

Louise turned her hand this way and that to evaluate the handiwork and deemed it good enough. Casper stood silently off to the side, the mare sensing the tension and throwing her head. Silently, the old healer made her way to the horse and gave it a reassuring pat on its neck before slowly turning towards our destination.

"Are you sure you don't want to take a break?" Seren asked quietly, her gaze trained on the ground as if she couldn't bear to look Louise in the eye.

"It won't change anything, will it? All that would do is make this blasted journey take even longer. Let's just get it over with."

With that, she jerked her head towards the road leading east. "On we go," she said, her voice bereft of emotion.

My pack felt heavy on my shoulders, digging into my flesh as we made our way onto the path. Someone had gone through the trouble of cobbling this road, the stones smooth and unnaturally chilled, even through my boots.

Aldric must have sensed my discomfort, because he tapped my arm and grabbed the leather bag from me, hoisting it over his shoulder along with his own.

"A gentleman mustn't let a lady trouble herself, eh?" Aldric said with a hint of his usual smirk.

Normally it would make me smile, but there was this overwhelming *pressure* in the air that I couldn't shake. We had turned off of the main road as Seren pointed out that we would be less likely to run into other people that way. Absently I began winding a lock of my pale hair around and around my finger, anxiety climbing the further east we went.

Casper sidled up to the other side of me as Aldric moved to the front of the group, his amber eyes assessing me in a way that felt too old for his years.

"There's something weird here, isn't there?" he whispered.

His words jolted me with surprise, causing me to stop in my tracks for a moment. Aldric hadn't mentioned anything.

"What do you mean?" I asked cautiously, increasing my pace so I didn't fall too far back from everyone else.

"I know you can feel it," Casper said seriously, his voice low.

"There's something weird going on. I don't know what it is, but something about this place is…strange. And the further we go, the stronger that feeling is."

"What do you feel?" I asked, goosebumps rising across my skin.

"It's just like…like a prickle on the back of my neck. Like there's something dangerous nearby. Kind of like when I was right over that bridge. It's hard to explain," he said in a rush, as though the words couldn't wait to escape.

"I know what you mean," I assured him, though I noticed we were lagging far behind. "But it's probably nothing. We need to catch up with everyone else."

Casper suddenly looked ahead as though he had forgotten about the rest of the group and jogged to catch up. After a moment, I followed.

After the sun began to dip below the horizon, painting the sky in swaths of crimson and plum, we finally set up camp in a clearing of trees. Stars were winking in and out of view in the cloudless atmosphere, almost as if the heavens themselves were trying to communicate something to me.

Aldric had already set up a fire with Casper 'helping' by finding kindling. Seren was checking in with Louise, and I was just here, existing, sitting on the soft grass with my back to a log.

The Serathine wound through my mind like a serpent, the image of my own rotting flesh haunting my thoughts. Then there was the whisper.

The twisted trees hide the disorder.

What did that mean? These trees? I looked around, but they looked normal to me. Nothing strange about them. No bends, no tangles, no contortions. Just regular wood.

If not here, then where? How could I find what they were talking about?

Was that even real, though? That place…was unnatural. There was something inhuman and yet distinctly *alive* about the Serathine. Just the thought of it had a shiver working its way up my spine. I tucked my knees towards my chest, wrapping my arms around them as though grounding myself.

A sigh escaped my lips, and I let my head fall back onto the log, gazing up at the sky as the colors leeched away into inky darkness.

Night was well and truly upon us.

CHAPTER 34

I nearly jumped out of my skin when Aldric put his hand on my shoulder. Judging by the drool running down my chin, I must have fallen asleep watching the stars. My cheeks burned red-hot as I hurriedly wiped the offending liquid away, my spine stiffening.

"As lovely as it is to watch you snoozing—which it truly is, darling, trust me—I need you," Aldric said, his eyes bright like moonlight itself in the darkness. His raven-black hair was a mess of waves around his head.

His words immediately sparked heat low in my belly, and when he offered me a hand, I placed my fingers in his.

"Let's go find someplace quiet, Onyra," he murmured, his voice sliding over my skin like a caress.

My pulse jumped in my throat, and I followed along as he led the way.

"Don't worry, by the way. I already told the others that I would be stealing you away," Aldric said, throwing a wink over his shoulder at me. My lips curled despite themselves. He always knew how to lighten the mood, even with the pressure in the air causing a buzzing at the base of my skull.

After a few minutes, we stopped in another clearing, a bed of moss spread over a patch of earth covered in shadow.

"I went to scope out the area earlier and remembered this little gem," he said with a smile, his fangs flashing in the limited light. "Wanted to make sure you would be comfortable."

I turned in a slow circle. Without thinking, my eyes had changed to accommodate the dim, allowing me to see better through the darkness.

"You keep giving me more reasons to fall even deeper in love, you know," he purred.

"What do you mean?" I asked genuinely confused.

"You're just amazing. Beautiful," he crooned. He buried his fingers in my hair, the tan of his skin against my snow-pale hair a stark contrast. He pulled the mass of waves until I gasped, and he took the opportunity to seal his lips to mine.

Melting against him, I moaned as I responded in kind. A growl raised from his chest in response, and warmth spread from my core.

After throughly ravishing my mouth, he tore away from me, panting. "Much as I would love to just devour you right here, I'm afraid I brought you here for another reason. We can't stay away from the group for long."

"We don't have to take long," I said breathlessly.

Aldric's eyes flashed in the dark, and his lips tilted up in a roguish grin. "Oh, but you are a temptress. But that will have to come later. And I do mean come later." He waggled his brows salaciously, and I couldn't help but giggle.

"Then what did you bring me here for?" I couldn't lie and say that I wasn't at least a little disappointed, but this eerie place wasn't exactly the most romantic spot I could think of.

"Well, I need to devour you…in a way. I need to feed, and it occurred to me you may not want me to go find a random throat to take."

The very thought had me scowling, and Aldric raised his hands as though to ward me off.

"Since I've been helping with the boy, I've been feeling a little more peckish than usual," he admitted. "I hope you don't mind."

He sat on the velvety moss, his legs spread in front of him. Aldric opened his arms to me and without hesitation, I dropped to the ground in front of him, curling into the space he offered me.

Peace sang through my body as Aldric embraced me, the oppressive air lightening in his presence as though it couldn't bear the bond between us. A sigh escaped my lips, and I nuzzled into his neck, inhaling his scent. The moss was slightly damp, but it barely even registered as Aldric began to slowly trace his fingertips across my body.

My arms, my legs, my back—and when he sank his fingers into

my hair, I nearly melted right there. A low, contented sound slipped out before I could stop it, and I felt Aldric smile against my hair.

"You're way too good at this," I said with a soft moan.

"I've had a lot of time to practice," Aldric murmured, his voice dripping with honey and mischief.

As my head lolled back, reveling in the sensations he offered me, I felt his breath at my throat. My mouth went dry with anticipation, but he didn't move.

"It's okay, Onyra. You can take it," I whispered.

As the endearment left my lips, Aldric shuddered.

"You make it so hard for me to stay in control, my love," he growled against my skin. I felt the warmth of his tongue tracing the flesh just over my pulse, and my back arched involuntarily, as though encouraging him to take what belonged to him.

The very thought sent a spear of heat through me, and I struggled to hold back a gasp. He peppered kisses along the column of my throat, shifting himself against me as I felt his arousal grow.

I held my breath and, after the barest hesitation, I felt a tiny pinch as his fangs sank into me. A rush of pleasure coursed through me, and the sound that erupted from me was borderline animalistic. But I barely had time to think as Aldric's free hand slipped under my shirt to cup my breast, squeezing.

He drew from me with single-minded intensity, stars bursting behind my eyes from the sensation bordering the line between bliss and pain. My arms wrapped around Aldric's powerful shoulders, holding him to me. His hand dropped to my rear, and he shifted my hips so that my core was flush against him.

The pressure of his hardness straining against me and the feeling of his lips sealed around my pulse was enough to undo me. I came apart in his arms. The sound that Aldric made was inhuman, and he quickly pulled away from me, his eyes intense.

As though I weighed nothing, Aldric had my back on the moss and his weight pinning me before I realized what happened. My legs cradled his hips, and he slowly, sensually ran his length along my core. Even through our clothes, my sensitivity was heightened, and my eyes rolled back in my head.

Warmth sluiced down my throat, and Aldric's eyes grew heavy-lidded as he slowly, salaciously dragged his tongue to catch the remnants of his feed.

Aldric nuzzled into the hollow between my shoulder and my neck, inhaling deeply.

"You frightened me earlier, you know," he said, his voice rough with emotion. "I cannot and will not live without you. You are my Onyra."

His voice was muffled against my skin, and my heart squeezed painfully as his words sank through the haze of pleasure I had been in.

"Oh, Aldric," I murmured, my hand stroking down his back as his muscles jumped in response. "You're my Onyra, too."

Aldric slowly stretched above me, his eyes unusually serious. "I mean it, Lyra. I love you. Wholly. Regardless of the gods' will, of my kingdom, of your magic. It's you. I've waited an eternity to find you."

Warmth suffused my chest, and my cheeks burned. "I don't

know what to say." I mumbled.

"Tell me you love me," he said, his voice strained.

My hand cupped his cheek, the rough stubble scratching at my palm. "Aldric, I care more about you than anyone. But I don't want to say it just because you ask. I want to say it because I've had time to learn what love is for *me*."

My heart shattered at the hurt in his eyes, but he slowly blew out a breath of air, the tension melting out of his body as he put his full weight onto my body. I cradled him as best as I could, wrapping my arms around his shoulders.

"I know, Onyra," he said, his voice achingly soft. "But I still cannot wait to hear those words leave your lips. I will do my best to be patient."

CHAPTER 35

The walk back to our little camp was awkward and too quiet. Aldric tried to show he wasn't affected, reaching out to hold my hand. But it didn't feel right, so I pulled away. The sharp stab of hurt flowed through our bond, but I didn't know what to do or what to say.

I cared about Aldric so much. He meant more to me than I thought was possible, even after such a short time. Especially after such a short time. He always built me up. He wasn't afraid of me or my powers. Even staying with me even when he shouldn't.

My eyes landed on him, silhouetted in the moonlight dripping through the tree branches. Aching inside, I wanted nothing more than to hold him and be held by him. And yet I couldn't say the words. Wringing my hands together, I stifled a sigh.

A tingle of warmth and reassurance reached me, gentle as a spring breeze.

Aldric stopped in his tracks and reached out to grab my wrist. He pulled me in close, the heat from his body enveloping me, warding away the chill in the air.

"It's okay, Onyra," he murmured. "Just don't pull away from me."

He tipped my chin until I was forced to meet his eyes. His eyes were molten silver, despite the lingering hurt that shadowed them. My chest tightened knowing that I had caused it.

The fear of saying or doing the wrong thing was getting to be too much—my eyes filled with tears.

"I'm sorry," I mumbled, jerking back from his touch. Wiping my eyes with my sleeve, I straightened my spine. "I don't know what I'm doing. There's no way of knowing how all of this will go. The gods themselves seem to want to damn me—or at least one in particular. And I don't know how to do this. T-to be with someone."

I gestured widely to the area we were in. "I'm used to being alone. Not having to care about someone else. There was Griffin, but even that…"

My words died in my throat. It felt wrong to compare how I felt between Aldric and Griffin. It was like comparing a candle to a forest fire.

"This is all new to me. But all I know is that I want you here. With me," I finished awkwardly, wrapping my arms around myself. Vulnerability didn't come easily. My brain was screaming at me to stop talking, but my heart refused to listen.

"I can't explain how I feel to you, but your arms feel like home. Your scent comforts me. Your dumb jokes are sometimes the only thing that can make me smile."

My eyes were trained on a rotting leaf on the ground, too

afraid to look at Aldric. I've never talked this much about my feelings before. How did people do this? Was I saying the wrong thing? Too much? Not enough?

My thoughts were tangled together like threads in a forgotten loom, difficult to track, to make sense of.

A distinctly masculine form filled my vision, getting so close that I had no choice but to take a step back straight into a tree. I glanced up in surprise.

Aldric's lips were quirked up, and he reached out to clasp my face, his thumb slowly rubbing my cheek. Leaning down, he spoke directly into the shell of my ear, his breath stirring the strands of hair and tickling my neck.

"What you describe *is* love, my Onyra. One day you'll realize it. But until then, I will be here."

Back at the camp, Aldric had gone to check on Casper and Louise. I settled into my bedroll a short distance away from the group. The way I felt was strange. That pressure crawling along my skin was back, a dull throbbing in my skull. It felt like too much to be close to them right now. The thick wool was enough to keep me warm against the autumn breeze.

My pack was within arm's reach—which was great, because I was starving. Louise had the forethought to ensure that we had enough food to last for our journey, barring any delays. I wasn't sure how Aldric was keeping Casper fed—and honestly, I didn't want to ask. I didn't want to know.

Rifling through the bag, I pulled out a small container of nuts and dried fruits. After devouring them like a gremlin while wrapped in my bedroll, I put the empty jar back into my pack and settled in for the night, the faint murmur of conversation and the crackling of the fire in the distance serving as a lullaby that sent me into a deep sleep.

The scent of seaweed and wet earth woke me with a jolt. And yet, what greeted me wasn't what I expected.

I was back in Starfall Veil. But how?

Turning in a slow circle, I stopped short as a familiar figure appeared. Ler.

He was leaned up against one of the strange multi-colored trees, the gentle glow resonating from the trunk highlighting his bare skin with odd patterns.

"What am I doing here?" I asked, crossing my arms. "What are *you* doing here?"

Ler looked me up and down, his rose-colored eyes especially piercing in the gloom.

"You need to hurry. I had to call you here because if I brought you to the river, the Sovereign would know. They'd expect it."

A shudder wracked me as his words sank in. "Why do we need to hurry?"

"You can sense it, can't you? The wrongness in the air?" He tucked a strand of his fluid-like hair behind his pointed ear. "Surely I don't have to explain everything to you."

A scowl formed on my face before I could fight it, and Ler cracked a hint of a smile, which seemed out of place on him. But it was short-lived. The deity's expression turned grave.

"It will only get worse. The decay is spreading."

My arms wrapped around my middle as if to protect myself from his words. "I am already doing what I can. We're already looking for Thorne."

"The Sovereign will not give up so easily. Be on your guard."

I opened my mouth to respond, but before I could, the world dissolved to ash, and Aldric was climbing in next to me. His familiar scent wrapped around me like a scarf and, despite the chilling vision, I snuggled into the comfort his presence offered.

Sleep eluded me even once the sky began to blush pink with the beginnings of dawn, but at least I had this.

Over the next few days of travel, I thought about ways to tell Aldric and the others about the vision I had. Both the one from my dreams and from the bridge. But at the same time, things were hard enough for everyone right now. Seren always wore a worried expression. Aldric had been more distant than usual. Casper seemed like he never knew what to say, so he was mute most of the time. Louise just looked…defeated.

How could I burden them with something that may or may not be true? There was no way of knowing for sure. At least, not yet. The closer that we got to the Werefolk city, the more my magic itched under my skin. My muscles tightened, a migraine blooming behind my eyes.

The strangest thing of all: no one else seemed to notice anything was off. So maybe it *was* just me.

That sense of wrongness only grew stronger as the city came into view in the distance. It was like the ground itself was saturated with disease and decay, spreading into my body from the soles of my feet. So when we heard laughter in the distance, I stopped short from shock.

There was no way.

How is this possible?

There was something insidious going on. The very earth here was emanating wrongness, and yet the sound of children playing and being scolded by adults was ringing out in the air. Like things were normal.

How?

I looked around for some place to sit and relieve my shaking legs, but there was nothing, so I sat directly in the grass on the side of the path. It was dry and itchy, poking my skin through the thin fabric of my pants.

"Are you okay, my love?" Aldric asked gently. He appeared, kneeling in front of me, as though teleporting out of thin air. Sometimes it was easy to forget what he was. But when he did things like this, it really pushed how far we were different into view.

I dipped my chin towards my chest, waving him off with trembling fingers.

"You guys go on ahead. I'll catch up in a minute. I just need a breather."

The group shifted on their feet as though the thought made them uncomfortable, but I shooed them away.

"Please go. I need a second alone."

Aldric's eyes searched my face, and I could feel a tender pull against our bond, as though he were testing my emotional state. Though he hesitated, slowly he stood back onto the balls of his feet and started to guide the group towards civilization.

"If you don't catch up in fifteen minutes, I will be back," Aldric said, not a hint of his usual playfulness in his tone.

Tired, I nodded again. "Please, go. I will be there soon."

My joints ached with the unnatural pressure in the air as though I was being poisoned just by proximity to this place. But the rest of the group looked strangely relieved as they resumed walking. This journey has weighed on them, though they tried not to show it. Best to avoid delays.

There was a flash of silver as Aldric looked over his shoulder at me one more time before turning forwards, striding along the path.

Closing my eyes, I laid down in the grass, ignoring the prickling of my skin from the withered turf.

Rest.

Just for a moment.

A hand covered my mouth, instantly filling my body with adrenaline. My eyes snapped open to find a hulking creature of a man standing over me, his expression grim.

"What are you doing back here?" he asked, his obsidian eyes glittering with rage. "Wasn't the pain you caused enough? I should kill you right here."

My heart beat a painful rhythm against my chest, and my breath began coming faster and faster as more Werefolk came into view. I tried in vain to pull his hand away from my face, but his grip was like iron. Panic filled me, and instinct took over. I attempted to slap the man away and, to my horror, my hand had become a massive, furred paw with dagger-like claws.

The man's face split like warm butter as the impact hit his cheek. He screamed, letting go of me and taking a defensive stance, blood pouring from between his fingers. I didn't have time to think. I needed to get away.

Jumping to my feet, I sprinted into the trees behind me. I knew they had to be giving chase, but all I could hear was buzzing in my ears. What did he mean 'back here'? I've never been here before!

I swallowed hard, my breath sawing in and out of my lungs

as I fought to get away, leaping over fallen logs and my skin lashing open as thin branches whipped past.

Glancing over my shoulder, the world tilted, and suddenly, I was looking up at the sky. Pain lanced through my ribs, and I realized I must have fallen. The men were shouting at one another, and the realization hit that this was my only chance to get away. Feathers sprouted from my skin as my body contorted, shifting and twisting until there was only a small bird where I had once lay.

The forest exploded in a kaleidoscope of colors, and a wave of disorientation hit. Shoving the feeling down, I tentatively flapped my wings before taking to the air. I needed to find Aldric. They knew who I was.

How?

The air was freezing against my delicate frame, and I struggled to keep momentum as wind whipped against me over the treetops.

Using a combination of my instinctive internal compass and the traces of the bond between Aldric and I, I managed to find the path forward. My wings were already tired, weighed down by the burden of energy saturating the land here. My body felt weak, but I couldn't give up here. If they knew who *I* was, everyone else may be in danger.

CHAPTER 36

The bright colors assaulting my eyes were dizzying, but eventually I made it to a rooftop in the city. Surveying the crowd below, I looked for anything familiar, but it was hard to tell in this form without being given time to adjust to what I was seeing.

I had to take a gamble. Hopping across the rooftop on delicate legs, I peered over each side of the building.

This was some type of industrial building. Towards the back of the building, there was an alleyway where it appeared they pushed product in carts for transport.

The sun was high overhead. The workers were milling out of the back door in droves. It must be lunchtime. Lucky for me, I supposed.

As the number of figures below slowed to a trickle, silently, I dropped to the cobblestone street. The shadows behind the door provided enough coverage for me to become human again—but I couldn't stay Lyra. If those guards knew who I was, chances are there are others in this city who might.

It had been quite some time, but I would need to change aspects of myself to make me unrecognizable here. Taking a deep breath, darkness flowed from the top of my hair to the tips, losing their waves until they were straight. My eyes became hazel. A glance at my hands showed a deep tan skin tone.

Clearing my throat, my voice became deeper, huskier. Adding a little extra weight around my hips and changing the shape of my lips to add some fullness completed the look. These minute changes seemed like nothing on paper, but in reality, they took a lot of concentration. There was already an uncomfortable tug on my belly from the strain, but I loosened the tether, allowing a small flow of my power to course under my skin and maintain this new form.

Tugging my clothing into place as well as I could—it was a good thing that these pants came with a drawstring or I may have been in trouble—I threw out my feelers to see if I could find a direction the group may be in. There was a distinct pull in one direction. Aldric.

His concern filtered through the bond, and I felt him growing closer as I stuck to the darkness, avoiding the bulk of people as much as possible.

On the side of another bland building a short ways away, I saw his inky mane of hair appear above the crowd, and my heart skipped a beat. Then, a thought hit me like an electric jolt.

Would he know it was me?

There were stacks of boxes in the alleyway, and I waited out of view behind them for Aldric to get closer. As my impatience grew, I took a peek around the crates to find Aldric looking down at me with a wry smile, causing me to yelp.

That earned the attention of a few passers-by, but Aldric used his body to block me in, herding me towards the wall. The hair on the back of my neck prickled as I heard footsteps approach. Aldric wasted no time, planting his hands on my hips and nuzzling at my neck. That familiar scent of wine and thunderstorms washed over me and I groaned just as an older woman's face appeared around the corner. She immediately went beet red and hustled off, muttering about people having no shame nowadays.

I felt Aldric smile against my skin, but he slowly pulled back to look me up and down.

"What are you doing?" he asked, cocking his head to the side.

"It's me," I said in an urgent whisper.

"Yes, I am aware, Onyra. I didn't ask who you are. I asked what you're doing," he said smoothly, a smirk on his lips. Then, his expression grew grim. "I felt your panic earlier and set out to find you, but you weren't where we left you. There was nothing but the scent of Were blood."

"They knew who I was. Those guards. I've never been here before."

I explained the rest in a rush, how I ended up here and why

I was looking for him so desperately.

"We don't know how much they know, or even *how* they know, so I didn't want to take any chances," I finished, my hands shaking.

Aldric took my fingers in his, grounding me.

"I would kiss you, but it doesn't feel right when it isn't your face," he murmured, causing my cheeks to grow heated.

Instead, he pulled me into an embrace, stroking his hand down my spine. The strength of his arms around me and the gentle cadence of his heart slowed my own back into a more steady rhythm.

"Where are the others?" I said, my voice muffled against his chest.

"They wouldn't have been able to keep up with me as I searched, so I left them behind at a cafe," he replied easily. "Louise said they would wait for my return."

"We should hurry."

With that, we strode off down the street, Aldric leading the way with a hand at the small of my back.

Making our way through a market district, Aldric stopped at a stall that was selling clothing. I cringed as I saw the prices, but he didn't balk, haggling with the purveyor with the skill of a royal who was not used to being denied.

My hands traced the different fabrics, a small sigh slipping through my lips. There were cloaks that were softer than should be possible, shirts, dresses in every color imaginable.

And yet, it was strange. There was that undeniable pressure in the air. Could these people not feel it?

Turning in a slow circle, there were families striding down the walkways. Older people hobbling their way along. Young folks striding purposefully as though they had somewhere to be.

The air was heavy, and yet, I seemed to be the only one able to feel it. Flexing my fingers, I took a deep breath to stay grounded. How it felt and what the reality was were conflicting. What happened here?

Is it related to why those Werefolk guards recognized me?

But how?

Those thoughts disappeared like smoke when Aldric reached for my hand, jarring me. Despite that, as warmth traveled up from my fingers, I couldn't help but smile at him. He would help me figure this out. Once we find the group, we'll be back on the right path before we know it.

Then, I realized Aldric had a parcel tucked under his arm.

"What is that?"

"You'll find out in just a few moments, Onyra." He winked at me with a playful smile on his lips.

Soon, the cafe that Aldric had mentioned came into view.

The Jittery Wolf.

That was certainly a name. In a place like this, it seemed to fit though. It was a well-kept red brick building with a hanging wooden sign. The sign had the cafe's name carved into it, along with a small painting of a wolf with a coffee cup in its paws.

The culture of this city was unlike anything I'd been exposed to in western Aethralis. Everyone seemed so much more cheerful and easy-going. The genuine happiness in the eyes of the passers-by and the number of children playing in the streets pointed to easier living than I was used to.

Despite how this place made me feel from a magical standpoint, from an emotional one, it made me feel happier, too. A genuine smile curled my lips as Casper came into view, but it died there shortly afterwards when I saw the guard I had injured earlier. His face wasn't as bad as I thought. When I was in self-defense mode, there had apparently just been a lot of blood.

He had a bandage wrapped across the wound, and his cheek was bruised and swollen where I had swiped him, but aside from that, he seemed not much worse for wear. Now that I got a good look at him, a pit opened up in my stomach. This was a huge Were, taller even than Aldric. He had muddy brown hair and deeply tanned skin.

My hand reflexively squeezed Aldric's, and his gaze followed mine, slowing our pace. He looked at me, and I felt the question he was asking even without words.

Is that the man who assaulted you?

I nodded, jerking my chin towards the gap between two buildings. Aldric ran his thumb over my wrist reassuringly, but it did little to stop the pounding of my heart.

"Why is he there?" I whispered, anxiety ratcheting my breathing up.

"They must be looking for people new to Mosswick," Aldric mused, running his hand over his stubble with a faint scratching sound.

"Mosswick?"

"That's the name of this place. They had a sign inside the entrance to the city."

Aldric looked me up and down, then peered behind me to see a wall between the two buildings.

"This is perfect. Here."

Aldric took the parcel he got from the clothier's stall earlier and handed it to me.

"I'll block you from view. Get changed quickly."

"Why here?" I asked, bewildered.

"You may not realize it, my Onyra, but you have a very faint scent of blood on your clothes. Despite your different appearance, they will still find you suspicious if they get too close."

Aldric shooed me further into the alley and then stood guard near the entrance.

Quickly, I stripped down and opened the parcel, throwing my old clothes into a nearby trashcan, shoving it beneath some rubbish.

The package's contents surprised me, and I glanced up at Aldric in shock. He never turned back though, diligently keeping an eye and ensuring that no one came through.

There was a cloak just a shade darker than my natural eye color, a gorgeous purple iris shade, with a dark eggplant-hued filigree around the edges. It had a soft, silky feel, with a delicate black fur lining. Underneath were a pair of pants and a flowy blouse, both reminiscent of soot.

Everything felt luxurious, and I felt slightly nauseated at the idea of how much this would have cost Aldric. But I didn't have time to think about it now, pulling the clothes on quickly. The cloak was heavier than it looked, warding off the chill in the air effortlessly.

I slipped my boots back on, adjusting the blouse as I went and joined Aldric at the mouth of the alleyway.

Aldric glanced down at me, and his gaze warmed.

"You look ravishing. I knew I had good taste, but damn the gods," he said, a wry smile on his lips. "I can't wait to see this on the *real* you."

A flush crept up my neck, and I worried the edges of the cloak with my fingers. Clearing my throat, I glanced down either side of the street. My senses were attuned to the injured guard, but I didn't see him anywhere.

The group was sitting at an outdoor table. Casper sat on one side, Louise and Seren next to each other on the opposite side. Seren was smiling, the tension eased from her face for the first time that I can remember since I've known her.

My heart squeezed painfully at the sight. She looked so

ethereal. Her smile was bright enough to light up a room, and the lines of tension around her eyes were gone, leaving her looking more youthful.

Casper laughed at something one of the others said, the sound shocking me. It was like…they were just regular people. Not on a perilous journey—just people who happened to be together.

A strange ache bloomed inside of me, watching them together like this. Aldric wrapped an arm around my waist, drawing me close.

But then he stiffened, shifting his body in front of me so I was no longer in view.

"What is it?" I asked.

Aldric held up a hand to silence me, crowding me towards a wall. He was so tense he may as well have been made from stone.

I scowled and peered around his arm, only to stop short.

A group of Werefolk, armed with blades and strapped with armor, were talking to Louise. She had her hands up defensively as though to ward them off, but one of the larger Werefolk gestured angrily with their blade and the group stood, falling into line in the middle of the guard.

They all began to stride off towards the Northern most part of the city.

CHAPTER 37

"Aldric, we have to help them," I demanded, trying in vain to push him out of the way. He stood unmoving, like a mountain.

"And how are we going to do that?" he asked, his dark brows drawing down. "We can't exactly fight in the middle of Mosswick. Not without drawing all Werefolk on us like flies to a carcass."

Taking a deep breath and releasing it, I realized he was right. Now wasn't the time to act emotionally.

"Let's just follow them. Maybe once we see where they're being taken, we can intervene or help somehow."

"That is something we can do, if we're careful," Aldric murmured, glancing back at the troupe as they marched off into the distance.

He grabbed the hood of my cloak and dragged it over my head, throwing my face into shadow. He then took my hand and placed it in the crook of his arm, leading us out as though we were just another couple on the street.

Aldric's long legs ate the distance between us and the guards, with me scrambling to keep up while also not looking like a crazy person running after him. I subtly adjusted my height so my stride could more closely match his without being too jarring for the people around us.

After about thirty minutes of walking, the Werefolk were approaching a large, prestigious-looking building. It had beautiful carved pillars made of marble. The double doors of the entrance were a deep walnut color, with the trim in a forest green. The rest of the building was made of clean, earth-colored bricks.

The roof was made with the same white as the pillars, bringing the whole aesthetic together. There were no signs or anything around, so we couldn't be sure what this building was. But the Werefolk did not hesitate, herding everyone in through the doors.

My stomach twisted painfully as they started to close the doors, a hint of saffron yellow showing between two guards as Casper's desperate gaze searched for any escape.

"W-we have to go in there," I stammered, my adrenaline rushing through me like a freight train.

"I don't think that is a good idea, Onyra," Aldric said, his muscles growing tense under my fingers. I pried my hand away from his arm and began to worry the edges of my cloak.

"We can't let them go in alone. I don't know what they want, but it has something to do with me. I just *know* it."

Aldric scowled, his eyes growing dark with his barely-constrained temper. "That's exactly the point, Lyra! You can't keep jumping in to save everyone else all of the time."

"I can't let them get hurt because of me, either!" I whisper-yelled back.

"And why not? You risked yourself with that blasted bridge and now you want to swoop in and save them again? What will that accomplish, besides putting yourself at risk?"

"They don't know it's me!"

Aldric angrily scrubbed a hand down his face, turning his back on me. He had never been this upset with me before. I didn't like it. But I wouldn't bow, either.

"I am going in there whether you want me to or not. They don't know who I am. I will just tell them that I am missing the rest of my group and ask whether they've been seen."

"Onyra—," Aldric stopped, exasperated. "Fine. But know that I will slaughter every being in there if they raise a hand to you in my presence."

His eyes glittered with dark promise, sending a chill up my spine. There was an ancient creature lurking at the edges of his gaze, desperate to be loosed.

I shuddered before taking his arm again, leading him to where our friends had been taken.

Aldric took the lead, keeping his body slightly in front of mine. He knocked at the entrance, three loud *raps*.

After a few moments, the wood creaked as the doors were pulled open.

"What is it?" the injured guard asked, barely contained vitriol in his gaze.

Aldric smiled easily, clearly used to pleasing people he disliked. "Pardon me, we seem to have been separated from our friends. Would you happen to have seen them?"

He described Louise, Seren and Casper to the hulking man, who scowled. But slowly, his face contorted with a grim smile.

"But of course. Follow me."

The Were gestured grandly as he waved us in. The room smelled of musk and cigar smoke. I wrinkled my nose and glanced around. This place practically dripped with testosterone. There were antique weapons mounted on the walls, along with trophies from hunting. Antlers here, an enormous stuffed bear there. It was really out of place compared with how the outside of the building looked.

I had expected more stuffy chairs, old paintings, crown moldings, that kind of thing. But I guess it suited Werefolk. They were known for being much more hands-on, more in touch with their roots than the rest of the Otherkind.

Aldric subtly pulled my arm, causing me to snap back

to attention. We were being led down a hallway lined in red and gold carpet, marble statuettes of Werefolk in various stages of Shifting placed on pedestals at regular intervals. This was more what I expected to see in a place like this.

There was a certain morbid beauty in the statuettes. The Were's faces were contorted with pain, but once the Shift was complete, they looked regal and powerful in their animal forms. A pang of sadness speared me as I thought of Griffin, but I shoved the feeling down. I couldn't afford to get distracted.

The hallway branched off with other doors, but we kept being led deeper and deeper into the core of the building. The lighting became much more muted, causing the statuettes to take on a grotesque feel, the shadows harsh and deforming their features.

After a few minutes, we stood in front of a rather unassuming-looking door. The injured Were cracked his knuckles against the door once, twice.

A figure appeared through a crack in the door—a small woman. I was surprised, given the state of this place. Didn't feel like somewhere you would expect to see such a delicate-looking person.

The Were leaned in to whisper something to the woman, and she nodded, opening the way for us to enter and stepping aside.

The room itself was dark and cave-like. The walls were stone, the ground packed dirt. It was incredibly strange to have a place like this in the middle of a building. This felt like more of a den than anything else. A shove at our backs had me stumbling forward, Aldric catching me before I could fall. He shot a dark look over his shoulder, but the door closed quickly.

There was a large desk in the middle of the room, with Casper, Louise and Seren seated in front. It smelled like damp fur in here, but I grew used to it quickly. Two more hand-carved chairs were shoved next to the others, and a monstrous-looking man gestured at us to sit.

"Join us, please," he said, his voice surprisingly pleasing despite his looks.

The leader of the Werefolk was a deeply tanned man, striped with thick white scar tissue as evidence of his brutal past. He had a mane of chestnut hair and bright, sky-blue eyes. His lips were thin and seemed to default to a frown. He wore a worn gray tee shirt and blue jeans spotted with dried mud. The Were was surprisingly clean-shaven, and the woman from before stood at his side.

She couldn't be much taller than five feet tall, and had bright red hair, her face covered in a spattering of freckles. She had eyes like rain clouds, unfathomably deep. Her hands were clasped in front of her, showing a diamond ring on her left hand. She wore a tight black dress with a dip showing her small chest, and a small slit in the skirt, exposing her pale skin.

"Since we have new guests, I'll start again," the man continued, his voice deep and gravelly. "My name is Cole. This is my territory. We had reported sightings of the transformation witch right about the same time as you all showed up. Do you know it? It attacked some of my men."

He put his elbows on the desk, steepling his fingers together. He had the same crushing pressure to his presence that I felt with Griffin when we first met. I kept my spine straight, refusing to show any weakness.

"We don't know about it. Why?" Louise said, her moss-green eyes steely.

A spark of respect shone in Cole's eyes at Louise's blunt response, and he leaned forward. "That witch bitch poisoned our city. People were getting sick wherever it went. We had to do a good old-fashioned witch hunt to chase that damnable demon from Mosswick. So I will ask again." He had a deadly calm about him, making his next words hit extra hard.

"Do you know that witch? Have you ever seen it? We will not tolerate any allies of that demon whore."

Aldric stiffened at my side, and I could feel his rage simmering below the surface, hitting me in boiling waves through the bond. I tried to return calming energy back to him, but it seemed to have no effect. Putting my hand on his thigh, he relaxed minutely, signaling to me that he wouldn't go after Cole right now.

"Poisoned your city?" I asked cautiously. "What do you mean?"

"My people were getting sick. I don't know how to explain it—it was like they'd go to sleep and not wake up." Cole scowled, his spine straightening and casting his face into shadow. "I am the one asking questions here. I gave you information as a courtesy. This is what it looked like."

Cole slid a brown sheaf of paper towards us, his eyes glittering. Nausea roiled in my stomach as my own face looked back at me from the illustration. There were minor differences, but there could be no doubt that it was me. How?

Louise glanced at the paper before sighing, looking bored. "I told you, we don't know any mages like that. I've never seen that girl before in my life. Did you catch her?"

"If we did, I wouldn't be asking, would I?" Cole snapped. "It'd be torn to shreds and burned if I had my way."

Louise cocked her head. "Where did she go? I want to make sure we don't run into her on our way out."

"Somewhere to the south from what my men told me. The ones that returned, at least." Cole leaned back, looking haggard. "But there's nothing down there anyway except some damn ruins. If we're lucky, maybe one of those buildings will collapse on it. It would be fitting for that bitch."

Seren piped up for the first time, her voice too calm for the situation. "What do you mean, it would be fitting?"

A shark-like smile twisted the Were's face. His wife put her hand on his shoulder, and you could just see some of the tension drain out of him. "It's that old magic kingdom. The last transformation witch cost them their kingdom. It would be right for one to die there."

His voice was bitter, but he leaned into his wife, dragging her onto his lap. He deeply inhaled the scent of her hair, and as she turned to look at him, my breath caught.

There was something in nestled into her curls.

A flower.

The spare room that I'd stayed in with Griffin. Those same flowers were in a vase there. He'd always kept them fresh and alive, swapping them for new ones every time they'd begun to wilt.

I'd always wondered why he would have flowers in a room he never occupied.

Was this who Louise had talked about—his mate?

My mouth went dry, and I swallowed hard.

It couldn't be. What would the chances of that be? This city was enormous. Plus, Griffin said he was from a small village. This was a bustling city. There's no way he could have been talking about *here*.

"Do you need anything else from us?" Aldric said, snapping me out of my thoughts.

The Were sighed deeply, his arms wrapping around his mate. "We will be watching you. *Closely*. Don't step out of line and don't stay long. If what you're saying is true, we have no qualms about you."

The delicate woman slipped from Cole's grasp, gesturing us to the door. But as she pulled the heavy handle, a child tumbled into the room, clearly having been eavesdropping.

"Tora!" the woman shouted, her voice deceptively light for how commanding her tone came across. Grasping the doorjamb, she leaned into the hallway. "Atlas! I told you to watch your sister. What happened?"

A young male Were came jogging up to her, a clearly exasperated expression on his face. There was something familiar about him. The way his chestnut hair fell across his face. As the boy angrily shoved his hair back, I saw it. Golden, sunshine eyes.

"I was trying! You know how she is. Tora was throwing a fit about not being in here with you and Dad," the young man spouted, full of righteous anger only an older sibling could muster.

"Well, take her and get out of here! You see, we're busy," the woman said back, scowling. "I'll come and play with you guys in just a few minutes. This was important."

"Yeah, yeah," the young man said, dragging his sister behind him.

"Eve, you got it?" Cole asked, rising to his feet.

"Of course," the woman said, waving Cole off. "Let's just get our guests out of here so I can be with my children."

Atlas's face kept replaying in my mind. The flower Eve wore in her hair. There's no way…was there?

Eve ushered us out of the room with all the hustle of a young mother, leading us back out the way we came.

"Thank you for being so receptive to this…interview, I guess you could call it," Eve said, a tired smile playing on her lips.

"You mean interrogation, right?" Louise snarked back. A deep laugh bubbled up from her chest. "Don't mind me. It's been a long trip. These old bones are tired."

Eve chuckled, nearing the exit to the street. We made it here faster than I thought, but my mind was clogged with a cyclical pattern of thoughts.

"I can imagine. You all have a nice time in Mosswick. We don't often get visitors here—we used to be much more hospitable before…" she trailed off, looking uncomfortable. "Well, before.

No need to get back into all that."

Eve began to pull the heavy door closed, but I placed my hand on the doorknob, stopping her.

"Wait. I need to know something. I met someone—a man. Griffin. Did you ever know anyone by that name?" I asked, desperation overwhelming me. I had to find out.

Recognition flitted over her face but was quickly locked away. "A long time ago. But that's not relevant anymore. If you ever see him again, don't mention me. I don't want to bring up old pain."

So it was true. What were the chances?

Atlas *had* to be Griffin's child. The resemblance was uncanny. A small part of me untwisted, allowing the guilt to melt away. He lived on in some way. Not all of him was lost.

The realization gave me the peace I didn't know I needed. Fire lit in my belly to find Thorne now.

To end this.

CHAPTER 38

After a tenuous night's sleep, under the watchful eye of Cole's guard, we departed from Mosswick to the east. As soon as we were far from view, I could finally release the disguise I'd been holding for over a day. My muscles ached like I'd been through a marathon, and my mana felt depleted.

I rolled my head on my shoulders, rubbing at my neck. Aldric was by my side in a flash, tucking me into his arms. He kissed the top of my head.

"It's so good to see you again, Onyra. The *real* you."

My arms slid around his waist of their own volition, and I melted into his embrace. This was nice.

Seren wasted no time, however. "When should we turn south?"

Casper finally piped up for what felt like the first time in days. "We're a couple of hours out from Mosswick."

He looked around at the sparsely forested area, his bright golden eyes sharp as a hawk's.

"I don't see a path south from here, so we'd have to make our own. But there aren't too many trees nearby, so it shouldn't be too bad."

Louise cracked a genuine smile. "It's nice to hear your voice, Casper."

A flush crept up Casper's face, and he refused to look the older woman in the eye. "There was just a lot going on, okay?"

Louise nodded, setting off through the meadow.

"I get it, kid. To be clear, I wasn't blaming you for being quiet. It's just nice to hear you talking." She didn't wait for a response, and Casper looked relieved, though his face stayed red with embarrassment.

The rest of us followed suit, carefully making our way through the tall grass.

Aldric went ahead to talk to Seren and Louise while I hung back. Casper slowed as well, his shoulders tense. I waited until there was a bit of distance between us two and the rest of the party.

Dropping my cloak's hood, I loosed my snow-white hair, finger-combing it as well as I could. Casper peeked at me, but seemed reluctant to talk.

"Are you okay?" I asked gently. "You've been awfully quiet the past few days."

Casper sighed. "I don't want to burden you guys with my problems. It's not a big deal."

I glanced ahead to see the others trailing off into the distance and took a deep breath. "Let me tell you something. I don't like to open up to people. I was alone for a long, long time."

Casper's golden eyes locked in on me, and I continued hesitantly. "There was a man I met in Haleshade—where we brought you and healed you—he changed all of that for me."

Curiosity brightened his eyes into tiny suns. "Who was he?"

"His name was Griffin. He was one of the Werefolk."

"Oh, like—,"

"Yes, like the folk from Mosswick. Then, come to find out, it looks like I met his fated mate."

Casper gasped, his attention rapt on my face. "Were you two a thing? Was there a betrayal?"

I couldn't help it—a small laugh escaped from my lips. "Nothing so crazy as that." Slowly my smile died, and my tone turned somber. "But the thing is, Griffin…he died. Trying to protect me from Thorne."

His gaze dropped to the grass, looking ashamed to have been so excited moments before.

"I'm sorry, Lyra. Are you okay? What happened?"

"This plague is around because of me. Thorne was trying to find a way to fix it, but he went too far. So now I have to stop him. To stop this gods' damned plague before it takes over all of Aethralis. That's why I'm so determined to find him. But there's something else."

"Something else?" Casper asked hesitantly.

"I think Atlas is Griffin's child."

"Atlas…" Casper murmured. Then, his face lit up with recognition. "That boy from Cole's?"

I nodded, shrugging my shoulders. "He looked a little too much like Griffin and not enough like Cole. Plus, that woman knew him. There's no way it's a coincidence, right?"

Casper snickered before he could stifle it. "I knew there was something going on. Didn't expect a surprise child though."

My lips quirked up. "It's a good thing. It means he gets to live on in some way. Makes the guilt easier to bear."

Casper touched my arm. His touch was exceedingly gentle and lingered for only a few seconds.

"I know I don't know you super well, but I don't think you should feel guilty. You're here now, and without you, I wouldn't be here. I'm glad things went the way they did. Even if that makes me selfish." Casper looked up towards the clouds, fluffy as cotton candy in a pure sky.

"Besides. If you had died, who would stop Thorne?" he mused. "Maybe Griffin knew that too, and that's why he sacrificed himself."

Something inside me eased with his words. This kid was more wise than I thought.

"Yeah, maybe."

I grabbed his wrist, tugging him along as I sped up my pace. "Let's catch up with the rest of our little band. No time to waste."

After catching up with Aldric and the rest of the troupe, we kept pushing through the heavy brush. No path opened itself to us, but we were determined.

I don't know how long we went before we saw it.

A monstrous tree in a clearing, with dead vegetation surrounding it.

It had huge roots bursting through the earth, bent and twisted as though they were writhing in pain. There were no leaves left on its branches, and it looked almost like the tree had been struck by lightning, with a thick black line bisecting the trunk.

The closer we got to the mangled wood, the more I felt it. Like a hum in the air, vibrating my bones. It gave a similar feel to the Glade where I had first been blessed with my powers. Almost like the ground itself was completely saturated with mana.

After glancing around, I saw by the startled faces around me that they felt it too. Everyone but Aldric, who looked unflappable as always. My internal reservoir of power was filling to the brim, and I got a momentary head rush. That feeling abated once Aldric put his hand on me though, almost like he was helping to level me out.

I glanced up at him in shock, but he didn't seem to feel it. Was he absorbing my power somehow through the bond? Vampires weren't affected by mana the same way that mages and the various Otherkind were. Maybe that's why he felt nothing off.

Holding my hand up, I took a deep breath. Was this what

Ler had meant about twisted trees? Were there more like this? Now seemed like a good time to discuss the visions I had been given with the party.

As I explained everything—the bridge, the dream, Ler's warning—Louise and Seren piped up with questions I didn't have the answers to, like why they didn't see the person on the bridge with me. Casper looked sickly pale, Aldric meanwhile was like a statue—tense, unmoving, but I kept going.

When I reached the last point about twisted trees, all four slowly turned towards the mangled trunk that loomed ominously in the distance, almost as if daring us to move forward.

"You said *trees* though," Louise murmured almost to herself, rubbing her temples as though warding off a headache. "If that's the case, there should be more like this one somewhere, right?"

Seren nodded, tucking her ink-black hair behind one of her ears. She crossed her arms, tapping her foot as she thought aloud. "So we're now headed south. There's this land heavily saturated in mana, and a perverse excuse of a tree. I think if we keep going this way, we should get some clues."

Casper had turned white as a ghost at the idea. "If this is what's happening to *trees*, what will it do to us?"

"There's no way to know, but we need to push on," Louise

said definitively, striding with more confidence than I felt past the mass of tangled roots and distorted wood.

Aldric called out, stopping Louise in her tracks. "You guys seem to be more affected by whatever this is than I am. Let me take the lead. I can keep an eye out, and that should give you all time to adjust."

She tapped a finger against her chin, considering. "Yeah, you're right. Get up here, bat."

Aldric raised his brows. "Bat?"

"I wouldn't be surprised," Louise replied flatly.

The absurdity of the moment broke the tension with a few quiet chuckles.

Aldric rolled his shoulders as though relieving tension, then took Louise's place at the front of the group, gliding far too gracefully through the thick branches and remaining foliage. The shadows seemed desperate to cling to him, causing my stomach to roil.

I took place behind him, with Seren, Louise and Casper taking up the back. We followed the path he laid out for us, careful to avoid any dangerous roots or dips in the terrain.

We continued that way for a while before we saw the next one. This one was even more polluted than the first. Its branches were gnarled like arthritic hands, reaching desperately towards the heavens as though requesting mercy.

There was something so disturbing about it, almost as though it were a living creature begging to be put out of its misery. A shudder took me, but we continued on, more and more of the woods being overtaken by these horrific scenes of wretched, twisted trunks.

After a few more hours, my legs were aching from traversing through this corrupted forest. We had to climb over fallen trees, through impossibly dense grass, and around thorned bushes that were just begging to pierce our skin. When we finally took a break, something had me absolutely crawling out of my skin.

There were no sounds. No bird calls, no wolves, foxes, heck even the skittering of mice in the bush. My ears rang from the weight of the silence, but it felt wrong to break it. Like we would be inviting something to find us.

"Rest up while you can. I'll take first watch," Aldric said, his tone hushed. Even he felt it. The gravity of something unnatural in the air.

Louise and Seren wasted no time, throwing out their bedrolls and settling in. The sun had barely begun to dip below the horizon, twilight slowly blooming across the sky as darkness reached its phantom fingers towards us, beckoning from beyond the safety of our campfire.

Stars winked into view, seemingly brighter than usual. And with them, the feeling of eyes on the back of my neck. We couldn't let down our guard now. Not when we were so close to Thorne's trail.

I think the gods knew that, too.

CHAPTER 39

I woke slowly, with a knot in my neck and my body aching from the bare ground beneath my bedroll. But there was also something comforting. A weight settled across my waist, cradling me gently. There was the scent of wine and thunderstorms surrounding me, cocooning me in a soothing embrace.

My hair shifted slightly with each even, deep breath Aldric took against me. Every part of me wanted to just stay here in his arms, but I knew we couldn't. Not yet. I slowly, carefully tried to extricate myself from his grip, but as soon as I shifted, his eyes snapped open and he clung to me even tighter.

"Onyra?" Aldric murmured, his voice rough with sleep.

His eyes were like slivers of moonlight against the dark circles that marked his exhaustion.

"You look awful. Did you get any rest?"

Aldric refused to meet my gaze and shrugged his shoulders slightly. "Enough."

"Did you? I couldn't tell by the puffiness of your eyes and how foggy they look." I crossed my arms, looking Aldric up and down critically.

His hair was a mess, as though he'd run his hands through the inky waves one too many times. He looked like he hadn't slept for a week.

Sighing, I slowly deflated, taking Aldric's hands in mine. He was hard to stay mad at.

"Why didn't you sleep when the others took watch?"

Aldric loosed a breath in return, weaving his fingers through mine. "I didn't trust it. The others, they're strong, but not strong enough to protect you if something were to happen. I need to make sure that *I'm* there. I couldn't rest without knowing that you were safe. But the 'off' feeling I had abated as the sun came up, so I caught a short snooze."

He gave my hand a squeeze and smiled when I returned it.

"Next time, I'll take watch so you can sleep. I can protect you too, you know," I said, only half-joking.

Aldric's smile turned salacious as he said, "I do like a strong woman. Not to mention so gorgeous it hurts my soul not to hold you. Oh, and then there's your wit and personality."

He released my fingers to swoon, and I couldn't help but laugh.

Louise was burying the fire with a little help from Casper. She looked terrible as well. The weight of the mana here must be getting to her. Strange. I felt better than I did when I went to sleep. Why would it be any different?

Maybe it was Aldric?

"Aldric, can you go hold Louise's hand for a moment?" I asked, curiosity getting the better of me.

"Already trying to pawn me off to another woman, are you?" Aldric asked with a serious look. But he cracked a smile when he saw my expression, dragging himself to his feet.

Louise held out her hand expectantly, almost like a queen awaiting a servant. Aldric bowed deeply before lightly grasping her fingers.

"Do you feel any better?"

Louise considered for a moment, then shook her head. Aldric released his grip on her and returned to my side, efficiently packing the bedroll and supplies nearby.

"Strange. I feel better when Aldric and I have contact. Almost like the weight of the mana here isn't as heavy."

Louise hummed and tapped a finger to her chin. "Can't say for sure, but maybe it's because of the bond? I've never personally known a mage and a vampire to mate, so I don't exactly have a control group to reference."

That could be. The only difference between Louise and I was that bond. Maybe he helped center my mana somehow? It made sense. Not really sure how that worked though. We may have to experiment further.

Then it occurred to me. One of us was missing. I glanced around the camp.

"Where is Seren?"

Surprisingly, Casper answered me this time.

"She went to see if she could find water. But that was quite a while ago. Seren should probably be back by now."

Aldric stiffened, straightening to his full, imposing height.

"When was this?"

Casper shrunk under the weight of Aldric's blazing gaze, but he shrugged.

"It was shortly after sunrise. She went further south. Said that her water skin was empty."

A hiss of air blew from between Aldric's teeth as he hefted our pack onto his shoulder.

"I'll lead the way. We have to find her, and fast. This place… there's just something wrong here. And not just the foliage," he said, waving a hand towards the twisted trees.

Louise lifted her own pack and threw Casper's in his direction. He clearly wasn't paying attention, because it smacked him in the ribs. Casper recovered quickly, however, and soon we were following the covert trail that Seren had left.

Aldric was like a bloodhound on the hunt, leading us this way and that with utmost confidence. The further along we went, the more mangled the forest became. There were fewer plants, and more of those mangled trunks, until we were surrounded by them.

Then, we saw her.

Seren.

She was sitting on the ground with something bundled in her lap. Her lips were moving, but I couldn't hear the words. Slowly, we approached, careful not to surprise her in case she was hiding from something.

But we couldn't have expected what we saw nestled in her cloak.

It was a deer fawn, looking to be a newborn. It trembled in her grasp, a weak bleat sounding from its small form.

"It's okay," she said, cooing to the fawn. She turned to look up at us. "It was just lying here when I passed by, and I couldn't leave it. The mother hasn't returned, and it only looked to be a few hours old."

Casper looked in awe at the small animal.

"I've never seen a deer close up before!" he whispered, clearly excited.

"Try not to spook it," Seren admonished, gently stroking the critter's fur to soothe it. "Fawn are delicate at this age."

It was a deep brown, with bright white spots mottling its torso. It had the cutest black nose and long, gangly legs. The fawn's ears were pinned back as though unsure, and it was curled into a ball, as tightly as it could get, clearly trying to stay out of sight.

"We need to get going," I whispered, gesturing at our surroundings. "Lo0k around, we've got to be getting close now. We can't be held up by deer, even if they are cute."

Taking a step closer, a branch snapped beneath my heel, and the fawn lifted its head in alarm. Its eyes, black as a void, zeroed in on me. Then it cocked its head slightly, as though assessing me. Something about it felt very unnatural.

A vertical slit on the creature's forehead slowly opened, revealing an orb, speckled with white and deep blue, like a condensed galaxy. Then it contracted, and nausea spiked through me as I realized.

It was another eye.

"Seren, get away from that thing!" I said, fighting the urge to yell. If there was one of these things, there had to be more.

To my horror, Seren merely cooed at the fawn, stroking its neck. But it would not settle, instead struggling on its unsteady legs to stand. Seren stood beside it, completely unphased.

"Seren, what are you doing?!" Louise hissed.

She looked at us as though *we* were the crazy ones.

"Don't you feel it?" she asked.

"Feel what?" Aldric asked, moving to stand in front of me.

I peered around his large frame to see Seren shaking her head sadly.

"Its soul is pure. Uncorrupted. Whatever is here is molding the flesh into something unnatural. I can only imagine how they suffer."

There was such sorrow in her voice it nearly drove tears to my eyes. She continued to run her fingers gently over the fawn as it struggled before collapsing into a heap again, clearly not strong enough yet to gain its bearings.

"Why is this happening?" I asked, a chill slipping down my spine at the implications.

"This place we're approaching is sacred in Starfall Veil. It's where the gods were born, where the Veil between us is the thinnest."

She looked over her shoulder as though seeing not the reality, but her memories.

"It's strange that everything is so…polluted here. Back home, it is verdant, Fae and animals alike drawn to the purity of the mana. But in Aethralis…it's like the earth has been soaked in blood and nothing is being done about it."

Her words caused my heart to twist painfully in my chest.

Was this Thorne's doing?

As if she could read my thoughts, Seren shook her head. "This goes deeper than just Thorne. This type of corruption wouldn't happen overnight. It takes hundreds—if not thousands—of years to get to this point."

"I don't know where the doe is, but we cannot afford to wait. Any delay will only cause more suffering."

Seren's face was a mask of melancholy as she crouched next to the fawn, pressing a kiss to its cheek.

"I'm truly sorry," she whispered. "Please live."

With a sheen of tears in her eyes, she cleared her throat. The fawn slowly laid its head down as if it understood, that ethereal third eye closing.

"Let's go," she said, pulling her forgotten pack onto her shoulder, a filled water skin dangling from the side.

CHAPTER 40

The next half-day's travel took place in silence. Each of us too afraid to open our mouths and speak for fear of breaking ourselves apart under the strain. Somberness flowed off of Seren in waves, so deep that it twisted your heart in your chest and made it hard to breathe.

But I understood her—which made it more difficult to say anything. The feeling that you understood your world and your place in it, only to have it all upended, leaving you in suspended animation, like a puppet on tangled strings waiting to be cut down. As though sensing the dark turn of my thoughts, I felt a surge of warmth through the bond, Aldric's hand gently sliding down my arm to weave his fingers with mine. When I glanced up at him in surprise, his silvery eyes were molten with unspoken emotion.

I held onto him like he were the only thing tethering me to this life. And he very well may be.

His touch ebbed some pressure within me I hadn't realized was there until it was gone. A sense of relief made my legs feel like jelly, and Aldric was quick to steady me as I stumbled. No one even looked up, lost in their thoughts as they were.

The sun was falling below the horizon, shadows stretching until they encompassed us all. Even the sky was like a dark void, the moon blotted out with thick clouds.

My eyes automatically adjusted to pull in every modicum of light, allowing for some limited visibility into our surroundings. The forest itself seemed to drown in the gloom, the surrounding air tense as though everything was holding its breath.

More than anything, the fear had gone. What was left was an all-encompassing emptiness. Thinking of Seren, I tried to look at it from her point of view. In her world, this place was rife with living creatures, bounding through lush greenery.

Here, it was like they poisoned the well, and the only thing nourishing the earth was the pile of corpses leftover. It must be agony for her, especially for a Fae. They're more attuned to nature than any of the Otherkind—of course she'd be taking it like this.

Aldric squeezed my chilled fingers, and I returned it back to him, his strength leeching into me. For Seren, for all of Magekind, I would purify this land of the sickness devouring it.

No matter what it cost.

We had walked through the night, stopping only as needed when our bodies were at their limit. The sun was just barely creeping over the horizon, offering the barest hint of light through the mangled branches of the forest. The clouds had gone, leaving a kaleidoscope of pastels in their wake.

There was a strange hope within me, seeing the gentle beauty through the tangled limbs of the surrounding vegetation. Aldric had been by my side the entire time, holding me tightly during the moments of brief respite. I'm not sure who needed it more—me or him.

A heaviness had descended upon us as we grew closer to our destination. There was no telling what would await us—and we all knew it. Death itself could be whispering sweet nothings to the wind, drawing us ever closer to its skeletal grasp, and we would be none the wiser.

The woods slowly began to thin, and my breath caught. Almost there. We had to be almost there. My body was screaming for relief, for an actual break, but I couldn't stop. Not yet.

Aldric placed a hand on the small of my back, silently supporting me as we trudged on, my feet feeling like lead. My pulse rang in my ears as we could finally see something beyond this accursed place.

Despite the misery my body was being put through, I couldn't stop myself.

I ran to see what lay beyond.

In the distance, there lay the remains of what used to be a powerful kingdom, left to fester in the rot.

The once-tall spires had crumbled, leaving only skeletal remnants of their structure behind. There was a wall surrounding the city's remnants, collapsed by the gravity of time. Shadows encompassed the damaged buildings like a living thing, leaving much to the imagination.

And yet…

There, barely visible through the shade, was a single lit window—a pinprick of a glow amidst the gloom, so small I could be imagining it. It took my breath away all the same.

This could be it. He could be *right there*. All we had to do was get there.

Adrenaline spiked through me with the force of a lightning strike, and my body began to move on its own. But before I could take more than a couple of steps, a grip of iron manacled my wrist.

"My love, we need to rest. *You* need to rest," Aldric murmured.

I tried in vain to extricate myself from his hold, but he didn't budge.

"Aldric, he could be—," I started, but Aldric quickly cut me off.

"Even if he were, you're in no condition to face him. Onyra, your feet are bleeding. Did you even feel it?"

Louise threw her pack to the ground. The sudden noise caused me to snap to attention.

"He's right, Lyra. Let's rest before we delve into the shit."

Louise sounded completely exhausted, her voice cracking. She plopped right down onto the dry grass, not even waiting for a response. The rest of the group followed suit, sighs of relief sounding through the air.

Deflating, I slowly lowered myself to the ground, my body protesting the movement. Aldric joined me, offering me the support I didn't know I needed. Carefully, so carefully, he removed my shoes and socks, and I was stopped short at the sight of bloodied blisters on my feet.

Aldric was right. I hadn't even felt it.

I was so single-mindedly focused. I was neglecting myself and the rest of the group. Wordlessly, Aldric went to Louise. He whispered something in her ear, and she fumbled through the contents of her satchel, handing him a single glass jar and something else I couldn't quite see.

A wave of fatigue hit me like a Feralumin as Aldric made his way back. I slowly lay on the hard, unforgiving earth.

My eyes slipped closed.

I just needed a moment.

A moment to breathe before we moved on.

That's all.

Warm.

My eyes slowly cracked open, and I stretched languidly. That movement was cut short by a grumpy-sounding moan from behind me and an arm pulling me tighter against a hard, male form. I felt surprisingly well-rested for how little time we'd been laying here, judging by the position of the sun in the sky.

There was a heavy leg thrown over my own, and the comforting scent of Aldric surrounding me. He had set up his bedroll next to my own so that we could lie together, and he had given me the pack to use as a makeshift pillow, judging by the lack of neck pain.

Gentle snoring rumbled next to my ear, and I couldn't stop a small smile from forming on my face.

This was nice.

Allowing the moment to linger, I let my mind drift, relishing the feeling of my Onyra clinging to me like a precious jewel he was afraid would shatter, even subconsciously. There was a faint smell of fire smoke and dry earth in the air.

Then, the sound of metal on metal clanking together caused my eyes to shoot open, the peace gone.

Louise appeared to be cooking something on a fire with what remained of our limited rations. I tried to sit up, but Aldric pulled me back into his embrace, a mumbled 'no' tumbling from his lips.

"Aldric, we need to get up," I said, shaking him gently.

"Orustus himself couldn't pry me from this bed," Aldric

mumbled, nuzzling into the spot between my neck and shoulder.

Louise must have heard him, because she sputtered, "Don't invoke the Unbound so casually. You want to give us bad luck?"

My brows furrowed. The Unbound?

Seren had been sitting quietly to the side, looking down at the remains of the once-grand Mage kingdom.

"The god of death," she whispered, her voice carrying on the wind. "Fitting in a place like this."

I shook my head. "No, no, no. We're not doing that. Absolutely not. We've got enough problems with enough deities. We're not adding to the list."

Everyone turned to look at me, shocked. There was a beat of silence and then Louise loosed a bark of laughter and everyone else followed suit, laughing until our sides ached and we were wiping tears from our eyes.

"We have to be crazy, right?" I said, gasping for air while the remnants of laughter rattled in my lungs. "This whole thing is crazy."

Louise smiled, highlighting the wrinkles around her eyes. "Absolutely. And I'm nuts for being here with you."

"Insane," Aldric said by way of agreement. "Kooky, if you will."

"Definitely got a screw loose, for sure," Casper said, his lips quirked up for the first time in ages.

Seren remained silent, and slowly each smile died like a candle being blown out.

Louise gave the meal a stir before heading over to where Seren sat, placing her hand on her shoulder. Seren glanced up at Louise in surprise before placing her hand over the older mage's.

"Thank you," Seren said earnestly. "Soon, this will all be over."

"It will."

CHAPTER 41

This was it.

The bones of the old kingdom lay just ahead of us. Our bellies were full from the meal Louise prepared, our bodies rested. As we packed up camp, Louise revealed that an entire day had passed while we had been asleep.

My shock was outweighed by a vague sense of gratitude. My body, my mind and my mana needed that rest. I knew it in the very core of my being. My feet were bandaged and in a fresh pair of socks. Boots were the only things I had to wear, but better than nothing. The feeling of the poultice on my feet was a sensation I had to get used to, but it soothed the ache until it was no longer at the forefront of my mind.

As we approached, the ruins loomed overhead, jutting into the bright blue sky like jagged pieces of broken glass. The scale of it stole my breath. Absently, I wondered how many had once dwelt in the cradle of these now-crumbled walls.

Aldric caught my upper arm, stopping me short.

"What is it?"

"Watch out, my dear. You almost stepped on someone."

I gaped at him for a moment before looking down, stifling a shriek. There was a sun-bleached skull smiling up at me from the red clay of the road. Without thinking, I clung to Aldric, who chuckled.

Then my gaze roved over the landscape, picking out the specks of alabaster dotting the landscape.

Just how many had died here?

Then I noticed it. Not all of these remains belonged to mages. There were some that had canine teeth that were too long, their skulls distorted, their fingers more like talons. Werefolk?

The gravity of the loss that occurred here, in this place, smacked into me like a train. Was this the site of the battle from a thousand years ago? It would make sense, I realized.

Of course, it would happen right here on the border.

The closer we got, the more my mind caught flashes of the battlefield. There were still claw marks in some of the stone, worn away by time. Swords jutting from ribcages, shields with the straps still tightened, armor left abandoned. Scattered around like fish scales, catching the barest hint of sunlight through the layers of dust and debris.

The very atmosphere seemed to thicken with untamed mana. No wonder this city had been so massive. It would have to be for this much power to be kept under control, I realized.

Louise grunted in pain, and my gaze shot to face, which was covered in a thin sheen of sweat. She looked pale and like she was struggling to catch her breath.

I rushed to her side, Aldric just behind me.

"Are you okay?"

"This is too much for me. The magic," she gasped out.

Casper took Louise's arm, the young boy trying desperately to keep her from collapsing.

One look at his sincere golden eyes and an unspoken understanding passed between us.

"I'm going to take you back to the campsite, Louise," Casper said with more confidence than I expected. "And I'll stay with you to keep you safe."

Louise tried to wave him off, but almost lost her footing. She grew weak very fast. Too fast.

"Hurry, Casper. Get her out of here," I said. "We'll come to get both of you when all this is done."

Casper gave me a mock solute and with almost preternatural speed, he hefted Louise into his arms—surprisingly strong for the frail boy I'd met just weeks ago—striding quickly back the way we had come.

I loosed a breath I hadn't realized I was holding, and Aldric gave my hand a reassuring squeeze before turning us back on our path.

The path to the end, one way or another.

Finally, we were at the rusted remnants of the gate into the kingdom. The bodies became more numerous the closer we got to passing the threshold and I was horrified to see mummified human remains, their faces twisted into masks of despair, clawing at their own skin. They still wore armor on their frail bodies, weapons forgotten to time strewn across the surrounding land.

Truly, this was a graveyard of a fallen era of the mages. A shudder skittered down my spine at the thought. Once we were within the walls, an unnatural silence fell on us like a weighted blanket. The pressure of the mana was stifling, my internal reservoir full to bursting. The tension eased as Aldric grabbed my hand, placing it in the crook of his arm as though we were just out taking a lovely stroll instead of making our way to potential death.

Seren glanced around, paler than usual, but still holding strong. The amount of magic the Fae could hold must be enormous for her to be this unaffected.

"Are you okay?" I whispered to her. It felt wrong to speak, like disturbing the dead.

She nodded, her emerald eyes wide.

There was a sense deep within that if we could see into the afterlife, we would be completely entrenched in a sea of souls, trapped here for gods know how long. Would they be screaming into the void? Grasping at the living in vain, desperate to move on? Or would they be resigned to their fate?

The thought was sobering, and a deep pang of sadness filled me. Aldric gave my hand a squeeze.

"Soon, we'll be free from this place," Aldric murmured. "And all the dead within it. This is a tomb dedicated to the mage's mistakes."

"We just need to find Thorne," I said, my voice ragged.

Where was that light? Most of the city had been in shadow, so it was hard to pinpoint.

Aldric tugged my arm, and we turned down a side road towards a series of dilapidated stone structures on the outskirts of the castle grounds, Seren following behind.

"How do you know where to go?" I asked, looking up at Aldric in shock.

"Just following the smell of rot," he said simply, as though it was the most obvious thing in the world.

We took another left, then a right, then after too many twists and turns, we landed in front of a surprisingly well-kept building near the heart of the city. It would have been pretty unassuming in the prime of this city. While it was multiple stories tall, there was no grandeur about it like you could see in the surrounding remains. No pillars, no flower boxes.

Aldric stopped in front of the stairs leading up to the door.

He leaned down so close I could feel his warm breath against the shell of my ear. "I think he's here," he whispered. "There is something alive in here, at least."

With a deep breath, I climbed the steps to the heavy wooden door that stood between me and whatever lay beyond.

It was time to knock on death's door—whether it meant his end, or mine.

WHISPERED SECRETS

The door handle seemed especially icy in my fingers as I pushed through the heavy oak entryway. The building was unlocked—not that I was surprised. Who would expect company in a place like this?

Aldric and Seren were tight on my heels when we crossed the threshold together. The building seemed fairly unassuming. Small motes floated through the air with casual abandon, catching the limited light flowing in. The windows were all caked with grime. The floor was coated with a fine layer of filth, causing footprints to stand out starkly against the dust.

Fresh footprints.

There was something else—a faint scent in the air that had me wrinkling my nose. The footprints led to several open doorways, and we moved as a group, checking each place carefully. A strange wave of recognition hit me as I realized these areas reminded me of Thorne's home. The frantically scribbled notes, the scattering of papers. The way the potion bottles were lined on shelves so carefully, and yet books were strewn haphazardly around.

My stomach twisted painfully. Reality was hitting me.

He was here.

Aldric insisted on taking the lead, keeping me close behind.

"I have the superior danger sense, not to mention

survivability. And this is no time to play games," Aldric had said, more serious than I'd ever seen him. He even pulled his hair back with a leather thong, highlighting his striking cheekbones. He looked like a warrior going into battle.

His insistence grated on me, but I allowed it, my eyes wandering from shelf to shelf, room to room. Each area was the same, with what appeared to be barely organized chaos spreading like bacteria on each surface. Upstairs was a sparse bedroom with dirty sheets and an unmade bed. There was a single, mostly melted candle on the lone bedside table. The windows had been blacked out with heavy curtains.

It reminded me of a cave. Or a den.

There were tracks across the stone that looked as though someone had been pacing the same path over and over. There were also mysterious dark stains and a sourness in the air that reminded me of the smell of the sick. The stains ranged from relatively fresh and bright red to deep black.

My mouth watered as nausea roiled in my stomach, and I backed out of the room before it made me vomit. Aldric wrinkled his nose in distaste and followed shortly afterwards.

"I don't know what in the world he has been doing here, but the scent of decay is so strong, it's like an unrefrigerated morgue," Aldric hissed.

As the food in my body threatened to rebel, I raced downstairs, desperate for fresh air. In my panic, I noticed it. More splotches of deep red. Small bits of flesh, writhing with maggots.

I had barely passed the threshold of the exit when I began

to heave, my stomach emptying all of its contents into the dry scrubs outside. Seren soon joined me, looking a sickly shade of green, though she managed to hold it together. There was a sheen of sweat on her brow, and she was holding a hand around her belly. Breathing hard, bracing myself with my hands on my thighs, I took a few minutes to compose myself.

Wiping my mouth with the back of my hand, I slowly straightened, dread creeping through me with increasing intensity until my fingertips tingled with adrenaline.

Aldric hadn't come out. He must still be looking in there, I realized.

Shoving the remaining nausea down, I steeled myself. No time to think about it, or I'll find every reason not to go back inside.

With renewed vigor, I stepped back into hell itself.

Standing on the threshold, I cocked my head, listening. But there was no sound. Aldric must be nearby, where else would he have gone?

Taking a deep breath, I steadied myself and realized I could feel a tug from deep within, leading me further into the derelict building. The closer I got, the more I could feel him. Aldric's presence. His aura was like a warm hug on a frigid night. A light to drive away the worst of nightmares.

That sensation only grew stronger until finally, he came

into view. Aldric was leaning with his back against one of the dark stone walls, his arms crossed. He looked casual as could be, though his face was solemn. It was so out of character for him it put me ill at ease.

"What are you doing?" I whispered.

"This is the only place I haven't checked. I know there's something in here. But I knew you'd have my throat if I went without you," Aldric said, though no smile crossed his face.

Seren crept up behind me, and I almost jumped out of my skin, my hand flying up to my chest as though to keep my heart within it.

"He's right," she murmured. "I think that's the way."

Staring at the wall, my brows furrowed, and my lips tugged downward. What were they talking about? There was no door.

Seren wordlessly walked up near where Aldric was waiting, and a warding sigil flared to life, its sickly yellow pulsating grotesquely.

This reminded me of the warding from the dungeons in Starfall Veil, which felt like an entire lifetime ago. Would it respond the same?

I followed, my throat suddenly dry. My hand raised towards the sigil, my fingers trembling. Pulling back, I made a fist to stop the shaking.

It's all been for this. Don't be a coward. Be strong. That mantra played through my head over and over. The next time I reached out, I was relieved to see my hand was steady.

The ward felt *sticky* under my fingers, almost as though it were trying to penetrate my skin. But within seconds, it crumbled into nothingness.

As soon as it was gone, it was like a curtain had fallen away, leaving a dank corridor with a spiral staircase leading into pitch darkness. Along with that was the smell of warm, rotting meat. But stronger than my drive to flee was my determination to finally end it.

To stop this curse.

CHAPTER 42

A sense of foreboding grew with each step we descended into the darkness. The air was thick with tension, and the sound of our footsteps reverberating off the stone seemed impossibly loud. With every whisper of fabric, every shuffle of our boots, I was gritting my teeth, half-expecting Thorne to fly up the stairs and attack us.

But there was nothing.

Eventually, after what felt like hours but was probably only a few minutes, we reached a heavy wooden door with an iron ring for a handle. It was incredibly dim with weak magical lighting interspersed on the walls, and I could barely make out Aldric's silhouette in front of me.

Aldric barely hesitated before pulling the heavy iron ring, the door surprisingly whisper-quiet. But the air beyond the threshold was rancid. There's no way something living could be in here.

But Aldric strode forward, entirely confident. Too confident. The space was cramped, little more than another hallway. There was an upturned side table and a dark smear on the stone in front of us, almost like something had been dragged through the door opposite where we had entered. Near the smear was what looked to be a bowl or beaker that had been smashed, shards of glass bearing the same residue that was on the floor and a scattering of papers.

Reaching out, I put my hand on Aldric's shoulder, pulling him to a stop. Something was wrong here, and I didn't know what.

But I needed to face it.

With more certainty than I felt, I rushed forward through the sticky remnants on the floor and pushed the door open before anyone could stop me.

I blinked in the sudden light, squinting. There were bright lights overhead, almost like surgical lighting. After a moment, I adjusted and looked around the room. This looked like a lab of some type. There were several abandoned workstations, dried plants of all kinds, and magical tomes littered everywhere, forgotten.

But what drew my attention was in the center of the room. The trail of viscera had coalesced into the form of a broken man. He looked to be barely alive, his obsidian eyes glassy and his hair streaked with red.

His flesh had sloughed off in chunks, at some points so deep that bone could be seen. He looked like a living corpse.

"Thorne?" I asked, gaping at the remains in front of me.

A ragged, wet laugh escaped his lips. "Of course. It would be you," he rasped.

"What the hell have you done? What happened to you?" I asked, reaching out before catching myself. I felt a prickle on my neck as Aldric and Seren approached from behind, silent from the jarring scene in front of them.

He was so decayed he almost didn't look real. How could he even still be alive?

"This is because of your power," Thorne ground out, his voice hoarse. "It was too much for my body. But I had to keep trying."

"Trying *what*?" I couldn't believe what I was hearing. What I was *seeing*.

"To right my wrongs. To fix the sickness. Find the cure," he said, coughing wetly.

A dark fluid dribbled from his nose, and as he reached up to wipe it, another patch of flesh fell from his arm onto the stone with a wet *plop*.

"After my other experiments failed, I started testing on myself. As you can see, it hasn't gone well," he said, chuckling darkly before breaking off with another hacking cough.

"You should have just left it alone," I spat. "The plague would have died out, eventually. It was isolated to our side of the Serathine. Instead, all you did was spread it farther."

"It was all for nothing," Thorne murmured, his voice cracking. "I am truly a failure."

"Yes. You are," I said, then sighed. "But that's all the more reason to stop holding on. It will be okay. We have found a cure. My friend Seren was sick, but she's fine now, see?"

I gestured to the Fae over my right shoulder, and Thorne's eyes filled with pink-tinged tears.

His lower lip trembled and wetness streaked down his mottled cheeks.

"How?" he whispered.

"She and I together can purify the tainted magic. You never would have found this out on your own. There is no other way."

Thorne's face went carefully blank and then a small smile appeared on his face.

"Then it sounds like I truly can let go. Thank you, Lyra. For what little it's worth, I am sorry. We never should have tried to change you."

I shook my head and stood, taking a step back.

Eventually his movements slowed, and his head fell back against the stone with a sharp *crack* as his body began to convulse. Seren reached past me for Thorne, panic on her face as though she wanted to help, but I stopped her.

Thorne went limp, his chest rattling as it loosed one final breath before going still.

A sick sense of relief filled me.

It was over. Finally.

Aldric reached out and pulled me away from the corpse, folding me in his embrace as though to shield me from the horror of what we had just witnessed.

Gripping his arms, I buried my face in his chest, surrounding myself in the comfort he offered. There was no way to know where we'd go from here, but at least we had each other.

The rest would come in time.

"Let's get out of here. This place is going to make me sick," Seren murmured, covering her mouth with her hand. "You two will have time to cuddle in a less disturbing place later. Plus, we need to get back to Casper and Louise."

She was right, of course. Aldric slowly loosened his hold on me, sliding his hand down my arm to weave his fingers through mine. He led me towards the exit, his grip strong and warm.

But it wouldn't last.

The lights flickered for just a moment, and I glanced up in surprise, only for a crushing weight to fill the entire space, leaving me breathless.

This wasn't a physical presence.

It was a magical force.

I whipped around and the sight that greeted me almost made me vomit.

A wet, gurgling sound along with the grinding of bone on bone sounded in the room, impossibly loud. What was once Thorne jerkily got to its feet, a dark aura flowing through the holes in its flesh.

A voice, multi-layered, flowed out of the corpse's open mouth.

"You will not escape me again, you defiant *wretch*!" they shouted.

Myrana. How could they be here?

In my shock, I stood there dumbly, mouth agape.

Myrana raised their hand, splaying their fingers towards me. An arc of what looked like liquid night flew from their fingertips like a whip.

Before I could react, Aldric shoved me roughly away, my back slamming into the hard stone of the wall. Stars exploded in my vision as the impact registered in my head, and I sat there, dazed, for what could have been seconds or minutes.

Faintly, I heard someone shouting my name, and my head lifted, my vision glazed in red on my left side.

Aldric. Where was he?

I felt empty inside, hollow, as though something precious had been lost.

There. A few feet away, he lay sprawled on the ground.

I squinted, slowly rising on shaky legs. That couldn't be right. Why was he laying down?

Like an electric jolt, my brain registered what I was seeing with horrifying clarity. I rushed to his side, collapsing to my knees.

"Aldric!" I screamed, my voice raw. "Wake up!"

I reached down to shake him, but what I felt had me reeling, jerking back like he had burned me.

Blood.

He had been flayed clean through, large slices into his body going all the way through to the ground.

He had been hurt worse, surely.

Aldric had to live.

But the echoing maw inside of me where his presence used to dwell whispered that my hopes were nothing more than a lie.

Seren stood in front of the door to the exit, shouting something, but the buzzing in my ears made her words muffled.

Numbly, I looked at the red staining my fingers before raising my eyes to the god—nay, the creature—before me, wearing a mangled body like a coat.

A rage like I had never known filled me, my entire being vibrating with fury.

There were no thoughts—I just ran towards them.

Shock flitted through their glassy eyes, but it was short-lived. I grasped their upper arms, my fingers digging into the rotting flesh until they reached bone, which ground against my fingernails.

"I hate you!" I wailed, my voice cracking with emotion. "Haven't you taken enough? Haven't you done enough?"

That familiar haughty look Myrana wore on Thorne's face shook me, but I refused to be cowed.

"Why are you here? You haven't taken enough?!" I hissed, my throat painfully tight as my eyes burned with unshed tears.

To my surprise, they laughed. They actually laughed, the sound mocking the agony they inflicted upon me.

"You aren't much without him, are you?" they purred, their smile too wide for the face they wore.

In that moment, as those words registered, I lost control.

My mana swelled within me, filling every ounce of my body. The white-hot fury choked me, and I ground my teeth so hard they may have cracked.

"I will destroy you," I muttered darkly, my grip getting stronger until I could hear the creak of Thorne's bones.

"You will be nothing but the dust under my feet, pissed away in the wind, you *monster*!" I screamed, my power siphoning Myrana's at an unforgivable pace.

My muscles strained, my organs aching as though they were being crushed, but I kept pulling. I could feel liquid dribbling down my lips, the taste of copper exploding on my tongue, and my vision went blurry, my head pounding.

Myrana tried to extricate themselves from my hold, but I was an immovable force and I could only scream all of my anger, my pain, my sadness, as my body tore itself asunder with the force of a gods magic.

It was too much.

I couldn't hold any more.

But I wasn't done. I couldn't be. Myrana still *existed* and that couldn't happen.

With a roar ripping itself from my throat, a massive burst of power flowed from my body in a shockwave, tearing what remained of Thorne into viscera and bone.

The workstations flew back against the walls with so much force, the wood shattered and splinters erupted through the air.

I heard the distant sound of a body hitting stone from somewhere behind me.

But I couldn't turn.

I couldn't move.

My body gave out, and the world tilted before going completely black.

CHAPTER 43

Aldric was adrift.

Floating aimlessly in a void of nothingness. There was no pain, no urgency. He couldn't even remember what he had been doing.

How long had he been here?

There was a vague sense of urgency hovering at the very edge of his consciousness, but he couldn't recall why. As his sluggish mind struggled to put the pieces together, something was pulling him back in.

Almost like a hand grasping at the very essence of his being and dragging him back towards reality. There was a voice, speaking words that reminded Aldric of the whisper of dried leaves against stone.

Try as he might, despite centuries of life, he couldn't place the language. It felt archaic and powerful, as though he shouldn't be allowed to hear it.

The force that manipulated his essence felt surprisingly gentle, and it laid a hand on his chest.

Aldric woke.

Everything felt fuzzy and sore.

Stretching his fingers, he sucked in a breath. Damn. The ancient dust bags had always warned him that First Death is awful, but Aldric hadn't prepared for this.

He brought a hand and scrubbed it down his face, his eyes slowly opening.

There was a wall directly in front of his face, obscuring his vision. What happened?

Aldric's memories were blurry, a whirlwind of information that he was trying to sort through a muddied lens.

His shoulder and abdomen burned like fire, and he slowly hissed through his teeth as he pushed to a seated position. It looked as though a bomb went off, he thought, shoving his dark waves out of his face. Reaching up, he slowly and carefully re-fastened his mane with the leather thong that was holding on for dear life to a few tendrils of hair.

Aldric's body was streaked with blood, the scent rich in the air. The remnants of his shirt hung off his torso in ribbons, so there wasn't any point in trying to wear it, he decided. The cloth was left forgotten somewhere on the cold stone.

Damn it all, but his stomach ached. A meal would help to heal him quicker.

There was a tantalizing aroma floating through the room, and his mouth watered involuntarily.

"What had I been doing?" Aldric mused aloud, his hand rubbing his chin thoughtfully.

A faint wheezing caught his attention, and he slowly got to his feet, navigating the debris in the room silently. For just a moment, a night sky appeared overhead, and Aldric rubbed his eyes, shaking his head. Then, it flowed like water behind him and descended into a still form in the hallway, left in a heap.

"I didn't know First Death could cause hallucinations," he said, chuckling darkly. But then the body in the hallway moved, sitting up before jumping to their feet.

"Ah, Seren. You're okay—" he began.

His words were cut off by the sound of a loud *crack*! The walls of the basement had begun to crumble under the force of whatever had destroyed this room. Dust began to rain from the ceiling, clouding his vision.

If Seren was in the hallway…

Where was Lyra?

He turned to ask the Fae, but she bared her teeth at him in what could be a smile.

"Her overconfidence will be what crushes her, you know," Seren said. Her eyes held a madness within them that surprised him. Before he had a chance to respond, Seren took off at a run, disappearing up the stairs.

Crushes her?

A gnawing pit opened up in Aldric's stomach, and his gaze flew around the room. There was an explosion of sound as one of the walls gave way, causing part of the ceiling to collapse. He covered his ears, but the ringing in his ears afterwards was still too loud.

Where the *hell* was Lyra?!

His bond with her had weakened when he experienced death, so it was hard for him to pinpoint her location in the mess. Taking a deep inhale, he tried to sort the myriad of scents in the room to find hers.

Then he realized. There was a different scent in the air—it was blood, but not just that. It was *Lyra's* blood.

Panic iced his veins, and he started throwing rock and wood aside, trying to make a path further in before the building collapsed. His mangled body was crumpling under the strain, but Aldric would give his life for his Onyra.

His fingers were scraped raw and bloody by the jagged edges of stone, but he barely even noticed. Though weakened, his vampiric strength was enough to open a small gap his body could fit through.

Once he pushed through, he narrowly side-stepped a hefty chunk of ceiling, which landed with another loud *boom*! It kicked up dust and particulates that stung his eyes and had Aldric coughing, but he pressed on.

There.

His heart squeezed painfully in his chest at the sight of his Onyra. For just a moment, Aldric was certain he saw a faint shadow hovering over Lyra, but as he rubbed his eyes, it was gone.

She was laying motionless, aside from the shallow rise and

fall of her chest. Aldric's heart was in his throat as he raced with preternatural speed to her side. Dropping to his knees, he flipped Lyra onto her back and shook her gently.

"Onyra, wake up," he said, his voice hoarse. "You must."

Adrenaline slammed into him with such force that the edges of his vision turned white, leaving only room for her.

His forever one.

"Darling, you *must* wake up," he said again, desperation coloring his voice. A grinding noise echoing in the room had his body as tense as a bowstring. He would run out of time if he stayed here.

Aldric glanced down at Lyra's body, the sight causing his throat to tighten. Her skin had split open in places, almost like whatever force had taken her had exploded from the inside out. She had blood running in rivulets down her face, from her nose and eyes. Her snow-white hair was streaked with crimson.

Lyra's head lolled as he hefted her into his arms. The grit of ground stone in the air made it hard to see. He had to rely on his other senses. Aldric's body was healing too slowly—his reflexes were not as sharp.

His feet barely touched the ground as he raced towards the exit. He cradled Lyra's body to him as though she were a delicate jewel. Careful not to jostle her too much, he leapt over the debris that had fallen from the ceiling.

There was a shudder in the air, like the moment before jaws snap around you. He couldn't afford to be careful. Aldric's skin tore as he narrowly escaped being crushed by falling rock.

A deep groan reverberated through the basement, and Aldric's heart sank as the exit came into view. The doorway had begun to crumble. His feet pounded the earth with rising urgency.

The doorway collapsed entirely just as he passed through it.

There was a discordant hum running through the walls, cracks tracing through the stone.

In a blur, he raced up the stairs. Dust hissed down, covering them in a fine gray coating. Lyra was disturbingly silent during the entire ordeal, driving Aldric's adrenaline higher.

Within moments, they were outside, and the building that stood as both a testament of Thorne's madness and his tomb—collapsed.

Aldric didn't hesitate.

Like an animal, he tore into his own flesh, lifeblood spurting from the wound on his wrist.

Carefully, he held his wrist to Lyra's mouth.

This had to work.

He cradled her delicately, her head falling back into the crook of his arm. Bits of dust and debris rained from her hair with that small movement. Dread coiled itself in his belly, filling his veins with ice.

Her breathing slowed further, and his chest seized painfully. Not like this. They had finally done it—Thorne was defeated.

She was safe.

"Onyra," he whispered, holding her tightly to his chest. "You can't leave me like this. I only just found you. Please."

Baring his fangs fully, he ripped further into his arm, blood now pouring freely.

He could ignore the physical pain.

But he could not—would not—live without Lyra. Were she to pass, he would soon join her in the afterlife.

"My love," he begged, once again offering himself to her. The dark liquid pooled in her mouth, and tears sprang to his eyes when he saw her throat working.

"Take all of me. Live for me."

He didn't know how long he waited, clinging to her still form, until her wounds slowly began to close and the color returned to her cheeks.

Relief flooded Aldric with such intensity he couldn't help but sob. Lyra's breathing eased, and he knew what he needed to do.

He had to get her to Louise.

S.D. GREDELL

www.ingramcontent.com/pod-product-compliance
Lightning Source LLC
LaVergne TN
LVHW091657070526
838199LV00050B/2189